SEX AND VIOLENCE

Sex and

Violence

A LOVE STORY

George Stade

Turtle Point Press
New York

Design and composition by Tag Savage
at Wilsted & Taylor Publishing Services

ISBN 1-885586-37-X
LCCN 2004113835

Printed in the United States of America

Author's Preface

This novel occupies in imaginative space an area homologous to the area occupied by Columbia University in actual space. But none of the characters have an intended resemblance to any professor, student, administrator, guard, or other denizen of the University. The action is set some time before September 11, 2001 and just before Viagra.

The Major players are as follows:

WYNN O'LEARY: expert on modernism, ex-football player, still big and strong, but has put on lots of weight since his wife left him, has "a little problem," the source of his bitter wit.

JULIETTE BERCEAU: Wynn's cousin at about four removes, turns up on his doorstep, asks him to take her in, has left her job as a gofer for the rock group Burning Jizz, wants to take courses toward a degree, wants "to get a life."

THE SMOKERS' CLUB: a group of professorial wits who gather for lunch in the small smoking section of the university cafeteria. These include KAY PESKY: upright and sympathetic, a feminist, wants a child but no husband, writes classic papers on such subjects as the codpiece; ZENO CONFALONE: married and with an air of dissipation, the lover of many; LISBET ARNO: a childhood refugee from Nazi Germany, "whose field is the whole of European culture," now a champion of Enlightenment values; MARSHALL GRICE: an expert in eighteenth-century literature, speaks in epigrams à la Dr. Johnson; LEONARD SISTRUNK: wealthy, black, gay, a fashion plate and pretense puncturer.

MURRAY WEINREIN: a shark out of water, chair of the department.

MONIKA WRIGHT: departmental administrator, was in a "Boston-marriage" type of relationship with the recently murdered vice-chair, has transformed herself from a tender plum into a tough prune, full of iron.

IRENE HOWLAND: lovelorn secretary to the chair.

ANGEL TERRASCO: around the time that Lisbet Arno's parents were going south over the Pyrenees to escape Nazi Germany, Angel Terrasco's parents were going north over the Pyrenees to escape Fascist Spain. Her father was an anarchist, an atheist, and a male-firster; Angel became a disciplinarian, a devout Christian, and a feminist.

TEDDY NAKATANI: brilliant graduate student, can't come up with a plausible dissertation subject, goes to Wynn O'Leary, whom he sees as savior and soul mate, for help.

HECTOR SUAREZ: lead detective in pursuit of whoever has been killing university professors; as a teenager played sandlot football against Wynn O'Leary; sardonic and smart.

SEX AND VIOLENCE

1

Dear Joel,

You will be sorry to hear that I have become a professor of English. It wasn't that I lacked the knowhow, speed, strength, size, or opportunity to play football. What I lacked was the killer instinct, still do, though I admire it in others. Except for that one little thing, I was temperamentally a natural for outside linebacker, a guy who reacts rather than initiates (except when he blitzes), a guy who can spot the intention in a form, or formation, a reader in short. But I could never get mad enough at the other guy to want to cripple him, even after a crack back, a leg whip, fingers through the face mask during a pileup. One guy even bit me on the chin, left me with a handsome scar, what with the infection and all.

When I was cut after a year on the development squad, I was surprised to discover that I didn't very much care whether I played football or not. In fact I've been sitting here trying to think if there is anything at all I do give a shit about. A well-turned sentence, maybe. A well-turned ankle, as they used to say, surely.

At least you had a goal, Joel: you wanted to play like Diz. And if you had gotten there, would that have been enough, to play like someone else, even Diz? And you knew that the bop you played was posthumous, put to its quietus by the fuzz box and a bunch of ithyphallic androgynes giving head to their mikes, Mick Jagger et al. So you turned to heroin. Well, that's too simple: we are not Englishmen, you and me. (According to my colleague, Zeno Confalone, there are two things that uppish Englishmen lack: "One is a subconscious. The other is a superego.")

Becoming a professor, I mean, was easy compared with what you set out to do. All it required was work, which came easy, for as I just said, I am by temperament a reader, a second-story man, a critic, someone who tells stories about other peoples' stories. Thus it was that I was able to spend a three-month vacation at Fern Hill Farm where I was supposed to begin my new book, but did not; thus it is that I drove back to the City on Labor Day, for registration begins tomorrow; thus it is that just as the roast pork shoulder in the oven began to release its perfume, I got a call from my chairman, or "chair," as we now say, Murray Weinrein. He is, I believe, the last New Yorker to have been named "Murray."

"Wynn," he said, "how's the body?" he said. He was alluding, no doubt, to this monstrous featherbed of fat I have wrapped myself in since Belinda and I went our separate ways, for like other men I too once managed to get married. Murray always tries to get the first dig in, putting you on the defensive, which is after all where I'm most at home.

"As usual," I said, something of a fib. Instead of writing, I spent the summer splitting stones, moving earth, pulling out stumps, getting some muscle back, but not losing weight, not giving up cigarettes.

"I hope you're well rested," he said.

"Why's that?" I said.

"I got a job for you," he said.

"What's that?" I said.

"I want you to be vice-chair," he said.

"What's wrong with Terry?" I said.

"She's dead," he said.

"Is it Terry?" I said. (In times of stress I sometimes sound like Pa.)

"Murdered," he said.

"Terry?" I said.

"Some time last night, or at least during the last twenty-four hours," he said. "Murdered," I said.

"So we need a vice-chair," he said.

"We will miss her," I said. Terry Jones was a distinguished, as we say, professor of medieval literature. Her essays on the visions and visitations of medieval Christian women are admired on both sides of the Atlantic. Her argument, radically simplified, is that the most hair-raising of these fantasies come out of a longing for an intimate and androgynous God. I can see her severe face right now: blue eyes, thick blonde eyebrows, freckles, lips tight, letting me have it for my pose as a mere aesthete, which didn't do me justice.

"Who killed her?" I said.

"The investigation is just getting under way," said Murray. "Monika only found her this morning."

"Poor Monika" (our administrator), I said.

"She'll survive," he said. "You've got to take the job."

"To what, exactly, do I owe this honor?" I said.

"You don't have any enemies with clout," he said. "You have not humped your load committee-wise. You will ride herd on these yo-yos who want to teach courses on matchbook covers or The Three Stooges. You'll write slick memos."

"I don't have an agenda," I said.

"I'll give you one," he said.

"I don't like administrative work," I said.

"If you did you wouldn't be qualified," he said. "I'll expect an answer tomorrow, in the affirmative."

"Where was Terry killed?" I said. "How?" But he had already hung up.

Murray would get on with football coaches. For him, too, winning is the only thing.

I am writing to you, although you are dead, because I can no longer write for anyone else, including myself, never mind why.

The date is September something or another, Labor Day, two months into my fortieth year, the time 5:49 p.m.

This morning, to beat the rush, I drove down from Uncle Alf's place, which is now mine, for Uncle Alf, like you, is dead. Did he ever lay a hand on you? Me neither. We were pretty children, but Uncle Alf was heroic. Imagine the raging desire, the fury and despair, if the only kind of sex you wanted, needed, was forbidden, scorned, derided, denounced from the pulpit. He died of a then-new disease called Acquired Immunodeficiency Syndrome or AIDS, and he left Fern Hill Farm and the whole 100 acres to his "beloved nephews," namely you and me, with the stipulation that if one of us predeceased the other, the whole shebang would go to the survivor. Materialize, and I'll gladly give you back your half. The lavender shutters, front door, and trim I have painted black, but otherwise the house is pretty much as it was when during those sun-bleached summers you used to teach me how to play football, to the peril of Uncle Alf's perennial border, valuable lessons as it turned out. Uncle Alf died slowly, stoically, tended in his last days by a guy named Stanley, who was not even a lover.

The car I drove down in is my latest memorial to the blue microbus, named "Blue and Boogie," in which you and the other Reboppers boppity-boppitied to gigs, out of key with your time, trying to resuscitate the dead art of bop, fat chance, only my version is called a Vanagon Carat, except Volkswagen stopped making it years ago. The removeable radio I bought to replace the original, which was stolen last spring, along with everything in the glove compartment, mostly little packages of salt and pepper and ketchup and mustard from fast-food joints, where I frequently, too often, eat, has a cassette player. (These zigzag sentences, juking around memories, are the sign of a dozy brain, but then I've had a long day.) In this cassette player I play cassettes. Some of these cassettes are, or were, yours. In any case I have been playing your kind of music. I have been playing, for example, the set Dizzy recorded with John Lewis, Sonny Stitt, and Skeeter Best, including "Blues for Bird," which you can't have forgotten, for you memorized Dizzy's whole chorus, down to the last furble, played the opening two phrases hundreds of times, until you got the mixture of lament and irony just right, for as Clark Terry said, you were the only trumpet man in history who tried to steal Diz's tone with his licks, but then it's not so easy to think of anyone who wanted to steal Clark's tone either. You will be sorry to hear that Dizzy, like you, is dead.

Six thousand people, and only in New York, and only for Dizzy, would you have gotten together such a variety of types, attended the memorial service. Some fine musicians blew their tributes. But unlike Bird, Dizzy had no surviving peer to play the blues for him. If you admired Diz so much, for the love of little Jesus (as Pa used to say, still says) why didn't you adopt his attitude toward drugs? It's for losers, said Diz, who had little patience for weakness, especially in himself. Well, I am no one to talk. I'm addicted to cigarettes, myself, for starters.

Terry Jones is dead, Diz is dead, Uncle Alf is dead, with Joel O'Leary in the grave, but I intend to live, in spite of the cigarettes, don't ask me why.

I opened the oven door and stabbed a fork into the half-baked potato, the size (roughly) of a shoe box, specific against cancer of the colon, so the skin would not burst, for if anything puts me into a rage, it is the pernicious habit of baking potatoes in aluminum foil, rubberizing the skin. I sliced the skin off the roast, put it in a rack, to make crackling, conducive of cancer of the colon, and all this alliteration is another sign of a dozy brain. I doused the succulent fat on top of the roast with garlic salt and pepper and sage. I stood there, breathing deeply, lit a cigarette, and to calm myself further brought my cassette player into the kitchen and loaded it with that great set Bird and Diz did with the Red Norvo All-Stars, including outtakes. Then the doorbell rang.

"Who the fuck is it?" I roared down the hall, roughly as long as a bowling alley, for years ago I blackmailed the University (with an offer from Dartmouth) into giving me this big apartment, the idea being that Belinda and I were about to have children, though we never did, never did.

I opened the door and there was a young woman, holding a shopping bag, green stone lodged in a nostril, green on her eyelids.

"Hi Cuz," she said.

"Beg pardon," I said.

"Don't you recognize me?" she said.

"Can't say I do," I said.

"Your mother has a sister, right?" she said.

"Right," I said.

"This sister has a daughter, right?" she said.

"Right," I said.

"This daughter has a husband, right?" she said.

"Right," I said.

"This husband has a sister, right?" she said.

"I guess," I said.

"I'm this sister's daughter," she said, "one of them. I'm your mother's sister's daughter's husband's sister's daughter. The last time I saw you was at Joel's funeral."

"There were a lot of kids running around. . . ." I said. "Juliette!" I said.

"You got it," she said. "except everyone calls me 'Jule.' "

"Hi Jule," I said.

"Can I come in?" she said.

I opened the door all the way and bowed as she entered. I had time while walking down the hall to remember her last name, "Berceau." Maybe you recall her father, a hard-handed Canuck who was not in control of his drinking. There was a time, a St. Paddy's Day, was it? When he started up with Pa, a mistake: something about how the Quebecois had it worse than the Catholics in Northern Ireland.

"Sacred blue," she said, "what's that?"

"That's Slam Stewart working his bow across a bass viol and humming in unison," I said.

She listened. "Fout," she said. "Now what is that?"

"Charlie Parker," I said.

"Never heard of him," she said.

"That chorus was historically important," I said. "It convinced swing musicians that bop was not a fraud. The test, as always, is how you play the blues."

"The group I worked for, those bastards, sometimes played the blues," she said. "But not like that."

"You eat?" I said.

"I think I had something yesterday," she said.

"Drink?" I said.

"It'll knock me out," she said.

Well, she was sagging, all right, never mind the perky chatter, her hair unstrung, her clothes a mess, a smudge along one shin, another along the rim of an ear. I poured her a glass of wine (strictly for company), and opened myself a bottle of beer and moved over to the stove, started some gravy. "You a musician?" I said.

"I took five years of piano lessons, my mother's idea, although my father wanted me to play the accordion," she said. "I can finger the usual three chords on a guitar. The group I worked for? Burning Jizz? I was really a kind of gofer. They grossed fourteen million last year and paid me five hundred a week."

She was mumbling. "You travel light," I said, nodding toward the shopping bag.

"The guy I was living with won't let me pick up my things," she said. "Maybe you could talk to him. A big important-looking guy like you . . ."

"Listen Juliette," I said.

"The room I had lined up?" she said, "well this girlfriend who was going to take me in, she took in her boyfriend instead."

I loaded up her plate with half the potato, a pile of pork, a mound of red cabbage. I gave her a bowl of salad. I put the bread and butter and gravy boat where she could reach them. Then I served myself and sat down. "You always eat like this?" she said, and it's been a while, Joel, since a nubile woman gave me that look, satirical but indulgent.

"Displacement activity," I said.

"I'll go over to Off-Campus Housing tomorrow, see what they got," she said.

"You're a student here?" I said.

"I register tomorrow, in the School of Advanced Studies, going to get myself a life," she said. ("Advanced" in this context means that the students have to be over twenty-one.)

"What are you going to study?" I said.

"The liberal arts," she said. "That's as far as I've got. I want to learn Homer, Plato, Dante, Zora Neale Hurston, and like that."

"You might want to try Lit Hum, Humanities, that is," I said.

"That's what I want, humanities," she said. "I haven't come across many lately. Pretty please."

"I can put you up for a day or two," I said, with a reluctance I can't now explain, except by the truth universally acknowledged that a single man in possession of good fortune soon becomes tight with his sympathies.

"Can I take a shower?" she said. "I feel grungy." She looked down at her plate. "I'm not much of a meat-eater."

I took her down that famous hall, lined on one side with floor-to-ceiling bookcases ("You read all those books?"), to the room Belinda and I had meant to convert into a nursery, never used, except by Belinda's twin sisters, relentless teasers, during their regular weekend visits to New York, refugees from Suicide Bridge and Cornell weather. I showed Juliette where the bedding was, in the drawer under the lower of the double bunks Belinda had ordered for her sisters, the sheets fragrant with cedar. I showed Juliette the bathroom on the far side of the nursery, as I still think of it, and the master bedroom, where I sleep, a smaller bathroom adjoining. And if I think of an unused room as a nursery, it is one more instance of a common occurrence, a past intention, never realized, usurping a present fact. Then I went into the kitchen to clean up, for of the two main classes of bachelor, the slob and the fusspot, I belong to the second.

I put on the classic "Bag's Groove" set, cut as you will remember, shortly before Miles' playing went astray, his brain addled by the condescensions of Jean-Paul Sartre and Juliette Greco, his bad nigger act a come-on to white would-be hipsters, his idea of hot stuff to quote Debussy's tame dissonances, rather than Diz. You should have seen him in his last years, wearing robes like King Wenceslas, playing with a fuchsia horn with an amplifier attached, for Miles, too, is dead. Belinda is too upright, supposing her sisters had been willing, to have merged with the three of us into the beast with four backs, for the secret life of every healthy male sprawls in a harem.

"Hey Cuz," I heard, realizing I had heard it once, twice, three times.

"What?" I bellowed down the hall, and you gets no bread with one meatball.

"Can you lend me a bathrobe or something?" she said. "I may have to burn these clothes."

I don't have a bathrobe, for when you live alone a bathrobe is superfluous, and when I was not living alone I used to hang around in my pajama bottoms after a shower, so Belinda could dig my muscles, which she never mentioned. I fetched a heavy flannel shirt, picturing the tails wagging around Juliette's thighs, and a pair of work-out shorts left over from my days of a thirty-two-inch waist. I knocked on the bathroom door. I expected her to open the door a few inches, so I could reach the togs in to her. But she opened it wide enough for me to see her reflection in the mirror on the medicine cabinet door, which was ajar. The mirror was lightly misted over. I saw her, that is, in a sort of visionary gleam, bright but indistinct: the head tilted forward, the shoulders rounded, the melodramatic tuck at the back of the waist, like a matador, the legs together from ankle to secret nook at the juncture of legs and apple-cheeked behind, which was thrust rearward, the arm curling out of sight around the door, her hand opening right before me, in the flesh. As a student of significant form I was particularly impressed by the curve that ran from the groovy delta at the base of her spine and swooped out and around and down under into that sacred grove, dark and deeper than any sea dingle. I was glad to see what looked like a birthmark on her bum, for I hate perfection.

I put the shirt and shorts into her hand.

"Merci," she said.

I found myself in my study, sitting at my desk, looking through the pile of mail that accumulated since my last visit to the City, in early August, to take care of business, the cassette player in my lap, transitional object for the millions. I put on the Massy Hall concert, Bird blowing a plastic horn he had just picked up (his regular horn in hock, I suppose), Bud Powell as drunk as Uncle Alf's Guernsey used to get from the fermented drops off the old apple tree in the pasture, Charlie Mingus and Max Roach on edge, the music glorious; for although equanimity, as our father James Joyce intimated, may be the greatest of virtues, it is not what's behind great jazz.

I read all the mail-order catalogues people send me, read them religiously, in a penitential spirit that is, for very little in them is going to fit me. It is an oddity of my corpulence that my hams and loins are about as lean as they always were. As for the rest, call in a teratologist. Therefore I almost always wear jeans, which have a low rise, for of the three categories of fat men, those who wear their belts above their bellies, those who wear their belts across their bellies, and those who wear their belts under their bellies, I belong to the last. The obscene practice of wearing one's belt above the belly, I believe, should be prohibited by law. I was looking at a picture of a bright red wool hunting jacket, for I hate blaze orange, but I was not seeing it clearly, for superimposed, as on a opalescent film, were rounded shoulders, a sharply indented waist, apple cheeks.

Juliette knocked on the study door, though it was open. "Can I watch television?" she said. "I guess I'm too tired to sleep." A towel was knotted around her hair into a turban. The flannel shirt reached down below her knees. The shorts, even if she was wearing them, were out of sight.

"Help yourself," I said, and couldn't I have given her a word of sympathy or understanding, for Pete's sake?

"I was wondering," she said, "could you call me 'Julie' from now on? Like, you know . . . a new life, a new name."

"Julie, it is," I said, and why not? The fiction of a new life can keep you going better than most truths.

"There's this one other thing," she said. "About my courses, which ones I should take. How do you decide?"

I suppose I looked impatient, for which sin I expect and deserve to fry in hell.

"Two courses is all I got saved up for," she said, " see how I do, what kind of work I can get."

"My office is 604 Hancock," I said. "Come there between two and five tomorrow, we'll sort it out."

"Thanks, Cuz," she said.

"You're welcome," I said.

"What are you listening to?" she said.

" 'Hot house' " is what it's called," I said. "It's based more or less on the chords of 'What is this thing called love.' "

"A good question," she said.

"Yes, indeed," I said.

"Do you know the answer?" she said.

"Yes, I do," I said.

"What is it?" she said.

"Goslings have a biological timer built into them," I said. "When it goes off they follow whatever is bigger than them and moves. Take away their mother goose and they will follow a pig, a black balloon, a tumbleweed, an ethologist. That's love."

"And that's what I want to learn," she said: "lots of big words. What's an ethologist?"

"A student of animal behavior," I said.

"You think humans are animals?" she said.

"We're not rhododendrons," I said. It would be interesting to know why I came on like that with this poor girl. Because living alone turns you into a pipsqueak? Because I have unresolved issues with the opposite sex? and what man or woman does not?

An hour later, maybe two, on my way to the kitchen for a snack, I stopped by what in the good old days was a maid's room, converted by me into a whatnot, at one end football trophies and stuff I didn't want stolen from Fern Hill Farm during the winter (firearms, boxes of ammunition, power tools, binoculars, a chainsaw), and at the other end a television set. On this set Julie was watching a documentary on Jeannette MacDonald and Nelson Eddy.

"That's what made bop necessary," I said. She didn't say anything. "And rock possible," I said.

"I used to love rock," she said. "Still do, I guess. That's why I went to work with Burning Jizz. Do you know I slept with one of those guys for three months before he told me he was HIV-positive."

My stomach dropped, no small matter. "Put a rattler in his guitar," I said.

"Well, I've been tested a half-dozen times since, and I've always come up negative," she said.

"Put anthrax in his harmonica," I said.

In the kitchen I cut two slices of pumpernickel from the middle of the loaf, where it's widest, spread Coleman's prepared mustard on one slice, spread mayonnaise, always Hellmann's, on the other slice, pressed lots of lettuce into the mayo, heaped pork onto the mustard, salted and peppered the pork copiously, slapped together the two slices with their loads, and cut the sandwich in half, for I believe that eating junk food has a bad effect on your character. Julie was standing in the doorway.

"Hungry?" I said, pouring myself a beer.

"No thank you," she said.

"Brandy?" I said.

"No thank you," she said.

"Glass of milk?" I said.

"No thank you," she said.

"I think I have the makings for hot chocolate," I said, "make you sleepy."

"No, that's all right," she said. "Do you write books?"

"Yes," I said.

"Can I read them?" she said.

"Sure," I said.

"Are you writing one now?" she said.

"I'm in between projects," I said.

"I've had some experiences . . ." she said. "They ought to go in a book."

"I'll bet," I said.

"Well, I think I'll try to sleep," she said.

"Good luck," I said.

I finished my sandwich, broke up some crackling and salted it, and peppered it, took a plate of the stuff and another beer to my office, pulled out a pad of paper and a pencil for I also eschew all mechanical and electronic aids to composition, for you can still feel the words through a pencil, even if at that one remove you can't breach lest the world end. Julie had aroused my itch to write, so I scratched it. Thus these unsolicited confidences. Can she possibly be dreaming that I'm going to write some abysmal postmodernist novel with her as the heroine?

Do you sleep, Joel? If I do, I guess it follows that you do. Do you dream? If so dream a little dream of me.

And so to bed.

2

I got up late,

and just whose business is it anyway? I used to roll out of bed, write all morning, ease on over to Whipple Hall for lunch, over which I lingered, teach classes, meet with students, read their prose, write them letters of recommendation, attend meetings, that kind of thing, earning my keep, riding easy in harness, since I had already done what I do for myself, which is write. (A page a day adds up to a book a year, said Robert Graves, now dead, but somehow it never does.) Then I'd modulate home, listen to music while supper was working, dealing with my extracurricular mail right there on the kitchen table. (If you write with a pencil or pen, rather than with a roomful of hi-tech apparatus, you can do it anywhere.) After supper I would read whatever books I was about to teach or write about, but not criticism, not often anyway, for it is my opinion that criticism should be written, but not read. What I wrote myself all those mornings, of course, was criticism. On Saturdays I cleaned house. On Sundays I did whatever else needed doing, although in the heat of inspiration, if that's what it was, I sometimes wrote on weekends, on evenings too, even on afternoons when I had no classes, let the students pester someone else. Oh, there were variations, football games on Sunday or on Monday evenings, the occasional evening out, few of late, fewer and fewer. And so the years and books accumulated, like piss in a bottle.

But I am no longer writing, except to you, and I have just started doing that, so what is there to get up early for?

There was a note on the kitchen table. It read, "Dear Cuz, see you at 2:00," signed "Julie," but you could see that the **i** had been added after the **e** was already written. A P.S. said "I made coffee." So I drank a couple of mugsful, maybe three, could have been four, while showering and the rest, making the fig at some asshole on the radio babbling that trendsetting cooks now used meat only as a garnish, making the bed. The pillow on the far side of the bed was still damp and there was a long brown hair curling back on itself in the middle of it, for I had not been in bed five minutes last night when I sensed someone in the doorway.

"Cuz," Julie said, "you awake? Could I sleep with you? I don't mean monkey business. I slept with that guy for two months after... I mean, you know, just *slept,* cause I grew up sleeping with my sister, and... I know you're a big guy and all, but I won't take up much room."

"Help yourself," is what I said, although it is not often that words fail me.

I contracted and concentrated, withdrew, and she lay down, her apple cheeks pointing my way, and fell asleep, as I estimate, in nine seconds. It took me longer.

I rumbled on over to Whipple Hall, on the ground floor of which is the university's main cafeteria, caisson walls, high ceilings, ditto windows, in one corner of which is the smoker's section, in one corner of which is a round table. There are the six of us who still openly smoke, in a department of forty-five or so professors, and notoriously gather here for lunch. In its campaign to banish smoking from the campus entirely, the college newspaper (*The Speculator*) refers to us as puffaddicts who feed on pish and quips, the idea being that among the poisonous fumes clever things are said, as with the old

Algonquin wits. There was Kay Pesky and Leonard Sistrunk, who said, "Heah cum de Vice."

Leonard, although he has the darkest skin I have ever seen on any human being, does not normally speak in the accents of any of the familiar black dialects, but in a faint and cultivated southern accent, and with a note of disdain, as though the hidden text of everything he said were "if you're looking for trouble, you've found it." He was wearing a tropical weight double-breasted black suit with chalk stripes and flecks of blue, green, and red, a purple shirt, a sky-blue tie, and ankle-high shoes that must have cost him six hundred dollars. (He got his money from his mother, who got it from her father, who was a mortician in New Orleans.) His lips are thinner than mine, which as you will remember are middling thick, as is his nose, but then his has probably never been broken. He wears a gold earring, size of a wedding band, in one ear, although there are three other holes in that ear, for when he really dresses up. The English Department had recruited him to be our senior African-Americanist, mainly at my instigation, for he had written a brilliant book on jazz in the literature of the Harlem Renaissance, as well as a three-part essay, later published as a short book (he doesn't like long ones) on jazz in the poetry of Langston Hughes, from traditional blues to bop. But once in place, he let it be known that he would teach exactly what he wanted, and only that, for Leonard is at war with the African-American establishment: "blowhards and schoolmarms," he says, "fags and fag-hags." He is himself a relentless seducer of handsome young men, not one of whom, among those I have met, ever wanted anything more than to be seduced by Leonard.

Leonard has a magnificent physique from the waist up, nor is he undeveloped from the waist down, but disproportionately thick of thigh, thin of calf. Once I dropped by his apartment to borrow a copy of Saintsbury's *History of Prosody* (in three volumes). He came to the door wearing only spandex tights. "Your calves always swell up like that in the winter?" I said.

He looked me over. "You stand there looking like a mournful and short-haired bison some fool taught to stand on its hind legs, and you talk about my calves," he said. "Come."

He led me to his workout room, two walls covered entirely with mirrors, a mat on the floor, a table to one side, on it a bottle of water, a towel, a CD player blasting out Louis Armstrong's "Low Gully Blues." Some day I will have to play for Leonard Dizzy's parody-tribute to Armstrong's version of "I'm Confessin'." He positioned us before a mirroring wall.

"Whose body would you rather have?" he said.

"I get your drift," I said, "but what would hold up my socks?"

"That's a racist remark," he said. "You Europeans, back there in the Paleolithic, needed fat around your shins during those long dark winters when you all became beserkers."

"I'm scarcely a European," I said.

He lay on the floor, extended his arms to either side, and brought one knee to his chin, slowly, under strain, the muscles that retarded the movement just giving in to those that advanced it, lowered it as slowly, did it again, but with the other leg. He brought a fist to his sternum, the same way, his whole body shaking with the effort, then the other arm. He moved into a series of combinations, both arms together, the right arm and the left leg, sweat breaking out. Then he began to writhe and roll, twist and turn, stretch and contract, grimacing horribly, flexing and relaxing every muscle from his superorbital ridge to the arches of his feet, one muscle group overpowering and submitting to the other, gasping, veins showing, a roiling, moiling, coiling and recoiling, zone of turbulence. He lay there panting.

"So that's how you do it," I said. "No free weights or machines."

"That's how I do it," he said.

"A little solipsistic," I said.

"Just me against myself," he said.

"It's a contest you can't win," I said, reaching down a hand, which he grasped, pulling him to his feet.

"Or lose," he said.

"All our victories over ourselves are Pyrrhic," I said.

"Anyone ever tell you," he said, "that sometimes you're a pain in the ass?"

"I've heard it said," I said, "but are you anyone to talk?"

"You are not my type, you understand, so my motives would be entirely altruistic," he said, "but you should let me fuck you up the ass some time, loosen you up."

"I could never go for a man with skinny calves," I said.

"Leonard," I said, by way of greeting him in Whipple Hall for no one calls him "Lennie," a clear mismatch between word and thing. "I'm not a vice-chairperson yet, got to meet with my handlers."

Kay offered me a hand and her cheek, which I bent over to buss, for Kay has cheeks well worth bussing. "I've got something for you," she said.

"Oh-oh," I said.

"My latest," she said, rummaging around in her immense handbag-cum-briefcase. "I want you to go over it for style." (Kay writes with a brick.) I glanced at the title of the manuscript she handed me: "Footman Beware: The Cult of the Calf, a Study of Class and Gender in Eighteenth-Century Literature and Culture." I would have to tell Kay about Leonard's theory of calf amplitude, for if you have class and you have gender, can race be far behind?

Kay is always writing these sexy articles (like her classic paper on why the codpiece went out of fashion), but that is where it stops. Because we are both single (although I wasn't always), maybe because we are both overweight (she less so), both of an age (she's younger), both blond (she more so), both listeners rather than talkers, colleagues would often invite us separately to dinner parties, but seat us side by side at the table. And indeed we became friends, or at least friendly, went out on dates, I guess you would call them. We would go to a university function, say, to a reading at P.E.N., to a publication party, to one of those awful art movies she likes, once to a performance of *Der Rosenkavalier*, which would have pleased me better had it been shorter, for if there is one thing I like even less than opera in general, it is camp in particular. And of course I would take her home, say goodnight on the stoop of the brownstone her parents bought her when she received tenure. She never invited me up for a nightcap, the usual euphemism. And I never kissed her goodnight on the lips, not because I didn't want to, not because she intimated that such a kiss would turn her off, but because it was clear that such a kiss would not turn her on either, for love is like a faucet, you can turn it off and on, for if you lack the killer instinct, chances are you also lack the instincts of a rapist. I have not become so much a cynic, however, to see this failing as the cause behind the other causes behind my failures with women. Kay is apparently a living refutation of Zeno Confalone's first law, which is that everybody gets some, somehow, with somebody, even if only with himself. (Zeno still uses the third person singular masculine pronoun to signify an unspecified someone, gender left open.) That is one more respect in which she is like me.

The human body with its accoutrements is the greatest signifying system the world has ever known, except for the world itself, which however can't know itself. I read bodies all the time. I have, for example, sorted out the styles in which people walk with their toes pointed out, seventeen of them, each expressing a different attitude toward the world, most of them being obnoxious, the exception being dancers. (I'll tell you, Joel, it's relief to write in this digressive manner, after all those uptight sentences about other writers, each sentence buggered by the one behind it and buggering the one before it, nary a pause in the schuss to the finish.) But Kay Pesky is unreadable, and not, I believe, just to me.

Consider her clothes, which never fit or suit her, a knit dress with broad horizontal stripes, riding up her thighs, or a black cashmere top, green kiwis embroidered on it, fur trim tickling her cleavage; or her hair, a different style each week, but never the right one, the wet golden retriever look, great honey-colored ramparts at her ear (slightly askew); or her lipstick, which she lays on thick but off line, bright red smears on her cigarette and coffee cup. (Her apartment, in which I have never been alone with her, is more of the same, the visual equivalent of a tin ear.)

Now consider her body, in which she is entirely at home. How balanced in motion, how graceful in repose. It is ample, but it is elegant. It is relaxed, but it is not slack, if you can dig where I'm coming from. I have seen her at some literary gathering, Joel, sitting on a couch, one leg tucked under her, an elbow propped on the armrest, her cheek propped on a hand, taking in everything, giving away nothing, her composure inviolable, the lines and masses of her body distributed as though upon a canvas for an exacting prince by a Renaissance master. (But her dress is bunched around her waist, her hair unraveling, lipstick on a tooth, a hole in her pantyhose.) When once I tried to compliment her about all this, the unfailing esthetic intelligence of her corporeal attitudes, she had no idea what I was talking about. She did not have a clue. Remind her that she has a body and she gets flustered. Body? What body? She is also the best dancer I ever faked a mambo with. When she jitterbugs with Leonard, sequins shimmering, mascara runny with sweat, the rug rolled up, the furniture against the wall, motherfucker, the others interrupt what they are doing to watch.

I think I would like to see her naked, Joel. I would like to see her without makeup, her hair simply hanging, still damp from a shower, starting to curl, her neatly intricate ankles and knees, the paleo-European calves swelling out on three sides of her tibula, the deep thighs, and ah, those plump, succulent hemispheres, for in my admittedly touched-up picture of Kay she has color on the bottom rounds of her cheeks, no lard-ass she. What I have seen of her flesh is bright: naked, she would glow in the dark. I would like to do her justice. I want to see her at her best.

I can't be the only one to have noticed that some people look wonderful in clothes, the mere thought of whose naked bodies can make you queasy, no need to name names, but think of Jimmy Stewart, say, or Audrey Hepburn (now dead). For me it is how you would look without clothes that counts, like how you play the blues. As to where that leaves me, for whom there is no enterprise in going naked, the less said, the better. (Not that there is much enterprise in my going clothed, either.) The flesh is wiser than the spirit, said D. H. Lawrence, who occasionally got something right. There is something about it, I mean, that can't be faked.

"Don't take on the vice-chair," said Kay, dropping her lug-all to the floor. "It would compromise your beautiful neutrality."

"Well, now, Kay," said Leonard, "if he were willing to push for another senior African-Americanist, take some of the pressure off me. Murray doesn't know pine nuts from Hibiscus."

"We need another senior feminist more," said Kay. "It's a disgrace."

Marshall Grice arrived precisely as the noon bells rang from the chapel tower, a sound I like (the silver circles brightening the air), then Zeno Confalone, then Lisbeth Arno.

"Esteemed colleagues," said Marshall Grice, chuffing his pipe, as square a specimen as you'll find in academe nowadays, although he headed the committee that recommended Kay for tenure.

"Zeno," said Kay, offering her cheek.

"Stunning dress," said Zeno, who is shameless: wide concentric swirls of lime green, fuchsia, and purple on a black background. Zeno himself always wears a lightweight black suit, white shirt, black tie.

"How was the flight from Rome?" Kay said.

"Flying used to be made bearable by the kindly stewardess who bent over to give the guy in the seat up front a drink," said Zeno. "Now they have flight attendants, old hags and young fags."

"*Chacun a son gout,*" said Leonard.

As for Zeno, imagine Marcello Mastroianni in *Divorce Italian Style,* only leaner, more dissipated, equally deadpan. His first name had been bestowed upon him by his father, who considered his son's birth something of a paradox, in that nine months before the son was born, the father had not yet been released from an Allied prisoner-of-war camp. So Zeno told me, but then he is a mythomaniac. He is also a relentless seducer of young women of an adventurous disposition, for Zeno is married. According to Leonard, who was in naval intelligence, Zeno was a daredevil helicopter pilot in Vietnam.

"I just had an experience," said Lisbeth Arno. This eminent woman likes her friends to call her "Lizzie." "Some kid just slapped me on the tush. Something, hanh?"

"Shocking," said Marshall.

"Congratulations," said Zeno.

"A student?" said Leonard.

"He looked too young," said Lizzie, "some black kid in a hooded sweatshirt and enormous sneakers. He was gone before I knew what hit me."

"The phantom tush-toucher," said Leonard.

The kid had selected an unlikely target, for whether seen from the front, back, or either side, Lizzie's sixty-five-year-old body is all straight lines. "Have you eaten yet?" she said to me.

"Not yet," I said.

"Let's get on line," she said. "I have to talk to you." So we wound our way around tables, nodding to students, none of whom were wearing enough clothes, the day being warmish, me leading interference, over to the food counter, her hand taking my arm, her head leaning toward mine. "You feel strong," she said. "Are you going to be vice-chairman?"

"I haven't decided," I said.

"They're trying to force me into retirement," she said. "I don't want to retire. I can't afford to retire. I haven't accumulated enough of a pension fund yet." After her first book, written in her beloved New York Public Library, a meditation on the obligations of citizenship hitched on to an account of what the death of Socrates had meant to this time or that place, she taught at Bard as an adjunct, punk salary, no side benefits. After her second book, which argued with Olympian detachment, that millennial delusions only became public and active among peoples who had been infected by Judaism or its heresies, Christianity or Marxism, or by its jealous and plagiarizing rivals, Islam and Fascism, she taught at the New School as an adjunct, puissant salary, no side benefits. After her third volume, a cool look at Joan of Arc, some of us conned Angel Terrasco, then head of the Appointments Committee, into recruiting Lizzie, piddling salary, middling side benefits, for she has no Ph.D., one of her attractions. The con amounted to no more than allowing Angel to believe that Lizzie was a feminist. It only worked because Angel never reads anything outside her field and in any case is oblivious to ironies that cut both ways, never mind this thing she has for militant maidens. I doubt that Lizzie's husband, Willi Heinfangl, has earned five thousand dollars in his whole life, though he must be near eighty.

"They can't do it—by law," I said.

"I know from personal experience how little people respect their own laws," she said. Lizzie was just a little girl when her family, which was Jewish, escaped over the Pyrenees, led by Willi Heinfangl, who was active in the Catholic opposition to Hitler, two steps ahead of the Gestapo. This could not have been long after Angel Terrasco's family escaped over the Pyrenees, going the other way, led by her father, who was an anarchist, two steps ahead of the Falange.

"You know I'll do what I can, which is not much, vice-chair or not," I said.

She smiled, showing a mouthful of archaic bridgework, but then Lizzie's mouth, by the usual standards, is too wide for her long, thin face. "It will be interesting to see you take up a cause," she said. "But you'll have more clout as vice-chair. Murray, you know, is ambitious: he won't cross the administration. Terry, for some reason, was always cool to me." The reason, I believe, was that Terry considered Lizzie a quisling for allying herself with "male supremacists" like Leonard, Zeno, and Marshall, with whom, oddly, Terry got on.

I got the chipped beef on toast, which students still call "shit on a shingle," and Lizzie got a cheeseburger and a Pepsi, for although her intellectual style is European, she is thoroughly Americanized in her quotidian practices.

Back at the table, we were all eating in silence until Marshall Grice said, "Who killed Terry Jones?"—what we were all thinking about anyhow. Marshall has the kind of face you might find on an old coin: lots of chin, a Native American nose, a lean face, longish white hair.

"It's got to be Murray," said Leonard.

"Why Murray?" said Marshall.

"He's in the last year of his second term as chair," said Leonard. "Terry was going to run against him."

"She would have gotten my vote," said Kay.

"All in all, she was at least a mensch," said Lizzie.

"How about that psychopath who goosed Lizzie?" said Kay.

"A goose it wasn't," said Lizzie.

"Of course," said Leonard, "some white woman gets killed, some black male had to do it."

"How was she killed?" I said.

"That is what we have been asking each other all morning," said Lizzie. "Nobody knows. Monika is sedated. Murray is *in camera* with the police."

"Are we really going to re-elect Murray?" said Leonard.

"Maybe you did it," said Kay, looking at me.

"Sure," said Zeno. "He wanted the vice-chair as a stepping stone to the chair and beyond. Can't you see him as Dean of Arts and Sciences?" They all laughed heartily at that one.

"All you have to do is look at the man," said Leonard, "to see that he is power-crazed." I should explain, Joel: part of the joke is that big as I am, I'm still seen as a pussycat.

"Angel Terrasco would gladly run, " I said.

"The Spanish Inquisition," said Zeno. Angel had once written a letter to Zeno's wife crammed with details (which she got wrong) about Zeno's infidelities. Zeno's wife (stout, glossy black braids pinned up) was outraged at the presumption of the woman. Zeno read the letter to us, one day at lunch, cracking us up, even Kay, who once told me that feminists like Angel were one of the crosses that feminists of Kay's generation had to bear. "Maybe we had better stick with Murray," Zeno said.

"We could do worse," said Marshall. "For him who would pursue honor, ambition is at first a spur but at last a bridle."

"Who said that?" said Kay.

"I did," said Marshall. "Doesn't anyone care who killed Terry?"

"We all know who killed Terry," said Lizzie. "Some junkie, some psychopath, some poor slob who wanted to steal her stereo and panicked when she walked in on him."

I sensed someone standing beside me, looked around, looked up, then got to my feet, for as Kay once said I make myself ridiculous by hanging on to the old sexist courtesies. (Zeno says that when applied with tact, nothing is so rude as courtesy.) The victim of my courtesy was short, freckled, demure-looking, brown hair parted down the middle, wearing too many clothes.

"Professor Weinrein said you would be here," she said, clearly meaning all of us, not just me.

Zeno, who kept his seat, made the introductions: "Fellow puff-addicts, meet Serena Crawfoot, freshly Ph.Deed by Yale, our new postmodernist."

"I believe, sir, that you did not quite say what you mean," Marshall said. "A postmodernist is not a student of postmodernism, but an instance of the thing. Professor Crawfoot, I presume, is a postmodernismist."

"Well, a little of both," said Serena.

"Sit down, girl," said Lizzie.

"And that is Lisbeth Arno," said Zeno, "whose field is the whole of European culture."

"I'm what you call a Zeitgeist-schmecker," said Lizzie.

"And on your right is Kay Pesky," said Zeno, "eighteenth century and feminist theory." (Kay nodded.) "And this old fart is Marshall Grice, eighteenth century, especially Dr. Johnson and his circle." ("Charmed," said Marshall.) "And on your left is Wynn O'Leary, modernist, or rather modernismist, as of today our vice-chair. (I took her hand, which closed down hard on mine, as though she thought that might be my style.) "Opposite you is Leonard Sistrunk, American Literature." ("For starters," said Leonard.) "And I, as you may remember, am Zeno Confalone, European Renaissance." Terry Jones, as vice-chair, had drafted Zeno for an ad hoc committee to search out and hire a junior expert in postmodernism, her justification an article he had written.

This article argued, in the tone of a character out of Nabokov, that long Renaissance narratives had preempted soap operas, the exemplary postmodernist form, in that they were digressive, polyplotted, resistant to closure, in that they followed the trajectory of female, rather than male, sexual desire, no implacable ascent to a climactic peak followed by a steep descent, all passion spent, but tardigrade at the onset, with pauses to look around, taking the crests as they came, wandering off rather than finishing fast, ready for another go-around. I took all this to be a put-on, although Zeno has never declared himself. This essay has become celebrated, the occasion of a special session at the Modern Language Association convention.

"I was hoping to speak to Professor Pesky and Professor Sistrunk," said Serena.

"You're one of us now," said Lizzie. "First names are indicated."

"Do you smoke?" said Kay.

"I can learn," said Serena.

Leonard offered her one of his gunpowder cigarettes, custom made, which he smokes through a filter, an innocent look on his face.

"Leonard, don't," said Lizzie.

Zeno, deadpan, offered Serena a light.

"Zeno, don't," said Lizzie.

Serena took a puff, holding the cigarette as you hold a straw when you blow the wrapper at the ceiling, but did not inhale, blew out the smoke, did not cough. Well, maybe we had gotten ourselves a new mensch.

I felt a presence behind me even before Murray's loud voice said,

"How can you eat in all this din, let alone think or make yourselves heard?"

"Sympathetic vibrations," said Kay.

"We feed on the energies of these students around us," said Lizzie.

"The Socratic method," said Leonard.

"All energy being erotic," said Zeno, Serena's head turning from speaker to speaker.

"Like vampires," said Kay.

"The blood is the life, said Dracula," said Serena, almost getting the hang of it, blushing.

"Madam, in the voicing of that sentiment," said Marshall, "Dracula had a distinguished predecessor."

"Careful, Lizzie," said Murray. "You're giving away professional secrets."

"Sir," said Marshall, "the open and only secret of our profession is that we need the students more than they need us."

I twisted around, something of a feat, displacing the table. And there was Murray, his pinstripe suit, his pencil-thin mustache, his off-white complexion, his shiny and slicked-back hair, parted just left of center, looking, as usual, like a tango dancer. Standing next to him was this blocky guy, his hair fleeing from stage front center to the wings, and where had I seen him before?

Murray turned to him and said, "They like to hear themselves talk." Then he turned to us and said, "This is Detective Hector Suarez. He is heading the investigation into Terry's death. I want you to accord him your fullest cooperation." Then he turned to me and said, "Wynn, he says he knows you."

"Swivel-hips Suarez," I said.

"Slim O'Leary," he said.

3

Dear Joel,

I was sitting at my desk, sipping beer, listening to "Funky Blues," arguably the best of the Jazz at the Phils, smoking all I wanted, writing you an account of yesterday's events, getting through the evening, when Julie, who should have been asleep, knocked at the door of my study, although I still hadn't closed it.

"You coming to bed soon?" she said. Her words scared back into its hole a notion I could feel rising within me, going to my head like a sneeze, that the only way to hold onto an experience is to put it into words, shit, is the only way to have it—not much of a notion, as I now see, now that I've put it into words. Bachelorhood is a drag, but so is living with someone, especially if her diurnal rhythms are in three-quarter time and yours are four-to-the-bar. I put aside my Scripto Fineline, no longer made, and I'll have to remember to get some 2B leads today, and went to bed, so Julie could sleep.

Therefore I poured myself out of bed early, re-revising my schedule, but not so early as Julie, for I did not want her to see my pajamas sticking out in front, like the cloaks of the Athenians in *Lysistrata*. I mean to continue this account before going over to my office, where I do the work that puts lead in my pencil.

No, you are not inconveniencing me, nor am I writing out of a sense of duty, the idea that the dead only achieve consciousness through the words of the living, as W. B. Yeats thought. I am writing because I have to, as you had to play the trumpet. I am able to do it, maybe, because when writing to you I do not have to accommodate my tone and range of reference to an imagined audience, standing at my shoulder, ready to rap my knuckles, for you scarcely constitute an audience. I am aware that I have mentioned things beyond your range, such as Zora Neale Hurston, or did you after all come across her before you dropped out of Fordham to lead the Reboppers, Sitting Bull trying to bring back the buffalo herds. We have learned in this century, in the literature of which I am a certified expert, that explanations only deepen the mystery, a good enough excuse for my not bothering to sift out what you might not be able to follow, for who knows how much the dead can follow.

My aim, as I am beginning to glimpse it, is to tell you how things go with me, how they go in the Department of English and Comparative Literature of a great university as this century stiffens into closure, for this century, in the literature of which I am a certified expert remember, has not been like one of Zeno's unending soap operas, but more like a tragifarce.

I must remember to arrange these verbal doodles into a story, for that's the only way you can follow a string of words, if they unwrap a story. Did you know that of the 4,000 or so human societies pawed over by anthropologists every one has tellers (or writers) of tales and listeners (or readers) who can't get enough of them, and interpreters to boot. Making up, taking in, and working over stories constitute what ethologists call a species-specific behavioral trait, a *sine con non*—and the justification of my existence, for let me tell you, it needs justifying. Just what my story is I haven't yet figured out.

You must remember my telling you about Hector Suarez, the shiftiest halfback in our league, who liked to run to his left, maybe because he is a southpaw, his big fullback leading the way, where I would be waiting for them. We got to know each other well, for football is an intimate sport. At the All-League award reception, Hector, who is tight with his family, brought his sister, Nilda, with whom I boogied all night long, Hector trying to stare me to death. Well, yesterday, after lunch, he and I were walking to Hancock Hall, where on Murray's orders, which I treated as a request, I was to provide Hector with a list of professional staff, a list of adjuncts, a list of graduate students in the department, a list of undergraduate English majors, rosters of Terry's recent courses, the names of students she had examined recently on orals and dissertation defenses, for the vice-chair is the keeper of the keys, and in general afford my fullest cooperation.

"How's Nilda?" I said.

"Like me, like you, getting fat," he said. "You may have noticed, women who grow up in poor families, get fat."

"And the men?" I said.

"They get fat when they're no longer poor," he said. "Then they slim down again, if they get rich. How's your brother?"

"Dead," I said. He did not say anything. I assumed that he assumed that if I wanted to say more, I would.

"He was a junkie," I said. What the hell, Joel.

"So I heard," Hector said. "Happens in the best of families."

"Meaning what?" I said.

"Meaning that if families like yours hadn't deserted the neighborhood the minute a few miserable Spics moved in," he said, "maybe it wouldn't have gone downhill so fast."

"What does that say for your poor miserable Spics?" I said.

"We needed time," he said, "which no one was willing to give us. You Micks had time."

"You ought to talk to my father about that, next time you want your earwax melted out," I said. "The point is, all our friends were all moving, my mother's pals at church."

"Well, we were Catholics too, motherfucker," Hector said.

"My father is a Catholic who hates all clerics impartially," I said. "My mother is a Welsh Presbyterian."

"Your brother was dealing on the side," he said.

"Fuck he was," I said.

"You don't think he could support his habit playing lip farts on his trumpet, do you?" he said. "A narco at the Two Six going after someone else caught him in the act."

"He caught bullshit," I said.

We were standing face to face outside Hancock Hall, one count away from forearm shivers.

"Hi, Professor O'Leary," said Felicia Zhang, an undergraduate with a brilliant smile.

"You get much of that young quiff?" Hector said.

"None," I said. We walked into Hancock Hall, into the elevator, into my office, in silence, Hector closing the door, which I never do when someone is with me, but then I can't see Hector bringing a charge of sexual harassment.

"Your sainted brother ratted on his supplier," he said. "It got him off the hook—with a little help from his friends, namely me."

"So I owe you," I said. "Is that it?"

"Somebody owes me," he said. "My father was shot by addicts in his cute little beaner locksmith shop, cost him more (in loans) to set up than he ever got out of it. They came away with maybe sixty dollars."

"Listen, Hector—" I said.

"No, you listen," he said. He leaned back in the chair across from my desk. Hector's smile is a bit on the evil side, maybe because his nasolabial groove is long and immobile. "This murder of a prominent lady professor is not your run-of-the-mill case. Whoever breaks it open is going to score some serious points. You see where I'm leading? You're going to tell me everything I need to know about this diploma mill. Where were you, day before yesterday?"

"Up yours," I said.

He smiled.

"Two hundred fifty miles north," I said.

He raised an eyebrow.

"On Labor Day morning two old-timers, Jack Longhenry and Hank Littlejohn, who look after my place when I'm away, stopped by," I said. "On the way down I stopped by a neighbor's—Ivan Grant—to say so long. This was about 9 a.m."

"These faithful retainers of yours," he said, "they got phone numbers? Put them here."

So I did, and don't sweat it, Joel, for we all deal in our addictions. I'm addicted to fictions, so I purvey them to students. What does it matter now? What does it matter? At least now you are off all hooks entirely (except mine).

Patiently, digging here, pushing there, getting dirty, as you pull out a stump, Hector extracted from me what he thought he needed to know and I pried out of him why he thought someone connected to the University had killed Terry. This much was fact: she returned from her vacation two days early. It was possible, then, that some local burglar who had been watching the place, but missed Terry's arrival, or had a bum tip from the super, or was brain dead and in need of a fix, broke in, bumped into Terry, killed her. The fire escape window was open, its latch hanging from a screw. The security gate was open, its latch jammed. But the day was warm, a new geranium on the sill, no sign of forced entry, and the latches had always been that way, according to the super. "Terry was not a timorous woman," I said. Nothing was missing, so far as Monika could see. No, Hector was not thinking burglar, especially considering the condition of Terry's body.

"Which was?" I said.

According to Monika—whatshername, Mrs. Wright—Terry called her around eleven on the day before Labor Day to ask whether they should get together. So on Labor Day, about the same time, Monika trips on over, carrying croissants and this little bag of coffee beans. That's what they do on Sundays and holidays, they have brunch, do the crossword puzzle, go for a stroll down to Filene's Basement, visit a museum, take in a movie, eat dinner out.

"They were getting it on together, right?" Hector said.

"I wouldn't know," I said.

"Don't fuck with me, Slim," he said. "We got this black secretary—"

"She's an administrator," I said.

"We got this black secretary," he said, " and we got this lady professor with short hair."

"Monika's a divorcée," I said. "She's got a grown-up daughter."

"What the fuck has that got to do with it?" he said.

All right. So the elevator man takes Monika up. She rings the bell. No answer, rings and rings, no answer, so she lets herself in, and if they're not sweethearts how come she's got a key? The first thing she sees is Terry's naked ass sticking up in the air.

Hector smiled. Someone knocked at the door. Come back at two, I shouted. You got to picture this, Hector said. She's folded over the armrest of the couch, legs hanging down, feet on the floor, upper body on the seat, face on its side, eyes open, looking at a doodad on the coffee table. In her back, almost up to its hilt, right between her thoracic five and six, is a trench knife, the kind they call a Ka-Bar.

"Wait," he said. "There's another wound in her back, way to the left, under her rib cage."

"So the killer is a southpaw—like you," I said.

A righty could have done it if he came at her from the side or left rear. You got to consider the angle of entry, which we don't know yet. From the blood flow we figure she took the first hit standing up. Then the perp positions her on the couch, pulls the knife out and drives it back in, through her spine, pulls down her pants—she was wearing these lounging pajamas, like Barbara Stanwick or someone—and pushes up her top. Pretty nice ass, considering her age.

I could have said something about respect for the dead, if I wanted to see Hector smile again. "Was she raped?" I said.

Her asshole was rough around the edges, a split, a smear of blood, but no sign of semen. But we took swabs for the lab to have some fun with.

"And it is your theory, I take it, that a morbid interest in the hinderparts of a woman," I said, "is limited to college men."

He pulled out a folded sheet of paper from the inside pocket of his jacket. "The original was rolled up and held by a rubber band and pushed into Terry Jones's mouth," he said. "It's on its way to the lab. This copy," and he handed it over, "I wrote out myself, down to the last jot and tittle, whatever they are."

The Song of the Wandering Anguish

I traveled through the haunts of men
A realm of men and women too
And heard and saw such dreadful things
As straight and narrowers never knew.

For there the babe is born in woe
That begotten was in sigh and moan
Just as we wash in tears the fruit
That once we sowed in rut and groan.

And if the babe is born a boy
He's given to a woman grey
Who nails him down upon a rock
Catches his shrieks in a box of clay.

She binds iron thorns around his head
She pierces both his hands and feet
She cuts his heart out at his side
So she can feel its blood and beat.

Her fingers number every nerve
Her jaws his naked member hold
She lives upon his shrieks and cries
And she grows young as he grows old.

Till he becomes a bleeding youth
And she becomes a virgin bright
Then he rends up his manacles
And binds her down for his delight.

Someone was knocking at the door. In a minute, I said, and I said it in a voice to rattle the window.

"Your everyday break-in artist doesn't leave around poems like that," he said. "Did the perp make it up or just copy it out?"

"The title is a play on 'The Song of the Wandering Angus' by Yeats, William Butler Yeats that is," I said. "For the rest, I would need some time, but it looks like the killer did to a poem of Blake's, I forget which, William Blake is who I mean, what he did to Terry's body—he fucked it over. There are words and phrases that Blake would never have used. Angus, by the way, was the Irish god of love."

"I know who the fuck Blake and Yeats are," Hector said. "Didn't I do two years hard at CCNY?"

"What happened to the scholarship to Syracuse?" I said.

"I needed to be at home," he said.

Someone was knocking at the door.

"There are students who need me to sign their programs and such," I said.

"Yeah, well, I've got to get to the autopsy," he said, getting to his feet. "As a student of human nature you'll be interested in this: when the uniforms arrived, your friend Monika Wright, the gay divorcée, was all crumpled-like in this armchair, staring at the ceiling, looking half dead. Then she suddenly jumps up with this wild look in her eyes and starts whizzing knickknacks at the walls. All the time she's shouting, 'Cocksucking, motherfucking, cunt-lapping, blue-balled bitching bastard of a whoremonger.' "

"She's normally very genteel," I said.

"Well, she was distraught, not her normal self," Hector said. "Then she starts unloading these haymakers at the uniforms. Jimmie Walsh there, he got a fat lip for his trouble."

Someone was knocking at the door, so I opened it, and there was Julie, in her defining posture, knocking to get in.

"Hi Cuz," she said.

"How'd it go?" I said.

"You'd think with all these smart people around," she said, "someone would make registration more logical."

On his way out, after winking at Julie, Hector said, *sotto voce,* "Get me those lists by tomorrow and see what you can make of the poem, but keep it quiet. Nobody's supposed to know it exists."

Julie had an appointment to see someone about an apartment, so we rushed through her registration packet, save the nuances for later. I was sitting at my desk, she standing beside me, her hip brushing my shoulder, a tendril of hair tickling my ear when she bent over to sign a form, which made me jump, and was she coming home for dinner? "Yes, thank you," she said, and I think she was about to kiss me on the forehead. But she didn't. Then for two hours I gassed with my advisees, the undergraduates tanned and full of it, the graduate students pale and wan, trading wisecracks, for somehow I do not have it in me to inspire awe.

Then, a new experience for me, I received petitioners. Murray Weinrein crossed one thin ankle across one thin knee, held his horizontal shin with two hands as a water-skier grips his tow bar, and gave me a long look. His face had the aspect of someone about to smile, but he didn't. You'll get nothing out of being vice-chair, but a course remission, which you don't particularly want, he said. Every decision you make will earn you real enemies and false friends. You will be equally resented by those you put on committees and those you leave off. As you try to delegate tasks you will learn The First Law of Administrative Work: those who want to do it thereby prove they are not qualified. If for the sake of efficiency you do something on your own, colleagues will wonder why you did not consult them. If you try to get them involved, they will not have enough time. You will find it impossible to put together a curriculum that does justice to all three divisions of the department, especially since no one wants to teach the courses we require our students to take. The administration wants more students in our courses, but is cutting our adjunct money in half and our professorial staff by five planning units. The students are agitating for courses that we have no one qualified to teach and which they will no longer want by the time we have hired someone. The vice-chair carries with it many responsibilities, but no power. You will measure out your life in meeting rooms, schmoozing and cajoling, because you cannot give orders. Unless, and here he sat back and came very close to smiling, you can impose your will by a force of personality no one yet knows you have. In any case, you will have to set aside work on your eagerly awaited new book, at least until you get the hang of things.

"OK," I said: "I'll do it."

"Good," he said. "I knew you would."

"For one year," I said. "I'll finish out Terry's term and that's it."

"I'll send in Irene," he said. "Tell her what course you're dropping, so she can get the word out." (Irene Howland's main job is as secretary to the chair and vice-chair.)

"That's all right," I said. "You can tell her yourself that I'm dropping the graduate seminar. And tell her to get together those lists that Suarez wants."

"I've created a monster," he said. "And your office stinks of cigarettes."

An assistant professor up for a tenure review stuck his head in the door and when I looked up skittered away. He has a curious way of walking. It involves furious motion from the waist down, corduroys swishing, and absolute stillness from the waist up, arms dangling.

Marshall Grice popped in for a companionable smoke. He did me the honor of comparing me to Cincinnatus.

Zeno Confalone and Leonard Sistrunk looked in, only to tell me that when the going got tough, they would be there for me.

Kay Pesky walked in and sat down, legs crossed, a highlight on her knee, one arm over the back of the chair, the other propping her head, a pencil in her topknot, which was leaning to the left. She had a friendly warning: Murray would use me up and throw me away, for if Terry Jones was tempered steel, I was silly putty. And there was Julie, knocking on the door, which was open.

"Come in, come in," I said. "Kay, meet my cousin, Julie Berceau. Julie, meet my colleague, Kay Pesky."

"Hi," said Julie, pulling a chair out from under my library table and sitting down, surprisingly at ease, as though Kay was a known quantity.

"I didn't know you had a cousin," said Kay.

"I have several," I said.

"Guess what our new assistant professor wanted to pump me and Leonard about," said Kay, ignoring Julie.

"The indomitable Serena Crawfoot," I said.

"She's writing an essay on fisting," Kay said. "I wish I had thought of it first."

"Fisting!" I said.

"It's when you stick your arm up some guy's ass to the elbow," Julie said.

"What does fisting have to do with literature?" I said.

"Wynn, Wynn, you *are* a dinosaur," said Kay. "Serena and me, we're culture critics, not just literary critics."

"This is, after all, a department of English and comparative literature," I said.

"Serena came across some article on a gay men's club," Kay said. "But a few women with a raised political consciousness are invited. What they do is, a man sits in a sling and gets hoisted to about shoulder height. Then a woman fists him."

I felt my scrotum tighten and my dangle shrink.

"A plurivalent play of signifiers," said Kay. "The man contests gender stereotypes by the mere fact of his being gay, more concretely by catching rather than pitching, as they say. The woman interrogates them from her side by penetrating the male. Together they reciprocally reverse the hegemonic gender code. That the site of desire had been displaced from the genitals to the anus adds up to a triple subversion of phallocentric ideology. But that's just the beginning."

"I wonder if those guys take an enema first," said Julie. "Otherwise think of what your arm would look like when you pull it out."

"Focus on the woman," said Kay. "What is she doing? She's enacting the black power salute, thus affirming feminist solidarity with blacks, thus dramatizing the status of women as niggers; thus defying the white supremacists who oppress blacks and women."

"*Chouette,*" said Julie. "Awesome."

"There's more," said Kay.

"Do you believe any of this?" I said.

"We have outgrown belief in belief," said Kay. "Besides, it's Serena's project, not that she sees all the possibilities."

"I must say," I said, "I prefer my sex less politicized."

"There's no such thing," said Kay.

"Does that mean there's also no such thing as nonsexualized politics?" said Julie.

For the first time Kay looked at Julie with something like interest, if not with approval.

I'd better disengage, Joel: time for lunch, office hours, a meeting with Hector Suarez.

Dear Joel,

I snuck (which sounds more sneaky than "sneaked") out of bed, my own bed, after Julie went to sleep, asserting my independence, to continue my account of yesterday's events, if that's the word, for already I am one day behind, although I wrote more pages in four hours this morning than I had ever before written in a week. You're a disinhibitor, is what you are.

I've got a cigarette in my chops, squinting through the smoke, burning out the Other, as that asshole Sartre said, sipping on beer, munching on a sandwich, the last of the roast pork, listening to Dizzy, Clark Terry, Freddy Hubbard blow one amazing chorus after another on "Chickenwing," Dizzy, as usual, bringing out the best in everybody.

Kay cocked an eyebrow when I said Julie and I were on our way to shop for dinner, Professor Bigfoot and Cousin Tip-Toe, an allegorical tableau of Appetite and its object. I sent Julie off to pick up whatever she liked for breakfast, lunch, and snacks ("Thanks, Cuz"), while I picked up the makings of a ratatouille, since she was not much of a meat-eater: peppers, big onions, zucchini, eggplant (but no garlic, for I have a braid of garlic hanging on my kitchen wall, next to the spice rack), and four big, thick, loin-end pork chops, for garnish. She met me at the checkout line with stuff made from grains, or starch, which as we learned in high school chem, turns to sugar in the mouth, with yogurt, hummus, bean curd, food from old civilizations gone in the tooth, unable to chew, goodbye Faust, so long tragedy. All our fashionable dishes aspire to the condition of baby food. As for me the only grains I normally eat are made into a gravelly loaf heavy as the kind of shot you put and out of which you could wring a pint of water, were you so inclined.

While I cooked, sipping on beer, listening to Miles and Bird play "Sipping on Bells," Julie sipping on wine, she dealt out the tableware, putting knife and fork both to the right of the plate, as though she had no mother, telling me about her day, about the rooms she went to see. One, about the size of a shower stall, was in the apartment of an old woman, and you'll be happy to help with the housework, won't you dear, $800 a month, no kitchen privileges. Another, a total mess, nice collection of beer bottles though, courtesy of the previous occupant, was in a university-owned apartment shared by three raunchy jocks, sweatpants cut off at the thighs, sweatshirts cut off at the hairy armpits, who wanted to know if she could cook, every kind of privilege *complet.* Stay out of that, I said. Maybe I could rent her a room, she said. I don't need the money, I said, for Belinda had too much class to go after a piece of my salary, and I put on a package of pinto beans, for tomorrow we would have brown rice and beans, with a few ham hocks thrown in (for garnish).

"I just wanted to know," Julie said. "Why did you sign me up for those particular courses? I don't mean . . ." And here, Joel, I'm afraid your brother suddenly let go of a lecture, for she had pressed the right button. I'll spare you the details, as well as the metaphysics, but here's the gist: Humanities, over two semesters, would take her from Homer to Dostoevsky, the deep background; the other course I put her down for, Style and Substance, was a composition course grafted onto a survey of English literature, the middle background, and in any case required for the degree. The latter should be followed, during the spring semester, by a survey of American literature, the near background. Then, next year, courses in modern literature, the foreground, revealing the age to itself. Then a course in non-Western literature, put it all in perspective. At the end she would have some idea of where she was and how she got there. Notice, Joel, I did not claim that literature makes you a better person: many great writers, and many more critics, have been complete shits. But it does make you more aware.

"Sounds terrific," Julie said, "just what I need. It must be very satisfying... but... what does an English major *do?*... after graduation, I mean. I know you're a professor and all..."

There's one of the things a man needs a wife for, to prick his balloon.

"About the degree," she said. "I've been thinking.... If I take two courses a term, that's twelve points a year, that's over ten years to get 124, and I don't have a job and I don't have an apartment and I don't have—"

"No tears," I said. "I can't stand tears."

"Who's crying?" she said.

"Have a chop," I said. "It will give you strength."

"This ratatat is delicious," she said.

"Ratatouille," I said.

"Oh, that's what it is," she said. "Your pronunciation threw me off."

"Imagine you have a degree," I said, "what do you picture yourself doing?"

"Well," she said. "I don't think I'm a word person." This was not the moment for me to say that the road to empowerment was cobblestoned with words.

"What kind of a person are you?" I said.

"I think maybe I'm a people person," she said. "I see myself among smart, decent people who have steady jobs, unlike my father, you know. . . ."

I told her to stick with the courses she had, for they would do her good, no matter what she majored in. I told her she could add introductory French if she wanted to speed up the process, for she would need a language to graduate anyhow. I told her that I had already spoken to my friend Zeno Confalone, a rousing teacher, to make sure she got in his section of humanities, for Zeno taught the course every other year, to refresh himself, he said, to support general education, he said, and to spite Angel Terrasco, although he never said so. Angel hated Humanities, which she described as "a course in male entitlement." She also said it was unprofessional to teach a text unless you had mastered the scholarship, and no one, least of all Zeno Confalone, had mastered the scholarship on all the assigned readings in Humanities. But then Angel's notion of professionalism is to teach a work of literature by summarizing what other scholars have said about it. I told Julie not to buy any books, for I had copies around of the ones she would need, and if she wanted to get a jump on her classmates I could give her a copy of the *Iliad* to read right then. I told her I would look into a work-study job or a student loan or I would lend her enough to get her by, or something.

"Thanks Cuz," she said.

"Eat your chop," I said.

"One more thing," she said. "Could you lend me a pair of socks until I can buy some tomorrow? One of mine has a big hole in it."

Safe in my study, enveloped in a protective cloud of cigarette smoke, listening to early Bird, and his solo on "K.C. Blues" has to be a couple of the most beautiful minutes in the history of music, I put together some notes for my opening-day lecture. Then I looked up the source of the poem left rolled up in Terry's mouth. It is the first six stanzas of Blake's "The Mental Traveler." Here's how they go:

George Stade

The Song of the Wandering Anguish

I traveld thro' a Land of Men
A land of Men & Women too
And heard and saw such dreadful
    things
As cold earth wanderers never knew.

For there the Babe is born in joy
That was begotten in dire woe
Just as we reap in Joy the fruit
Which we in bitter tears did sow.

And if the Babe is born a boy
He's given to a woman old
Who nails him down upon a rock
Catches his shrieks in cups of gold

She binds iron thorns around his
    head
She pierces both his hands & feet
She cuts his heart out at his side
To make it feel both cold and heat

Her fingers number every nerve
Just as a Miser counts his gold
She lives upon his shrieks & cries
And she grows young as he grows old

Till he becomes a bleeding youth
And she becomes a virgin bright
Then he rends up his Manacles
And binds her down for his delight

I traveled through the haunts of men
A realm of men and women too
And heard and saw such dreadful
    things
As straight and narrowers never knew.

For there the babe is born in woe
That begotten was in sigh and moan
Just as we wash in tears the fruit
That once we sowed in rut and groan.

And if the babe is born a boy
He's given to a woman grey
Who nails him down upon a rock
Catches his shrieks in a box of clay.

She binds iron thorns around his
    head
She pierces both his hands and feet
She cuts his heart out at his side
So she can feel its blood and beat.

Her fingers number every nerve
Her jaws his naked member hold
She lives upon his shrieks and cries
And she grows young as he grows old.

Till he becomes a bleeding youth
And she becomes a virgin bright
Then he rends up his manacles
And binds her down for his delight.

I had meant to make this an all-nighter, over the bent world brooding, everyone else dormant, my consciousness the last stay against all-out oblivion, telling you what I did, what I saw, after breaking off this morning's letter, but suddenly I felt sleepy, although it is just round about midnight—on which for the duration of that dash I listened to Bird chime the changes. There's a chilling breeze on the back of my neck, for Julie must have opened the window when I wasn't looking, a premonition of fall, and the warmth emanating from her apple cheeks beckons. I'll leave it for you to sustain the world with warm breast and ah! Bright wings.

4

Dear Joel,

Although I struggled out of bed early, Julie was already gone, my socks with her, a banana skin on the kitchen table, a bowl now empty but for the two now soggy flakes of the crunchy horrible she had for breakfast, a note leaning against the cereal box, and on it written one of Ma's Druidical superstitions: "Breakfast is the most important meal of the day." But she knows how to make a pot of strong coffee, does Julie. I like that in a woman.

I'm back here in my study, the cigarette smoke gathering nicely into a veil between me and the outside world, Bird and Diz thickening the air with "Melancholy Baby," Bird making the most of that corny interval from "my" to "melancholy," Diz doing things with rhythm no one had ever tried before. "Rhythm's my bag," said Diz, but melody was his carryall and harmony his backpack. I suppose they had to end with the quotation from "Country Gardens" to let the squares know that what went before was something of a put-on. But bop is like modernism in this: the most serious moments can occur during the put-ons, Eliot's footnote to *The Waste Land,* Joyce's mythophilologicoproprogenitive micturations.

I was late for lunch, for writing to you has a sedating effect on me, for usually I am one of those impossible people who is early for everything. Everybody was eating already, except for Zeno, whose chair was empty. Next to Serena Crawfoot's plate was a pack of Kools, Kay's brand. I was still thinking about how to start off my class, which is six hours in the future from the present in which I am writing, but a day in the future from the time about which I am writing, although sometimes I confuse the two, the past usurping the present, the present taking over the past, as with some owlish New Historicist, the future in any case dispossessing both of them, so I said to Leonard, "Here's one for you: scan the second line of this:

> It gathers to a greatness, like the ooze of oil
> Crushed. Why do men then now not reck his rod?

"It's Hopkins, of course.... But where does the second?..." Leonard said, counting: "da bum, da bum, aha! Crushed. Why do men then now not reck his rod? You have to lean on every syllable."

"Bingo!" I said.

"A Jesuit priest shaking his finger at some darling boy in short pants," said Leonard, "stroking his rod."

"Yet let not each gay turn thy rapture move," said Marshall Grice.

"Sir, all puns are corn, a coarse ground of wheat," said Leonard.

"And ten low words oft creep in one dull line," said Marshall.

"The Age of Reason," said Lizzie, "was the age of wonders. Everything has gone downhill since."

"As soon as I get a chance, I'm going to read some poetry," said Serena.

"All right, wise guy," said Leonard, looking at me, "here's one from your own barren field. How does the last line of this grab you?" and he recited these winged words:

> Reflected in my golden eye
> The dullard knows that he is mad.
> Tell me if I am not glad.

"I'll be damned," I said. "Well, Eliot had a good ear, even if he did become a Christian."

"And no birds sing," said Kay, getting into the act.

"Purgatoried, I should say, is more likely," said Marshall, pointing his pipe at me. "What did you learn about Terry's murder from Detective Ortiz?"

"Suarez," I said. "The evidence points to a college man."

"Why not a college woman?" said Kay.

"She was killed with a trench knife," I said, "not a woman's choice of weapon."

"Good old Wynn," said Kay.

"You've been living a cloistered existence," said Lizzie.

"Just what I've been telling him," said Leonard.

"I have a Shrade folding hunter in my handbag," said Serena.

"Suarez called it a Ka-Bar," I said.

"Yes, yes, I carried one across France and Germany," said Marshall. "And if I had gotten close to George Smith Patton Jr., I would have tickled his kidney with it," and he thrust forward with his pipe. Marshall, as it then struck me, is, like Hector Suarez, a southpaw.

"Some of us had them in Vietnam, even aboard ship," said Leonard, "but a grunt told me they were on the unwieldy side when it came to cutting of ears."

"As a conveyer of gossip, Wynn, you have long been a disappointment to me," said Marshall. "From now on have Lopez talk to Lizzie."

"Suarez," I said.

"That's right," said Leonard, "leave it to Lizzie."

"She'll MRI the heart of darkness," said Kay.

"Our myriaminded metamystery sleuth," I said.

The point of this badinage, Joel, is that Lizzie is writing a book and teaching a course on the mystery story, which she sees as above all the form in which Western Humanity set out to track itself down, starting with *Oedipus Rex*. The absence of anything like the mystery story during the Christian dark and middle ages she takes as evidence of an Asiatic interlude.

"Think of what a wonderful Watson you would make," said Kay, looking at me.

"I have just dragged myself through one by Ira Lovecraft," said Lizzie. "Are there no editors any more?"

"The beanbag!" said Leonard, for such, in reference to her shape, is Zeno's name for Amabelle Bloor, who writes detective novels under the pseudonym of Ira Lovecraft. She is a professor in the English Department of our sister institution across Broadway, where her hatred of all her colleagues is warmly reciprocated. Angel Terrasco, prodded by Professor Bloor, has been trying to get us to pirate her away for years.

"We are all in it," said Lizzie, "thinly disguised as fools and knaves. The exception is Wynn, who turns out to be gay, which makes him all right."

"It's not fair," said Leonard.

"The plot is that a character very like Angel wants to bring a distinguished feminist into the Department," said Lizzie, "but characters like Zeno and Leonard through a series of dirty tricks rabble-rouse an opposition. Wynn, however, out of a disinterested concern for justice, kills Zeno and Leonard. The main task of her amateur detective, a feminist sympathizer, a twit teaching at CCNY, where he is insufficiently appreciated, is to frame Marshall. In a euphoric ending, the distinguished feminist is hired and Marshall is led away. A Schweinerie, no?"

"Egad," said Marshall.

"And me?" said Kay.

"You and I are described as 'masculinist toys,'" said Lizzie.

"Makes me want to reach for my Schrade folding hunter," said Serena.

"There are, however, a number of *mots justes*," said Lizzie. "I thought that Wynn, as a feinschmecker of prose, would appreciate this: 'What do you mean? He puzzled.'"

I had one petitioner of note, Angel Terrasco herself. She suddenly appeared in the doorway to my office like a messenger from the chthonic powers carrying bad news. She is tall, broad-shouldered, no flesh between the skin and bone of her pale face, her stiff, black frizzled hair, now streaked with gray (when did that happen?) flaring out on either side from the back of her head like Dracula's cape, no ornamentation except for arterial-red lipstick and a delicate little gold cross on a chain. The currents of my emotional life must flow out of murky pools, for I used to lust after Angel, but that was fifteen years ago, when I was a graduate student, indiscriminate in my hankerings.

"I expected better of you," she said.

"What did I do now?" I said.

"You will not keep Murray in his chair by doing his work for him," she said. "He has thoroughly discredited himself."

"I understand he's doing a good job on all those committees, kicking ass, trying to save our benefits."

"I had hoped you would not turn out to be just another old boy," she said. "That's the rule, isn't it? Never snitch on another man to a woman. You know very well I'm not talking about his silly committees stumbling around drunk on their own self-importance."

This was not a good time for me to say anything, not even that I had no idea what she was talking about. She sat down, took a cigarette out of my pack, leaned forward so I could light it, settled back, inhaled to her deepest depths, a tendril of smoke curling out of her crotch, her eyes fluttering closed, for Angel, whose self-control is excessive, is one of those people who can smoke three cigarettes a week and never get hooked.

"I want you to sign this," she said. There was a short text, beneath it a column of signatures that ran down the page, down a second page, halfway down a third. I saw the signatures of Bertil Lund, our senior medievalist now that Terry is dead, and of Malcolm Tetrault, the assistant professor with the funny walk who is up for tenure. The text, which was addressed to the university senate, demanded immediate enactment of a statute forbidding sexual relations between faculty and students and between faculty and administrators.

I lit up to avoid meeting Angel's eye. My theory had always been that in rebellion against her father, who was an anarchist, an atheist, a philanderer, and a male-firster, Angel had become conservative, pious, puritanical, and a feminist. Her father got revenge by coming down with some obscure neuromuscular disorder that keeps him in a wheelchair. Her mother's choice of passive resistance is to play the all-around incompetent, mangling her twenty words of English after fifty years in the States. Angel took them in, pays their ways, answers her father's self-pitying tantrums with the cool condescension of a professional nurse in charge of an ill-bred child she doesn't particularly like.

"I do not believe in regulating sexual relations between consenting adults," I said, and I am not the first man who clutched at a slogan to hoist himself out of a jam.

"It's no skin off your nose," she said.

"Even I have been known to act on principle," I said.

"The principle is this," she said: "unless male lust is regulated, no other regulation will hold. The primitives that your precious modernists looked to as paragons of polymorphous promiscuity in fact regulated every aspect of sexual behavior. That's how they could remain stable for thousands of years until they collided with the degenerate phallocentric post-renaissance West. The modernists' valorization of the primitive was not a response to the alleged Victorian erotophobia, but a symptom of the accelerating license that was not careening toward disaster fast enough to suit them." (And right there Angel gave me the idea of how to start off my first class.) "Look at the lives around you. It's disgusting. What do you thinks AIDS is, if not a warning? Never mind that no one heeds it. Do you know that nearly half the births in New York City are out of wedlock? And that is in spite of the legalized murder we call birth control."

"It takes two to tango," I said.

"What countervailing force does a secular girl or young woman have in her equal to the demonic rages of male lust?" she said—"especially when their minds are stuffed with twaddle about romantic love. Especially when millennia of male propaganda have defined women solely as receptacles for penises and babies? Don't you play the let-it-all-hang-out-liberal with me."

Sure it is a peculiar sort of feminism that allows for no slack in the Church's line on abortion and irregular sexual arrangements. Sure it is her feminism does not derive from Enlightenment ideas about the unity of mankind, the rights of women, the right of all men and women to equality under the law. The Enlightenment is to Angel as the Middle Ages are to Lizzie—anathema. Nor can you say that Angel is simply a man-hater, for on the whole she does not much like women either. She shook out another of my cigarettes, lit it from her stub, settled back, took a drag that left smoke seeping out from under her toenails, her eyelids fluttering.

"I'll think about your petition," I said.

"Waffling is your métier," she said. "You will be recruiting a committee to hire a replacement for Terry. I want to be on it."

"Let's see if we get authorized to hire anyone," I said, "and then the Department will have to decide whether it wants a junior or a senior."

"There is no question that we need to hire another senior feminist," she said. "And I know just the one we need. I have not yet forgiven Terry Jones and your friends for blocking the appointment of Amabelle Bloor."

"Terry is beyond the need for forgiveness," I said, unless it is for saying that Amabelle Bloor is the one case of motiveless malignity she had actually met.

"I hope you put that Spanish detective on the right track," she said. Angel is sensitive about her Spanish surname, which nevertheless earned her a scholarship to college, a fellowship to graduate school, and her first job. The rest she earned by some hard-hitting scholarship on Mary Shelley and the impact abroad, especially in Spain, of *Frankenstein*, which she reads as a novel of protest against the victimization of women by men.

"Which track is that?" I said.

"Whom do you know that hates lesbians?" she said.

"You?" I said.

"I am now going to quote your friend Zeno Confalone verbatim: 'the difference between male homosexuals and lesbians is this: whereas gays envy women, lesbians hate men. It is simple justice to respond in kind.' He was drunk, of course, but *in vino veritas*."

"Zeno doesn't really hate lesbians," I said. "He just pretends to resent them as rivals. Of the shapely ones he says that a good behind is a terrible thing to waste."

"Some young hoodlum just slapped me on mine," she said. "I wouldn't be surprised if Zeno put him up to it."

"The phantom tush-toucher," I said.

"In a civilized country they'd cut off his hand," she said.

"A public spanking by his victims would be more appropriate," I said. "A spank for a spank."

"It has been impressed upon me that for the sake of the department I ought to run against Murray," she said. "Should I do so, I will expect your support."

"Well, as vice-chair," I said, "that would put me in an awkward—"

"This time you will not be allowed to waffle," she said. "A trimmer, you must know, is an object of universal contempt. A sinner at least through a conscious offence against the Light affirms Its existence and in risking hellfire acquires a certain moral gravity. I am giving you a chance to redeem yourself."

"From what? for St. Siobhan's sweet knees?"

"Malcolm Tetrault is already sounding out the juniors," she said. "Bertil Lund and Amabelle Bloor are sounding out the seniors. I want you to speak to your smokers' club."

"What do you expect me to say?" I said.

"You might remind Lizbeth Arno that the administration will not renew her contract without an unequivocal recommendation from the chair," she said. "Are you willing to count on Murray?"

"The ACLU—" I said.

"She is not a regular line professor," she said. "Her contract, which I looked into, is renewable every three years. Should I become chair, I could under certain conditions be persuaded to recommend an extension."

"You are asking me to become a bagman for a bribe," I said.

"That is how the political game is played," she said. "You might point out to Zeno Confalone and Leonard Sistrunk that there are students who under pressure judiciously applied would consider bringing charges of sexual harassment. I am looking into it."

"But that's blackmail," I said.

"Whatever I am, I am not a waffler," she said. "You might get Kay Pesky to understand that she is overdue for a show of feminist solidarity. A new chair will have to decide whether or not she is ripe for promotion from associate to full professor. Then there's her catamite, that Serena Crawfoot person. . . ."

"You're wrong about—" I said.

"As for Marshall Grice," she said; "he has convinced himself that he is a just man. Very well: you might ask him in the name of justice whether or not it is about time that a woman occupied the chair. Malcolm and Bertil are taking the others to lunch one by one to ask them precisely that question."

"We are in for an interesting time," I said.

"You can tell them that as a sop to the old boys I shall keep you on as vice-chair," she said.

"I have to think about all this," I said.

"You'll keep on trimming until there is nothing left," she said.

The beans with sofrito and ham hocks were simmering, the water ready for the brown rice, the leftover ratatat warming, garlic in the air, when Julie breezed in, sighed ("What a day . . ."), dropped her bookbag on a chair, poured herself a glass of wine, set the table, and that bookbag, at second glance, is my carryall, which I don't remember giving her. She turned down the volume on my boombox, which was playing a sampler of the churchy blues, by various hands, that Blue Note used to release, good listening, amazing all-around competence, some of the sides really cooking, but just the same, muzakification has set in.

Julie had just come in from an apartment east of the fashionable East Side, riverratsville, seven feet wide by thirty long, a kitchenette at one end, a loft bed at the other, shower in the hall, a smell of cats, $680. Another she had a look at was on Amsterdam in the Nineties, old women in black in chairs on the stoop, young women with memorable derrieres, talkative old guys brown-bagging it, young guys hustling controlled substances, $800.

"And by the way," she said, "Professor Confalone is cool. He took me to lunch."

"Cocksucking, motherfucking, cunt-lapping, blue-balled bitching bastard of a whoremonger," I said, but in a mumble.

"I didn't catch that, Cuz," Julie said, as the doorbell rang.

I led Hector Suarez down the hall ("You read all these books?") and into the kitchen, where he lifted his nose and closed his eyes, a mock-exalted expression on his face: "Spanish soul food," he said.

"Julie, this is Detective Hector Suarez," I said. "Hector, this is my cousin Julie Berceau."

"Hello, Cousin Julie," said Hector, smiling evilly.

"I *knew* you were a cop," said Julie.

"Oh yeah?" said Hector.

"You got that look that comes from hassling people," she said, setting an extra place before I could do anything about it. So Hector ate with us, drinking beer ("Dos Equis, no less. You've come a long way since you Micks used to have wet dreams about Miss Rheingold."), treating Julie as though he knew all about her, but nothing good, scornful of the brown rice, eating two of the ham hocks I had in mind for myself.

"I got those lists you wanted in my study," I said.

"That department of yours is a snake pit," he said, "what it looks like to me."

"Go ahead, I'll clean up," said Julie, getting domesticated, not necessarily a good thing.

We sat on opposite sides of my desk, Hector pulling out a cigar, the corners of his mouth up, the middle down, while for a minute or two we blew smoke at each other. This was not an exchange I was going to win, his firepower being heavier, so I opened the window, clearing the air between us. He began to ask me about the people I work with, and you will remember Pa saying that a snitch was a crab louse on the body politic, but I also wanted Terry's killer taken down, so I waffled, sticking to the facts.

Hector wanted to know whether Terry went both ways, whether she had "lovers" besides Monika, whether anyone wrote her threatening letters, made threatening calls. I thought not, I said. She ever make it with a student? I thought not. He asked me what I knew about people on the lists, students she had flunked or barely passed or disparaged on evaluation cards, administrators she had bearded, colleagues she had crossed, a thieving janitor she had denounced. I said I knew no one on the lists who hated or loved Terry enough to kill her.

"How about this secretary, this Irene Howland?" he said. "I hear she was afraid of our Terry."

"She's afraid of everything," I said.

"What about this departmental aide, is his title, this Jap. Tatsuo Nakatani?" he said. "I see he's been a graduate student for ten years."

"He calls himself 'Teddy,'" I said, "but the other students call him 'Jug,' maybe because of his ears, maybe because he's a first-class juggler, does card tricks, sleight-of-hand stuff. He's also a computer whiz. His people, by the way, have been in this country longer than yours or mine."

"How'd he get on with Ms. Jones?" said Hector.

"You've got to understand," I said. "Nakatani has submitted a half-dozen dissertation proposals during the last couple of years—to a half-dozen different professors, all of whom turned him down. He appealed to Terry. She told him that to date all his proposals had been bizarre. When he came up with a sensible proposal she would find him a sponsor. Terry never had much patience with the department's waifs and strays. She probably suggested that he find another line of work."

"Could piss you off," said Hector. "Ten years of your life down the drain."

"I've never seen Nakatani in a snit," I said. "Mostly he wears a kind of smile, as though he knows something the rest of us don't."

So maybe Terry was killed by a crazy, but he'd have to be of the organized type, because he brought his weapon with him, because he didn't leave any traces of himself, even though there were two months' worth of dust on everything. If a crazy, did he kill Terry because she was a lesbian or because she was a professor or because she was a certain physical type, or was she just a target of opportunity? This kind of crazy, according to a course on sexual homicide Hector had taken at the John Jay College of Police Science, is driven by a fantasy. Pressure builds up in him until he has to act it out. When he comes across someone who fits the bill, say a brunette with her hair parted down the middle, a prostitute, a nurse, a lady professor, he rips her out of life and shoves her into his fantasy, some scene he's been carrying around in his head. He plays the producer, director, and male lead. What the victim is really like has nothing to do with the part she has to play.

"Just like a writer," I said, "except that a writer acts out his fantasies in words."

"I wouldn't know about that," he said, "but a crazy is like possessed; he's taken over entirely by a need for that sense of power he gets from manhandling his victim. He's your basic pip-squeak."

"So the victim is a stand-in for someone or something else?" I said.

"You could say that," he said.

"So is a character in a novel," I said.

He flashed me his famous smile, looked at his cigar as though something was wrong with it. "You're telling me that writers are crazies?" he said.

"The good ones," I said.

"The difference is that a writer's stand-ins only bleed commas," he said, "which I never yet seen stain a carpet."

"We're talking magic here," I said. "Eat the lion's heart and you become lionhearted. Shoot a deer, which in the imagination of the hunter is always feminine, and you kill the woman in you. Stick a pin in a simulacrum of your enemy and you've poked holes in him. Magic is a metaphor, through which crazies and writers do their thing, one thing standing for another."

"You always was full of shit," he said, "and all these books you been reading is no substitute for Ex-Lax. What I'm thinking is maybe we got some guy pretending to be a crazy, trying to throw us off. With all this noise about serial killers lately, you can see how he would get the idea."

"No one pretends to be crazy who isn't," I said. "You've got to have the inclination."

"Thank you, Professor O'Leary," he said. "The main point is that an organized crazy can also pretend to be sane, makes him tough to sniff out."

You had to consider the possibility that Terry was the first or the last in a series, said Hector. He had already sent the case files and crime scene photos to the FBI, see if there had been other killings with a similar "signature," as they say, see if one of the eggheads at Quantico could draw up a profile of the killer. Meanwhile Hector was trying to figure out why there was no semen anywhere in Terry, although there were traces of a lubricant, so far unidentified, in her rectum—something was jammed up there, but not anything left in the apartment, far as he could tell. He was also trying to figure out how the killer got in, not in Terry, but in the building.

"Elementary, my dear Suarez," I said. "The lock on the door is ancient. The innards must be all worn down. You take the knob in one hand, pull the door toward you, place your other hand flat against the frame, give the door a sharp, sudden push with both hands, and it opens. A former lady friend who lives there showed me."

"You and me, we're going to take a walk, check that door out," he said.

"The killer is across the street," I said, "sitting on one of those benches against the park wall, under a hanging sycamore branch. He waits until the tenant lets himself in, crosses the street, looks through the door glass to see whether the doorman, who doubles as an elevator operator, is at his desk. If not, he pushes in, buzzes Terry's doorbell. She opens the door, says what do *you* want, gets an answer, turns around to lead him through her foyer, gets stabbed."

"That's not all she gets," Hector said. "The knife is sharpened by someone who knows what he is doing, on the back too, along what they call the false edge. He shoves it in, jerks the handle one way, then the other, so the blade slices from side to side. Under the skin Terry was just about cut in half. Could a professor do that?"

"I don't see why a lot of reading should smother the old berserker howling in our genes, wanting out," I said. "Usually professors do their damage with words. But sometimes words are not enough."

Hector pulled out a cigar, unwrapped it, licked one end, put it in his mouth, lit the other, took short pulls on it, the smoke writhing around his face, took a long pull, turned his head to the side, his usual boorishness (a matter of choice rather than ignorance or stupidity) in abeyance. The cloud of smoke poured up, over the books, defying gravity. He leaned forward, put his elbows on my desk, said, "How about you? Are words enough for Professor O'Leary?"

"Sometimes I go hunting," I said.

"I got people looking into the possibility Terry was killed by a burglar, a crazy, an enemy or lover outside the university," he said. "But I'm leaning toward a university connection. So what have we got? We got maintenance people. We got security. We got administrators, inside the department and out. We got undergraduates and graduate students, majoring in English or something else. Myself I'm concentrating on the department, and in the department I'm concentrating on professors. I haven't ruled you out either."

"I'm flattered," I said.

"Nearest we can figure she was killed twelve to eighteen hours before Monika found her," he said. "That gives you time to drive down to New York, kill Terry, drive back to your hideaway."

"Why would I do that?" I said.

"Maybe you're a crazy pretending to be sane," he said.

"That would have to mean I was a crazy pretending to be crazy while I killed Terry," I said.

"You got it," he said.

I've got to cut out, Joel. One thing I never do is arrive late for class.

5

The class went fine,

thanks. Giving a good class must be like blowing a good chorus. Afterward you feel pleasantly depleted, all that anxiety let out, shaped into an offering, a solicitation to others, in whom it survives, if it survives at all, no longer a part of your life, but of theirs, transposed energy, always sexual energy, according to Zeno. Does that mean that all this time I've been fucking my students over?

After class I sat in my office, processing paper. Julie knocked on the door, although it was open, two women her age behind her, one already blushing, the other looking ready for a fight. Classmates of hers in Style and Substance, is how Julie introduced them. Would I mind, she said, but they sort of came up with the idea of eating together, in that Ethiopian restaurant, supposed to be reasonable, then studying together, going over their first assignment together, "The Miller's Tale"—did I know what it was about?—listen to some music maybe, these new CDs Heather (the blusher) had, the latest sounds out of Seattle. I gave them my blessing, and if we had been on speaking terms I would have said to myself, That's what she needs, woman friends, keep her away from Zeno Confalone.

So it is that I'm in my study, home alone, two hero sandwiches on a platter, one sausages and peppers, one steak and onions, a beer freshly opened, a cigarette freshly lit, ready to put something on, and it's got to be "Funky Blues" again, *Nachtmuzik,* matches my mood, cause I'm feeling funky. There it is: A-Do Wah a-DoWah a-Do-Wah a-Dahaha, Oscar Peterson barrellhousing, Bird kansascityfy-ing, both superhuman, but Charlie Shavers climbing Jacob's ladder toward them, showing the world why he was one of Diz's favorites. Remember how he keeps hitting that high note, holding it, falling away from it a la Louis Armstrong, hitting it again, coming down dirty. Just thinking about it, waiting for it, I can feel the sweat gather in my armpits and crotch.

I'm listening to Peterson comp. He's throwing in all these beautiful little ideas, enough of them for a middling musician to make a career out of. How does anyone get so inventive? Remember that ten-inch LP you had of Peterson playing boogie-woogie? He's the best, yet he never had the cult followers, you know, speaking in tones of hushed reverence, of Thelonious Monk and Bud Powell. The reason, I suppose, is that he never cultivated that formidable air, working the audience over with a cold stare, fuck you Whitey, never went crazy. Is Peterson queer? That might explain it, for the world of bop was relentlessly macho. I can think of only one female bopper, outside of singers and piano player, and she was a lesbian trombonist. (Can you imagine kissing a female trumpet player with big lips, man, do a chorus of "Flight of the Bumblebee"?) Diz, on a celebration for his own seventieth birthday, said that playing with Peterson was like coming home. He meant a number of things, among them that Peterson's playing, with its blues base, is at the source, cornucopiasville, but also that he is accessible, as a musician and a man, for which the jazz cultists won't forgive him until he's dead. Do you think that is why, unlike Angel and Leonard and to a smaller degree Kay and Zeno, I have never generated any charisma, because I am too accessible? Available Jones the Confessor, that's me.

I do not believe that Hector seriously considers me a suspect. We accessible types are not murderous. It is possible, of course, to be a resentful-aggressive type pretending to be accessible. Then there is Sartre, from whom France has yet to recover, who said that you are what you do: an aggressive person is one who does aggressive things; there is no latency. I protest that my testosterone levels are as high as anyone's, that I'm a latent father of thousands. Tell me, please tell me, that I am not one of those despicable types whose aggression takes the form of turning the other cheek.

"You got a hunting knife?" is what Hector said the other night, still coming on as though I was a suspect. He was rummaging around in a little gym bag he had brought with him.

"I have several," I said.

"Got one like this?" he said, and he lateraled something across the desk—which I caught, for you do not lose old habits all at once. "Was one of these did in Terry," he said. "Go ahead, take it out, try it on for size."

I slid the black, Parkerized blade out of its sheath slowly, with respect. The blade is saber-ground and long, seven inches at least, with fuller, a swage, the cutting edge rounding up to a high point. The handle is made of dark brown leather rings squeezed together under such pressure you cannot see where one ring ends and the next begins. I hefted it, slashed through the air. It feels good in the hand, Joel, as though hand and knife had evolved reciprocally, each shaping the other. The point of balance is about an inch behind the finger guard, where the pointer finger grips, where I like it, the handle heavy enough to make the blade feel alive, responsive, intelligent. I could feel its power move all the way up my arm, like a surge of blood. "Too much blade for a hunting knife," I said. "You want something not much bigger than the finger you lay along the knife's spine when you slit open a buck's belly, from sternum to genitals, as though you were drawing a line with your finger. You want to be able to slice off its genitals, to search in and sever its windpipe, without cutting your other hand. You want to be able to core out its rectum without nicking the intestine, tainting your meat."

"That so?" said Hector. He went on about this trapper who wrote a letter to the Union Cutlery Company of Olean, New York. He claimed he had used one of their knives to "kil-a-bar." Hector had this theory that people who spent too much time alone, bachelors and such, developed an overheated imagination, and he smiled. (I think it's Darwin who somewhere says that the smile evolved from the snarl.) Anyhow, the company officials thought the phrase had a certain ring to it, so they brought out a line of knives under the Ka-Bar trademark. Once World War II got under way, the company submitted a Ka-Bar "combat-utility" knife to the Marines, who couldn't get enough of them. They were first used in the Pacific, mainly to pry gold teeth out of dead Japanese soldiers, was Hector's guess. Naturally the other branches of the military wanted their own, so all those gold teeth lying around Europe wouldn't go to waste. The demand was more than Union could supply, which meant that other cutleries got a piece of the action. Did I see that word stamped across the blade, right next to the finger guard? "Hylas" is what it says, for Hylas Cutlery, Hylas, New York. If someone asked Hector to name a city, he sure as hell could do better than "Hylas." How did I like the sound of Hectoria.

"It's classical," I said, "like lots of the place names upstate. There's Troy, Ithaca, Camillus—hang on a minute." On my desk is a row of reference books held upright by heavy brass bookends that Leonard Sistrunk picked up for me at a flea market, two bison leaning forward, trying to butt heads, but held apart by the books, a symbol, no doubt, of the pretty fable that book learning holds back the archaic lusts and rages, like Plato's charioteer. I picked up the classical dictionary, looked up "Hylas," read. "I thought so," I said. "Hylas was Herakles' punk, kidnapped by nymphs, never heard from again. Herakles went berserk, something he did from time to time. He had lots of testosterone, what made him a hero."

"He kill any lady professors?" he said.

"He once killed a priestess," I said, "pretty much the same thing."

According to the company historian—who "sounded like Norman Bates over the phone"—Hylas alone sold fifteen million knives to the military during World War II, and they are still making the Ka-Bar type, selling it too, and not just to the military. "What did soldiers need all those knives for? I thought modern wars were fought with guns and bombs."

"More magic, I'd say," I said. "It's hard to get an imaginative grip on a bomb. But did you ever carry a knife? It makes you feel complete, dangerous, and ready for anything, better than a gun because more intimate, more like a part of you."

"Now what part would that be?" Hector said. "You been thinking about this, or do you professors always carry around some loose bullshit to spread as needed?"

"It's how I make my living," I said.

"I'm sending this historian the knife that killed Terry," he said, "see if he can figure out when it was made, trace it from supplier to retailer to buyer, fat chance." He took back the knife, sheathed it, placed it back in the gym bag. "You got something to eat? I need to be fortified before I listen to your interpretation of the poem, which I been putting off. I never was big on poems, on interpretations neither."

On the way to the kitchen we stopped by the whatnot or miniden, where Julie was sitting on the recliner, the television set on low, a book in her lap, which she closed on her finger, Cedric Whitman's *Homer and the Homeric Tradition*, for Julie is learning where to find things in my library, but not where to put them back. A simple matter you would think.

"What's on?" Hector said.

"It's a new show called *Metermaids: The Untold Story*," she said, "but I haven't really been following it. I just put the set on for company."

"How do you like Cedric Whitman?" I said.

"It's very interesting," she said, "but, well, it's a man's idea of heroism."

"What's a woman's idea?" said Hector.

"Getting through the day," Julie said.

Hector and I had to settle for bean sandwiches on pumpernickel, flavored with ketchup and pickled jalapenos. While we ate, in my study, I gave him copies (typed by Irene Howland) of "The Mental Traveler" and the killer's assault on it. "You've got a nice clear handwriting," I said, "the unmistakable sign of someone who doesn't do much writing," getting a dig in of my own.

"Our handwriting guy looked the original over," Hector said. "Most is like it was written left-handed, except there's something ain't kosher about it. What it is, the letters don't rightly flow into each other. OK, what's this our friend wee Willie Blake is trying to say?"

"It's not so much that he's trying to say anything," I said. "The poem is more like a cycle of images ... a vision of how it goes with us ... how it must go with us, being what we are ... being where we are, in a fallen world ... how it goes for instance between men and women—if you travel through their minds—a fight to the finish, all passion spent ... almost ... because when it's over, it begins again ... new passion rising from the old ... a repetition compulsion ... and the endless beginning of prodigies suffers open ... also how it goes between the imagination and actuality ... each taking over and then being overcome by the other ... dying each other's life, living each other's death ... unless—"

"Stop!" he said. "You need some coffee or something?"

"All right," I said. "Look at the killer's changes, the sites of transgression. If he is speaking about himself, he has hung around queers and hung around straights, but he looks down on those who walk the straight and narrow. Sex is a woe and a horror: so is what comes out of it: life, his life. His mother crucified and castrated him, but he gets back at her every time he fucks a woman, a stand-in for his mother. The word 'fuck,' by the way, derives from an old Indo-European stem meaning 'fight.' That's the killer's poem, with the poetry removed, for your convenience."

"If you say so," he said, "but your interpretation doesn't exactly give me much to work with, how I'd recognize this guy if I saw him."

"You are looking for a male Caucasian twenty-five to thirty-five years old," I said. "He is neat and economical in his movements, hypercontrolled, the type that used to be called 'anal.' He has not been able to establish an enduring relationship with a woman, or with a man, for that matter. He can get along with people on a workaday basis—he might even be persuasive, something of a con man, but his work, if he works, is not as prestigious as he thinks he deserves, as his talents, intelligence, and education, as he sees it, warrant. He lives by himself or with an older female relative. His father, you will find, was distant or absent, his mother too close. His violation of Terry after her death suggests an inhibition or an incapacity. How's that?"

"You've been reading Robert Ressler," Hector said.

"Everybody is interested in serial killers," I said.

"He's full of shit too," he said. "And we haven't got a serial killer. Yet." He crumpled the paper towel he had been using as a napkin, stood, shot the napkin into my wastebasket, finished his beer, said, "Let's check that door," stretched and yawned, said "I need some sleep."

I looked in on Julie, who was curled up in the recliner, asleep. On the television screen some plump blabbermouth was lurching around the stage and rapping

> Love yo ass, hate yo sass
> You want to gas, I'm gonna pass
> Gimme that sass, gonna kick yo ass.

Behind him a line of girls were writhing and whirling, bent forward slightly at the waist, knees flexed, singing "oop boop, yakata yakata." They were dressed in tight black union suits, except that instead of a trap door, there was wide-open mesh. I watched for a while, then turned off the light and led Hector out and over to the walk along Morningside Park.

A steamy haze thickened the night air, for it was once again warm out of season, and my eyes were tired, so the street lights looked like so many balls of scintillating gas. Big old spooky trees reached out of the park, thirty feet below, to lean their branches on the surrounding stone wall, as though to rest them until some prey came within reach. I looked into the treetops for the yellow eyes of a lemur or something. I've seen hawks, owls, crows, once a raccoon, in those trees, especially in the one that is long dead and leafless, poking up above the others. Oh, don't the moon look lonesome, shining through the trees.

We lit up and strolled uptown, to a point diagonally across the street from the house in which Terry had lived (and died). Here the wall curves out over the park and back again, thus forming a semicircular platform, an observation deck or turret-top, for from the park below the half-round wall here must loom up like one of those towers the Irish built as protection against Norse berserkers, the kind our incendiary grandfather was supposed to have hidden out in once. This area just west of the park is called Morningside Heights for a reason: at the base of the wall, three storeys below, the ground slopes down steeply to Morningside Avenue across the park, southeast Harlem. From where we stood Hector and I could see over row after row of tenements, here a mosque, there a church, to the Triboro Bridge, spiderwebbed with blurry lights, the sky a chemical pink, indistinct music.

If you were to go down the steps from our tower top, walk along the dark and dangerous path that slants downtown and across the park, go out the other side onto 116th Street and continue east, you would pass through a black neighborhood, vacant lots and burnt-out buildings, into a Hispanic neighborhood, crowded streets, music and bright colors, into a mixed area, in which a few remnants of the old Italian neighborhood huddle together. There, while you were still a child prodigy, your hair neatly combed, you used to go for trumpet lessons with Carmine Caruso. You told me, as I recall, that he had been a violinist, never played the trumpet, but was the best trumpet teacher in the city, guys from Canada flying down once a week to study with him. You don't have to be good at something, as

I am no good at writing poetry, to be good at teaching it. Well, the analogy doesn't exactly hold, for I do not teach people how to write poetry, but how to read it. I don't know, there's something ignominious about being only a teacher.

"Terry's killer may have had the park in mind, in case he had to make a quick getaway," I said. "Who'd follow him?"

"Get himself mugged," Hector said. "The guy I'm picturing doesn't know his way around Morningside Park. The other day Patrol rousted two guys barbecuing a cat over this cozy little campfire. Last week they found three headless white chickens and a white goat, sacrificed by voodooers. People get tired of their pit bulls, they turn them loose in the park."

There was a sudden ruckus right below us, animal snarls and human curses. We looked over the wall, but couldn't see much. This part of the park, above 116th Street, has not been tended since 1968. The lamplights are out, the stone slab steps split and tumbled, the concrete walks in rubble, deep in garbage, in fallen leaves and branches, mere tunnels blocked or narrowed by encroaching brush. The weeds are crotch-high, bushes and vines hugging each other to death. I saw shadows shifting, an upright figure whirling this way then that, two figures low to the ground, ah yes, a man swinging a tree branch, saying, "Get the fuck out of here," two dogs circling, feinting toward the man, retreating into the brush, yip-growling.

"There's a doorway set into the wall down there," I said, "used to have a black iron grate over it, now hanging loose. Inside is a little room for park attendants to store their tools, back then when New York could still afford park attendants. Stray dogs use it for a den."

"A bum trying to beat two mutts out of their flop," he said, "*that's* how it goes with us, forget your poetry and its 'virgin bright.' Fuck it." He turned and started across the street, a sudden loud yelp sounding behind us with a dying fall.

"Those dogs could be guarding a hidden treasure," I said.

The door to Terry's house opened the way I said it would, the doorman jumping up from behind his desk, a scared look on his face, reaching for his walkie-talkie. "Relax," Hector said, showing his badge. "You better see that lock gets fixed before Professor Jones's family finds out about it. I can see a big-bucks lawsuit." As we walked out, he said, "The university own the building?"

"Yes," I said.

"Figures," he said. I walked him to his car, which had not been broken into, and then walked home, the streets empty.

I turned off the television set, cradled Julie in my arms, carried her into the bedroom, her hair tickling my cheek, lay her down on my side of the bed, pulled the covers back on her side, lifted her over, took off her shoes (black high tops), and began to pull off her socks, my socks, when she kicked violently, sat up, all over rigid. "What are you doing?" she said, more fear than anger in her voice.

"Putting you to bed," I said.

Her face relaxed into a dreamy smile. "Thanks Cuz," she said, "but I've got to take a pee first."

While she got herself ready in her bathroom, I got myself ready in mine. I was already lying down when Julie returned, wearing my flannel shirt, said "Good night, Cuz," got into bed, turned onto her side, pointed her behind at me, and within a minute was breathing deeply. I lay on my back, asking the ceiling whether I had it in me to kill someone, up close I mean, with a knife, for it is easy to kill someone by pressing a button that releases a rocket.

You sneak up behind some guy, lunge forward and at the same time swing your left arm over his shoulder, cup his chin in your hand, yank his head back, almost losing your grip, because you haven't got his chin centered, because you are sweating, because he is struggling, stomping your instep, elbowing your belly, but you reach over his other shoulder with your right hand, the one holding the knife—and slash your own left hand or wrist, a balls-up. All right, you sneak up behind some guy, lunge forward and at the same time swing your left arm over his shoulder, cup his chin in your hand, yank his head back, and drive the knife in underhand, right below his rib cage, the pommel recoiling against the heel of your trusty right hand, what the killer did to Terry, except left-handed—maybe. Nothing to it, except she reaches back to scratch your face, your skin and DNA under her nails. But suppose she, he, is facing you? Think of Homer's heroes, slashing and jabbing up close, careful of their footwork, for to slip on blood or trip on a fallen comrade would be fatal, the terror of a short sword descending on you, the horror of the other guy's blood splattering on your face, the taste of it. My imagination shuts off, closes down.

Whereas I have to wrestle myself to sleep, Julie sleeps the night through without moving, far as I can tell. At least she is in the morning as she was the night before. But last night while I was still projecting scary pictures onto the ceiling, she suddenly turned over, mumbled "Diomedes of the great war cry," and threw her arm halfway across my chest. I lay there feeling my heart beat against her hand.

Here's the line I handed my students in English 3636x, British Literature of the Modernist Era (1880-1940):

Settle down chillen, while I tell you a story, a free improvisation on changes recorded by the anthropologist Lauriston Sharp. There once lived in western Australia a tribe that called itself "The People," so as to distinguish themselves from other people, whom they called "The Others." The People were divided into three, the Flaker clan in the north, the Staker clan in the south, the Maker clan in between. Before they collided with Europeans, as with a wrecking ball, The People had lived the same way for thousands of years, far as we can tell, for The People preferred to reinvent their past as needed, which is harder to do (unless you are a New Historicist) when it is written down.

Sure it is, in any case, that they had side-stepped the tedium of farming, the bother of domestic animals, the crowded and craven despotism of Neolithic culture. The People hunted and fished and gathered and raided The Others, and a very good time it was.

For The People, as you can well imagine, did not suffer from ontological insecurity, nor from anomie, accidie, abulia, bulimia, acid reflux, or gender role confusion. Serial killers were unknown. The People knew who they were and what to do and how to do it, there being no other way but theirs, for they were The People. But just to make sure, the social space was thick with instruction, with precept and example, with parable and saying, with cautionary tale and taboo, all of it dramatized in ritual, mimed in dance, chanted in hymns, and painted on pots, while the exacting eyes of the totemic powers, of tutelary ghosts and ancestral spirits, the wakeful dead, looked on, looked on, and the wakeful dead looked on. Fables of origin and myths of law-dropping heroes were devised, the present casting a shadow over the past, to show that as it was in the beginning is now and ever shall be, world without end, man. Barring ecological disaster, and The People had no memory of one, change, if it occurred at all, was gradual, unnoticed, untraumatic, a breeze.

The People had no chiefs: quotidian problems, the only kind they had, were calmly debated by a council of drunken elders, not because old men are wise, but because they are not good for anything else. The elders would talk and talk, for however long it took, until they all agreed upon a solution, the rare holdout thereby exposing himself as infested by a demon and therefore in for an exorcism, a particularly painful type of purge, the idea being that evil spirits entered you from below, but enough of that. *Enough of that.* There were no malcontents, or if there were, they learned to grin and bear it or how to act out their malcontent through one of the traditional roles designed to turn malcontent into spectacle.

Shamans, for example, were deferred to in person, as capable of infesting you with a demon, but derided behind their backs, as hysterics and sissies. Berserkers, however, were spoken of in tones of affrighted respect, as making manifest the awful power of the dingo-demon that possessed them.

The People, in short, were altogether all together. Every component of their culture was to every other, to paraphrase William

Coleridge, as form is to content in a poem. (He meant, of course, a pre-Modernist poem, not knowing any other kind.) Whatever was religious was also political; whatever was political was also economic; whatever was economic was also domestic; whatever was domestic was also educational; whatever was educational was also medical; whatever was medical was also magical; whatever was magical was also artful; whatever was artful was also practical; whatever was practical was also religious, down to the way you killed your enemy or dressed out a kangaroo or scarred your cheeks or cuddled with your spouse. *Coitus a tergo,* for instance, and any other kind was considered perverse, was religious in that imitated the demiurge (a large bat), who in that position quickened Mother Earth (an immense kangaroo) into life; it was military in that The People's word for lovemaking derived from an archaic stem that meant "to cleave your enemy with an axe"; it was political in that it recapitulated the relations between the sexes, the man up, the woman down, as God intended; it was economic in that it was thought to ensure conception, and in those halcyon days children were considered an asset; it was a form of art in that it had to be enacted with a certain style and between ritual preliminaries and sequelae, which I will not go into here. What above all held the people together, believe it or not, was a short-handled axe called the Kilakang.

Heads for the Kilakang were made by the Flaker clan up north, whose turf was flinty. The Flakers were skilled at picking out likely chunks of flint, at polishing them, at chipping off flakes until the finished product was sharp and shapely, like an intelligent dancer. Handles for the Kilakang were gathered by the Staker clan down south, whose turf was swampy. The Stakers were skilled at searching out a kind of swamp ash, the wood of which is tough and straight-grained, in harvesting, peeling, curing, and storing the ash stakes, turning woods into goods. Heads and handles for the Kilakang were brought together by the Maker clan in the industrious midlands, whose turf was coniferous. The Makers were skilled at extracting and heating spruce gum, at cutting and treating strips of pine bark, for the bond, one capable of withstanding the most exuberant of chops. But that was not the end of it, not by a long shot, for the owner of a new Kilakang, his most valuable possession, unless he already had others, would color and carve designs all over it, some common to The People, some restricted to his clan, some special to his totem, some contrived by his family, some peculiar to himself. The finished Kilakang, you might say, was synecdoche for The People as a whole: it summed them up in shorthand. The finished Kilakang was also a thing of beauty, let me tell you, to which museums throughout Australia will testify.

Just the same, a strict morality governed their use, for The People had not reached that stage at which the good and the beautiful become incompatible, never to be reconciled, never, never to be together again. Only an initiated male could own a Kilakang; only an initiated male could make one, or any part of one; only a Kilakang could be used as a tool to make a Kilakang, for The People lacked the knack of making sacred wine out of secular water. A man's prestige and status were determined by the quantity and quality of his Kilakangs, even more than by the quantity and quality of his wives, although the two were related: no self-respecting woman would marry a Kilakangless man; but her self-respect depended upon her dad's being able to spring two or three of them for a dowry. Women, who did all the work, had to borrow Kilakangs from their husbands; and they had to return them at night, as issued, or receive a drubbing, administered, we are told, more for the sake of appearances than to give pain or receive pleasure. Any boy wanting to practice the manly arts had to borrow a Kilakang from an initiated male relative; and he had to return it too, or receive a ragging, more painful than any drubbing, so we are told.

At his initiation ceremony, the post-pubertal male was stripped naked, made woozy with fermented honey, scarred (lines radiating from the mouth, like cat's whiskers), dragged through a tunnel representing the earth-kangaroo's womb, wrapped in swaddling clouts, given his first Kilakang, and told how at the beginning of things the bat demiurge slit open the earth-kangaroo's belly with a Kilakang. He then extracted the first man, told him to go up north and gather flints; extracted the second man and told him to go south and gather stakes; extracted the third man and told him to stay put, dammit. All the while drunken elders whirled Kilakangs tied to lengths of braided bark overhead. The resulting noise was described to the women, who were barred from the ceremony, but who braided the bark, as that of tutelary ghosts moaning mysteries. We are told that the women did not laugh at this pious fraud in the presence of the men.

After nine months, the initiate, now a man, could carry a Kilakang on the raid or hunt; he could use it to gather wild honey or scar a cheek or perform a rite of exorcism, for which activities the heads and handles of Kilakangs were the only permitted instruments. He could go on business trips to other clans, find himself some trading partners, who would become closer to him than parent or sibling or wife or child, closer than wife or child, wife or child. He could wheel and deal during the four great yearly festivals at which the clans gathered, to drink fermented honey, to arrange marriages, above all to trade heads, handles and whole Kilakangs. These partnerships, these exogamous marriages, these festivals, all dependent on the Kilakang, are what kept the clans from trying to exterminate each other. And so the uniform centuries accumulated, like rain in a roadside bottle—

Until missionaries from England arrived. They set up camp, three huts with tin roofs, in Maker turf, right next to the sacred grove, the bosky cleft in the earth-kangaroo's belly from which all living things were expelled, mewling, gasping, chirping, blinking at the light, finding their legs, swimming downstream to the ocean, flapping their fledging wings. These missionaries, who were as shrewd as they were naïve, saw immediately what the Kilakang was to The People. They ordered crates of mass-produced hatchets from Manchester. They then gave these hatchets to The People as bribes to attend services. The old men held out, but the young men, who at first derided Jesus as an hysteric and a sissy, wanted those hatchets. But even the young men were horrified when the missionaries, beaming with righteousness behind their wire-rimmed glasses, handed out hatchets directly to women and children. Soon these earnest innocents were traveling north and south, accompanied by troops with repeating rifles, to bribe the Flakers and Stakers. What was the result of all this benevolence? Things fell apart entirely.

Hatchets and Jesus and repeating rifles were just too much evidence that The People's way of being human was not the only way, nor even the most auspicious. The myths and beliefs of The People, balanced on the edge of a Kilakang, devolved into mere fictions, suspended over the void. Those precepts and parables and sayings, that elaborate morality of the Kilakang, received wisdom of any kind, what does it all amount to, anyway? A swindle perpetrated and perpetuated by the old boys to keep themselves in fermented honey and the rest of us in line. The dances and hymns and paintings on pots demystified themselves into mere décor. The components of The People's culture became not only distinguishable, but separable, a jumble of juxtapositions, like the shore after a storm. The past no longer justified the present; the present no longer stabilized the past; both became unknowable. They changed from day to day, like everything else. The totemic powers and tutelary ghosts and ancestral spirits turned into vampires. Women no longer only laughed behind their husbands' backs. Nor was any woman cowed by cautionary tales of how vampires kissed erring women into monsters of appetite who sucked the life out of husbands and children. She rather hoped she'd meet one. Parricide became a problem.

The People forgot how to carve and color Kilakangs or where to look for raw materials. Trading partners became cutthroat rivals. Trading festivals became drunken brawls. Initiation rites went out of style. So did exogamy. But the fashionable set began to scar both sets of cheeks. The demimonde underwent exorcisms just for the fun of it. Even respectable couples experimented with the missionary position and other perversions. For the first time ever, some of

The People got fat. Malcontents began to pop up all over. Many people no longer deferred to shamans; worse, others began to take them seriously. The elders no longer could agree. Strongmen rose to replace them. They led their followers in raids not against The Others, but against their fraternal clans, as the missionaries wrung their hands. To the extent that reality is a social construct, it collapsed. To the extent that the self is a social product, it dissolved. The People had become modernists.

And there you have my story. I hope it got to you, for that is above all what a storyteller wants, to get it on with his listeners, if you know what I mean. The next thing he wants is that his listeners apply his stories to their lives, for that is why we have stories, to apply them. He does not want interpreters, for to appropriate is not to apply. My claim is the storyteller's claim, that his story applies. The Parable of The People, so I claim, and for the sake of your grades you better believe it, applies to that modernism with a small "m" that has overtaken many people at many times, in many places, ever since the shy Neanderthal was overtaken by the berserker Cro-Magnon. But it also applies to that big-bang Modernism, with a capital "M," that began going off in *fin de siècle* Europe, Britain, and North America. That Modernism, my friends, the Modernism that knows itself for what it is, the modernism that swallows up all the others, has yet to reach its boundaries in time or space. It is still happening here, there, everywhere, to you and to me, which is why the best of us lack conviction and the worst are full of passionate intensity.

As a responsible scholar, I should tell you that the touts of postmodernism, or post-mortem modernism as I think of it, undead modernism, modernism routinized or campified, think differently.

Your assignment for next time is to read, think, and imagine. Read Pater's conclusion and Wilde's introduction—you see them there on the reading list—for the aesthetic maneuver is the supreme response to the advent of Modernism. You substitute the work of art for everything else that has been lost; you substitute private whim for public wisdom, for the good and the true, the useless

Kilakang hung up on a wall where you can see how the carved and colored designs refer only to you—or to themselves. Next, I want you to think: what in turn-of-the-century Eurocentric culture corresponded to the Kilakang, what to the hatchets, what to the missionaries. Then I want you to imagine: imagine yourself a young modernist Flaker or Maker or Staker. How would you react? With Thomas Hardy's gloomy uncertainties? With Conrad's ironic nostalgia for all we think we lost? With Woolf's ontological insecurity? With Eliot's absurd leap backward into faith? With Yeats's absurd belief in whatever absurdities gave him metaphors for poetry? With Waugh's satire of everything new? With Pound's search for a leader? With Rhys's drunken despondency? With Joyce's understanding that neither the worldview of the Cross or of the Kilikang is true, that truth is a hole, but one whose outline you can only begin to make out when you have spotted all the errors surrounding it?

Would you become a revolutionary? An exile? A cool observer with a superior smile? An as-if philosopher? A serial killer of missionaries? For just before The People became extinct, a serial killer appeared among them, a Flaker named Jack who used an antique Kilakang to rip open the bellies of women who fraternized with missionaries.

Any questions?

Tell your kid brother the truth, Joel, and don't pull any punches: do you think I'm going crazy? It's true that something gets into me when I go before a class. Giving that class put me up, but writing it out has been a downer. I can't go to bed, and I didn't realize how late it is, because I have to wait up for Julie, to let her in, because she doesn't have keys . . . maybe a snack. Between that last sentence fragment and this sentence, which I mean to finish, I have been sitting here in a trance or fugue or daze or who knows what for over a half hour. I'm trying to remember—there's the doorbell, there she is, there's Julie.

Back for a last word while Julie takes her shower. She and her friends broke each other up, taking turns reading "The Miller's

Tale," wetting their pants, she said, laughing all over again while she told me, making me laugh, getting it on with her audience. You will want to know whether I believe in my little story, the Parable of the People, for professors do not always believe what they tell their students. The answer is No, not in the way I believe in my kneecap or in the Pythagorean Theorem, no equivocations from me about how we have outgrown belief in belief. But I do believe it applies, that much I do believe. There's Julie shouting, "I'm ready, Cuz." Me too, and how about you? Are we getting it on together?

6

Dear Joel,

Even in the old days, three months ago, when I was a different man, for the self, so my modernist masters tell me, is discontinuous, not one thing at one moment and the same thing at the next, not even one thing at one moment and another thing at the next, but several things at one moment and several other things at the next, but not several things at one moment and several entirely different things the next, oh no, that would be too easy, for if the self at any one moment is composed of the elements A,B,C,D,E, it may at the next moment be composed of elements A,G,I,J,K, and still one moment later of elements C,K,M,P,X with neither a clean break nor a common denominator, no common denominator—even in the old days I did not write criticism every morning, and who the hell this "I" is, I haven't the faintest.

On mornings when what one of me had in his mind to write needed to simmer in someone's subconscious for a day, I would go into the office early, have a fourth cup with Irene Howland, catch up on the gossip. Irene came in an hour before anyone else, made the coffee, warmed up the computers, so that she could leave an hour before anyone else, for Irene is a great attender of classes, all over the city. From time to time she has mentioned classes in furniture refinishing, country cooking, leather crafts, dog grooming, blacksmithing, taxidermy, ceramics, rug braiding, flower arranging, bee keeping, and autohypnosis, that I remember. Somewhere, not quite at the back of her mind, Irene pictures herself married to some character out of an L.L. Bean catalogue, a country lawyer, a veterinarian, strong and gentle, the two of them surrounded by dogs, children, a big stone fireplace, functional antiques, a butter churn, a spinning wheel, the smell of baking bread.

Such types being hard to come by in New York City, Irene has shown a willingness to settle for less. She had only been working in the Department for a month when she fell in love with an assistant professor who at the time only had eyes for squash. Irene took lessons, carried with her a $300 gym bag with attached sleeve for the racquet, skipped lunch for the courts, built a rep for her serve, broke a tooth on an opponent's backhand. But when this assistant professor, out of politeness, asked her about her game, she was too shy to answer, except in monosyllables. Then she fell in love with a neo-hippy graduate student: a course on tambourine-playing, hair long and parted down the middle, a mother hubbard, marijuana and tofu, bare feet and an infected toe that nearly required amputation. For love of Teddy Nakatani she plunged into Yukio Mishima and origami, both of which, as it turns out, Teddy loathes.

For love of Murray Weinrein, Irene made herself into the best secretary in the history of the Department, proof that even unrequited love exists for a reason. There were courses in office management and computer programming and accounting and whatnot, a slow modulation of the Department's record-keeping into changes as logical and life-giving as the cycle of fifths, and still Murray's attitude toward her was a distant and humorous condescension. Other units of the university tried to seduce Irene away from us with promises of a raise in rank and salary. But Irene remained constant: she is not venturesome or fickle; she would not leave Murray; with us, she is not only accepted, but respected, as she might not be elsewhere; she has wanted only to be wanted and to serve, and the Department has provided what she wanted, thereby earning her eternal loyalty. Now, if it could only provide her with a man.

I have auditioned for that role, but only in my imagination, where it's all at, anyway. Irene is a handsome woman: WASP features (a bit thin of lip), glossy chestnut hair thick and wavy and tumbling onto her shoulders, a firm and shapely body from all that squash, from aerobic classes, from classes in dance, for Irene spent years wearing black, a severe expression, and a bun, trying to look like Murray's wife Yvonne, a celebrated beauty, a former ballerina with posture and poise and attitude to match. Marriage to Irene, as I used to think the matter over, would have its attractions. She would not be a competitor, but an ally. She would not show contempt when you fail or resentment when you succeed. She would spend the few spare moments in her busy day thinking up ways to please you. She would learn to cook whatever you like to eat. You would have a spiffy apartment and a balanced checkbook. She'd type your manuscripts, go to the library for you, move the car. In sex she would get pleasure by giving it. And so on.

Why then, you may well ask, have I never made a move on Irene? Well, for one thing, she has never made a move on me, never takes on a stricken look when I approach, never took a course in bebop. What Irene sees in me is my Aunty Wynn personality, confidant and comforter and advisor, and only that. Still, she would have responded, all right, had I made the first move, so desperate is her need. For another thing I do not like the set of her shoulders. Whereas Julie lets her shoulders droop forward, as though to throw them back would be pretentious, Irene hunches her shoulders up, scrunches her neck down into them, as though ducking a cuff to the back of the head, one reason why she never reminded anyone of Yvonne. For myself, I find it easier to tolerate distortions of the spirit than of the flesh. Finally, I would not trust myself to resist at least verbal violence with Irene. Meekness brings out the berserker in me, but only in my imagination, where it's all at, alas. As it is, my impulse is to sit her in my lap, stroke her hair, massage her trapezius, say relax, everything will work out, some day your prince will come, except that my lap is already occupied by my stomach.

When, this morning, I walked into the Departmental office, looking for coffee, Irene greeted me with one of her appeasement smiles, although I had no intention of hitting her. "Morning Rene," I said, releasing a torrent of words: it was so nice of me to come in early, she just had to talk to me, there was no one else, could we go into my office, where it was private, she would bring the coffee, and did I want a donut? I guided her by the elbow into my office, saying not a word. She sat on the other side of my desk, holding her cup with both hands, her head bent over the cup, her lips just above the rim, looking at me through her eyebrows: "I've been sleeping with Murray," she said.

And why not hit me with a stun gun, while you're at it? For a long time, no words, either of commiseration or congratulation, would come. Finally, I said, "I see."

She ducked her head another notch, although I still had no intention of hitting her, glanced at me to make sure that was so, and said, "All summer long, every Monday night, Murray drove in from Sag Harbor, leaving Yvonne and the kids."

"I see," I said.

"He's doing this report on the faculty benefits package, already three hundred pages long," she said. "He had to be in the office, where he could get at things, where I could help him."

"Of course," I said.

"Every Tuesday, Wednesday, Thursday we worked together, just the two of us, to eight, nine, ten o'clock, long after the others were gone," she said. "I never felt so close to anyone. We're a great team, you know."

"I believe it," I said.

"We would order in Chinese food," she said, "or eat at one of the local greasy spoons and go over the day's work. There would be columns of figures all over the table."

"I get the picture," I said.

"Once when it was rainy out and we were both, you know, sort of goofy with fatigue," she said, "numb with numbers you might say, I invited him to my apartment for a nightcap. We couldn't go to his place because neighbors—"

"Say no more," I said.

"It was the happiest summer of my life," she said.

"I'm glad to hear it," I said.

"This has been the most miserable week of my life," she said.

"Oh, oh," I said.

"He acts like it never happened," she said. "Once school started. . . . He won't even talk to me about our relationship. He puts on this breezy manner, what would you call it, *affable* is what he is, never an intimate word, a touch."

"Well, with Yvonne in the city. . . ." I said.

"I don't care about the sex," she said.

"What I meant was. . . ." I said.

"He could put his hands on my shoulders," she said, "look me in the eye, and say he's sorry it has to end, it was wonderful while it lasted, we will always be friends, and kiss me on the forehead. I put myself to sleep at night picturing it. At least he could give me an understanding smile when no one else is around, a wink for Christ's sake, a slap on the ass even, but no—there has to be this complete erasure of everything we had together . . . of me." Her face was reddening.

"You're not going to cry, are you?" I said.

"I don't know what to do," she said. "I'm not crying," but one silent tear trickled down her cheek. "I've got to do something. I can't go on like this."

"There would be serious repercussions if this got out," I said. You know, Joel, there are times when I suffer a deficiency of the sympathetic imagination.

"Yes, Yvonne would feel she had to leave him," she said. "I know that. Anyone who invests so much in her own beauty. . . . I don't want that. Murray loves the kids. I don't want to hurt anyone."

On that point you have to believe her, Joel. Irene is entirely without weapons. She never strikes back. There's no malice in her, no resentment or spite, the usual armature of the weak. You have to like that about her, but it can make you mad, makes me mad, anyhow.

"I was thinking of other repercussions," I said. "Twenty years ago we all would have cheered you on. Now. . . ."

"I don't have anything left over to worry about Departmental politics with," she said. "I'm fading out of existence. I don't know how to save myself."

"What you've got to do is change your thinking," I said. "Look at it this way: you and Murray had something going. Fine. You gave each other . . . what? comfort, companionship, affection, pleasure? Wonderful. So it has to end—like everything else. Not so good. Still, you gave him, he gave you, nobody owes anybody, and you got something you otherwise would not have had. What more do you want? Call it quits, count your gains, move on to something else." Sure, and the next thing I'll be telling paraplegics to take up hopscotch.

Someone was knocking at the door.

"It's this feeling of being negated," Irene said, "of this black hole where you live getting bigger and bigger."

I got up to see who was at the door. Irene tucked her elbows in and ducked her head, hunching herself against whoever was knocking, and there was Monika Wright.

"I'm looking for Irene," she said. "The Departmental office door is wide open, and no one's around. That's how street vendors get all those books and office supplies they sell."

Irene jumped to her feet. I opened the door all the way. "It's my fault, Monika," I say. "I asked Irene in. She's been bringing me up to date on—"

"That's my job," said Monika. "Professor Jones was very efficient. After her first year, she and I wrote out a detailed schedule of the vice-chair's responsibilities. It's one of the things I want to talk to you about."

"In a minute," I said. "We're nearly finished," and I closed the door, for although I could see the cracked logic in Monika's resenting Terry's successor, namely me, I did not have to give it a field to romp in.

"Thanks, Wynn," Irene said when we were both sitting again. "That detective thinks Monika killed Professor Jones."

"Suspicion is his métier," I said.

"Well, Monika does have a violent streak in her," Irene said. "You know, I think Terry, as she said I should call her, was beginning to fall in love with me, a little."

"I may not understand," I said, "but I can sympathize. I don't know if you heard, but—"

"I know, your wife walked out on you," she said.

"You could put it that way," I said. "Can I do anything to help?"

Irene looked at me for a long time. Once, twice, three times, she started to speak. Finally, all she said was, "Nobody can help. I've got to do something myself."

I walked into the Department office, two doors north. If what she has in mind is for me to take Murray's place, I shall have to turn her down, no help for it. The rest of the staff had arrived, Teddy Nakatani juggling packs of three-by-five index cards, each pack turning over once on its way up after leaving his right hand and turning once more on its way down before falling into his left hand, which flipped it into his right. He scooped up a stapler with his left hand, flipped it into his right, and sent it after the cards, then scooped up a tape dispenser and sent it after the stapler, his hands now a blur, cards and stapler and dispenser revolving in a rotation in a widening arc. Then he shot me a pack of cards, which I caught one-handed, for in all modesty, I can still pretty much catch whatever is thrown at me.

"This not a dissertation proposal," I said, for I decided right then that it would be best for Teddy if with Teddy I came on stern.

"I wrote up something last night," he said. "Your class inspired me."

"By now you should be giving undergraduate courses," I said, "not taking them."

One by one he caught the stapler, the dispenser, the pack of cards. The other pack landed on the bridge of his nose, where, with little shifts of his head, Teddy kept it balanced on edge. He tossed it over his shoulder, as a seal might toss a ball, kicked it back with the flat of his foot, as a mule might kick its tormenter, caught it with his left hand, balanced it on a finger, let it fall over flat on his hand, and with a bow presented it to me. "Honorable sir," he said. Then he straightened. "I wanted to see if you are the man to sponsor my dissertation." He had that look on his face, the look, let me see, well, the look of a man who has an impulse to laugh at you, but holds back, for the aristocrat knows that only the weak need to be rude.

"At your service," I said, with a bow.

"It is Robert Graves, is it not, who speaks of a service that is perfect freedom," he said.

"He was talking about service to the White Goddess," I said, "whom you do not in the least resemble."

"You know her personally?" he said. "But now I remember: she is described as having a fluorescent white belly with no belly button, an image that for some reason gives me the shivers. What significance do you see in Leopold Bloom's query as to whether Aphrodite had a rectum?"

"*Has,*" I said, "not *had,* for Aphrodite lives. The significance is that Aphrodite, like Celia, shits, and is all the better for it. Monika!" I shouted toward her inner office: "You ready?"

"Coming," she said.

"May I request a conference?" Teddy Nakatani said.

"We'll see how long Monika keeps me on the hook," I said.

For a couple of hours Monika and I faced each other from opposite sides of my desk, sipping coffee, while she explained my job to me, how to move through or around the minefields and booby traps and pitfalls lined with dung-smeared bamboo.

"I'll be here to remind you as things come due," Monika said.

"You could just give Irene a schedule," I said.

"No one does my job but me," she said. "While we're at it, you ought to call a get-organized meeting of the curriculum committee for next week."

"We don't yet have a curriculum committee," I said.

"Better get cracking," she said. "I have to send bulletin copy in to the printer before Christmas."

Monika has worked up her acerb manner in imitation of Terry's famous severity. She has also shucked thirty pounds, upscaled her costume (tan linen slacks tight around her bum, feathered belt, sage cotton sweater, a cravat around her neck and anchored to the sweater with a small cameo brooch), processed her hair, sifted much of the Harlem grit from her speech, got into reading, learned to drink her coffee black, no sugar. You could see it happening during the first year of their friendship, the plump and deferential Baptist in flowered dresses drying down into the lean, don't-fuck-with-me feminist she is, as the tender grape becomes the tough raisin rich in iron, longer lasting too.

Monika is now a well-defined personage, no doubt about that, but she is only an efficient administrator. She does not transmit those subliminal erotic currents that energize a workplace. All the same Monika and Irene are evidence that love, requited or not, can inspire self-renovation, as pre-modernist poets used to say, as Plato used to say, cozying up to some pretty peach-fuzzed ephebe. Their similarity, if that's what it is, does not prevent Irene, so I gather, from feeling that Monika has something like a Kilakang stake up her ass, although Irene has not said as much, maybe not even thought it, given her inhibitions. But I could be wrong, for as Kay Pesky says, my female intuitions are butch.

Probably that's what I need, to fall in love, except that I have lost the knack, although the lust lives on, lives on. For lust is to love what the blues are to elevator music and the body to its furnishings, the real thing, the evolutionary force field through which we live and move and have our being. And I don't expect that mincing pipsqueak St. Paul to agree, and if you think—

"I hope you are not giving Irene an excuse for falling in love with you," Monika said, apropos of nothing, except my musings, which I refuse to believe her feminine intuition sniffed out even before I got through musing them.

"She needs someone to talk to," I said.

"Don't we all," Monika said.

"Doesn't she have any women friends, family?"

"How can she have any women friends, the way she is?" she said. "Terry used to talk about helping her.... I met the father once, smooching around to check up on Irene, bothering us with questions, till I sent him off with a hornet in his ear. He's an activist minister who thinks his work is so important everybody in his vicinity has to cater to him. I know the type well. Didn't one of them give me a baby? And that's all he gave me. There were lots of those fools around during the sixties, still are."

"She's all alone, Monika," I said. "Maybe you could—"

"So am I," she said. "Wait till she finds someone, the only one, then loses her."

"You have a daughter," I said.

"My daughter disapproves of me, won't give me the time of day," she said. "You're alone too, only you don't know it."

"That's where you're—" I said.

"You think you have friends, that they're enough," she said. "Let me tell you, you will need an ally inside that office, and that sorry sister Irene Howland ain't who you need."

"I don't think of myself as a combatant," I said.

"Goes with the job," she said. "You ought to get out of the vice-chair if it don't fit yo ass." I was taking the descent (or ascent) into down-homeisms as a compliment when Monika really surprised me, for we had never been tight. "Did you ever think that in this whole department, with all its professors and associate professors and assistant professors and instructors and adjuncts and administrative staff and poor relations, only you and me come from a working-class background?"

In academe nowadays there's a nouvelle cachet in coming from the laboring classes among people who don't come from them, or got out from them, quick as they could, but I don't think you and I can claim it. Ma and Pa have to be considered middle class, in their outlook anyhow. Didn't Pa advance from driver to assistant regional manager of UPS? By the way, Pa retired last year, still careful with his money. He spends his time pestering the Ancient Order of Hibernians and wondering whether I'm queer, why I don't get married again. Ma wants more grandchildren. Sissie's three kids are not enough for her. You would have been a great uncle to them, Joel, which I am not, for I am awkward with children. You would have been a great father, too, the way you used to teach me things.

"It gives us a certain perspective," she said. "Tell me you don't know who killed Terry Jones."

"Naturally I have my suspicions," I said, although in fact I do not, "but—"

"You've got to tell Suarez that Angel Terrasco killed my Terry," she said. "I can't do it. I got a, what is it, phobia of talking to cops, can't get past it. Besides, he sees me as a suspect, when I would have died for Terry, like *that.* Besides he's a racist."

"He's not big on Anglos either," I said. "You've got to understand: suspicion is his métier."

"You can talk to him," she said. "You know where he's coming from. You've been there."

Sure, the proletarian professor, *c'est moi.* "You got any evidence?" I said.

"You don't need but eyes and ears to know she's crazy," Monika said, "the way she carries on. That low-minded, high-handed bitch, treats me like shit—since Terry and I became close. With Terry gone she'll try to get me fired, if I give her an excuse, putting Suarez on to her. The fact is, if she gets the chair, I'm on my way, anyhow. You've got to stop her."

I was trying to figure out what form my waffling would take, when Monika said, "I'll bet you didn't know she was a champion fencer in college."

"She can still stick it to you," I said, "but she does it with words."

"The Spanish are all big on knives," she said, deflating. "My mind has been going around like a cat with a burr in his butt. You got a cigarette? I gave up smoking for Terry, but now..."

We lit up, smoked for a while in silence. "Tastes lousy," she said, getting up, crushing out the cigarette.

"Can you spare Teddy Nakatani for a few minutes?" I said.

"You taking on his dissertation?" she said.

"If he's found a subject, I'll find him a sponsor," I said.

"I've got to ride herd on an office full of lunatics, and no Terry to ride herd on me," she said. "Any of those poets you write about ever notice that love is a discipline, not a debauch?"

"The idea is on record," I said.

When I looked up, Teddy Nakatani was standing in the doorway. He could have knocked or something, but he didn't. "Come on in," I said. He entered, started to close the door. "Leave it open," I said. He sat. "Where's your proposal?" I said.

"Now where is it?" he said. "Ah, yes." He came around to my side of the desk. "Excuse me," he said, reaching inside my jacket, pulling out a scroll, a roll, a half-dozen sheets of paper held by a rubber band. "Right next to your heart," he said, returning to his seat, almost smiling.

He probably had the scroll up his sleeve, for Teddy almost always wears a long-sleeved white shirt. On very hot days he wears a short-sleeved white shirt. On cold days he wears a denim jacket over his white shirt. On freezing days he wears a black sweater between his denim jacket and his white shirt. He does not go naked from the waist down. Rather he invariably wears unnaturally clean Levis and those obsolete low-cut white sneakers called tennis shoes, although no tennis player wears them. His socks I believe, for I am not in the habit of inspecting people's socks, are black.

I unrolled his proposal, spread it out, and began to read. The epigraph was from Simone de Beauvoir:

> But when woman is given over to man as his property, he demands that she represent the flesh purely for its own sake. Her body is not perceived as the radiation of a subjective personality, but as a thing sunk deeply in its own immanence; it is not for such a body to have relevance to the rest of the world, it must not be the promise of things other than itself: it must end the desire it arouses. The most naïve form of this requirement is the Hottentot ideal of the steatopygous Venus, for the buttocks are the part of the body with fewest nerves, where the flesh seems an aimless fact: the taste of Orientals for fat women is of similar nature; they love the absurd richness of this adipose proliferation, enlivened as it is by no project, with no meaning other than to be there. Even in civilizations where sensuality is more subtle and ideas of form and harmony are entertained, the breasts and buttocks remain favored objects, because of their unnecessary, gratuitous blooming.

"Poor Simone," I said, "the teacher's pet snitching on teach because he put his hand on her ass." But I never would have taken Jean-Paul for an ass-man. Mind-rape, I would have said, was more his thing. "Do you know that poem by Yeats in which Anne Gregory is told that men will never love her for herself alone, and not her yellow hair?"

"Intimately," Teddy said. "As an Oriental, or as an Asian, as we now say, I must protest that I have no taste for fat women. It would be fruitless, I suppose, to dispute the implication that Orientals entertain no ideas of form and harmony."

"She's French," I said: "cultural chauvinism is her métier."

"While we are at it," he said, "I must inform you that I have sought entrance to this august chamber in part as an Oriental minister nullipotentiary."

"How's that?" I said.

"*Your* teacher's pet, Felicia Zhang, is trying to organize the university's Asian students, a hopeless endeavor, I should say," he said. "I do not know whether you observed that she is attending your class."

"Her smile lit up the room," I said.

"After your entertaining lecture, as we were leaving, she and two colleagues approached me," he said. "In that I am the Department's senior Asian student, I was entrusted with the commission of placing before you a negotiable demand."

"What's that?" I said.

"They want you, as vice-chairman, to hire someone to teach Asian-American literature," he said. "For undergraduates they are remarkably well informed. They are aware that a perk of the vice-chairman's office is the appointment of adjuncts."

"I suppose they already have someone in mind," I said.

"I am given to understand that there is no shortage of candidates," he said. "My impression is that the field of Asian-American studies is one of rapid growth and low yield." He scratched his armpit vigorously, an unexpected gesture from so fastidious a man.

"Such a course would draw a lot of students," I said. "As an administrator I'm for it. Have Ms. Zhang or one of her group—what do they call themselves—write me a formal request, a petition even, with lots of signatures—let them come on strong, so I have something to work with."

"They are as yet unnamed," he said. "I suggested 'The Asian Students Society,' or ASS, but they were not amused."

"Why are you so disdainful?" I said.

"I am indifferent," he said. "They are predominantly Chinese, Taiwanese, and Koreans, a few from Indochina, none of whom have any love for the Japanese. No one has any love for the Japanese. You don't know what it's like: everyone loves the Irish."

"Professor Confalone likes to say he can pity anyone except someone who pities himself," I said. "I never think of you as very Japanese."

"I wonder if I might have one of your cigarettes?" he said. "I left mine in the office." We lit up. "It is so difficult to find a place in which to smoke nowadays. I envy you your office. One thinks of it as a sanctuary." He held his cigarette between finger and thumb, but reversed, palm toward his face, hiding his chops when he puffed. "I am Japanese enough to have grandparents who were interned during the Second World War."

"My grandfather was also interned," I said, "in his own country."

"No doubt he was a subversive," he said. "My grandparents were, are, not. They wanted, want, nothing more than to be considered good Americans. My parents want the same. They are long-established artichoke farmers outside San Jose, active in numerous booster organizations. If this is not their country, which is? Ask their neighbors and the response would be equivocal."

"And what do you want?" I said.

"I am a disappointment to my parents," he said.

"So long as you don't disappoint me," I said. "Let's see what we have here." I began to read:

> A man with a utilitarian interest in a woman's bum is a pervert. But a man who truly loves a bum loves it as an end in itself. It is not what a bum surrounds that attracts him; he has no taste for abasement; he has no itch to violate. His love is not the sort that is a function of ontological insecurity: he does not in his character of bum-lover need to demonstrate his existence by observing its reflection in the discomfort of others. Nor is it what emerges from a bum that's at issue: there is nothing regressive, aggressive, or ingressive about bumphilia. A bum-lover loves a bum for what it is in relation to what he is, another sort of bum.

I looked up at the top of the page at the title: *Bums and Boobs, Bubs and Bums; An Essay in Phenomenological Anatomy and Literary Classification.* "I have read the first paragraph," I said. "I fail to see what it has to do with literature."

"I mean to establish two new categories of modernist writers," he said, "the bum and the boob, the ass-man and the tit-man, the anal and the oral. It will be an essay on style, rather than biographical criticism."

I read on:

> He is a bum because he refuses to define himself by a love of the good or the useful. He contributes neither to the cohesion of the group, the perpetuation of the species, nor the pacification of females. He pursues his vagrant love as one acts upon a choice, not as one complies with necessity; no social or psychological compulsion, no biological urge, has fixed the seat of his affections. When he loves what he loves he is not doing something else as well. He loves what he loves as a substance, not as a symbol, as a signifier of only and entirely itself. His love is a service that is perfect freedom.

I looked up again. "I have sponsored some offbeat dissertations in my time," I said, "but this. . . ."

"I have heard that you favor syncopation," he said. "One glance at *Dissertation Abstracts* is enough to see that my thesis is in tune with those recently defended in the nation's most prestigious institutions. You must forgive me: I do not ordinarily mix my metaphors."

I read on:

> His sexual interests, that is, are apolitical, as he, so far as he is a bumphiliac, is amoral; his love is beyond good and evil, or behind them. He does not do his thing to demonstrate a point, as does the exhibitionist; or to display the triumph of artifice over

> nature, as does the fairy; or to protest the complicity of society with biology in making invidious distinctions between the sexes, as does the dyke; or out of timidity, as does the child molester; or to parody the severity of official morality as does the sado-masochist; or to have in fantasy what he cannot have in the flesh, as does the masturbator; or to affirm that uptight is all right if the woman is supine, as do the righteous right prone; or to place beneath him women who in social status are above him, as did Don Juan, whose modern equivalent is the black Negro among white ones; or to subvert society at large by organizing in small its prototypical obverse, as does the communard polygamous pan-sexualist, a Charles Manson or Jim Jones. On the contrary, there is nothing demonstrative, tendentious, polemical, argumentative, ideological, or adversarial about the bum-lover's love of bums.
>
> Bumbumery negates all causes by turning it back on them . . .

I sat back in my chair, took out a cigarette, put it to my mouth, paused and offered one to Teddy, which he withdrew from the pack and flipped toward the ceiling, so that turning slowly end over end it rose and fell, right between his lips. We lit up. "It won't play, Mr. Nakatani," I said. "This is not a dissertation proposal—you must know that. What else it is I am not prepared to say."

"The regrettable truth is that I have no topic," he said, collapsing. "For some reason my mind stalls when I try to drive it in that direction. It is not a writer's block, but something anterior."

"Maybe you are in the wrong business," I said.

"I am not," he said, suddenly attacking his armpit as though an invisible hand had turned the switch on a mechanical toy. "Don't say that. Haven't I trained myself like an Olympic athlete, denied myself like a novitiate? Even Professor Jones said that if she could read poetry as I do her career would have taken a different turn. Professor Sistrunk—" The flush faded from his cheeks. He sat back. The near-smile returned. "From your bibliography, which I have studied," he said, "It is clear that you have never suffered through a like malady. I mean to survive it—with your help. I am placing myself at the disposal of the omnivorous sympathies for which you are so justly celebrated."

Let us hope that my malady, whatever this is, is not the same as Teddy's, whatever his is, a nasty double rhyme.

"Then why this?" I said, tapping *Bums and Boobs* with the back of my fingernails.

"I was trying to catch your eye," he said. "I was hoping you would find the point of view congenial. From certain suggestions in your lecture, from other indications, I gathered that you—"

"Don't say it!" I said. "Who the fuck do you think you're fucking with? One fucking more word and I'll twist your fucking ass—" I caught myself halfway out of my chair. I sat back, took a deep breath, lit a new cigarette from the old, puffed on it, put a near-smile on my face. "You know, Mr. Nakatani, sometimes you really do presume."

"I am not a timorous man, Professor O'Leary," he said, "but when your neck swells and the veins stand out on your forehead, you are truly frightening."

"It's good of you to say so," I said.

"I did not mean to presume," he said. "I was trying to establish rapport."

"Do you believe any of this?" I said, once again backhanding *Bums and Boobs*.

"We are not children," he said. "Belief... confessional criticism ... another fashion to which I have been unable to accommodate myself. I put a spin on my material that I hoped would lead to meeting of minds. (I find that I alliterate at times of stress.) I am not too proud to admit that I need help."

I swiveled around in my chair, put my feet on the radiator, and looked out the window, so that I could think, for of the two categories of thinker, those who find an inspiration in what is right before their noses and those who find there only an impediment, I belong to the second. Did I hear the word "Please," low, hoarse, as though spoken by someone imprisoned inside Teddy Nakatani? I swiveled back to my desk. "What do you know about Sato's sword?" I said.

He blinked. "Junzo Sato in admiration gave Yeats a five-hundred-year-old sword," he said.

"Yes," I said.

"It was wrapped in a piece of silk torn from a court-lady's dress," he said.

"Yes," I said.

"He kept it on his writing desk, by pen and paper," he said.

"Yes," I said.

"A potent symbol to Yeats," he said, ". . . and to me. What is the phrase? 'Emblematic of sex and violence.'"

"'Emblematic of love and war,'" I said. "What happened to that famous ear of yours?"

"Yes, of course," he said. "A forgivable slip, since one might say that the one is a euphemism, or even a synecdoche for the other."

"One might say so, but not Yeats," I said.

"You are aware that in Lucretius, whom Yeats read, the nature of all things is explained by the unending opposition of Venus and Mars," he said.

"In Yeats it is more often by their conjunction," I said, and I quoted these memorable lines:

> The sword's a cross; there He died:
> On breast of Mars the goddess sighed.

"There's your subject," I said.

"Sex and violence?" he said.

"Only in part," I said. "Your subject is Yeats and japanoiserie. Chapter I: What did Yeats's Britain know or think about Japan? Was there a special Irish take? Chapter II: What contact, direct or indirect, did Yeats have with things Japanese? Chapter III: what was his own take in general, in his plays, in his prose, in his poems? This chapter will play to your strength, the close reading of poems. Chapter IV: How did the Japanesque mesh with Yeats's other preoccupations? Chapter V: You stand back: is what Yeats did with Japan lamentable or admirable?"

"I am indebted to you," he said. "Without being aware of it, I have already considered these matters."

"It is time to do more than consider," I said.

"This not a neutral subject for me," he said. "It provokes emotions that—"

"Too hot for you to handle?" I said.

He jumped to his feet, reddening, scratching his armpit, his hand moving like the hindpaw of Uncle Alf's collie, Alice. "I am going on the assumption that your malady is an immunological reaction to dissertations that are merely academic."

"I shall not disappoint you," he said.

"I want a weekly progress report," I said.

"You will see," he said. "We have more in common than you are willing to admit."

There you are, Joel, a typical morning on the job. Some fun, hanh! (to quote Lizzie). And professors have the nerve to complain that they are underpaid. Well, we're like dentists in that the incomes of doctors and lawyers give us an inferiority complex. I am myself probably making more money than any other member of the family since the O'Learys materialized from the mists of County Donegal, like a swarm of Irish Snopses. No, it's not the money (or even our social status as licensed figures of fun) that makes me feel as though I were floating on a dead sea on a dark night. It's that we never know whether we are doing anything, no tangible outcome, no bone set or case settled or button sewn or baby born or ditch dug or record cut, like your "Llareggub," which has become a jazz standard, which brings me and Sissie royalty checks that grow bigger every year. Pa is pissed, not because you made me executor, but because you willed all the income from your music to Sissie and me. Sissie is pissed because I won't let Nike use "Llareggub" as background music for a television ad. Normally I can stand back from this sense of futility, take a long view, from which all effort is futile, humankind extinct, the dead earth drifting away from a cooling sun through cosmic debris, in widening gyres.

I thought this account might help you pass the time, for you have a lot of time to pass, for no matter how much of eternity you have to pass through, there is still more, still as much more, no end to it, ever. I picture you as getting along easier without heroin than without the six hours a day practice, whizzing through three octaves of the Phrygian mode in every key, or the all-night jam sessions, twenty presto choruses of "Ko-Ko" in five flats, making that bitch of a bridge on "Bebop" every time, cutting most everybody, even Freddie Hubbard giving you a nod. What is this cat Gabriel like? Would he lend you his horn? You could teach all those harpists the changes on "Dizzy Atmosphere," liven up the place.

I am just penciling in time myself. Julie said she would be home by one o'clock, and here it is one-thirty. I see that I have been writing without a break for ten hours, without anything to eat, in fact. I must be coming down with something. I was locking the door to my office, ready for lunch, when Murray Weinrein placed himself in my path. We have work to do, he said. After lunch, I said. He had taken the liberty of ordering lunch in, he said, a corned beef on rye with mustard and cole slaw (Celt-Hebraic cuisine), for me, pickles and a Dos Equis. For him, cottage cheese and tea with lemon. So for three hours we distributed colleagues among committees (a ticklish business), distributed their names, that is, for it will be my job to twist arms or kiss asses, each according to his needs. We drafted memos, decided what to do with a four-by-six-foot portrait of a professor emeritus, now dead, that his widow had donated to the Department, dreamed up an administrative post for Professor Derwood Bobbie, so we could give him a course remission, so he could drop his seminar in Victorian poetry, for which only one student had shown up. We studied a complete list of the professorial staff, calculated likely years of retirement or dementia (in the case of senior staff), and likely years of expulsion (in the case of junior staff) listed their fields of expertise, looking for holes to hire into, should the administration permit us to hire.

We were encroaching on the Appointments Committee's turf, but what were a chair and a vice-chair for, Murray said, if not to facilitate the decisions of their constituents, for nothing simplified the decision-making process like a fait accompli, for after I had been on the job a while, he said, I would learn that it was as important to make a pretense of democracy as to prevent it. That being the case, I said, taking on his tone, I had a fait accompli for him to hand on to the Policy Committee. I wanted him to send a letter to the Administration recommending that Lizzie Arno's contract be renewed. I would draft the letter, put some oomph into it. He said he would think about it. Do this for me, I said, one hand washing the other. His hands were already clean, he said. Playing the sly boots, taking a cue from Angel Terrasco, hinting that I had leverage, I told him to be nice to Irene, for she was going through a difficult time. He was always nice to Irene, he said. I pointed out to him that Lizzie's new book—there's the doorbell. I have to remember to get Julie a set of keys tomorrow.

I'll just say goodnight while Julie takes her shower. She was late because after studying she and her friends went to the Other End for a beer, a toast to the Wife of Bath. Professor Confalone was there. He bought them all drinks. He's awfully nice. He seemed really sympathetic about the obstacles students in the School of Advanced Studies have to face. He said that any time they have a problem, they could take it to him. Sure, and if you've got a migraine, take it to the guy who works the guillotine.

"Ready, Cuz?" Julie is shouting down the hall. Well, yes, I think I am.

7

Dear Joel,

Forgive me for not writing yesterday, but I was up and doing, and as Willie Yeats used to say, you can perfect the life or the work (by which he meant his writing), but not both. I cannot say I have perfected either, for my life is a shaggy dog story, no punch line imaginable, and my writing is like flap copy for a lost work by an apocryphal writer, but I *can* say, yes I can, that Julie showed me some action. Right about now she ought to be crossing the Triboro Bridge, on her way to Jones Beach, with her girl friends, in my Vanagon, a so-long to summer, but one day late, for overnight the temperature dropped twenty-five degrees. I can't doubt she meant it when she said she really wished I would go with them, but even if the thought of how I would look in a bathing suit does not bother her, it does me.

I woke up early yesterday morning, but got up late, telling myself to move it, but no one listened. I kept running pictures of myself sliding out of bed, letting Julie sleep, build up her strength, for I would put her to work later, Saturday being the day I clean house. There she was, still on the far side of the bed, her backside still pointing my way. But she must have moved, after all, for when

I sat up, my mind on something else, and lifted the cover, to get out from under it, I saw that the flannel shirt was up around her waist. I snapped my eyes away, not because I am an honorable man, but because a sudden shock coursed through me, from sternum to scrotum, deep-throating a cattle prod. I gathered up my things and tiptoed out of the bedroom, light on my feet as the hippopotamus in *Fantasia*, and dressed while the coffee dripped, still shaky. By the way, remember that first night when I thought I saw in the bathroom mirror a birthmark on one of Julie's golden delicious cheeks? Turns out to be a butterfly tattoo.

I carried a mug of coffee and my cleaning stuff, the Ajax, the Mister Clean (mesomorphic cleansers), a scrubbing brush, a sponge, and old toothbrush (for between the tiles) to the large bathroom, the one Julie has been using: hair in the sink, the toothpaste cap disparue, the soap dish soggy, lipsticks here, their tops there, socks, my socks, and two pairs of my briefs hanging to dry on the shower curtain rod. I may have said "fuck this," loud enough for someone to hear, had anyone been listening.

One of Julie's feet, a congenial foot, a brawny foot, a foot you could depend on, broad across the ball, shortish of toe, plenty of arch, was outside the covers, hanging defenseless over the rim of the bed. I ran a finger along the underside of it, from heel to ball. Nothing happened. So I did it again. The foot retracted, toes curling, then relaxed, slid back. My scientific curiosity thus aroused, for as Leonard observed, I can be a pain in the ass if I set my mind to it, I did it again. Julie thrashed over on her back, arms flailing, and sat up, her eyes wide. "You can't—" she said, then saw what she was looking at, namely me, then the dreamy smile: "Morning, Cuz."

"Let's go after your things," I said, for I did not like the idea of her wearing men's underwear. It did not sit right, if you know what I mean.

I was taking my suit out of the closet, for I only have one, the cut never quite in, or out, of style, when Julie returned from the bathroom. "I was thinking, Cuz, maybe a suit isn't a good idea. The only thing that impresses Torrie is someone who is more out of control than he is. He doesn't pay his child support, starts fights with metermaids, uses a gizmo to get cable television for free, that kind of person. Do you have a denim jacket without sleeves? You know, like a biker, let him see those arms."

"Torrie?" I said.

"Well, his name is Thorwald," she said, "but he doesn't like anyone to call him that."

I put on a midnight blue shirt, birthday present from Kay, a silver tie, present from a visiting scholar from Italy, whom I showed around, and a belted, black leather jacket, Christmas present from Sissie. She got it from her husband who got it from a friend who was helping a friend sell off the goods from a truck a friend had heisted. It seems there was no demand for this one jacket, size extra-tall, XXL. Such in any case, is the tale told me by our idiot brother-in-law, with the air of an inside trader explaining how he made his first 100 million.

"That tie makes you look like a character in what was it, *Guys and Dolls*," she said. She pulled down on the tie, so she could reach, removed it, opened the top four buttons of the shirt, went to her room, came back with a gold chain, pulled my head down, put the chain around my neck, where it fit like a choker, for Julie's neck is by no means a size 17, led me to the bathroom, ran three inches of water into the sink, swished around a bar of soap until the water was foamy, and, dipping a comb, slicked back my hair, on both sides, so it could harden. Then she scratched around the hair on the top of my head until it hung over my forehead in a jumble of curls, accentuating the bison-effect no doubt. She stood back. *"Formidable!"* she said. "Now you look like one of those guys who hang out in front of the Ravenite Social Club."

I looked in the mirror, tried on a sneer, but only managed to look apologetic.

"Do you have black pants made out of that shiny material?" she said.

I made do with my charcoal grays and the black shoes, shiny enough, that I keep for formal occasions.

We putsi-putsied downtown in the Vanagon, detouring around a street fair, Julie telling me that Torrie was a D.J., not the kind that has a radio show, but the kind that jockies discs where people dance. The chances are that he would still be asleep, catch him off guard.

We double-parked in front of a brick building that had been painted white around 1910, from the look of it. Julie pressed a bell in the entranceway, and when nothing happened, pressed again, and when nothing happened, pressed once more, leaning on it. "Go away!" said a voice, remarkable for how much snarl it could compress into three syllables.

"It's Michelle," said Julie, in a voice I had never heard come out of her before.

"Come back later," said the intercom, the snarl deepening into a growl.

"It's this cush gig I heard about," said Julie. "Four days work, good pay. I just want to give you the guy's number before I go to work."

The buzzer sounded and we pushed on in.

Before us was a long narrow staircase, about three normal storeys' worth. We started up, Julie saying, "Michelle's his new girlfriend, from California. She wants to be a singer. She's a nice person, but she can't remember the words and she hits every big note a quarter-tone flat, makes your teeth itch."

On the landing was a green door, next to it a bell, which Julie pushed. For a while no one came, and a good thing, for I was incapacitated by loss of breath. The door opened three inches, one eye peering over the chain, first at Julie, then at me. "Fuck off," said whoever was attached to the eye, and the door began to close. I stopped it with a forearm shiver, for of the two categories of people, those who like their doors closed and those who like their doors open, I belong to the second. The chain did not hold: the door swung open until it hit flesh. I shouldered my way in, followed by Julie. The guy in front of me, no longer young, had the build of a sixties rockster, shortish and stringy. There was a red circle, size of a doorknob, over his ribs. Thorwald, for who else could it have been, was naked from the waist up and from the ankles down. He was wearing maroon jeans. Julie told me later that at this point I was wearing a truly nasty smile, made her nervous. Well, I don't know: to bring that kind of smile off you need an upper lip like Hector's, which I don't have.

The room behind Thorwald was square, much larger than your average studio and smaller than the usual loft. The wood floor was wavy, as though there had once been aisles between the sewing machines, for the greenhorns to walk along. Along the right hand wall, beyond the bed, were two partitioned-off areas with doors set into the unpainted particleboard, beyond them a kitchen sink and a stove. Along the back wall was more audio and video equipment than any decent person would want. Against the left-hand wall were a dresser and a desk, in front of them six cardboard cartons, three of them open, the flaps hanging like a beagle's ears.

Now I can usually regard a messy bed, grubby sheets, with equanimity, but this one riled me. It was king-sized and unusually low, as though someone had sawed off the legs three-quarters of the way up. It was not against the right-hand wall, nor was it midway between the right-hand and left-hand walls, nor a quarter of the way from any wall. It was just there, anywhere, saying up yours to form, balance, proportion, a postmodernist bed. I could feel my neck swelling, Julie's chain sinking into the flesh.

"Don't make trouble, Torrie," said Julie, "we're just getting my clothes and things."

"Where's my three months' rent?" Thorwald said.

"The check's in the mail," said Julie.

"Does it talk?" he said, nodding toward me.

Before I knew what was happening my arms shot forward, the heels of my hands catching him just below the shoulders, as many an offensive tackle had caught me, on those plays when I was the designated blitzer. He backpedaled until a calf bumped into the bed. He sat down abruptly, teeth clacking. He jumped up and charged, head down, risking the vertebra in that skinny neck of his, for five inches below the surface, my stomach is granite.

At the last second, he slanted his head and came into me shoulder first, grunted, rebounded, fell to a knee. I leaned over, gripped him by his hip bones, lifted him over my head, as you would carry a surfboard, his face to the ceiling, walked over to the bed, shifted my grip, and brought him down, hard, his face to the sheets. "Oof," he said, and bounced surprisingly high, so that I caught him in midair, one hand in his fork, the other around his neck ("kack," he said), and lifted him over my head, as you would hold a barbell, his face looking up your way, Joel, shifted my grip, and brought him down, putting my back into it, his face toward China. This time he hardly bounced at all, for one already shortened leg of the bed collapsed. I took hold of him by his pigtail and waistband, lifted him over my head, buttons popping off his fly, his face toward St. Mary the Intercessor, shifted my grip, and brought him down, putting my back and stomach into it, his face toward Beelzebub, and something went "nok." "Oo, oh, ah, ow," he said, "you bastard, you broke my wrist."

I was leaning over to pick him up again, when Julie jumped on my back, wrapped her legs around my waist, put a hammerlock on me, and pulled me half upright, her free hand pounding my shoulder. "Stop," she said, "enough. No more. Oh, will you please stop: you'll kill him." Thorwald crawled off the bed, his pants around his thighs, and what can you expect if you wear maroon jeans with a button fly, and started toward one of the doors. He crawled pretty well for a man who could only put one hand into it. I stepped onto the bed and walked across it, Julie still hanging on, tightening her choke hold, pulling my hair, saying "Stop, stop, stop, stop, stop, stop," but I didn't, even when another leg on the bed collapsed, nearly tipping us over.

Thorwald made it to the door, jerked it open, scurried past it on three points, sat on the potty, for behind the door was a bathroom, pulled the door to, and I could hear the lock turn, just as I got there, Julie twisting an ear, pulling my nose. I kicked the door, a flimsy affair, breaking a panel across. Another kick, and the pieces fell in. Did I ever tell you that I was our emergency place kicker, for when our starter got hurt, as well as first-string weak-side linebacker and occasional tight end? "Help," said a wee, weak high-pitched voice from within. "You're losing it, Cuz," said Julie. "Come on now, back off." I hammered in a top panel of the door with the base of my fist, and reached for the lock, when Julie put her cheek against mine, and in a low voice said, "Please, Cuz, please, for me." So I stopped, went for the cartons, Julie releasing her hold, sliding off, patting my back, saying, "Whew!"

While I carried cartons to the landing, Julie took a clock radio off the dresser, an antique lamp (bronze nymph holding up the fixture) off the desk, an elegant little mirror off the wall. She looked in the open cartons and said, "I knew it: he's been wearing my clothes." She went to the partitioned-off area next to the bathroom, ignoring Thorwald, whom I could see through the breaks in the door, reclining in the tub, holding his wrist, head back, eyes closed, and she opened the door, behind which was a closet, at the back of which was a big pile of clothes, for Thorwald, so I gathered, has a phobia of laundromats. Julie pulled out a flannel shirt, a sweatshirt, tee shirts, a cotton sweater, a denim jacket, a striped jersey with hood, flowered suspenders, a paisley vest. She held up an argyle sock, stiff as a strip of *bocalhau,* and dropped it. "He can keep whatever is in the bathroom, too."

We pockata-pockatated uptown, but had to stop halfway around Columbus Circle for a light. Outside the open window of my trusty Vanagon was a group playing, and damned if they weren't stating the theme of Miles's "Doxy," which I had never before heard live. There was a break, and the trumpet player hit a high note and came down in lovely clusters of blue notes, as the light changed to green and I felt the poison seep out of me. We turned on to Broadway off the Circle and then on to Amsterdam at Seventy-Second Street and then back to Broadway at Ninety-Sixth Street, for I had just thought of something.

"I didn't think you had it in you," Julie said, speech after long silence.

"I didn't think I could let it out," I said.

"Did you ever hit a woman?" she said.

"Not yet," I said.

"Don't do it, Cuz," she said. "It's not the same. I've seen guys two days after a fight, one all red and purple around the eye, the other all green and yellow at the side of the mouth, having a drink, rubbing shoulders, big buddies again. It's different when a man hits a woman. The hurt doesn't heal."

"Be good, and I won't spank you," I said.

"Not even if I ask?" she said, lightening up, putting a hand on my shoulder, giving it a squeeze, the leather jacket creaking.

"What was that about rent?" I said.

"He walked in on me while I was packing those cartons," she said, "and he said what the fuck you doing and I said I'm moving the fuck out, I've had it, and he said fuck you are and I said fuck I'm not and he said all right you owe me three months' rent, and I said you didn't say anything about rent when I moved in, and he said I'm saying it now, and I said I haven't got it, cause he'd already gotten his money's worth out of me, and he twisted my arm behind my back and pushed me out the door. He kicked me in the butt, too."

"Whatever did you see in him to begin with?" I said. "A pipsqueak like that."

"I didn't have any other place to go," she said. "I know you're not supposed to be prejudiced and all, but it felt creepy living with that drummer who was HIV-positive, even after, you know, we stopped having sex."

"Maybe you ought to practice sleeping alone," I said. "You know, first one night a week, then two, then three. . . ."

"It's not just that," she said. "I was trying to save on rent money, so I could go to school."

"Well, anyway, I'm the beneficiary," I said.

She squeezed my shoulder, making the leather creak, but she had a wistful look on her face, and a good thing I only glanced her way, for a bicyclist cut in front of me, from the inside lane, and if I hadn't braked, the reflexes still there, my Vanagon would have had itself a new bumper ornament. The look on her face, as I read it, signified that she thought I was just being polite, although she herself was too polite to say so. Well, was I? The pleasure of her presence in bed was offset by the displeasure of an arousal unassuaged. I should have been a pair of ragged claws.... But Yeats speaks of a couple passionately in love, who abstained, on behalf of "that sweet extremity of Pride / That's called Platonic love." Bah: Platonic love is the result of an aversion that outweighs desire, twisting your neck away from Dracula's kiss. Shaw said that marriage is popular because it combines the maximum of temptation with the maximum of opportunity. Wrong on both counts. Yeats also asks whether the imagination dwells most on a woman won or a woman lost. Just what am I talking about? I haven't won Julie or lost her or married her or fallen in love with her, Platonically or otherwise, banish the thought.

We stopped by a street vendor, from whom I bought Julie four pairs of socks, and stopped at a locksmith, for a duplicate set of keys, which I presented to Julie. "Thanks, Cuz, thanks," she said.

I can't blame Julie for not wanting me to help her unpack, although I had no intention of snatching a quick feel of her underclothes. I lurked in the doorway, peeping in, like the Frankenstein monster, swaying from foot to foot, while Julie set up her sound box, slid in a CD, some guy mournfully wailing words I couldn't make out. "You ought to like this group, Cuz," she said: "They're Irish." Well, I did— in a way, thinking that the interest of rock was more in the words, which escaped me, and in the personality of the group, which I didn't know, and in an attitude, which was not mine, than in melody, harmony, or rhythm, Dizzy's bag.

Julie placed her lamp on the desk, propped her mirror on the dresser, hung clothes in the closet, hung a beret on one handlebar of her bike, an Elmer Fudd plaid cap on the other, rearranging things, moving in, marking her territory, so I could no longer think of the room as a would-be nursery. I broke off, prowled the hall, replaced Cedric Whitman, found myself in the kitchen, where the refrigerator reminded me that I hadn't eaten for over twenty-four hours, peered without seeing into the pantry, discovered a jar of scotch marmalade in my hand, dark and bitter, the way I like it, a gift, and the image of the giver flashed before my inner eye, gave me an idea.

My phone is on the kitchen wall (I forget why), an extension in the bedroom, no answering machine (because I am a dinosaur). I reached for it, holding the jar of marmalade under an arm, and called Katriona Campbell, Dean of the School of Advanced Studies, or SAS, pronounced "sass." Her husband, Marty Cline, said she was in her office, Saturday or no Saturday, trying to catch up. On the way out, I stopped at the doorway to Julie's room, formerly the nursery, and just stood there, as though kept out by an invisible barrier, something out of science fiction, listening to the sounds, making out the words, and looking in. Julie was reaching for the top of the closet, a floppy hat in her hand, while the Irishers wailed "love is a blindness," reaching up, up, her bust rising, "love is a clockworks," stretching up, up, her calves swelling, "and cold steel," her can canted, and finally with a little hop, pushed the hat halfway onto the shelf, "fingers too numb to feel," the hat teetered, toppled, fell over her face, between her hands, onto the floor.

"I've got to go out for a while," I said.

"When you come back, we can clean up together," Julie said. She picked up the hat, stepped back, and scaled it onto the shelf, as you would throw a Frisbee.

"Let's declare a holiday," I said. "If you're not busy, we can eat out."

"What's that under your arm?" she said.

I let the jar of marmalade slide down my arm into my hand. "A gift," I said, "and it's the giver I'm going to see."

"A girlfriend?" she said. "Are you going to return it?"

"An ex-girlfriend," I said, reaching through the barrier to place the jar in her hand.

As I made my way to Lightfoot Lee Hall, past the statue of Paul Revere, past the guy in a Norfolk jacket who comes on campus twice a day to feed the squirrels and pigeons, past the suntanned knees of coeds sitting on the steps to the rotunda, I thought about rock and roll, of which I disapprove, for a number of reasons, not so much for what it is, as for the sake of what it displaced. Anybody concerned for the moral and physical well-being of humanity must see rock and roll as an adulteration of the rhythm and blues that begat it and died for it, like one of Frazier's sacred kings. Rock and roll began as rhythm and blues without that swing, without which it don't mean a thing. Who or what was it that beat the beat out of whites? The Vietnam War? You must have noticed, although I never heard you say as much, that only during the swing and bop eras, in the whole history of the world, or at least since Australopithecines left Africa, only then and here did the prevailing popular music among whites, never mind that it was invented and best played by blacks, swing. So kiss my ass, Momma Cass. Pearl Jam, go on the lam. To Guns N' Roses here's halitosis. As for you, Led Zeppelin, watch what you step in. And may we open our sensorium to the swinging spirit of St. Diz.

I stuck my head into the doorway of Katriona Campbell's office and said, "May I come in?"

Without looking up, recognizing my voice (for smoking two packs of Pall Malls every day, like playing jazz trumpet, puts static in your voicebox), she said, "When did I ever refuse you anything?"

"Giving is your métier," I said, walking in, sitting by her desk.

She turned her bold brown eyes toward me, tossed back a coil of brassy hair, accepted a cigarette, allowed me to light it, looked me over: the hairdo, the black leather jacket, the gold chain.

"You've changed your style," she said.

"I'm living with someone," I said. "She's re-doing me."

"Congratulations," she said.

"Thank you," I said.

"Who's the lucky woman?" she said.

"A student at the School of Advanced Studies," I said.

"That's two wise decisions she's made," said Katriona.

"I want you to give her a tuition exemption," I said.

She fell back in her chair, tossed back a coil of springy hair. "Now I know what Marty means by chutzpah," she said.

"Faculty spouses and children get tuition exemptions as a matter of course," I said.

"So marry her," she said. "Adopt her."

"She's struggling toward self-reliance," I said. "That's why I can't pay her tuition."

"Self-reliance, is it?" she said. "She had better be self-reliant if she's going to make it with you. And what's so self-reliant about a tuition exemption?"

"I never refused you anything I had to give," I said.

"You had what I wanted, but you didn't know how to give it, or even that I wanted it," she said. "You don't know what a woman wants. And you don't know how to take what a woman wants to give."

"I assume women want what men want," I said.

"Meaning sex, I suppose," she said. "You're hopeless."

"Give me this one thing," I said.

"I can't do it," she said.

"It won't cost SAS anything," I said.

"I can't do it," she said.

"You did it for Trudy Stone, Bernard Berenson Professor of Art History," I said.

"What's that you say?" she said, sitting forward, two coils of hair slipping over an eye.

"You gave Allerby Tuckus, 'Allie' I believe she's called, a tuition exemption," I said.

"I know what the blue blazes she's called," she said. "How did you get wind of this? Kay Pesky, I bet, the feminist grapevine."

"Kay knows I'm a mausoleum of other people's secrets," I said.

"You listen to me, Wynn O'Leary," she said, pointing a finger.

"Those two have been together for nearly twenty years. They're as married as you can get without a license."

"Is the duration of . . . an arrangement the test?" I said. "You've been married for one year, Zeno for over twenty. Who's more married?"

"Trudy Stone came here as you did," she said, her voice clear and cold as a xylophone. "I told her what I told you. A week later she comes back with a letter, says she's going to send it to the *Voice*, the *Observer*, the *Chronicle of Higher Education*, I forgot who-all else, talk-show hostesses." Life had come back into her voice, a note of outrage. "She named me by name, made me out to be a sexist, a homophobe, an Aunt Tillie, a quisling, a pettifogging stickler for the letter, which killeth. And we were just kicking off our five-year fund-raising campaign. We didn't need that noise."

"I can write letters, too," I said.

For some reason that amused her. She sat back with a big smile on her face. "Give it up, Wynn: that's not your style," she said.

"I've been taking lessons in realpolitik from Angel Terrasco," I said. "Pretty soon I'll be capable of anything."

"Dear old Angel," said Katriona. "She stopped by yesterday. The whole time she looked at me as though I was covered with botflies."

"Yes," I said. "She was kind enough to say that signing her petition would be no skin off my nose."

At that, Katriona laughed. Then, pulling back the two coils of hair, she said, "Give me one of yours. There's more vitamins and minerals in them." We lit up. "What Angel really wanted to know is are there any complaints of sexual harassment against Leonard Sistrunk."

"What did you tell her?" I said.

"That all such matters are strictly confidential until formal charges are brought," she said. "I can tell you that there are none."

"Did she ask about Zeno?" I said.

"Even Angel doesn't have the chutzpah for that," she said.

"Everybody knows that Zeno and I had a fling"—she blew smoke in my face—"off the rebound from you."

"I was making you miserable," I said.

"You were making yourself miserable," she said. "My misery was only a pale reflection of yours." She stood up, went to the window, turning her back to me. "Masculine vanity, that's what got between us."

"I like to think of my faults as personal rather than generic," I said.

"I had a real feeling for you, Wynn, and you misread it as pity," she said, turning to face me.

"I can't bear it when people are nice to me," I said. "I was having homicidal fantasies."

"How about your new friend?" she said. "Does she make you feel homicidal? Or has she solved your little problem?"

"You know I never speak about my love life, or the absence thereof," I said.

"Yes, holding back is your métier," she said.

"When have I ever refused—" I said.

"You tell your roommate—what's her name, anyhow?" she said.

"Juliette Berceau," I said.

"Juliette, no less," she said.

"'Julie,' for short," I said.

"How old is she?" she said.

"Mid-twenties," I said.

"Robbing the cradle, are you?" she said.

"She's the kind of person SAS was invented for," I said: "She's smart, but uneducated, but determined to make a life for herself."

Katriona sighed, came over to her desk, rested her cheek in her hand, looked me in the eye. "You can tell her that she's got a tuition fellowship," she said, "renewable every semester so long as she maintains at least a B-minus average. I'll send her an official letter."

"I owe you," I said.

"You owed me already," she said. "I'm having a Dean's Day this spring: you're going to be one of the speakers."

"I'm not very good at that sort of thing," I said.

"Next year you will teach a section of Style and Substance," she said, "to show SAS students that the vice-chair of the English Department cares about them."

"Come on, Katy, I always have a dozen or so SAS students in my lecture course," I said.

"I'm arranging back-to-school seminars for New York alumni," she said. "You're going to preside over one of them."

"You want me to pass around the hat, too," I said.

"And now that you're vice-chair," she said, "maybe you can get some of those hoity-toity, airy fairy, prima-donna Marxist colleagues of yours to teach courses in the evening, when real working people can take them. Let *theoria* become *praxis*."

"Anything else?" I said, standing.

"I'm thinking," she said, getting out of her chair, coming around the desk. "I want a sit-down with the Policy Committee. I've got a list of demands. And you might remind them that I have an equal say when it comes to faculty raises, adjunct money, and planning units." I should explain, Joel, that departmental resources are allotted in consultation with the three Deans of SAS, the College, and Graduate Arts and Sciences, or GAS, pronounced "gas."

"You're better off sending those demands to me," I said. "I can present the Committee with faits accomplis, save then all those decisions and revisions which a minute will reverse."

She walked over to me, gave me a hug, making the leather creak, put her head on my chest. I kissed her where a vague part showed through her crisp, crinkled hair.

"Has your new squeeze put you on a diet?" she said.

"I redistributed my weight a little this summer," I said.

"Are you sure you didn't break off with me to get back at women for what Belinda did to you?"

"I like to think that my spites are as personal as my other faults," I said. "And Belinda didn't do anything to me... exactly. She was running for her life, or at least her sanity. Sooner or later, you would have done the same."

She bit me on the chest, hard, right through my shirt, disengaged, stood back.

"Ow," I said.

"Is that so?" she said, cuffing me on the shoulders, as I had cuffed Thorwald. "And that's why you wrote me that awful letter?" She cuffed me again. "And do you now plan to commit suicide because sooner or later you're going to die? That's what life is, love too, putting off the inevitable." She cuffed me, smacking leather.

I couldn't help smiling at her vehemence. "I've gotten used to living posthumously, you know... almost," I said.

She gave me a long look, now holding me by the shoulders. "That means your popsie hasn't turned the trick," she said.

"You know I never speak about my love—" I said.

"Spare me," she said. But she hugged me again, put her head on my chest.

"Don't bite," I said.

"Some Romeo you'll make," she said.

Walking home across the campus, leaping up (about two inches off the ground) to make a nice one-handed catch of a stray Frisbee, placing the legs I saw in one of twelve categories (shorts are in fashion this year), for of the five kinds of men, legs-men, ass-men, tits-men, face-men, and façade men, I belong to the first four, remembering that I had better read Kay's article ("Footman Beware"), remembering suddenly that I had forgotten to ask Katriona what we should do to get Lizzie's contract renewed, stopping dead in my tracks. I had meant to tell Katriona that Lizzie Arno is the best friend an SAS student ever had... unless that had become me. God save I'm not becoming some do-gooder.

I've just come back from the kitchen, in one hand a mug, a twelve-ouncer, of coffee, in the other a slab of pumpernickel slathered with butter, back from answering the phone. Kay Pesky wanted to know whether I wanted to go with her this coming Saturday to take in some music, try out the new local Thai restaurant afterwards. The performers are a professor from East Asia Languages and another from physics, who in general make beautiful music together, as Kay put it; they are going to play some duets over at the Treat Paine Auditorium, and to a sold-out house. On the program was stuff by Mendelssohn and such, Schumann, or was it Schubert, I didn't catch which, maybe both, in any case music by and for people who have never lifted anything heavy. I think it would be fair to say, Joel, that of the two classes of people, those who most hate singing violins and those who most hate tinkling pianos, it would be difficult to say which had the greater claim to justice.

Usually I accept these chaste offers to escort Kay on her outings in pursuit of culture, for she is acute where I am obtuse, as I am sharp where she is dull, makes for good talk. And I like the way she holds my arm when we cross the street or reaches up a hand for me to pull her out of a taxi, the feminist ban on the old sexist courtesies in abeyance. But not this time. It was not just the prospect of salon-keeper's music and then having my roast pork tricked up in coconut and pineapple, but some obscure and unassigned reluctance. I told Kay I was going to the country, baby, I can't take you, to get Fern Hill Farm ready for winter, a lie. I should have thought of something else, because now I'll have to drive up there. Well, maybe Julie would like to come along.

Kay, of course, has too much class to coax or sulk, or sound disappointed, or even to ask whether I had read "Footman Beware."

I put on *Thelonius Monk's Greatest Hits,* starting with "Mysterioso," to get the taste of those Romantische Teutons out of my mind's mouth.

That's today. But yesterday, letting myself in, I was looking forward to that moment when I would spread out before Julie, like Sir Walter's cloak, that costly tuition remission. "Thanks, Cuz," she would say, giving me a hug, which I would be careful not to return.

Would she notice the wet spot on my shirt where Katriona had bit me? I went right to the doorway of her room, whence issued some amazing sounds.

"Sacred blue!" I said. "What's that?"

"I can't believe you've never heard it before," Julie said.

"God in a cat-gut!" I said.

"It's Jimi Hendrix at Woodstock," she said, "playing the 'Star Spangled Banner.'"

"Even I can recognize 'The Star Spangled Banner,'" I said. How come you never told me about this, Joel?

"He sums up the whole of the sixties," she said. "The sixties were something. I wish I had been there."

I listened: the stuff Hendrix does after "the rockets' red glare" and after "the bombs bursting in air" for a moment brought back all the rage and regret, the love of country and hatred of those who were in charge of it.

"Well, weren't they?" she said. "Something, I mean."

"I lived through the sixties without much experiencing them," I said. "We jocks in the Southwestern Conference were not exactly at the cutting edge of the counterculture. I graduated the year the sixties ended, 1974."

"The Southwestern Conference is all those states with a lot of sand in them, right?" she said. "Why go there?"

"The Longhorns courted me with flattering ardor," I said, "turned my head."

"I wish some college would court me," she said.

"Well, SAS is making some kind of move on you," I said: "they're going to offer you a tuition scholarship."

She lifted her head slowly and then looked up at me with that appeasement smile of hers. "I don't . . . ," she said.

"You'll be getting a letter from Dean Campbell," I said. "You won't have to pay tuition so long as you maintain a B average."

She stood up. She looked stricken, you would have to say, as though I had just informed her that through some neglect of some little duty she had wiped out a whole village in India.

"You can take as many courses as you want," I said, and "oh, I suppose you'll have to fill out some financial—" when she rushed from the room, swivel-hipped to avoid brushing up against me, out into the foyer, and out the front door, which she slammed. Some character in E. M. Forster, I think it is, wonders whether men and women are not, in fact, members of two entirely different species: they accidentally got mixed up with each other, way back there, thus the mutual incomprehension.

I trudged into my study, prowled around the walls, pulling out books and sliding them back. Nope: Oscar Peterson is not gay. Nat Hentoff describes him as living contentedly in a penthouse with his wife and two kids. Good for Oscar. I was all restless, jumpy, anxious, jangled, impulses bouncing around inside me at all angles to each other, as when you pour out a bucketful of ping-pong balls onto the floor.

I put on another of those Blue Note compilations, *Funk and Blues* it's called, and sat at my desk, fidgeting. As you will remember Horace Silver managed to get some honest swing, soft swing, swing without cojones, but swing, into "Senior Blues." I let my pores open to the rhythm, let it seep in, organize me. Halfway through Donald Byrd's solo, my impulses settled down, ping-pong balls floating on a dark and rippled lake, deep as the blues, only the stray current or snapping fish to agitate the surface.

The next track, Art Blakey's "Moanin'," was even more like it, man, the rhythm riding me, as on a spirit gyroscope with a pulse in it, as in an undertow with a beat in it, as wrapped up in the arms of a great mother who surged forward in her rocking chair on the offbeat, relaxed backward on the downbeat, her naked breasts pressing up against me and releasing in tempo. I fell into a kind of trance during Lee Morgan's magnificent solo, picturing his old woman looking for him, finding him in a bar with his new woman, shooting him dead. Like you, Lee was one of Dizzy's legitimate heirs, in spite of the licks he adopted from Fats and Brownie, but he was her man and he was doing her wrong. When I came to, those interior twitches and itches had fallen into a sine curve with only sporadic spicules and spikes, my head bobbing, my feet keeping time, my head clear and empty, my shit together.

I had forgotten that the next track was Jimmy Smith's "Back at the Chicken Shack" (the best little whorehouse in Nevada), my alien-tester. If you can sit still while listening to it, you're an alien. It pulled me right out of the chair, got me motoring, got me really dancing for the first time in maybe ten years, my body memory taking over, the whole room shaking. Remember that trill Jimmie holds for eight bars with his right hand, his left hand a whole rhythm section worthy of Basie? Remember that shoulder shake you taught me, said you learned it from Geoffrey Holder, my latissimus dorsi in those days of four percent body fat waving like the wings on a stingray, those watermelon thighs stretching the seams on my bell-bottomed jeans? I swung out of it, whirled, and there was Julie standing in the doorway. She had a shopping bag in each hand, tops of bok choi sticking out of one of them, a nice smile on her face, a bit wistful maybe. What I mean is that it wasn't derisive or pitying, not that it did much to ease my embarrassment, face and neck hot and swelling.

Julie stepped into the room and began to dance, mirroring my moves, a broad smile on her face, but gradually sinking back into herself, eyes out of focus, communing with the rhythm. Julie is a minimalist dancer, Joel, making the most out of less, her chin tucking and pointing no more than an inch either way, one shoulder then the other just perceptibly coming forward, fists in front rotating like maracas in a tight little circle, hips subtly revolving, pelvis flickering toward me, her heels barely lifting off the floor, one coming down as the other goes up, never missing a beat, are you kidding? I didn't miss many either, for all my lumbering around, if I may say so myself. With the diminuendo restatement of the theme and then the fadeout, I became aware of myself, breathing heavily, sweating lightly, feeling good. Julie stretched her hands out to me, palms up.

I assumed, naturally, that she wanted to dance some more, so I fast-forwarded past all that slack and slick stuff to "The Sidewinder," your favorite (and mine) from the early sixties, before everything got tragic, Lee Morgan's masterpiece (and the inspiration for your "Llareggub"), as driving, rocking, rollicking, and joyous a blues as ever made life seem worth living. I just stood there, holding Julie's outstretched hands while the rhythm section led us into it, the bass going like this:

and the piano and horns, as I hear it, going like this:

We stood there, letting the beat, a beneficent daemon, possess us, until the horns came in to announce the theme, whereupon Julie turned herself on. She moved as before, except that I was holding her hands, except that she began to raise her knees and then to backstep, in tempo, pulling me with her. She pulled me out of the study, down the hall, into the bedroom, the whole world hardbopping with us. She pushed me, as I had pushed Thorwald, so that I sat on the bed. She pushed me again, again on the offbeat, so that I stretched out on the bed, my feet still on the floor. And then, Joel, and then she went into a striptease, as Lee Morgan took off on his once-in-a-lifetime solo, her hips rotating, her pelvis throwing uppercuts at the rhythm:

She reached back over her shoulders to unbutton her black turtleneck jersey and pulled it over her head in time with the bass clef figure. She reached back around her ribs to unhook her bra, shaking it off with her shoulders in time with the treble clef figure, thereby releasing her breasts, and all the while Lee Morgan soloed like a man who is tipsy, knows he is tipsy, likes being tipsy, but doesn't want to let on, his control the more deliberate the closer he comes to losing it, although he never quite does, all the while enjoying himself immensely. Julie stepped out of her shoes, pulled off her socks, my socks, teased down her denim skirt, shimmied out of her half-slip, seesawed out of her panties, one thumb hooked in them on either side, and danced in place, her brawny feet just lifting off the floor. She whirled around and bumped her apple cheeks once, oh my, and twice, oh my oh my:

What happened then, Joel, is what I hoped and feared would happen. As Joe Henderson's raunchy and raucous saxophone took over from Lee Morgan's carousing trumpet, Julie stepped between my legs, bent over into a right angle, and unbuttoned my shirt. She put a hand under my head, lifted me to a sitting position, and pulled down my shirt, but not off my arms, so that I was like manacled in it, all the time moving to the beat. She unhooked the gold chain and rubbed my neck over what must have been a thin red line, as though someone had garroted me. She pushed me down onto the bed and played the tom-tom on my stomach:

She stepped back, lifted one of my legs, pulled off a shoe, a sock, lifted the other leg, undressed the other foot, unlatched my belt, unbuttoned my fly, pulled off my pants, pulled off my briefs, patted, stroked, pecked my pecker, said, "Hello there." Then she lay down on me and dug in with a kiss that made the rockets red glare and the bombs burst in air. It had been a long time, Joel.

My arms were still caught in that dumb shirt, so I hugged her with my legs, the idea being to touch as much of her surface as was possible, for although like other men I have often daydreamed of just lying there while a woman made love to me, now that it was happening, it didn't feel right, though it certainly felt good. I threw my arms out and up from under me, thereby ripping the shirt apart, giving me room, even if my arms remained ensleeved. I rolled us onto our sides, still holding the kiss, for if as Leonard says I am a classic case of anality, I am also a textbook case of orality.

And now, instead of just letting Julie kiss me, instead of just holding on for dear life, I began to kiss back. I began with her shallow hollows, under her lip, behind her jawline, behind her clavicles, under her arms, around her navel, in front of her hipbone, where her thighs join her trunk, behind her knees, behind her anklebone, taking at least five minutes on the way down. I am assuming you will agree, Joel, that the beautiful body of a beautiful woman is the center and symbol of all human value in the universe.

On the way up I kissed, licked, sucked, bit her bland expanses, the calves, the shins, the thighs in front and behind, the apple cheeks down and around, the belly, the back, the brow, for, as I am sure you will agree, the beautiful body of a beautiful woman is the origin and paradigm of all visual and tactile beauty. I moved down again, lingering at the creases and crevices, especially at the salt licks under her breasts until I arrived at the Source, where I lingered longer. From some change in viscosity or temperature or perfume, I could tell that Julie was getting there. "Holy Sebastian, Cuz," she said, "will you stop beating around the bush?"

She grabbed me by my new curls as Perseus grabbed Medusa, and pulled me up, my belly sliding over hers, for we were both in a righteous sweat. I braced myself on my forearms, as a sex manual I read at age fifteen said a considerate man does, still wearing the sleeves of my shirt, but you would need longer arms than mine to prevent a stomach like mine from squashing the woman. She reached down and positioned me in the doorway to her inner sanctum. When I didn't move, she said, "Groove, dig, bop!" so I thrust home:

and went limp entirely, the moment my head poked in beyond the doorway. You understand, Joel, we are not talking here of a gradual softening, as of a balloon with a pinhole, but of an instant collapse, as with a wind sock suddenly becalmed.

It took Julie a couple of seconds to realize that nothing was happening. Then her eyes opened wide and her face took on a kind of startle-scared look. She quickly rolled me off her, onto my back, and stroked my corpus spongiosum, from scrotum to urethral meatus, to be scientific, once, twice, thrice, which did the trick, for so far as getting it up is concerned, I am prodigal. She straddled me, her seat off the saddle, like a horsewoman about to post, and reached down a hand to position me in the gateway to her hortus conclusus. Then she descended and I ascended, like a horsewoman and her trusty steed:

whereupon I crumpled, at the precise moment that my snake's head butt into the garden.

Julie dismounted, bent over, and gave me long, light licks along my stalk from root to bud, once twice, thrice, four times, which did the trick, for when it comes to standing ready, I am a minuteman. She put her mouth gently, delicately, over my spout, as over a floating soap bubble she did not want to break, upon which I collapsed utterly, as when a woman holding up her stocking by the toe, suddenly lets it drop to the floor. "I get it," Julie said.

Julie, as before, brought the dead back to life, took a firm grip on my balls, for it is time I eschewed euphemism, fell back, pulled me on top of her, so that I was astraddle her sternum, placed my prick between her tits, which she pushed together with her hands, from either side, a bratwurst in a bun. As soon as her flesh, like a gracious host, received mine, the boorish guest shrank back, withdrew, like the head of a turtle.

Julie threw her arms out to the sides, for as Dylan Thomas said, the bed is a cross place, smiled grimly, pushed me off her, onto my back, rolled on top of me, kissed the corners of my mouth lightly, ran her tongue between my lips, from side to side, featherly, kissed my neck, ticklingly, reached down to see whether my homunculus was erectus, which it was, prodigiously, gripped it as though to jerk me off, and thus put to my little man his quietus, precipitously. She slid off me, propped her head on her left hand, her left elbow on the bed. "How long has this been going on?" she said.

"Nine years," I said.

"I know how you feel," she said. "I had to wait until I was nine years old myself, before I first got laid."

"Are you making fun of me?" I said.

"Lighten up, Cuz," she said. "It's not as though you were missing out on anything important." She put her right hand on my stomach.

"Can you do yourself?" she said.

"Well, yes. . . ." I said.

"Go ahead," she said, "while I take you round the world. It will feel just as good."

"It's too humiliating," I said. "But let me bring you off," stirring, getting in position to go down on her, "that much I can do."

"Not now," she said, pushing me back on my back.

"Don't you like to come?" I said.

"Course I do," she said. "It makes you feel all relaxed and cozy."

I rolled over onto my stomach. She climbed aboard, stretched out her body over mine, rested her head on my shoulder, slid her arms under my chest.

"Is that why your wife left you?" she said, "because she couldn't handle your problem?"

"We left each other," I said, "because I couldn't handle my problem and because she couldn't handle the way I couldn't handle it."

"Well, did you, you know . . . experiment?" she said.

"We tried between her thighs, under her armpits, behind a bent knee—" I said.

"That's not very imaginative," she said. "Poor Cuz."

"Poor Belinda," I said.

"Maybe it's connected to why you're sort of, well you know . . . *thoughtful,*" she said. "Did you ever think of that?"

"No subject wants to become its own object," I said.

"Why didn't you ever, like, go to a therapist?" she said.

"I did," I said. "I went to a shrink, very highly recommended. He kept asking vot I feldt about *him.*" I have to tell you, Joel, that to have a well-built woman bouncing on your back in a giggle is by no means the worst feeling in the world, even if the giggle is at your own expense.

"I guess I've finally got what I always wanted," she said, giving me a squeeze.

"What's that?" I said. "I'm all ears."

"What every woman secretly wants," she said.

"Half of humanity is waiting impatiently for your answer," I said.

"An impotent boyfriend," she said.

P.S. I took a break a couple of hours back, to get myself something to eat, but the cupboard was bare, of anything worth eating that is, not even a can of Spam. How long is this that it's been since I had a meal. Three days? As for yesterday, after presuming so far as to call me her boyfriend, Julie said relax, she would fix chow, and I remembered the bag of groceries standing in the doorway to my study. While she cooked, I dozed, frightful images coursing through my brain. A big fake gorilla, of the kind you see in old horror movies, an earnest look on its face, sat on the corner of teacher's desk, facing the students. From the corners of the classroom, men materialized. They were dressed like gangsters in the comic books of my childhood, their suits and fedoras impossible shades of green, purple, blue. They pounced on the gorilla, bit out chunks of its flesh. The gorilla did not resist, an appeasement smile on its face. "Soup's on," Julie shouted down the hall.

I put on jeans and tee shirt unsteadily, walked down the hall woozily, my ears clogged, my head turgid with blood, so it felt, my eyes dimmed. The food was artistically arranged: cutlets of grilled soybean, I suppose it was, in a circle around a mound of stir-fried vegetables striped with red peppers, deep-fried zucchini in a circle on a platter around a mound of rice stippled with scallions, the whole smelling of garlic, which ordinarily I like, if it's on a big venison roast, say, glistening with bacon fat. "Looks good," I said.

She heaped my plate as high as I would have heaped it myself, and she put on her plate as much as you could stick in your eye without blinking, to quote Ma.

"Don't you like it?" she said. "It's low-cal, no saturated fat, no salt."

"It's delicious," I said.

"Then why aren't you eating?" she said.

"I don't feel right," I said.

She looked me over. "Yes," she said. "I never thought I'd actually see someone who was green around the gills."

"I never get sick," I said.

"Eat the rice," she said. "It will settle your stomach."

"I'll try one of these," I said, lighting up.

"You know, Cuz, maybe I shouldn't say this," she said, "but smoking is for losers."

"It's my one refusal to comply," I said.

"There's your problem right there," she said. "You're always holding back, how you feel. You never express your feelings, so your body does it for you."

"Bailey's balls," I said (quoting Pa), "not you too. Next thing you'll be asking vot I feldt about *you*."

"What just now happened . . . or didn't happen," she said, "it's had to upset you, but you didn't let on. Now your stomach is upset."

"What didn't happen just now . . . ," I said. "Another refusal to comply, maybe." But with what?

"Well, how do you?" she said. "Feel about me, I mean. I want to know."

"All kinds of ways," I said.

"Good ways?" she said.

"Don't make me fall in love with you," I said, "for your sake."

"You shouldn't be afraid of your own feelings," she said, and her tone was just a mite complacent. "You'll see: I'm going to fix you up."

I stood up suddenly ("Oh-oh," she said) and ran to the bathroom, because I felt as though I was going to be sick, which I was, in a paltry kind of way, my stomach being empty. Then I lay down, as I lay down a little while ago, after finding that the cupboard was bare, as I was still lying down when Julie burst in, back from the beach, salty, sandy, and sunburnt.

"Look what I've got," she said, and she pulled a book out of a shopping bag: *Human Sexual Inadequacy.* Inadequate? Yes, I guess I was, am. Then she pulled out *Disorders of Sexual Desire.* Disordered? Sure, why not? And she pulled out the last of the library books: *The New Sex Therapy.* Does "new" modify "sex" or "therapy," I wonder. And then she pulled out a couple of spanking new books from the bookstore: *Heterosexuality,* which set her back twenty-seven fifty (plus tax), and my favorite, for in sexual matters I prefer pictures to words (after the real thing), *The Illustrated Manual of Sex Therapy* (second edition, at twenty-two ninety-five plus tax). "You're really in for it now, Cuz," she said. "These books tell you exactly what we gotta do."

As I write this, Julie is out in the kitchen, eating cold grilled soy cutlets, or whatever they are, and cold rice (I told her I had already eaten), the sex books piled beside her plate, as one by one she skimmed through their introductions.

I am weary, but not tired, which is what happens if you do nothing but write all day long. I am going to sit back, close my eyes and listen to some sounds until Julie is ready for bed. John Milton and in this one respect his disciple William Yeats both say that when angels make love, we are not talking about a few delicious sensations here and there, but of an incandescence of their whole bodies entirely. Is there anything to that?

8

Dear Joel,

I got up with Julie (for a change) feeling cool and clear and mean, ready to see things as they are, not as I want or fear them to be, assuming that's possible, and sat down with her for breakfast. But I did not eat any of her cereal. What is this that it's called? Mucilage, I believe.

"I'm going to register for French," she said.

"Good," I said.

"Don't be grumpy," she said. "Do you want me to fix you some eggs?"

"We don't have any," I said.

"Toast?" she said.

"We're out of bread," I said.

"Can I borrow a copy of *The Odyssey*?" she said. "That's what we're doing in Humanities this week. You have six or seven of them."

"Use the Lattimore translation," I said. "It gives you a feel for the Greek original, I'm told."

"Don't you read Greek?" she said.

"I don't read Linear B either," I said.

What she did then, Joel, was get up from her chair, walk over to my end of the table, bend from the waist, like a dancer, put her cheek against mine, wrap her arms around me, pat me on the back. I could see right then that she was going to be tough to get the better of. But maybe it was time for me to get rid of this adversarial notion of the relations between the sexes.

Irene Howland, looking mournful, was waiting for me when I got to my office. She placed some papers on my desk. It had been a hassle, she said—some of the other departments kept lousy records—but she had put together lists of all the out-of-department orals boards and dissertation committees Terry Jones had served on during the last ten years. Lieutenant Suarez had already picked up his copies Friday afternoon. He kept asking the staff all these questions about students that might have a grudge against Terry. Monika was on her high horse and wouldn't tell him anything. Suarez also questioned everybody about some black kid who goes around slapping women on the behind. Trudy Stone complained to campus security, who are working with Suarez, after her companion was slapped on her recently installed hipbone. The whole time Suarez was there Jug Nakatani was doing tricks with this big handkerchief.

"Terry earned her keep," I said, scanning the lists, which were long.

"I can understand why some women turn to other women for comfort and support," she said. "Do you think Monika is a warmer person when she's away from the office?"

"You've got to toughen up," I said. "Take pride in being self-sufficient and alone. Amid a place of stone, be secret and exult, because of all things known, that is most difficult, said W. B. Yeats."

"I don't know how you do it," she said.

"I beg your pardon," I said.

"Jug has been sweet," she said. "He could see I was desperate. I get the impression he knows what it feels like. He asked me out, to that performance, piano duets—you must have heard about it—this coming weekend."

"I've heard," I said. "Sit down a minute."

"He knows one of the performers, Medori Tashiro," she said, sitting.

"She has an international reputation," I said, "but not for her piano playing."

"This past weekend was horrible," she said. "I did something stupid."

"What's that?" I said.

"I don't think I should tell you," she said, "but at the end of it, last night, before I knew what I was doing, I sat down and wrote Murray a long letter."

"What was his response?" I said.

"He hasn't read it yet," she said. "It's on his desk."

There was a knock on the door, which, before I could say Come in, opened: and there was Monika, looking wrathful. "What are you two up to?" she said.

"These lists . . . ," said Irene.

"The vice-chair is in conference with his secretary," I said.

Irene got up from under Monika's stare and walked out, her head down and forward, her shoulders up.

"You're looking for trouble there," said Monika, jerking her head toward the door through which Irene had made her exit.

"What's on your mind?" I said.

"You don't want to know," she said. "I had a bitch of a weekend. Terry and I . . . Here's some lists you're going to need." She sat down, helped herself to a cigarette. The first list was of the faculty's standing committees, their composition, how many tenured faculty, how many untenured, if any, how many students, if any, graduate or undergraduate, how many slots to be filled, if any, and of which rank. The second list was of the committees I would have to form this semester and their composition. The third list was of all the teaching staff, next to their names the committees they had served on during the last five years, if any, the idea being to spread the work around evenly. Fat chance: asking some of my colleagues to do committee work was like asking the coloratura to move the piano.

"The first priority is the Curriculum Committee," she said, "then there's the tenure-review committee for Mal Tetrault," which committee, Joel, I am tempted to stack against that meeching malcompoop, for power corrupts.

"You have some recommendations, have you?" I said, and so we moved the pieces around, undoing and redoing the work Murray and I had already done, back there during the Pleistocene, when I last had enough food to pack in a thimble, as Ma used to say.

"Suarez was here last Friday," she said, "sticking his garbanzo into everything."

"You want him to find Terry's killer, don't you?" I said.

"We could do it ourselves, you and me," she said. "Between us we know all the players. I spent the whole weekend racking my brains."

"I'm no good at nosing out other people's sins," I said. Zeno, quoting Yeats back at me, once said that I lacked the imagination of evil. Oh, yeah?

"Did you speak to Suarez about Angel Terrasco?" Monika said.

"He would only think I was trying to divert suspicion from someone else," I said, "like me, like you."

"You may not realize it," she said, "but you're the one person who can clinch Murray's re-election." She reached for another cigarette. I lit her up.

"Well, if I do a good job," I said, "with your help, of course—"

"That's not what I'm talking about," she said. "Those buddies of yours in the Smoker's Club, they listen to what you say, right?"

"In one ear and out the other," I said.

"Tell them this," she said: "there's Lois Barker and Freddy Macready: they're black. Ziggy Sensum is openly gay, unlike some other sneaks around here I could mention. They'll listen to Leonard Sistrunk."

"Possibly," I said.

"The younger feminists, they'll listen to Kay Pesky," she said.

"Probably," I said.

"All those people in Shakespeare and the Renaissance, you could get Zeno Confalone to browbeat the young ones and sweet-talk the seniors," she said.

"Or the reverse," I said.

"Yeah, and you can get Lizbeth Arno and Marshall Grice to go after the old boys," she said. Monila's lips are very attractive when she relaxes them at the corners so that they curve up rather than down. "Remind them Angel recruit these feminists been whupping they ass these last ten years and some."

"Professor Derwood Bobbie, I understand, has come to cherish that warm feeling in his southern zone," I said.

"And you," she said, "you can rope in the creative writing staff, get them to a meeting for once, get them to vote, vote the right way. If they'll listen to anybody, they'll listen to you. Terry used to say you were the last professor of English who thought writers are more important than critics."

"It won't work," I said. "Squeeze professors forward and they squirt sideways. They're 'contrary,' what my father used to call me."

"A herd of sheep is what they are," said Monika.

"Penned-up strays, more like," I said.

"You can't just sit back and let things take their course," she said. "It's irresponsible."

"There are times when to do any one thing is to do the wrong thing," I said.

"You speak to your pals, hear," she said.

"I've already got messages for them from Angel Terrasco," I said.

"I miss Terry so bad," she said, "I don't know what to do with myself. Deep down I don't give a fuck who's chair."

"Yes you do," I said.

"Peekaboo, I see you," said a voice. I looked up, over Monika's shoulder, and there was Murray's head, hanging sideways in the doorway, his body hidden by the frame. You don't often see Murray clowning around, allowing other people to laugh at him. He's no good at it anyway, lacks the touch. Somewhere along the way Murray must have decided to back out of any game he couldn't win. My guess is that he went for the chair, for administrative work, when it dawned on him he would never be a popular teacher, or an important critic, for that matter.

As for Murray's criticism, he began as an expert in the history of the novel: he then became, in the following sequence, a narratologist, a phenomenologist, a neo-Freudian, a structuralist, a post-structuralist, a neo-Marxist, and a new historicist. His last collection of essays applied feminist theory to the same half-dozen novels he always writes about. It was mauled by feminist critics for encroaching on their turf, for in academe, as in the Serengeti, territoriality is the instinct that orchestrates the others. One of those feminists was Angel Terrasco, who had already written an article complaining that male critics ignored feminist scholarship. "May I come in?" he said.

"Stand and deliver," I said.

"The password is 'emphysema,'" he said, straightening up, walking in, looking at Monika: "Don't tell me you're smoking again."

"Only in here," she said. "Where was it, this place Terry told me about, there's a sign over the entrance says 'Do what thou wilt'?"

"Yes," he said. "Rabelais' Abbey of Theleme. It's what we all do anyhow."

"Only," I said, "if you postulate an unconscious that wills us to do what we otherwise don't want—" I said.

"Wynn," he said, "has anyone ever told you that sometimes you're a pain in—"

Monika abruptly stood up, ground her cigarette in the ashtray, said to Murray, "You've got a meeting at eleven," said to me, "Remember what I told you," and walked out.

"What have you two been cooking up?" he said, sitting down, smashing out Monika's cigarette, which was still smoldering, and crossing one skinny ankle over a knife-edged knee.

"Your goose," I said. "Aside from that, the vice-chair was in conference with his administrator."

"I happen to know that Monika is a loyalist," he said. "What about you?"

"Kay has been advising me not to compromise my beautiful neutrality," I said.

"To do nothing is to do something," he said. "If you're not part of the solution, you're part of the problem." Remember that slogan, Joel? Murray was a student radical during the sixties, occupied a building at Princeton, but came out voluntarily when his cadre of three deserted.

"What is it you want me to do?" I said, lighting up another.

"For one thing you could help me with Irene," he said, looking rueful.

"Oh, what's the problem?" I said.

"She's all alone, having a bad time," he said.

"Like yesterday," I said, "like last year, like five years ago."

"There's a new . . . ," he said. "She wrote me a letter . . . of course I can't repeat. . . . Well, she's in a state."

"Yes," I said.

"You're the only straight male in the department who's not married or living with someone," he said.

"Actually—" I said.

"You are straight, aren't you?" he said.

"I never speak of my love life, or the absence thereof, except to a person I'm having it with," I said.

"You could talk to her—" he said.

"I have been," I said.

"—make her feel wanted," he said. "Take her to lunch. There's a piano recital—"

"She's already going with Teddy Nakatani," I said.

"Another loony," he said. "The office is full of them, something in the air."

"Put a sign up over the entrance," I said. "Abandon all hope, ye—"

"This not a laughing matter," he said.

"I'll introduce her to my cousin, who's staying with me for a bit," I said. "She's about Irene's age, an expert in affairs of the heart."

"What makes you think it's an affair of the heart that's Irene's problem?" he said.

I have to admit, Joel, that I was half enjoying this. I took a drag on my cigarette worthy of Angel Terrasco, let the smoke seep out of my nose, then blew out the last of it toward the ceiling. "Isn't it always?" I said.

"You're going to kill yourself with those things," he said, fanning smoke away from his face, although there wasn't any near it, "and everyone around you." Then he gave me the kind of look you call penetrating, although I'm pretty sure my own look was what you might call impenetrable. "I know I can count on your discretion," he said.

"There's something you can do for me," I said.

"Surely I don't figure in your affairs of the heart," he said, sitting back, "assuming you have any."

"I want you to write a letter," I said. "I want you to write a letter to the Administration. I want you to tell them that if they don't renew Lizzie's contract the Department will take to the bullhorns."

"You listen to me, Wynn," he said, leaning forward, gripping his ankle as though to row, row, row himself. "I like Lizzie, too. But as chairman my first responsibility is to an institution, the Department, not an individual."

"E. M. Forster once wrote," I said, "that if he had to choose between betraying his friend and betraying his country, he hoped he would have the guts to betray his country. Substitute the word 'department' for 'country' and the principle still applies."

"E. M. Forster was a sentimentalist," he said, "like all fags. My idea is to pry a line for a senior feminist out of the Administration in exchange for Lizzie's line. That ought to appease Angel."

"Angel is unappeasable," I said.

"What did I ever do to her?" he said, sitting back.

"Her resentment antedates any offense against her," I said. "It's primal."

"One more loony," he said. "Going after a senior feminist is still the right thing. Kay's swamped."

"Kay will always be swamped," I said, "because between Kay and her students, it's an affair of the heart. She will not thank you for dumping Lizzie."

"I suppose not," he said. "There was a time when we all thought you and Kay—"

"In fact I can see her talking to the younger feminists," I said. "They'll listen to her."

"I suppose," he said. "Are you taking her to the recital?"

"And I can see Leonard talking to Lois Barker and Freddy Macready and Ziggy Sensum," I said. "They'll damn well listen."

"It's possible," he said. "I've been so busy I forgot to have Irene pick me up tickets."

"And it's not hard to imagine Zeno browbeating all those juniors in the Renaissance and sweet-talking the seniors," I said.

"Or the other way around," Murray said. "I see where you're going."

"Dump Lizzie, and you'll have Marshall Grice buttonholing the old boys," I said.

"It's Derwood Bobbie I should dump," he said.

"The creative writers will listen to me, if they'll listen to anyone," I said.

"In one ear and out the other," he said.

"There's a lot of votes there," I said.

"This is not like you," he said. "I didn't know you could think this way. I always took you for the original apolitical man."

"Politics is an epiphenomenon," I said. "I act on what's behind it."

"What's that?" he said.

"Impulse," I said.

"There's something inhuman about you, Wynn," he said. "you sit there in your massive repose, moving only so much as to light a cigarette," which is what I then did, "and you talk to me about *impulse.*" He pulled himself forward by his ankle until his head was hanging over the desk. "You can't fool me. Behind your . . . imperturbability you care about the Department. You can't just sit back and let Angel usurp the chair. It's irresponsible. You know damn well Angel would be a disaster."

"This country survived Nixon and Reagan," I said. "The Department will survive Angel."

He released his ankle, stood up, walked to the door, closed it, walked to the chair, sat, jerked the chair closer to the desk, picked up my letter opener, a very pretty little knife I had made myself from a strip of circular saw blade, lifted my cigarette out of the ashtray, and sliced off the burning end. "I can tell you that the Weinrein Comprehensive Benefits Coordination, the WCBC as it's come to be called, is winning praise where it counts," he said—"the Ad-Hoc Committee, the Council of Chairs, most deans, the vice presidents, the president, the trustees. Harvard and Yale are studying it toward their own reorganization."

"You don't have to tell me that you are good at what you do," I said.

"I should add that much of what's best in it would not be there without Irene's input."

"Irene's a jewel," I said.

He felt the edge of my letter opener, tested it further by shaving a few hairs off his wrist, then dropped the tip on Teddy Nakatani's so-called dissertation proposal, *Bums and Boobs.* "Sharp," he said. "I am going to put a further strain on your celebrated discretion: by the end of the next year we will have, for the first time, a Vice President for Arts and Sciences."

"Long overdue," I said.

"I have been led to believe, by hints, winks, significant looks, pregnant silences, that I am the man for the job," he said. "And I am."

"I'll wink it from the rooftops," I said.

"How would it look if my own department voted me out of office?" he said, and he slit the air in front of his throat across with my knife. "I would automatically lose the clout that comes with being chair of the university's largest department," and he jabbed the knife at me, "lose my position on a dozen crucial committees" (another jab), "lose the chairmanship of the Council of Chairs, which I have laboriously shaped into an extension of my will." He picked up the top page of Teddy's proposal and ran it through. "What the fuck is this?" he said, reading the title.

"You could do the statesmanlike thing," I said, "step down voluntarily this spring. Monika, Irene, and I would organize a party in your honor. You could tell us who the people are that count, so we could invite them. I'll make a speech in extravagant praise of your accomplishments as an administrator, with references to Cincinnatus."

He replaced the top sheet of Teddy's proposal and tapped the tip of the knife on it, as one by one he checked off his points. "I need this year and the next to maneuver my plan through," he said; "otherwise a pack of deanlings will gut it, till it's no longer the Weinrein Comprehensive, etcetera. After that, when I move up, you will be in line for the chair. Angel will not challenge you if you promise her the vice-chair. Your one problem will be to replace Irene, because I mean to take her with me, if we can keep her from sliding into an abyss of self pity. That's why it's so important that you—"

"I don't want the chair," I said.

Very deliberately, Murray picked up the top sheet of Teddy's proposal, sliced it down the middle from top to bottom, placed the halves next to each other, where the whole sheet had been, and lay the knife on top of them. He sat back and smiled broadly, stretching his mustache. "A person who wants nothing, if you can imagine the existence of such a monster, would be tough to handle," he said. "There's no way of getting a grip on him—unless he also fears something. What do you want? What do you fear?"

"I want Lizzie's contract renewed and I fear it won't happen," I said.

"There's my grip," he said, standing up. "I have a meeting to go to, for a change," and he walked to the door, turned my way. "For the time being, at least, I will put off bartering Lizzie for a senior feminist," and he opened the door, strolled out.

Don't be too hard on Murray, Joel. He's a shark out of water. If he'd gone into business, he'd be a CEO somewhere. People with voracious ambitions may gobble us up, but they may also spew out something of value in their wakes, a St. Mark's or Declaration of Independence or diagram of the double helix. Think of your own ambition. I call you up before me, your black shirt buttoned up to the neck, your leather vest and leopard skin beret, your *chulo*, tall and skinny, a long drink of water as Ma used to say, rocking your head just perceptibly to the beat as a sideman takes a chorus, then stepping into your horn, sliding one foot forward, like Diz, as you find your groove, trying to make it in the black world of bop, already extinct. I remember your scorn for the West Coast white boys, for Chet Baker, "that wispy, wishy-washy, whispering swish." Without your self-consuming ambition, we would have no "Llareggub," no "Skeltonics," with those eerie augmented chords, nor your solo on "Yesterday," those Picardee thirds that fill up my chest with some nameless emotion, which comes over me now. Oh yes, and at the back of your brain, where you burst all those blood vessels blasting F-sharp over high C, you thought that turning yourself into a motherfucking junkie would make you a soul brother. Did Diz ever try to turn himself into a honkie, you dumb fuck?

Calm down now. Take it easy: some day I'll give myself a heart attack, like any other fatso. I stepped out of my office, on my way to fetch Teddy Nakatani, prod him toward his dissertation, but there was Felicia Zhang, sitting in one of the chairs against the hall wall, from where, once each semester, the fire marshall makes us move them. She was dressed in shorts and a tank top, although the day was cooling, for Felicia's is a soul of summer.

"Hi," she said, with a smile, and the psychobiological equivalent of sunshine rinsed out my chest.

"If I had known you were waiting . . . ," I said. "Come on in."

"No problem," she said. "I've been doing my homework," and she held up a copy of Pater's *The Renaissance.*

"How'd the Conclusion grab you?" I said, sitting down, lighting up.

"It's sort of wistful," she said, crossing a leg, plumping out an already plump calf, a sandal dangling off her heel. "Am I right that Pater wasn't getting any? I mean to resort to art so as to burn with a hard gem-like flame—was he afraid of women?"

"It was the era of limp dicks," I said. Don't worry, Joel, Felicia is not the sort of woman to report a professor for making an off-color pleasantry.

"Without your lecture it would never have occurred to me that Pater's aestheticism comes out of a crisis-cult mentality," she said.

"You don't buy it?" I said.

"Oh, I do," she said. "Where you lead, I follow. Wait, I even composed a sentence in your style. Wait," and she pulled a sheaf of papers from between the pages of *The Renaissance,* looked through them, read: "What is Pater's Mona Lisa but a woman ripped from life and imprisoned in a mirror?"

"A cracked looking glass," I said, "except Pater's Mona Lisa was ripped from a painting, not life. There are no women in life like Pater's Mona Lisa, alas."

"Yes," she said. "We all forgive you for being an unreconstructed chauvinist, cause you try to suppress it. But your assignment was not an easy one for us gals."

"It wasn't meant to be easy," I said.

"You didn't give us enough about the women of the Kilikang to work with," she said. "We were supposed to imagine ourselves—"

"I gave you more than my source gave me," I said.

"No problem," she said. "I had family history to fall back on.

Here, this is for you," and she handed me the sheaf of papers. "I wrote out your assignment instead of preparing it orally."

"Your family made Kilikangs?" I said.

"My grandfather had the smokehouse in a small fishing village," she said. "When Japanese soldiers arrived it was like when missionaries came to the people of the Kilikang."

"I should have said that my little parable was an old story endlessly renewed," I said.

"A Japanese soldier pinched my grandmother's nipples," she said, "but his officer had him taken away to be punished. How, I don't know. My grandfather's theory is that this officer felt it was dishonorable to abuse inferior beings. After the surrender, the officer committed suicide. I heard that story a hundred times."

"Love and war," I said.

"Sex and violence," she said.

"That reminds me," I said, "I met with your emissary."

"Jug told me," she said; "I knew he would win you over."

"He's hincty about your organization," I said. "He thinks you all dislike him because he's Japanese."

"That's just Jug's paranoia," she said. "We all love Jug. He's amazing: the other day he was telling me the right way to make pressed duck."

"I'm trying to press a dissertation out of him," I said.

"It will be brilliant," she said. "He helped me with this draft of the letter you wanted," and she pulled out a sheet of paper from between the pages of *The Renaissance.*

"We thought you could point it up any way you want, then give it back, and we'll retype it and then sign it," she said. "And here's a list of people in the area who can give a course in Asian-American literature."

"Where you lead, I follow," I said.

"Professor O'Leary," she said, "are you an aesthete? I hope you don't mind me asking."

"About aesthetical matters, I am," I said.

"How about ethical matters?" she said.

"I always think of ethics as a branch of morbid psychology," I said.

"We love it when you say things like that," she said, getting up. "See you tomorrow," and she walked out, throwing a smile over her shoulder, so that its afterglow lingered. Murray asked me what I wanted. I want a woman like Felicia Zhang, maybe five or ten years older, to light up my life.

I went out the door again, again to fetch Teddy, Tetsuo, Jug Nakatani, but I was intercepted at the doorway to the main office by Irene Howland.

"He read the letter," she said in a whisper.

"Was his response satisfactory?" I said.

"He said I was too young to be acting menopausal," she said. "He said I should take the initiative and ask you to go with me to that piano recital." She paused, looked at me with her head tilted to the side: "Would you have gone?"

"If you don't mind my wearing earplugs," I said.

"I've got to do something," she said.

Teddy was standing next to his desk, explaining to a pregnant GAS student, in obstetric and hair-raising detail, what she should do if the water breaks and she can't get to a doctor.

"Come with me," I said, before the student fainted.

We faced each other across my desk.

"May I have a cigarette?" he said. "I left mine on my desk."

We lit up. "Do you have something for me?" I said.

"My undying admiration, of course," he said, holding his cigarette the way you hold a dart.

"Where is your dissertation proposal?" I said.

He looked around the room, stood up, walked over to the right-hand bookcase, and pulled out a copy of my first book, *Yeats and the Seven Sons, or, Poetic Minority in the Age of Paleo-Modernism.* (The seven sons are John Davidson, Austin Dobson, Ernest Dowson, Ralph Hodgson, Ralph Thompson, and William Watson.) He opened the book, pulled out a neatly folded sheet of paper, unfolded the paper, sat, read out these winged words:

> Bumbumery negates all causes by turning its back on them. It presents itself in a relation of subversion to all politics and moralities just because it refuses any relations with them whatsoever. Because it serves none it subverts them all. Because its only cause is itself, it eludes cooption. No policy of liberalization by the prominent powers can strip bumamoria of its offensiveness to the oppressing decencies, precisely because the amorist of bums has not assumed a posture of offense to begin with. Only he is a privateer when Big Brother puts up a blockade around eros.

"This is just more of what I told you will not do," I said. "What happened to Yeats and things Japanese, Sato's sword, love and war, and all that?"

A spasm of bewilderment ran across his face. He scratched his armpit with the sudden mechanical motion of a lizard flicking out its tongue. "I had a harrowing weekend," he said. "I need someone to talk to."

"Irene is a good listener," I said.

"I have the greatest affection for Irene," he said, "but it is with you I need to talk."

"So talk," I said.

"This is not the occasion," he said. "May I visit you at home?"

"Knock out an outline," I said. "I don't care how sketchy. Then we'll see."

"I shall not let you down," he said. He started to rise, then spotted the first page of *Bums and Boobs,* which as you will remember, Murray had poked holes in and cut down the middle. Teddy held up the two halves. "Words failed you?"

"That's the work of another critic," I said.

"My observations were for your eyes only," he said.

"In the usual way, the critic did not read your observations before cutting them to pieces," I said.

"It's very strange," he said. "You will remember what happened when Dorian Gray slashed the picture of Dorian Gray across."

I think it is safe to say that my neck swelled and the veins on my forehead showed themselves.

"I don't want to overwel my staycome," he said, and took off.

I need your advice, Joel, for if these loonies around me need someone to talk to, so it appears does the loony they are around. That must be why I'm writing these letters. Well, well, look who's pretending to know his own motives. I want you to tell me this, brother mine, whether I am getting the job done, getting it done right, so far as Teddy Nakatani is concerned. There is a danger that I might lose my grip, Murray's word, my hold on him, by coming on so strong, Terry's mistake. Maybe I should stroke him, radiate some pedagogic eros, play on what he thinks is an admiration for me, his seeing in me something he sees in himself but that is neither here nor there, a cracked looking glass looking for its reflection. Yes, I know, we are alike in that neither of us can get down to writing criticism, but the crucial difference is this: I have already made my bones. Of the two kinds of professors, those who get turned on by students who come on as disciples and those who get turned off, I belong to the second, unlike Diz, who had an amused tolerance for his ephebes, including you. Discipledom always seems to me like a species of parody.

No, I don't think so, not a chance, just like you to come up with that one, of course Teddy's not queer for me, where did you get that idea? I surmise he's just another celibate, like James Duffy in *Dubliners,* or John Marcher, a postmodernist limp dick. So am I, you say? Damn you, Joel, of the two kinds of male celibates, those who don't do what they want to do because they can't and those who don't do what they want to do because it horrifies them, inactive pedophiles say, or abstaining necrophiles, I belong to the first. And Teddy? Who knows? Who cares?

Felicia Zhang, by the way, is not a disciple. Felicia is not a mirror, but a lamp.

It was too late for lunch with the Smokers' Club at Whipple Hall, so I stuffed the lists into my elegant leather famous-designer attaché case, five bucks from my favorite street cadger, who said to me, "I'm a bum, like my father before me, like his father before him, probably all the way back to Abraham, who was black, did you know that?" for I mean to study those lists, see who was on the Policy Committee, what slots were open, then stack it, make it an instrument of my will, and followed my stomach to the Academy Market, where I found myself behind Kay Pesky on the checkout line.

While we talked, the woman before Kay on line watched with empty eyes while the checkout clerk rang up her goods, packed them, said "$22.78." The woman came to herself, spread open her carpetbag, pulled out her purse, snapped it open, pulled out her wallet, zipped it open, pulled out a twenty and a single from the fold, squeezed open the change purse, slid out the coins, said "shit," slid back the coins, pushed the bills back into the fold, zipped up the wallet, dropped it into her purse, snapped together her purse, dropped it into her carpetbag, rummaged around, pulled out a checkbook, opened it, came to herself, rummaged around, pulled out a fountain pen, removed the cap, filled out a check, filled out the stub, ripped out the check, passed it to the clerk, who said "ID?"

The woman spread open her carpetbag, pulled out her purse, snapped it open, pulled out her wallet, zipped it open, flipped through the plastic windows, held her driver's license up to the clerk, who squint-eyed it, said "Expired." The woman flipped through the plastic windows, found her university ID, held it up to the clerk, who must have been satisfied, or did not much care whether the check would bounce, for it was unlikely that Academy Market gave her a piece of the action, or who in wondering dreamily whether to let this woman pass or empty the carpetbag over her head, decided on the former, as more economical of her energy.

"You've been avoiding me," Kay said, but with a smile.

"The vice-chair has been in conference with his staff," I said.

"You've got to get out of that as soon as you can," she said, "for your own sake."

For my sake, Joel. Leave it to Kay. I put my arm around her shoulder and pecked her on the forehead, right there in the Academy Market, though no one was looking. And suddenly I felt abashed. It's been arrant pip-squeakery for me to resent Kay for not inviting me up to her apartment after our dates. She deserves better, and I like to think that resentment, the most abysmal of emotions, is not my métier. And when you stop to think, what (or who) could come of it, given my little problem . . . and I was shook to smithereens (only morally speaking of course, for my façade is quake-proof) by a thought that roared through me like a twister: Kay had somehow heard of my little problem or guessed it: her refusals were for my sake. Her idea was to let me save face, enable me to go on facing her with the face I needed, preserve my façade, preserve, if I am not once again kidding myself, our relationship. Kay did not want me to resent her as the occasion and reminder of a limp dick. And there I was, resenting her anyhow. I felt my face redden, a very different sensation from feeling your neck swell.

"Come up to the country with me," I said, and praise the Lord for my professorial absentmindedness, or I would have already asked Julie. "Murray's looking for tickets to the recital; you can sell him yours." And Julie could ask one of her new friends to sleep over, study together, make popcorn, for I am not my cousin's keeper.

"I already gave mine to Zeno," she said. "No, I think Serena and I will take in a movie. She's lots of fun, you know." On the other hand, it might be that Kay just does not care much for sex, with me or in general. "Come along with us. Come on, Wynn. In your honor we'll eat at Dallas Barbecue instead of the new Thai place."

Without thinking, without asking myself why, I said, "I can't."

Behind Kay, the woman spread open her carpetbag, dropped in her checkbook, said to the checkout girl, "I want this delivered." So the checkout girl gave her a label to fill out. The woman spread open her carpetbag, rummaged around in it for a pen, pulled it out, removed the cap, began to write. "How about a cup or a glass right now?" I said.

"I can't," Kay said. The woman slipped her arm through the handles of the carpetbag and trucked on off. Kay moved up. "I'm on my way to a lecture. You know Meg Bachrack? From Duke? Her title is 'Theorizing the Bustle.' She wrote me in advance to say it takes off from my essay on the codpiece. I don't suppose you want to go."

"I can't," I said, in reply to which Kay smiled knowingly. She paid for her cigarettes and Pecan Sandies, then waited while my stuff was rung up, paid for, so we could walk out together.

"How's your cousin?" said Kay.

"Flourishing," I said.

"Is she going to the country with you?" she said.

"I haven't asked her," I said.

"There's something private I want to talk to you about," she said.

"Tomorrow after lunch?" I said.

"We've both got classes," she said.

"So we have," I said.

"When you've got time," she said, put a hand on my shoulder, pulled me down, pecked me on the cheek, walked uptown (the blouse showing beneath the wide-shouldered waist-length corduroy jacket of her skirt suit, which, in my opinion, did an injustice to the flesh it covered) toward the entrance of our sister institution, at which, I presume, Ms. Bachrack was going to theorize the bustle.

Once home I immediately went to the kitchen, put on a smoked pork tenderloin to boil, ripped open the bag containing my lunch, two pastrami sandwiches on rye with mustard and coleslaw, honest New York sandwiches in that the layer of pastrami was thicker than the two pieces of bread surrounding it put together. I hesitated, taking in the aroma, feeling the liquid gather in my mouth, then took a bite, the size, roughly, of a hockey puck. As I chewed, I understood for the first time, some lines by Willie Yeats:

> So great a sweetness flows into the breast
> We must laugh and we must sing,
> We are blest by everything,
> Everything we look upon is blest,

for during those millennia while protohumans were evolving into us we were carnivores, for nothing is so sweet as to satisfy the lusts of and for the flesh. That's right, and I'll remind you that male carnivores only get fat when they're deballed.

I went to my study, and to the sounds of Lee Morgan's "Rumproller" album wrote the beginning of this letter, and I must remember to bring Irene and Julie together, returned to the kitchen, removed the pork tenderloin from the water, poured in two large cans of sauerkraut, a diced green apple, a chopped large onion, too many caraway seeds, returned to the study, wrote some more, to the sounds of Diz and Little Jazz, especially on "I Found a New Baby," and I must remember to study Monika's lists, stack the Policy Committee, make it an instrument of my will, returned to the kitchen, put the sauerkraut into a Dutch oven, put the tenderloin on top of the sauerkraut, put too much Coleman's prepared mustard on top of the tenderloin, put the Dutch oven into the American oven at 325 degrees, returned to my study, wrote some more, to the sounds of Jazz at the Philharmonic, especially Basie and rhythm on "Lady, Be Good," and I must remember to brief the Smokers' Club on my meeting with Angel and Murray, returned to the kitchen, put on thick slabs of rutabaga to parboil, returned to the study, wrote some more, to the sounds of Bird, with outtakes, collected under the title *Now's the Time,* and I must remember to stroke Teddy next time I see him, returned to the kitchen, put the slabs of rutabaga around the pork tenderloin, on top of the sauerkraut, put too much pepper on the rutabaga, returned to the study, wrote some more, to the sounds of Bennie Goodman at Carnegie Hall, especially to "Sing, Sing, Sing," in which swing reaches its climax, just before bop deballed it, and I wonder what Kay wants to talk to me about, and wrote some more, until Julie came home.

People who say that meals should be social occasions are right. Conversation is good for the digestion, not that I said much, for while Julie sampled the sauerkraut and rutabaga and ate postmodernist goo from little plastic containers, she told me about her day, how she loved *The Odyssey,* and could the person who wrote it have been a woman? How I was Odysseus, but was she Nausicaa or Circe? —"Both," I said—pleased and amused in that Julie, unlike professors, read righteously, not scrutinizing the words for evidence of bad faith or trying to subdue them with a theory, but living through them, and while she nibbled and noodled I ate slice after slice of pork tenderloin, thus living through some words by the bard of the land of our father:

> My body of a sudden blazed:
> And twenty minutes more or less
> It seemed so great my happiness,
> That I was blessed and could bless.

Her French teacher was a character, she said, a graduate student who should have been a priest: thin, buttoned up, stern, especially with female students, well, you know, like ascetic. He said her accent was corrupt, but redeemable. In Style and Substance, she said, after Chaucer (and did I believe that *amor vincit omnia?),* they were moving on to Renaissance love lyrics, and was it true that John Donne's poems were randy? For she had never known that highbrow literature was so sexy. And by the way, she said, helping me clean up, put the leftovers away, she had spent lunchtime reading around in the sex books, and it was scary how many things could go wrong, she had no idea, but she couldn't believe that the women who were having all those orgasms were having anything *she* would consider an orgasm, but anyhow she had figured out what was wrong with me. In a day or two she would be ready to begin therapy, fix me up, leave it to her, so I better get plenty of rest, and she squeezed my shoulder.

Julie got to the TV den before I did, so instead of watching Monday Night Football I worked on this letter, the time I'm writing about nearly catching up to the time I'm writing in, but it never will, for never, never will the numerable past catch up to the absolute zero of the present. Julie finished *The Odyssey* with one eye on the fall premiere of a new television series for football widows: each week a heartwarming made-for-TV movie, based on a true story, will show how an ordinary woman grew as a person and married a doctor by turning into an asset what could have been a heartbreaking disability, such as growing a head out of your elbow or an attack of *proctalgia fugax.* The teaser did not say what a true story is, nor, for that matter, what an untrue story would be. Right now, Julie is taking a shower. No, she isn't, for there's the door of the bathroom opening. "Ready, Cuz?" she says, or said, for her words are already in the past. Certainly I'm pajamaed and beshowered and dentificed. Fold your wings, Joel, and rest your head on a cloud, till we meet again.

9

Here's the way you read a poem,

by which I mean any verbal form, any fiction, a tragedy, a farce, a tall tale, the story you told Uncle Alf about the time between sets at a jazz festival, you spritzed Kenny G's horn full of Reddi-wip: you apprehend element A. The mind consciously or subliminally separates from its context a word, a phrase, a sentence, a line, a couplet, a rhyme, an image, a scene, a snatch of conversation, a meaning. That's element A. You apprehend element A in one way rather than in another because of your experience in life, in literature, or because of the situation. You apprehend the opening lines in *Hamlet* in one way if you were ever on watch at Da Nang, say, another way if you never were, one way if you venerate Shakespeare, another if you are a New Historicist, one way if you are at City Center, another if you are in a junior high school auditorium.

Element A propels you on to element B as the dominant seventh chord propels you on to the tonic. You apprehend element B in one way rather than in another not only because of your experience and the situation, but because of how you apprehended element A. Element A, that is, conditions your apprehension of element B, just as element B in retrospect conditions your reapprehension of element

A. After the ghost of Hamlet *pere* appears, we see why Bernardo and Francisco had been so jumpy. I trust I have made myself clear.

If element B is to element A as the tonic is to the dominant fifth, element B is to element C as the dominant fifth is to the tonic. Element B propels you on to element C, which you apprehend in one way rather than in another, not only because of your experience and the situation, but also because of how you apprehended elements A and B. Elements A and B, that is, condition your apprehension of element C, just as in retrospect element C conditions your reapprehension of elements A and B. When Hamlet *fils* appears, you comprehend the watchmen and the ghost of Hamlet *pere* in a new way. And so on until you run out of elements, although if you look hard enough, you will always find new ones or recombine and subdivide the old ones. All that, you will agree, is elementary.

Once you have taken in the last word, the concluding couplet, the punch line, the hero raised on a dais, you can see every element as conditioning, even creating, the others and conditioned by, nay created by, the others. Everything the mind isolates for attention, a character trait, a setting, a stanza form, leads to and follows from everything else, an authorial comment, business with a prop, an off-rhyme, in both directions. Nothing, as you see it, can be dropped out or added, nothing changed or rearranged. The poem, as you see it, is like the society of the People of the Kilikang before the missionaries arrived, as I read them.

That's how you see it. But to see it that way you had to play some tricks on yourself. You had to ignore this and exaggerate that, overlook this and look beyond that, take it that a cigar is just a cigar here but that a stovepipe hat is a symbol there, rearrange widely distributed elements into a mosaic of your own aspect, for no verbal form is a ball bearing; there are always loose ends and parts that do not quite fit. Nevertheless, you apprehend the whole as a whole, even if you apprehend it as a different whole at different times, as your interior condition and external circumstances change, even if you know that different people apprehend it differently, and let's not get into the problem of whether when I apprehend it one way and you apprehend it another we have one IT variously apprehended or two ITs that are indistinguishable from the apprehensions themselves, for that is how the reading mind works, if you are an ordinary reader. Literary critics, of course, are capable of anything. (Of the two categories of critic, those who pull elements apart and those who smush them together, I belong to the second.)

I have run through these banalities for a reason. I want to ask you a question. Is my life a poem, what that asshole Sartre, pilfering from Georg Simmel, calls an adventure? Can you read it? I can't. Is there a whole to apprehend? I need to know, well let's not get hysterical about it, let's say I'd like to know. Reading over these letters to you has revealed my life to me as I have never seen it before. To wit: I am fat. A colleague has been murdered. I listen to bebop. Leonard wears a purple shirt and expensive shoes. My cousin barges in on me. I teach modernism. You are dead. Murray eats cottage cheese. Katriona Campbell bites me. I can no longer write criticism. The murder was committed with a Ka-Bar. I need a haircut. My secretary is on the verge of a breakdown. I have a sexual problem. I write with a mechanical pencil. I get drawn into departmental politics. I buy socks for Julie. What's the opposite of "esemplasy"?

I spent the morning preparing my class on aestheticism and Oscar Wilde, then meandered toward lunch. Coeds were still wearing shorts, although the weather was cooling again, after heating and cooling twice already. The guy in the Norfolk jacket was feeding bread crumbs to bubonic squirrels the color of weathered stone, city dwellers. A long-legged pigeon-toed black kid in a hooded sweatshirt gave me a smile of complicity in some crime I don't remember committing. I nodded to Amabelle Potts, who was standing by the statue of Nathan Hale, leaning on her cane, surveying the scene with baleful disfavor, how she surveys everything. Her cane is stout, as it has to be, to bear her weight, which is not distributed in accordance with any familiar contour of the human body, the dells and swells in her shapeless flowered dress all in the wrong places. The cane is topped with a steel knob, size of a baseball, for crushing the skull of any would-be rapist, so she told me once, as though in warning. She pursed her wrinkled lips into a smile, a smile I believe she thinks sweet, for Amabelle reserves her true smile for the misfortunes of others, especially when she has caused them. I swung into Whipple Hall, past two students sitting on a bench, each with one arm around the other, each in turn licking the other's nose, a form of petting hitherto unknown to me.

Leonard Sistrunk, looking glum, was sitting at his usual place, reading the *Speculator*, his feet, shod in the hide of some reptile or amphibian, on my usual chair. His suit was of a blackish green, his shirt a fudgy brown, his tie a freckled beige. He moved his feet, thighs bulging, and placed the paper on the table.

"It says right here," he said, placing his pointer finger on a column in the *Speculator*, "that the Sixty-Niners have demanded a lounge for their exclusive avail. If the gays have one, they want one. Justice must be served."

"The Sixty-Niners?" I said.

"The title is an expression of their sexual position," he said.

"One good turn deserves another," I said.

"They have sent an open letter to the Ancient Order of Hibernians," he said, "demanding that they be allowed to march in the St. Patrick's Day parade under their own banner."

"They can't all be Irish," I said.

"Irish is as Irish does," he said.

"The Irish orientation, I would say, is toward self-abuse," I said, sitting, sliding the grilled chicken sandwich off my tray, for I promised Julie I would try to get through one whole day without eating fatty meat, the best kind, as everyone agreed until just last week.

"I have with me here, Dan," said Leonard, speaking into an imaginary microphone, "the distinguished vice and ethnoethosexzoologist, Dr. Winsome Leering. Dr. Leering, what is your comment on this extraordinary turn of events?"

"And what about voyeurs, bumamorists, trichomaniacs?" I said, speaking into the imaginary mike. "Is there no one to speak for us? Are we once again to be marginalized, denied our place in the sun?"

Leonard nodded, as though in confirmation. "Over to you, Dan," he said, "and get your filthy paw off Connie's immaculate ass." He crushed the *Speculator* into a ball and placed it on my tray. "I thought that poking fun at queers was no longer permissible," he said.

"They hate us youth," I said, biting into the sandwich, its texture roughly that of the balsa wood out of which you helped me make model airplanes.

"My fiftieth birthday looms like a cloud over Chernobyl," he said.

"You don't look a day over forty-nine," I said.

"I'm in love, a symptom of my dotage," he said, "and I don't want to be."

"Can't you take something for it?" I said. The sandwich was gone, scarcely enough to fill the cavity in your bicuspid.

"He's blond, pouty, petulant, capricious, and to me the entirely beautiful," he said.

"It will pass," I said.

"That's what I'm afraid of," he said. "And that's how I know I'm getting old."

"Monika told me that love is a discipline, not a debauch," I said.

"Bah," he said, "not when it's working right."

"When one is in love one begins to deceive oneself," I said. "And one ends by deceiving others."

"Poor Oscar," he said. "Now that I think of it, Alistair reminds me of Lord Douglas."

"Alistair!" I said.

"He spells it differently every time he writes his name," he said, "poor duckie, can't find himself."

"Lord Douglas was an arrant pip-squeak," I said.

"Wilde knew that, and it did him no good," he said. "I know the same about Alistair, and it doesn't change anything."

"All Western civilization, I have been told, is based on the premise that knowledge will set you free," I said. "And you negate three thousand years of it for a piece of ass."

"Et tu?" he said. "What would you negate for the right piece of ass?"

"All time and space, shattered glass and toppling masonry," I said.

"Thank goodness I came to you for comfort and support," he said. "Someone else might have said an encouraging word."

"Come on up to Fern Hill Farm with me this weekend," I said. "We'll sight in our rifles, shoot some skeet, load up on terpines."

"Alistair wants to go to that piano recital," he said, "but there's no tickets to be had. You can't imagine the sulks. How about I bring him with us?"

I sat back, lit up. "You're not testing me, are you?" I said. "You'll have to remember that I am not one of your lovers. You know damn well he'd be as comfortable to have around as sand in your condom."

"Peace, Brother," he said. He put his hand on my neck and pulled me toward him until our heads bumped. "It was sweet of you to ask me along."

"Just don't catch your death from this guy," I said.

"As long as you don't do it in the streets and scare the horses, to quote Lady something-or-another," said Zeno Confalone, looking haggard.

"Wasn't she on Oprah Winfrey the other day?" I said.

"A little male bonding, is all," said Leonard, releasing my neck. "You ever been in love, Zee?" Only Leonard and Kay called Zeno "Zee."

"Once," said Zeno. "I'm still paying for it." Zeno always looks haggard. I've seen him after three days at Fern Hill Farm, well-fed, well-rested, easy on the booze, and he still looked haggard. It's a condition of the soul visible through his body. The only time he doesn't look haggard is when he looks ravaged. For lunch he was having a large container of black coffee.

"My dears," said Lizzie Arno, sitting down, looking indulgent.

Lizzie, who is built like a plank, a one-by-eight, had a bacon cheeseburger, a pile of fries, a large Pepsi, and for dessert, lime Jello topped mit schlag.

"We've been asking ourselves what love is good for," said Leonard.

"The propagation of the species," said Marshall Grice, as the chapel bells struck noon (silver circles brightened the air). Marshall had a plate of rice and cottage cheese, with unbuttered toast on the side, for his stomach is delicate. On a diet like that you could starve and get fat at the same time.

"In love and work lies our salvation," said Lizzie, "such salvation as there is. Freud, as usual, was right."

"What's the news from Chief Inspector Gomez?" said Marshall.

"Lieutenant Suarez," I said.

Kay Pesky and Serena Crawfoot arrived, laughing at something one of them had said, I guess—Kay with a salad and a brownie, Serena with a stuffed pork chop that only a lifetime of self-discipline prevented me from snatching.

"He seems to be looking for a disgruntled graduate student," I said to Marshall.

"Is there any other kind?" said Leonard.

"Sir," said Marshall, "graduate students are like soldiers: a license to gripe is a perquisite of their service."

"I just introduced Serena to an admirer of yours," said Kay.

"I'll get a dissertation out of him yet," I said.

"Who?" said Kay. "I'm talking about Amabelle Bloor."

"The beanbag!" said Zeno.

"And what mistaken idea of me does she think she admires?" I said.

"Her latest whodunit depicts you as a virtuous gay," said Serena, "if you know what I mean."

What it means is that Amabelle thinks I ain't misbehaving by choice, a limp dick by scruple.

"Sounds boring," said Zeno. "What's the point of being queer if you're virtuous? The whole point of being queer is that it's so much easier to get laid."

"There's that," said Leonard.

"Sir," said Marshall, "virtue may look boring to the vicious; vice may look exciting to the virtuous; both will be wrong." He scraped around in his pipe with a three-pronged tool.

"I am here before you as an envoy extraordinary," I said, "also known as a gofer."

"What does Munoz want?" said Marshall.

"Suarez," I said. "Angel wants me to recruit you all for her campaign."

"So she's decided to run," said Kay.

"Officially, she's still testing the waters," I said. "You can expect an invitation to lunch from Bertil Lund or Malcolm Tetrault or Amabelle Bloor any day."

"I've already got one from Amabelle," said Kay.

"So that's why Malcolm invited me to the piano recital," said Serena.

"I am authorized to tell Kay that it is time for her to make a show of feminist solidarity," I said.

"Well, I suppose she's got a point," said Kay.

"Angel also said that as chair she could see to Kay's promotion," I said.

Kay stiffened, but there was a hurt look on her face. "I am not a whore," she said, her voice trembly.

"Of course, you're not," said Lizzie. "The idea!"

"I've never sucked up to anybody for anything," said Kay. "My father. . . ." Serena put her hand on Kay's arm. Kay's father fled Poland to the States during the Partition, landed a job as a porter in Bickford's, designed a gadget for simplifying the flush tank, sold the rights to a plumbing supplier (for a job and a piece of the action), formed his own company when his employer went bust, devised other gadgets, got rich. He is now the main supplier of flush tanks, bidets, urinals, showerheads, valves, and other things especially designed to save water. He is stern, reserved, courteous, mangles his English, taught his kids how to behave by example rather than precept, encouraged Kay every inch along her arduous way, quickly wiped away the tears that ran down his face when, at the graduation ceremony, Kay officially became a Ph.D. Kay's upright character is related to a loving respect for her father. How come you could never get along with Pa, Joel? He's not that bad a guy.

"As for Marshall," I said, "I am instructed to say that as someone who considers himself a just man, he should realize it is time a woman occupied the chair."

Marshall puffed three times on his pipe. Then he leaned forward and said:

> "Justice requires that a woman occupy the chair.
> Angel is a woman.
> Therefore Angel should occupy the chair.

We begin with a *petitio principii* and go downhill from there."

"You are implying, if I understand you correctly," said Leonard, "that Angel has an undistributed middle."

"No one has ever seen the hide nor hair of it," said Zeno. "She wears *lederhosen* in the shower."

"A *quaternio terminorum,*" said Marshall.

Said Zeno:

> "Nothing is better than a piece of ass.
> A piece of bread is better than nothing.
> Therefore a piece of bread is better than a piece of ass.

I read that somewhere so it must be true."

"Angel went over to Katriona Campbell's office to see whether any complaints of sexual harassment had been filed against Leonard," I said. "Katriona was not forthcoming."

"She was looking to blackmail you, Len," said Serena.

"According to Angel, that is how the political game is played," I said. "I do not believe I have misquoted her."

"All feminism tends toward the condition of Andrea Dworkin," said Zeno.

"Come off it, Zee," said Kay, still tight and white around the mouth.

"Angel believes that with pressure judiciously applied some student could be persuaded to come forward with charges against Leonard," I said.

"It's an old story: a middle-class white woman going after the job of a black male breadwinner," said Leonard, deadpan, so we could not tell which way the irony cut, for Leonard's bread had long ago been won, by his grandfather.

"You can inform Professor Terrasco," said Serena, "that if she pulls any of this stuff I'll tell the world she chased me around my desk begging for a kiss."

"You'll do no such thing, child," said Lizzie.

Zeno placed one of Serena's hands between his, looked her in the eye, said, "Will you marry me? And if not, at least let me take you to the recital."

"I want to do a Mata Hari on Malcolm Tetrault," said Serena.

"Madam," said Marshall, "the sages of all ages agree: the untenured who meddle in departmental politics thereby perpetuate their condition."

"That's what I'll tell Malcolm," Serena said.

"I am further instructed to inform Lizzie," I said, "that if she wants her contract renewed, she should do the right thing by Angel."

"Why, that's a bribe," said Serena.

"It's too bad," said Lizzie. "She has now made it impossible for me to support her."

We smoked in silence for a bit, sipped on our coffees. "I don't suppose there was any message for me," said Serena, looking disappointed.

"She believes that where Kay leads, you follow," I said. "She implied a . . . relationship."

For some reason, surely reprehensible, I was happy to see and hear Kay snort with derision. Serena reddened.

"There, there," said Leonard, patting Serena's hand. "Angel's problem is sex in the head, the zone best left unerogenized, knocks you into a tailspin."

"Like a hand grenade in the cockpit," said Zeno.

Certain puns occurred to me, but I held fire.

"And what inducement was dangled before our dear vice?" said Marshall.

"She offered to keep me on as vice-chair," I said.

"Poor Wynn," said Kay, and she patted my hand, a regular epidemic.

"I should add that Murray's initial plan was to barter Lizzie's line for authorization to bring in a senior feminist," I said. "He has now put that plan in abeyance, pending. . . ."

"These people are devourers of the world light," said Lizzie.

"Are there further communications from the chair?" said Marshall.

"From Monika," I said. "She foresees Angel coming down hard on her from the chair. Her idea is that we have influence and should use it, Leonard on Lois, Freddy and Ziggy, Kay on the feminists, Zeno on the Renasissancesters, Marshall and Lizzie on the old boys, me on the creative writers, to begin with."

"And me?" said Serena.

"The best way to lose influence is to use it," said Leonard. "Tell Ziggy to do one thing, he's sure to do another."

"I don't know," said Kay. "It feels somehow . . . underhanded."

"I like it," said Zeno.

"I will not be used," said Lizzie. "We must each of us do what is right, as individually we see it."

"Do right, fear no man; don't write, fear no woman," said Zeno.

"We are not in the realm of spirit," said Marshall, "but in the real world—"

"An English department is not the real world," said Leonard.

"—where to exist is to be used," said Marshall, "where the difference between right and wrong is thinner than the thinnest of skins."

"Sir, do I understand you to accuse me of being thin-skinned?" said Lizzie.

"Centrifugally, Murray has been a good chair," said Marshall. "Other departments have been practically dismantled or put into receivership; we are intact; it's Murray's doing; no other professor has his clout with the administration."

"It's true," said Zeno.

"At the cost of his soul," said Lizzie.

"Centripetally Murray has been a good chair," said Marshall, "in that he has pretty much left the department's internal affairs up to his second-in-command, first the indomitable Terry Jones, and now her worthy successor. He is about as good as, under the circumstances, we can get, which is good enough."

"If Malcolm gives me any lip, I'll tie him into a double half-hitch," said Serena.

"How about you, Wynn?" said Kay.

"We have months to go," I said. "Until then, I'll waffle."

For some reason, once again there was silence, except that Serena, who had not learned Kay's repose, tapped out a beat on the table with her fingertips, and Marshall made little pops with his pipe. Then Leonard said, "The right thing to do is this: since we have a quantity of influence we use it to run Wynn O'Leary."

"Bravo," said Lizzie.

"I don't like it," said Kay. "Don't do it, Wynn, this is not right for you," and I'll be damned if the woman didn't pat my hand again. I was wishing that she would let me speak for myself, if only to agree with her.

"And Kay for vice-chair," said Serena.

"A knockout one-two punch," said Leonard.

"Administration is not my métier," I said.

"Bosh," said Marshall, "any of us could do it. It is a lighter task and a lesser accomplishment to subdue people than to subdue words, your true métier, dear Wynn."

"Let's just see what happens for a while," said Kay. "Angel's ham-handed ways may turn everybody off before she even announces."

"If not, Amabelle's table manners will," said Zeno. "Are you really going to have lunch with her?"

"Yes," said Kay.

"I begin to see possibilities in an O'Leary-Pesky ticket," said Marshall. "But I don't think Murray has earned a slap in the face, let alone a knockout one-two punch."

"Murray's problem is all the people in the department, especially the youngsters, who don't know the players," said Zeno. "They will naturally act on the assumption that the progressive thing is to vote for a woman. It is not underhanded to raise their consciousnesses."

"Still, our stock would go up nationwide if we had a woman for a chair," said Kay.

"Who cares what a bunch of professors of English think about us?" said Zeno.

"Or about anything?" said Leonard.

"Come on guys, let's Win with Wynn," said Leonard. "He'll have the best kitchen cabinet in the annals of academe, shape this place up."

"False modesty won't work with us, Wynn," said Lizzie.

"All right then, drop your plow and raise your standard," said Marshall.

"I like the idea of being a kingmaker," said Serena.

"Come on, Wynn," said Lizzie.

"Come on, Wynn baby," said Leonard.

"Kay's right, let's see what happens for a bit," I said.

"You don't want to jump in at the last minute," said Leonard, "look like a spoiler."

We blew smoke at each other for a while, figuratively as well as literally.

"Have we decided to watch and wait, then?" said Marshall.

"I'm for taking action," said Serena, "any action."

"We should each take whatever action he sees fit," said Lizzie.

"Or she sees fit," said Serena.

"You are not holding back out of misplaced delicacy, are you," said Marshall to me, "or worse, on principle? He who forgoes an advantage on principle soon covets the advantage and turns against the principle."

"The principle is self-preservation," I said, "otherwise known as laziness. I'm not up to slugging it out with Angel."

"Sir, the burdens of a man with friends to share them weigh on him lighter than they weigh," said Marshall.

"Friends can also be a burden," said Kay. "Come on, Wynn, we have classes to meet. I'll walk out with you."

As we stepped out of Lightfoot Lee Hall into the warm sun, Kay stopped, turned to me, said, "Do you want to have supper after the party? We could have our private little talk."

"What party is that?" I said.

"Don't you read your mail?" she said: "the chair's annual reception."

"I forgot," I said. "I'd love to have dinner with you, but no coconuts and pineapple in my barbecued pork."

"What did you say to Angel's innuendo about Serena and me?" Kay said.

"How could I know what to say?" I said.

"I want you specially to know that there are certain lines I don't cross," said Kay. "The Old Testament is not the last word on morality, but it's the first: there are certain things you just don't do."

"It's not a question of morality," I said. "Morality has nothing to do with it," and now I was holding forth. "You've got to follow your inclinations. There are only two sexual sins—rape and abstinence."

"What I wanted to say was, once you cross certain lines there's no going back," Kay said. "You have changed how you think and feel about yourself, irrevocably. I just wanted you to know."

"When is this then that it is—Thursday?" I said.

"At six," she said.

"See you then," I said.

"I'll have a surprise for you," she said. "I hope you like it."

"Give me a hint," I said.

"You're not having an affair with your, ah, cousin, are you?" she said.

"Banish the thought," I said.

"Not that it's any business of mine," she said.

"You could make it your business," I said.

"We'll talk Thursday," she said.

When I came home from class (which went well, thanks), Julie was already cooking, stirring a sauce of soy "milk" to put on the mussels, which she apparently thought of as a species of vegetable. "Hi, Cuz," she said. While she cooked and I went through the mail, writing checks, skimming catalogues, she chattered on about her day, music to my ears. Professor Confalone was in top form, she said, and she was sure she passed his weekly short-answer quiz. He kept mentioning this essay on *The Odyssey* by George Dimock. Did I have a copy? I told her where to find it. Her friend thought *The Odyssey* was a crock, but she liked it, much better than *The Iliad.* She thought *The Odyssey* read as though written by a woman. I told her about Samuel Butler and T. E. Lawrence, and Robert Graves, who all thought the same. She said I was like Odysseus and she was like Nausicaa. Except that Odysseus was a hero and Nausicaa was a virgin, I said, but Julie was reading in the right way, was Julie.

"All the female characters are aspects of one complete woman," she said. "I know I have it in me to be a witch, a virgin, a bountiful goddess, a siren, a stay-at-home wife. We all have."

"Let's hope they don't all come out at the same time," I said.

"Professor Confalone asked me for a date," she said. "He's got tickets to that piano music everyone is going to. Are you going?"

"No," I said. "Are you?"

"I couldn't," she said. "I sort of thought we had this, you know, understanding, me and you."

"I have to go to my place in the Adirondacks this weekend," I said: "do you want to come?"

"Do you go by Middleburgh?" she said.

"I can," I said.

"Could you drop me off?" she said. "I've been thinking, now that I'm settled, going to school and all, I have something to face my parents with. It's been six years."

"I remember your father as something of a hardcase," I said.

"He always spoke well of you," she said. "He always said you were the least useless of the O'Leary brats." She poured mussels into the sauce and spooned rice into a casserole dish.

"What turned you to vegetarianism?" I said. "Worried about your health? The old have never gotten older, and the current crop grew up eating all the meat they could get."

"It's the animals, Cuz," she said. "I can't bear the way they are forced to live—and die."

"During the crucial stage of human evolution, when we became what we are, we hunted big game."

"I thought the idea was to become better than we are," she said. "That's why I'm going to school."

"Human nature does not seem to have improved much during the three thousand years for which we have a semi-continuous record," I said.

"Well, we don't have bear-baiting," she said. "You can't hang a twelve-year-old for stealing a loaf of bread. Slavery is illegal. Women have rights. Now you have to invent a justification for going to war; you can't just go on a rampage to earn a rep. Human nature may not have improved, but our laws and customs are less brutal—you have to invent pretexts to justify brutality. I've thought about this."

"The result is universal hypocrisy," I said.

"Better universal hypocrisy than matter-of-course brutality everywhere," she said.

"This is arguably the most brutal century ever," I said.

"I love it when we have conversations like this, Cuz," she said. "Will you still talk to me when we've solved your little problem? Maybe then you'll be a little less... I don't know—grim. I don't think you're really a grufgrump by nature."

Because the class went well, I was in a good mood: I did not take offense at the implication that my considered ideas were mere by-products of a disability. Besides, the thin dress that Julie wore as she bent over the stove, the sink, the chopping board, had a beneficial effect on my disposition. Why do men like women's asses, Joel? Do you now have complete knowledge of everything, like Spinoza's dreary god? One anthropologist, who likes to get a rise out of his readers, says that at one period in human evolution, women in heat *presented*, as do female baboons (and, he said, so do low-ranking males). The female behind, then would be a sexual releaser, as it surely is, for every human physical or behavioral trait at one time helped us get along in our conspecific or extraspecific environment or is a by-product of an adoptive trait, as lower back pain is a by-product of upright posture. But why then do men like women's tits and legs? Nothing in this area is self-evident. Maybe you're even in a position to tell me the secret of secrets: what physical and behavioral traits do women like in men? Stop, don't tell me. I don't want to know. After such knowledge, what forgiveness?

You'll have to forgive these aimless doodlings. My brain's been addled by the toxicity of my own words, written down continuously since supper, which was good, once I added some hot mustard to Julie's sauce. And my mind was half-following a train of ideas set going by an album of Dizzy's, *Dee Gee Days*. Those lame arrangements and corny vocals are to Dizzy's career what those sides with strings were to Bird's. America's two greatest musical geniuses of all time were trying to make themselves some walking-around money by appealing to what they thought was popular taste. Both in their solos fly free of the musical sludge enmiring them, as a seabird might shake free of an oil slick. But note that Bird's instinct was to go middlebrow, whereas Diz lowered his brow to goofy novelties and roadhouse blues. Once again, I have to side with Diz. The enemy is not lowbrow culture, but middlebrow gentility. I know: as the dutiful son of a lace-curtain Irisher, I'm in no position to squawk. You at least were not dutiful: you did your bit, for bop is the implacable enemy of everything soft, tame, easy, and genteel. It's music with a stomach, as they say in the Mafia—and used to say during the English Renaissance.

Julie just popped her head in through the study doorway to ask how I would like it if we took our showers together. I think she's gotten the idea from those sex books that her job is to demystify the female body for me, remove some of its charge, or mana, so that I can approach it without fear and trembling. I don't think it will work. After all, isn't penetration of the mystery what we're all about? Or is violation of the sanctum sanctorum? I hope so. Talk to you tomorrow, pal. I'm off to wash away my sins.

10

Dear Joel,

I missed chatting with you these past two days, but a desultory life, such as mine, is one that more plotted lives sweep up into their stories, to swell a progress, start a scene or two. To exist is to be used, says Marshall, and a good thing, or I'd have no contact with other people at all.

My day at the office on Wednesday was routine, getting the job done. I read two dissertations in progress, one entitled *Professorial Protagonists: The Academic as (Anti-) Hero*, the other an elaboration of a theme by your kid brother, entitled *The Body Lost and Found: Virginia Woolf and James Joyce.* I read a make-up paper by an SAS student whose husband was busted last spring when he held up a mom-and-pop grocery: Mama-san stuck a snub-nose up his nostril and said, "You shoot: I shoot; you die, maybe I live." I read a makeup exam by a blind student whose scanner had broken down, so he said. I wrote to an alumnus of Graduate English who suddenly became rich when his father died and bequeathed him a vacuum-cleaner factory (the idea being that he endow a named [with his name] dissertation fellowship). I called and chewed out an assistant professor who, instead of showing up for her class (UC 3269: Deadlier than the Male: Women, Narrative, Murder), had her teaching assistant show movies. My note to Malcolm Tetrault told him that I wanted a packet of his publications toot sweet, my tone implying that he had better watch his step. I sketched in a re-do of the undergraduate major in English (drop the required seminar in theory, add a required survey of the lyric poem, musing in rhythm). I wrote eleven letters of recommendation, for this is the time of the year when undergraduates get ready to apply to graduate school and graduate students get ready to apply for jobs or grants, poor babies, for both are scarce. I prepped a student for her orals, the major field late nineteenth- and early twentieth-century literature, her special interest the abnegating male character, refuser of life's feast, from Oblomov to James Duffy. I received a call from Marshall Grice, who said, and I should keep this under my hat, that he would retire, effective next fall, if I could get a guarantee of a regular appointment for Lizzie in his place. I said that he who forsakes an office to benefit a friend soon covets the office and turns against the friend. He said that parody is the tribute paid by envy to accomplishment. I said that we ought to hold off for a while. Our fates are in your calloused hands, dear Wynn, he said. I received a call from Bertil Lund, who wanted to know if I was free for lunch. Not this week, I said. I ate a curried chicken sandwich at my desk. I answered a letter from a woman who after twenty-five years on first a commune and then a homestead in New Hampshire (Live Free or Die) raising vegetables and (mostly other people's) children, was thinking of returning to graduate school, but didn't know how to go about it. The main office transferred to me a call from a secretary (to an advertising exec) who wanted to know whether she should use two periods or one when a sentence ended with "Inc." I answered a call from a man who was writing an article for New York magazine on the vogue for sadomasochism and who wanted to know whether I could recommend any of the department's "culture-watchers" for him "to tap into." He asked whether I had any thoughts on the subject. I said that sadism was masochism by proxy, the sadist being a masochist who was too much of a pip-squeak to take his pain straight. May I quote you? he said. No, I said.

Why do I write this stuff down? Because I want you to know about it, I guess; but that can't be all. Let's see, two things happen when you put an experience into words: One, you falsify it. Two, you fix it in words, in your mind, recover it, make it your own, get closer to your own experience. Well then, consider this: putting an experience into words is itself an experience, distinct from the experience you are putting into words. Wait a minute, we are actually dealing with three things here: one, the experience; two, the experience of putting that experience into words; three, experiencing that experience as written down and therefore falsified. The experience you make your own is not exactly the one you had. So what? It is arguably better to have and hold a falsified experience than none at all. Besides, reporting my quotidiana to you gives me pleasure, no, that's going too far, let's say it relieves tension, as when the man with a hand-washing compulsion is released from his cuffs.

I'm sitting here falsifying my life at the big oak kitchen table in Uncle Alf's old house, the cast-iron stove radiating heat, for I cut wood nearly every day this past summer, the cast-iron kettle letting off steam. Through the window I can see the light rain mixed with heavy mist descending, engulfing the big old maple by the garage. For some reason I feel spooked, nervy, scooped-out, vulnerable. Leaning against the wall behind me is my fine old Winchester Model twelve, a box of OO shot shells on the table, in case a werewolf lurches out of the mist.

On the way up I left Julie off by a big old barn by a big old farm, the barn now converted into a year-round flea market. But I did not hang around until her parents drove out of the hills to pick her up. Instead of returning to the Thruway, I meandered north through the Catskills, digging the trees putting on their outlandish fall colors by way of preparation for going naked, then the ghostly hamlets, the clenched faces and misshapen bodies of the locals, who would hate me if they knew me, who hate me anyhow.

When I came home Wednesday with a sack full of short ribs, Julie was already throwing something together, chickpeas, dried tomatoes, buffalo mozzarella, parsley, garlic, safflower oil, and the feminists go on about the horrors women suffer for the dubious benefits of living with men. (I put the short ribs in the freezer, for another time.) “Hi, Cuz,” she said. “Tonight’s the big night. We begin our walk, hand in hand, down the roads to your full orgiastic potency. Are you ready?”

Certainly I was willing, in a way, if not exactly ready. Do you remember that trembly feeling you got in your stomach when you first realized you were finally going to get laid? Not that I expected to get laid, or that it would be a first if I did. The point is that it’s childish to attach so much importance to something so ordinary, something that occurs millions of times a day, all over the world, between all kinds of people, including those who are no good at anything else. In spite of my desire to believe in the biological basis of human behavior, I have to admit that with us, what should come naturally seldom does.

I was in my study browsing through a Smoky Mountain Knife Works Catalogue (they have a Ka-Bar for sale) and listening to your old Pete Rugalo album, and what a lovely solo that is Lars Fagerquist takes on “Oscar and Pete’s Blues,” when Julie knocked on the open door, and as I looked up, said, “Now’s the time.”

Frazer, in *The Golden Bough,* tells us how the ancients used to pamper a bull before leading it off to sacrifice, aromatic oils, a garland, a hairdo for the tail, and that was exactly the wrong analogy for me to think of even in self-mockery, as Julie led me to the shower, pulling me by my pizzle, lathered me all over, rubbed in some kind of skin cream, smelled like Brazil nuts, pushed me out, said, “Get into bed, I’ll be right with you,” and then, ten minutes later, came out of the bathroom in a cloud of steam, wearing lipstick, perfumed, hair piled on top of her head, skin gleaming, laughing-eyed Aphrodite.

"Here is what we do," she said. "I lie on my belly and you feel me up all over, any way you want, your hands, your mouth, it's up to you."

"Now you're talking," I said.

"Then I turn over and you do the other side," she said.

"Let's get started," I said.

She pushed me down. "Wait," she said. "There are rules."

"I'm a confirmed anarchist," I said, who nevertheless almost always complies.

She sat down on the bed, put a hand on my stomach. "Rule one," she said: "you're supposed to keep your mind on what you're doing, *tu piges?* 'Sensate focus' it's called. You focus on your sensations. You don't daydream or anything."

"No daydreaming," I said, sitting up. She pushed me down.

"Rule two," she said: "You're not supposed to stand back and look at yourself. It's called 'spectatoring,' seeing how you're doing, worrying about your hard-on, judging your performance, *compris?* 'Performance anxiety,' my books say, 'is a component of nearly every type of male sexual dysfunction.' They all agree about that one."

The neophyte is led into the sacred cave, torchlight red on the glistening walls, and he knows he is about to be drugged and mutilated, but he also knows that if he does everything right, and only then, he will receive the secret words and the magic touch that change you forever. So he's a little anxious: you can't blame him for that.

Absentmindedly, Julie plucked out a few of the sparse hairs around my navel. "Rule three," she said.

"Hey!" I said, moving her hand south to my exterior plumbing. Let her pluck that.

"You're allowed to be selfish," she said, kissing my navel to make it better. "Don't do something just because you think it will turn me on. And don't worry about turning me off either, what I'm thinking, am I disgusted, bored, laughing at you, got me?"

I grabbed her wrist and pulled her down on me, kissed her. She immediately rolled off, then onto her stomach. I sat up, straddled her legs, bent over and kissed a gleaming cheek. "That reminds me," she said, looking up at me with one eye, for the right side of her face was flat against the sheet, "you're not supposed to touch any hot spots."

"Is this a hot spot?" I said, kissing the other cheek.

"It is to you," she said.

I moved up, so that my dangle rested along her cleft, leaned forward, ran my tongue along the shallow groove from hairline to cervical vertebra, called "the atlas," nuzzled with my nose the crease between jawline and neck, lipped an earlobe.

"That's the spirit, Cuz," she said. "Remember that you're not trying to get anywhere, make anything happen. All you're doing is what you're doing, not something symbolical of something else."

I did not respond with one of my patented gruffisms, in the first place because my mouth was full, in the second place because her voice had become a hot spot too.

I sat back and felt up her trapezius. I felt up her deltoid, her bicep, taking my time, circled a forearm with thumb and forefinger, slid my hand down to her wrist, and damn, can you believe that I had never before noticed how complicated, intricate, elegant, a healthy young woman's wrist bone can be? Not that in those respects the wrist bone even approaches the anklebone, as a careful inspection proved. I did not then, nor do I now, believe that the rules required I tell Julie she had become one big hot spot all over.

I took a break just now to throw some wood into the firebox, turn the ribs over, paint them with sauce, open a bottle of very good Saranac amber, put on some music, that comical set Bird and Diz did with Slim Gaillard, lighten my mood. It's still drizzly out, dusk darkening the fog, a feeling of things closing in. Two owls call back and forth:

"Screw you."

"Screw who."

"Screw you."

"Screw who."

Well, I don't think I left any of Julie's surfaces unstroked or unkissed, except maybe the soles of her feet and her rosebud. Then Julie did me, in what you might call a businesslike manner, but I have never come across a woman in either life or literature who felt for a man's body what a man feels for a woman's, even if the man's body is young and sculpted, rather than middle-aged and fat. Maybe it's just as good that women don't care much about the kind of shape we're in, or they'd never go to bed with us at all, given how most of us look.

Julie's massage, what it amounted to, left me glowing, my joint jumping. We were lying side by side, facing each other. I hooked my arms around her, closed on her cheeks, one in each hand, pulled her toward me. She put the palms of her hands on my chest, like a demure heroine in an old play, looked me in the eye. "Behave, Cuz," she said. "The one thing we can't risk right now is a failure." A current of rage flushed through me, probably engorging my face and neck, making me a hard-on all over, for Julie got a worried look on her face. "You've got to be patient," she said. "We're going to make it together yet." Here I've been waiting for nine years and the woman tells me to be patient. Suddenly an idea, like a possessing demon, took hold of me: only rape would make me whole. Who did this bitch think she was playing with? "I know what you're thinking, Cuz," she said, pulling herself up against me from nose to knee, laying her cheek on mine. "Think how you'll feel if it doesn't work. In fact think how you'll feel if it does work: first you'll hate yourself, then you'll hate me. Or the other way round."

I must have let out a considerable sigh, for a cluster of Julie's curls riffled, as in a breeze. I flopped over, onto my back, pulling her with me, her breasts spilling onto my chest. So that's how we lay, phosphenes shooting across the underside of my eyelids. I think you would be wrong, Joel, to say I was awash in self-pity, for self-pity, including my own, brings out my sense of humor, and I wasn't laughing. Besides, I had just spent an hour cuddling with a congenial and beautifully embodied young woman. What more could you want?

Julie peeled herself off me, went into the bathroom, left the door open, so I could hear her tinkle. In honor of a similar occasion, James Joyce privately called his collection of lyrics not *Chamber Music* but *Chamber Pot Music,* closer to the bone than tinkling pianos, at any rate. But then Joyce had a thing about urine and feces—H. G. Wells said he had a cloacal complex—as he did about snot, navel fluff and toe jam. I do not recall him alluding to conkleberries. All these, as products of the human body, are akin to poems, plays, paintings and big ideas, thus refuting the old saying that you can't polish a turd. He rather liked the fact, which distresses idealists, that *inter urinus et faeces nascimur.* And didn't Yeats have Crazy Jane say that love has pitched his mansion in the place of excrement? What is it with these Irishers? I rolled over on my stomach, for I did not want Julie to see the effect her tinkle was having on me. After all, I'm an Irisher too.

Julie climbed aboard my back and stretched out like a surfer, her pelvic hair tickling my coccyx, her head hair tickling my ear. "Let's talk," she said. I may have groaned. I'm pretty sure I groaned.

"That essay by George Dimock, 'The Name of Odysseus,'" she said. "Is he right?"

"I've sworn off literary criticism," I said.

"I'm surprised at you, Cuz," she said. "Isn't the point of literature that it teaches you how you're supposed to live? That's what I'm trying to find out."

"Literature is life, but criticism is not literature," I said.

"Well, this George Dimock essay is about how you have to live if you want to be someone," she said. "I want to know if you agree with him."

"I don't," I said.

"Come on, Cuz," she said, "why are you holding out on me? Is it because I'm too dumb?"

That's right, make me feel like a complete shit, entirely. She goes out of her way to give me what I need, lets herself get felt up all over by a fat sex fiend, and I won't give her a little of what she needs, won't even spare her a few words, although they wouldn't cost me anything, for words are like muscles in this: the more you use them, the more you have.

"I remember I used to consider the essay important," I said, "but I can't remember what's in it, must be something I don't want to know."

"Well, George Dimock says that the name of Odysseus is cognate —that's the word, right?—with a Greek verb that in *The Odyssey* means to cause pain, give grief, do damage, make trouble. When Odysseus tells someone his name he's saying 'call me Trouble.' "

"You've got to be skeptical of arguments based on etymology," I said.

"Etymology?" she said. "What's all this got to do with bugs?"

"You're thinking of entomology," I said. "Etymology is the study of word derivations."

"Thanks for not laughing at me, Cuz," she said, giving me a squeeze.

Oh Joel, what a mob of emotions surged through me then, and I thought I had outgrown them all. If this frail makes me fall in love with her, I'm going to kick her out on her butt, take a cue from Thorwald. "A misplaced entym is nowhere near as funny as a mislaid hard-on," I said. "But you didn't laugh at me."

"That's right," she said: "cause we care about each other."

"Let's get back to far-famed Odysseus, that polytropic man."

"OK, forget Odysseus—what's an etym anyway?—but when you think about it, Odysseus *does* odysseus everybody, you know, in the sense of causing them some serious pain. He masterminds the sack of Troy, right? He gives grief to his mother—who dies of it—to his father, to his wife, to his son, all of whom suffer like in physical ways, not just mentally, and then think of poor Argus. Ajax won't even talk to him, even in Hades, because of the way Odysseus crossed him. He puts Poseidon in a major snit and then blinds his son, that big dope Polyphemus, brushes off Nausicaa, which had to hurt, brings disaster upon the whole Phaeakian people, pulls sword *on a goddess*, good old Circe, walks out on another goddess, Calypso, kills what is it? 108 suitors and a bunch of servants. And this is really awful: He just comes across these people called the Cicones, kills the men, ransacks the city, carries off the women, and divides them up like so much *loot,* can you imagine?"

"Easily," I said: "it's one of my favorite fantasies."

"You're kidding," she said.

"That's what men want," I said: " an endless supply of sex slaves."

"What would you do with them?" she said.

"That's a low blow," I said.

"I didn't mean your little problem," she said.

"Odysseus, remember, is a hero," I said. "He's not plain folks like you and me. A hero is someone who's not afraid to go after what he wants, no matter who he has to odysseus along the way. Is that a good way to be?"

"Homer and George Dimock, not to mention Professor Confalone, seem to think so," she said. "You've got to odysseus and accept being odysseused if you want to be somebody. That's how Odysseus earns his name."

"One way or another, you're going to wind up odysseused anyhow, like it or not," I said.

"The point is not to hide from it," she said. "You've got to sort of welcome it, even. You can't play it safe, or you'll wind up calypsoed. According to the etymology, to be calypsoed is to be covered over, 'engulfed,' says George Dimock, like being pushed under underwater, the way my sister Dominique.... If Odysseus had stayed with Calypso, he would have had ease, comfort, safety, heavenly sex, and immortality, think of it! *Immortality.* But he leaves her. The reason is, if he had stayed with Calypso he would have become a nobody."

"Like any uxorious man," I said.

"What does 'uxorious' mean?" Julie said.

"From 'uxor,' *wife,* it means pussy-whipped, tied to your woman's apron strings," I said.

"What's wrong with that?" she said.

"It's a kind of lotus-eating," I said; "it's living on a fantasy island, like the Phaeakians."

"I thought about that," she said. "Can you be a hero if you're—what's the female equivalent of uxorious?"

"Narcissism," I said.

She cuffed me on the back of the head.

"Tell me what you wanted to ask, then I'm going down on you, scarf some pussy-whip," I said.

"Whoa, big fella," she said, pulling me by the hair, as Athena pulled Achilles. "I'll put it in a nutshell," she said: "Odysseus tells Polyphemus that his name is 'Nobody,' right?"

"Right," I said.

"Then he odysseuses him," she said: "he tricks him, blinds him, steals his sheep, makes his getaway. Right?"

"Right," I said.

"So Odysseus is in his ship moving out," she said. "All he has to do is keep quiet and he's safe."

"Right," I said.

"But what does he do?" she said. "He shouts out this put-down of Polyphemus."

"No class, like a lot of football players nowadays," I said.

"Now Polyphemus knows where he is," she said. "He throws a huge rock, a mountaintop actually, that causes a wave that nearly calypsos Odysseus."

"Death to all blowhards," I said.

"Odysseus is moving out again and his men are trying to keep him quiet," she said. "But he has to stand up and let loose with a brag: the guy who poked a stick in your eye was me, Odysseus, sacker of cities, out of Ithaca, son of Laertes, a complete ID."

"That's the heroic style," I said.

"It's how Odysseus moves from Nobody to somebody," she said. "It's how he forms his identity."

"I doubt that the Greek notion of personal identity was the same as ours," I said.

"I know," she said. "It was based more on recognition, reputation, honor, things like that. Professor Confalone told us. But I was thinking, does it make any difference? In one case—let's see if I can say this. In one case, you recognize yourself in the way others keep seeing you, right?"

"Right," I said.

"In the other case you recognize yourself in what you keep doing," she said.

"In both cases you distort what you think you see on behalf of the narcissism that keeps us alive," I said. "I sometimes think of personal identity as a fiction."

"Professor Confalone said that too," she said, "a necessary fiction."

"What else did he say?" I said.

"Well, for example, he said that Poseidon symbolizes the forces of nature and Polyphemus symbolizes uncivilized human nature," she said. "Do you agree?"

"You could say that," I said, "among other things."

"Then here's my question," she said: "to have a life do you have to dis other people and nature? I mean, including human nature, including your own nature, like your need to sleep, like your sexual urges, like your hunger for a juicy steak from the sun-god's cattle?"

"I've already dissed my sexual urge," I said.

"Come on, Cuz," she said.

"Not having a life, I wouldn't know," I said.

"Oh, pooh," she said. "Ninety percent of the men who have ever lived would have traded their lives for yours."

"Not if my little problem were part of the trade," I said.

"That's what's so stupid about men," she said: "they base their self-esteem on who or how they fuck."

"Normal men do," I said.

"What about the others?" she said.

"They drive themselves to become religious leaders," I said. "Then they think they have the right to fuck whoever and however they want."

"Would you odysseus someone who stood in the way of something you really wanted?" she said. "I mean something you needed to establish your identity. I mean something that would leave you calypsoed if you didn't get it."

"Right after college I wrote down a number of resolutions," I said, "like some figure of fun in a novel. One of them was to get through life without seriously harming another person."

"What about football?" she said.

"If I harmed anyone," I said, "the harm was an accidental by-product of my need to tackle him."

"I thought the idea was to hit the other guy hard enough to, sort of discourage him," she said, "and anyways, you sure odysseused Thorwald."

"I don't know what came over me," I said.

"You did it for me, right?" she said. She reached her arms under me, gave me a hug, rested her head on my shoulder. And that's how we both dozed off. . . . Now for some spare ribs.

Dear Joel,

It's Saturday morning and still raining, wild apple wood popping in the firebox, smelling good, the coffee by my elbow smelling better and strong enough to dissolve a spoon, the kettle wetly whispering like the voices in a paranoid's head, cigarette smoke closing round me, Diz and Bird bouncing off each other those wild solos on "Perdido," thou lost one, my belly full of the cold spare ribs I had for breakfast, a meal I don't usually eat, in spite of Julie's admonitions, and if you think I can hold out on her for long, no matter how absurd her whim, it is only because you have not properly estimated how impossible it is for a man like me to refuse a woman like Julie anything, although it would not be literally be true to say I was pussy-whipped . . . yet.

I don't know why I filled up so quickly last night. It was not because I stuffed myself with appetizers, condiments, garnishes, side dishes, and desserts, like some interior decorator. There were two large tomatoes cut into wedges and floating in oil and vinegar, a sliced purple onion. There was the round loaf of pumpernickel that I cut into hemispheres, out of which I scooped the pith, and around the inside of which I smeared butter. And of course the ribs, the ribs. And that's all. Maybe the reason is that instead of listening to bop, which sharpens your appetite for everything that gives you strength, I watched television, which is enervating.

I don't see you keeping track of such things, but since you died the Russian empire has gone the way of all the others, its constituent parts in the throes of rebirth pangs. In a number of these parts Catholics, Muslims, and Eastern Orthodox types are all looking to smite each other. It would be a boon to the rest of us if they wiped each other out. Think how much better the world would be, would long have been, had there never been any missionaries to anywhere, ever. My idea of a useful missionary is one simmering in a cannibal's cooking pot. These thoughts, although that's too grand a word for them, were abruptly cut off by something I noticed on television: the Muslim combatants were using cast-off G.I. gear, including Ka-Bars.

This observation uncorked a vision: a battered fiberglass box in a corner of the barn: it is behind a wrecked hand cultivator, a coil of untrustworthy rope, the cast-iron door of a Franklin stove no longer with us. Munching pumpernickel, I walked through the rain to the barn, uncovered the box, pulled it out, opened it: a meat saw blade, an axe head, an adze head, a much-nicked chisel, an immense auger, whether for peg-and-hole carpentry or for ice-fishing I couldn't say, a bladeless plane, and a Ka-Bar, still in its sheath.

Merely for the sake of something to do, I spent yesterday evening restoring that Ka-Bar: applications of neatsfoot oil to the leather rings, applications of WD-40, then a wire brush powered by my hand drill, then extra-fine emory cloth, then steel wool, to the blade and hilt. The Parkerizing came off with the rust, so after some work with first a coarse, then a medium, then a fine whetstone on the cutting edge and on the top "false edge," I got my bottle of gun bluing. I worked on it until the color was a pale blue, as smooth to the touch as the inside of Julie's thigh. It could never have looked so good when new. It is here on the kitchen table, next to the box of shot shells, as I get myself ready to tell you about Thursday night's extraordinary turn of events.

Don't even try to make me feel guilty for not asking Julie to the Chair's welcome-back party. What was I supposed to do with her after the party, when Kay and I went to dinner? I assumed, no presumed, that Kay's promised surprise was for my ears only. Have you ever noticed how involvement with women turns the most straightforward of men into double-dealing machiavellian intriguers? Anyhow, Julie was better off doing her homework, or so she was understanding enough to intimate: "I'd feel out of place," she said; "but someday I want to meet all your friends." So it was that I walked into the Graduate Students' Lounge, a nice room (two-storey ceilings, floor-to-ceiling windows, deep chairs and couches and library tables along the perimeter, a piano) with no woman on my arm.

Monika Wright, Irene Howland, and Teddy Nakatani were hovering, with the air of a hostess who has not yet received a compliment, around the end-to-end library tables on which they had set up munchies. There were bowls of pulverized chickpeas and eggplant for smearing on crackers; fingerfuls of the raw vegetables some people call *crudités* for dipping into the mash; skinny French bread sliced into pieces the size of a half-dollar; platters of smoked, sliced turkey product, fat-free; no-cal "cheese"; the kind of mustard that has wine in it; big bowls of popcorn; sliced sweet pickles, and in a city where you can get the best real pickles in the world, plump black olives. No mayonnaise, no salt shaker, no meat. That's how our class eats out nowadays.

I nodded to the crew, said "looks good," stood by the tables, scanning the room, palming a fistful of olives with the attitude of a man whose head didn't know what his hand was doing. About half of us (cum spouses) had arrived, the double doors continuously swinging in and out with new arrivals. We are not exactly stylish, but living in New York keeps the professional class up to a certain standard. There was Marta Confalone, heavier still than the last time I had seen her, in a black slacks suit, her thick, glossy hair piled in rolls and curls and coils above her handsome face, standing back on her heels, her bold eyes daring anyone to sympathize with her for Zeno's infidelities. There was Yvonne Weinrein, her back to Marta, not three feet away, sipping a glass of white wine, striking a pose, showing off her posture, though no one was looking, her hair severely pulled back, like a dancer's, her neo-flapper's dress a-glitter with beads and sequins and bits of mirror. Harriet Grice walked between them, hooked them each by an arm with hers, pulled them around until they were facing each other, said something to make them laugh. Alcohol loosens Harriet's satirical tongue. She looks the classic faculty wife of yore: tweeds, opaque stockings, clunky shoes, stiff, chopped-off battleship gray hair, no makeup. But once, standing behind her on the checkout line in Academy Market, I saw her slice open a package of chop meat with an unpolished nail, finger out clumps of meat and chomp them down raw. Her practice, at gatherings such as this, is to circulate rapidly, stop with someone to say a quick word or two, and return to Marshall as though to make sure he wasn't getting into trouble, then start off again. Marshall always seemed glad to see her return, an arm around her shoulder, a quick press of his cheek to her hair, must be like nuzzling a porcupine.

Murray's people who count were already there, including the deans of GAS, SAS, and YOOK (University College, or UC). When I caught Katriona Campbell's roving eye, she winked it. Well, here was my chance to talk to her about Lizzie's contract renewal. But first a drink. I moved to the bar, a library table on which were rows of bottles of white wine and a few stray bottles of the real thing. White wine is the drink of choice among people who care more about style than substance, Joel, although the other night, glancing at the TV, which Julie was watching with one eye while reading with the other, I saw some guy in a white smock say that according to recent studies, red wine was better for you. It's enough to cause panic among all those people who own liquor stores and wine cellars, stocked with the white. I don't want anyone to take a serious financial hit, but you tell me, is it out of line to hope they have to drink it all themselves? Strong hands closed on my biceps. "I have a bone to pick with you, Wynn O'Leary," said the voice of Angel Terrasco.

I turned around to face her. "I have just been subjected to a homily on political deportment by Marshall Grice," she said. "Why did you betray my confidences to your profligate cronies?"

"I only told them what you told me to told, to tell them," I said.

"Don't you play the stuttering innocent with me," she said. "There is more left of your brain than you pretend. You well knew I meant for you to take them aside one by one and intimate by indirections what was in it for each of them to support me. They are not in a condition to face political realities without buffering. I have often noticed that heavy smoking works on the brain like certain antidepressants. It produces apathy in some users and a low-grade paranoia in others. Neither is conducive to an alert and responsible participation in the political process."

"Teddy Nakatani also alliterates when he's agitated," I said.

"What are you talking about?" she said. "Is this some new form of waffling?"

"Angel," I said, "as vice-chair I have to remain neutral. I can't be one of your campaign handlers."

"It won't work," she said. "You are under the delusion that a hopelessly split department will turn with a craven sigh of relief to safe and solid Wynn O'Leary. Flighty people have a touching faith in the ability of big, fat men to maintain an even keel. They believe that in self-preservation you have learned how not to rock the boat. I won't let it happen."

"I don't care who is chair," I said, a lame snatch of doggerel, "so long as it is not me."

"I understand that you are shacked up with a student," she said. "Perhaps I should have a little talk with her."

"A misunderstanding," I said. "My cousin is staying with me until she finds a place of her own."

"I'm not surprised," she said. "It's a short step from fornication to incest."

"I need a drink," I said.

"I want to talk to you about the peremptory tone of your letter to Malcolm Tetrault," she said.

"So he went boo-hooing to you, did he?" I said. "Now I really need that drink."

"We can have a smoke out on the steps," she said.

"First a drink," I said, starting to turn.

"Wynn," she said. "I need your help. There are some things a man can do better than a woman."

That stopped me as would a rearward yank of a rope around my neck. "Whatever might that be?" I said.

"Winning over another man to a good cause," she said.

"What's the matter with Bertil Lund and Malcolm Tetrault?" I said.

"Whatever it is that makes a man one of the boys, they don't have it," she said. I looked her over, trying to figure out what was going on. Angel was wearing black boots like d'Artagnan's, a long flared black skirt, a long-sleeved black satin turtleneck blouse too tight around the shoulders, a delicate little cross on a gold chain, her stiff frizzy hair hanging down and away from her head like a miniature cape.

"We can drink to that," I said.

"I don't drink," she said, and she marched off, her boots clomping.

"Wait," I said, but she didn't.

Leonard Sistrunk was standing at the bar, pouring himself a glass of bourbon, neat. He was wearing a white double-breasted suit, well maybe there was a touch of gray in it, a cobalt blue shirt with button-down collar buttoned down with pearly buttons, a white tie, and three earrings. I held up a plastic glass for him to fill, for the occasion called for something more substantial than beer.

"You missed the demonstration today," he said, pouring.

"I was finishing off my masterpiece," I said, "a proposal for a revised English major, as logical in its changes as the bridge of 'Ain't Misbehaving.' "

"A new student organization, the Missionary Positioners, had a dustup with the Sixty-Niners and the Gay and Lesbian Alliance," he said, "hitting each other upside the head with outrageous placards. They also want a lounge of their own. They also have petitioned the Ancient Order of Hibernians."

"Now they've gone too far," I said. "That kind of pervert offends everybody."

"The trouble I've been having with Alistair," he said, "I've been thinking of forming an alliance of my own, the Limp Dicks."

"The A.O.H.," I said, "will welcome you with open arms."

Over Leonard's shoulder I saw Kay Pesky and Serena Crawfoot come in. "What?" he said, turning to see what had made me react.

Kay was radiant, I mean glorious, I mean visionary, although no vision could equal it, reality as usual more arresting than any substitute. I must have been in a susceptible mood: her sudden appearance had the effect on me of a football helmet to the solar plexus. Man, there hasn't been any moon-luminous skin like that since Marilyn Monroe died. And her outfit showed plenty of it: a black sheath hanging loosely from spaghetti straps cut short above knees as intricate and trim as a good sonnet, a pair of shoes consisting in each case of a sole, a high heel, a couple of straps. And that's all she was wearing, far as I could see.

Her calves curved out boldly from below those famous knees on both sides of her shinbones and then narrowed modestly to ankles as neat and complex as a good triolet. Her toenail polish matched her lipstick. Her shoulders, her shoulders! They glowed as from a source of light beneath the skin. There is more flesh on them than fashion would allow, but the flesh is shaped by a musculature hitherto concealed from the world. I shall not discuss her cleavage out of consideration for your fleshless condition. I shall only record an impulse to dive into it. Kay had finally hit on the right hairstyle for her, a French braid, the hair drawn back to show off those world-historical Slavic cheekbones. She saw us and smiled broadly, oh Joel! And nudging Serena, walked over.

"Hello there, big boy," she said, " 'lo, Leonard."

"Hi, guys," said Serena.

"I like your dress," said Leonard, beating me to the draw.

"Zee brought it back from Italy," she said.

I cursed him, but silently.

"He said that anybody as white as I am should wear black," she said.

"And anybody black as I am should wear white, then?" said Leonard. "In December, too? Where is that wop?"

"You two would make a striking couple," said Serena and who asked for her two cents?

"Your hair is perfect," I said, trying to recover lost ground.

"Serena put it up for me," said Kay, nodding to that lady-in-waiting, who blushed.

"You ought to let Serena style your hair, Wynn," said Leonard. "There's no reason why you have to look like a hick."

"I'd love to," said Serena. "I see flowing locks down to the shoulder." Yeah, and if she's so smart, why doesn't she do something about her own hair, cut short, parted in the middle, curving under her chin like the bottom halves of parentheses?

"Make him look like Custer's last stand," said Leonard.

Just to be touching her, I took Kay by the elbow. "Drink?" I said.

"Seltzer," she said. "I'm on the wagon."

I filled her glass, filled Leonard's and mine.

"I'll have one of those," said Serena.

We held up our glasses to each other and turned to the spectacle of our colleagues at play.

Harriet Grice was still circulating, in a figure eight, Marshall at the point where the lines crossed, a little shaky on her pins, spilling her vodka. Zeno Confalone was saying something to make Felicia Zhang smile, a good reason for saying something. Felicia was there as head of EMU (pronounced "eemoo"), the English Majors Union. From their attitudes, I would say that Amabelle Bloor, wearing a flowered tent, leaning on the skull-crusher knob of her cane, was laying down the law to Bertil Lund and Malcolm Tetrault. Her head was forward, her pursed and wrinkled lips splatting out words. Amabelle must have come with Angel, for who else would have brought her? From their attitudes, I would say that Marshall Grice was saying something to make Monika Wright and Irene Howland feel good about this party for which they had done most of the work. Derwood Bobbie and Willi Heinfangl, the latter pale and frail, were exchanging what I took to be their usual banalities wrapped in Christian Humanist smiles. Teddy Nakatani was earnestly explaining something to Ziggy Sensum (ponytail and flannel shirt), how to build a cuckoo clock from found materials, maybe. I once again reminded myself to seek Teddy out, say something friendly to him. Lizzie Arno and Katie Campbell were face-to-face, leaning forward, the better to hear, until, in unison, they turned solemn and speculative eyes my way. Murray Weinrein in tango dancer's haircut and striped suit was standing next to the provost, counting the house.

The hum, burble, and susurration rose in pitch and volume. Here a shriek, there a bellow, of laughter, there a titter that ran the mixolydian scale. There was no tink, clink of glasses, I am sorry to say, for we were drinking out of plastic. Groups broke apart and reformed, singletons flowing around them like a virus in the bloodstream looking for a compatible cell to invade. Harriet Grice dropped her glass, bent over to pick it up, could not find it among all the legs. Lois Barker, cheerful to a fault, sat down at the piano, began to pound out some eight to the bar. Ziggy Sensum pulled Lisbet Arno away from Katriona Campbell, whirled her around, fell into a fair imitation of the Lindy Hop. Lizzie, laughing at herself, unsolicitous of her own dignity, hampered by her tailored skirt, confident of the steps, but with the lumpish European sense of rhythm, let it all hang out. People began to clap in tempo, but on the downbeat. Zeno Confalone, deadpan, boogied with Felicia Zhang, smiling brilliantly.

Kay, letting me have an elbow in the ribs, said, "Come on, let's show them how."

A sense of something heavy and disorganized fell on us in mid-stride, an irregularly spreading silence, a voice in protest, another querulous and questioning, a laugh sounding out like a broken guitar string. The revelers, in a widening circle, moved back from something in the middle of the room, knocking Harriet Grice on her behind. It was Hector Suarez, looking like that portentous figure in Poe's story. He swung his head around, searching for something—for me, as it turned out. He came over, put a hand on my shoulder, looked at Kay, said, "I've got to borrow the professor here," steered me through the swinging doors.

"You going to read me my rights?" I said.

"There's a couple of things you could maybe clear up for me," he said.

"I think of it as my professional duty to muddy the waters," I said, for like other professors, I get pompous with strong drink.

"We got us another murder," he said.

"Triple Jesus!" I said: "Who?"

"Irenaus von Hartmann, Lamont Ingersoll Professor of Religion," he said.

"Is it Blinky?" I said."

"Blinky?" he said.

"His nickname," I said.

"There's another poem—I guess that's what it is—and I want you to look it over," he said. "And I want to know how Blinky and Ms. Jones fit together."

"First thing tomorrow morning," I said.

"First thing tonight," he said.

"Can't," I said. "I've got a dinner date after the party."

"Break it," he said.

"Not this date," I said.

A slow evil smile took over his face. "I can see what you mean," he said. "Does Cousin Julie know about your blonde bombshell there?"

"What's it to you?" I said.

"Don't be a hard-on," he said. "What's the matter, you don't want to see this guy caught? Who knows, you could be next."

"Unless I'm the perp," I said.

"Don't make me beg," he said. "You don't want to put people in that position. They never stop looking for ways to get back at you. Besides, it lacks class."

"Why me?" I said. "There's still other people around who can read a poem."

"You're the only civilian knows about the other poem," he said. "I want you to rub them together, see what kind of sparks fly. That's one thing. The other is you're the only one of these ninnies here I can get to talk my language."

Something in my attitude must have signified indecision (my métier), for Hector said, "You make your excuses while I speak to your boss and his helpers. I'll say this, when it comes to keeping records, compared to the English Department, those people in Religion are nowhere."

Kay accepted my invitation to step out for a cigarette. "I've been cutting down," she said, as she took one of my smokes. "I start smoking an hour later every day. I'm up to three p.m."

"You on a health kick?" I said.

"It's related to the surprise I have for you," she said. "Have you been trying to guess what it is?"

"I've been thinking of nothing else," I said.

"Don't bullshit me, Wynn O'Leary," she said.

"There's been another murder, Kay," I said. "Suarez thinks that as vice-chair I may be on top of some information that will help him link the two cases."

"My God," she said. "Anyone we know?"

"Blinky Hartmann," I said.

"Poor little guy," she said. "If there ever was a harmless human being, Blinky.... Does that mean our dinner is off?"

"I can tell Suarez to go fuck himself," I said. "One day won't—"

"I was counting on candlelight, a nice restaurant, a new dress, a phrase whispered in your ear," she said, " 'brandy at my place.' "

"I'll tell Suarez to stick—" I said, starting to turn.

She pulled me back. "Listen to me, Wynn," she said. "I want to have a baby. I've been obsessing about it all summer."

"I know the feeling," I said, for I was too flabbergasted to come up with the needed words.

"I want you to be the father," she said.

Are you laughing at me, Joel? You do realize, don't you, what she was offering me? The answer is rebirth, a new life, never mind access to her flesh, no insignificant matter. For myself, I was not laughing. I was flustered and I was ready to strangle my limp dick.

"I believe you have good genes," she said, while I was still trying to figure out what I could say that would be equal to the occasion. "I don't think you are fat by nature, but by, because of... disappointment. I've already started working out with a personal trainer."

She lifted her face to give me a long, serious look, and I may be imagining it, but it seems to me that had I bent just a little bit I could finally have kissed her on the lips. "I can see that I'm going about this the wrong way," she said. "I was always too busy going after straight A-pluses, and then tenure, to learn pillow talk. Any junior high school student could do it better."

The best part of me reached me out to give her a hug, a touch vehement maybe, and I didn't give a shit who was looking. "I can't father a child and then walk away from it," I said. Do you think, Joel, that a fairly strong man can knock himself out with an uppercut to the jaw?

"You don't have to walk away," she said.

"Uncle Winnie to my own child?" I said.

"You can be as involved as you want," she said. "I've got the top floor of my town house closed off, that's right," in the attitude of someone who had just thought of something, "three rooms, your own bath." Then she caught herself, looked off into the middle distance. "I'm not asking you to marry me," this proud woman said, and in a little voice that would break the heart of anyone in possession of such an organ.

I gave her a squeeze, a failure of imagination, made her vertebrae pop, and the two women smoking on the other side of the stoop can report me to Anita Hill if they want. "Just a little shperm," Kay said, her mouth smushed against my breast pocket. "Let go," she said, and pushed off.

"I'm at a loss, Kay," I said. "No one's ever paid me such a compliment before."

"I ovulate in twenty-three days," she said. "It's best to get to work a couple of days before, that's what my book says. That gives you three weeks to make up your mind. If you don't like the idea, I can get Zeno to help me out at a moment's notice."

I had a vision: I broke Zeno in half, then broke the halves into half, then tossed the pieces into the Hudson River, amid the other debris.

She placed her hand, her fingers spaced, on my ample bosom. "I was just thinking what with us both being blonde and getting along so well," she said, softening, "and my father says you look like a stand-up guy, which phrase," and here her lips loosened into something very close to a smile, "stands at the apex of his lexicon of praise."

"I have a little problem . . . ," I said.

"Now's the time," she said, "and there's no reason for you to look so hangdog. This way I can have my baby in the spring. If it's a boy, we'll call him 'Joel.' During the summer baby and I can get to know each other at my father's place on the shore, where the living's easy. You're invited, of course. And next fall you can give me a two-day schedule. I'm not going to be an absentee Mama."

"I can see you put a lot of thought into this," I said.

"That's what I want you to do," she said.

"If thinking could solve my problem," I said.

"Hush," she said, putting a finger across my lips. "Go now and do your guy thing with Suarez. I'll catch something to eat with Serena."

"Well . . . ," I said.

"Hush," she said. "We'll talk after the weekend."

Well, well, here it is way past my lunchtime. That's what comes of eating breakfast. I'm going to clean up and go out for an early supper. There's an aspiring diner I go to, not because the food is any good, but because I like the waitress who works the smoking section. Of course she has a nice ass. Don't ask foolish questions. I once told her she had a New York face, by which I meant quick and sharp, and she said, well, you got a mountain man's body, comfy on a cold night. I know she would go out with me if I asked. And what then? Say, Joel, how do you like the idea of being reincarnated as my son?

11

Here I am again,

my belly full, a middling cure for anxiety, the Ka-Bar before me, the model 12 behind. My favorite waitress, twitching her masterpiece of a derriere, said try the stuffed pork chops, so I did: two large shoulder chops under mounds of ready-made stuffing, a half-bushel of mashed potatoes with a crater full of gravy out of a can, a concoction of winter squash and stewed tomatoes, all served on a crowded platter the size of Achilles' shield. To my left a salad, to my right corn fritters swimming in ersatz maple syrup. Do you think that slimming down, laying off the sauce, giving up cigarettes would make me whole again? Getting in shape might restore my old self-confidence as a physical entity, without which confidence no man can be an adequate lover. Naw, women would just get wary of me again. Besides I only began to get fat *after* two years of sexual failure, after Belinda and I split up. You have to understand, my hooking up with Kay would bring material advantages, as well as the other kind, shall we call them "spiritual"?

She has more than enough money for both us of us, and baby makes three. I could retire, or at least take a year off, write your biography. Its plot: white boy tries to make it in the black world of bop.

Do you remember that horrible scene you told me about, when Max Roach and Oscar Pettiford denounced you for feeding off black music, appropriating its angers? You would think they'd be used to it. No, what am I talking about?—I'd write a film script, the score's the thing, put together from a closet full of tapes you left me. Picture it: as the credits come on we hear the Reboppers play the opening bars of your jazzification of "Bolero."

The screen is dark, but somehow has a pulse in it. Phosphenes glimmer, flash, streak. Screen right: the credits blink on. They are written in blue neon tubing. They continue to blink off and on while at screen left Sidney and his bass viol suddenly appear, in an amber light. He plucks a note; then up a fifth, down an octave, up a fourth, repeats, keeps repeating till you feel slightly delirious. Suddenly Spider and his drums appear next to Sidney in the same amber light: Tat tatata Tat Tatata tatata Tat, lightly, brightly. Carol and her vibraharp appear on the other side of Sidney. She is wearing a black sheath, spaghetti straps, shoulders gleaming, playing chords on top of Sidney's bass figure. Smoky and his rowdy tenor blink on, screen center, playing the A theme, sticking to the melody. He fades, some bars of the rhythm playing alone, upping the volume, until you appear in his place, blowing your funky first statement of the B theme, funky to begin with, a gas, man.

Here's my definition of funk: It's 2 a.m. You're in a roadhouse tavern in Mississippi. Outside it is still 85 degrees in the moonshade, for the moon is full, the air turgid as it can get without relieving itself in rain. Inside, there is no air conditioning and the joint is jammed. The atmosphere is all smoke, sweat, and pheromones. For five hours you've been digging the blues, drinking beer, dancing dirty. Consider the condition of your crotch and armpits. That's funk.

And that's what you put into your first statement of the B theme. From there the Reboppers build, Sidney dry-humping his bass, Carol's shoulders slick with sweat, Spider laying down a beat on the rivet cymbal that grabs you like an undertow, his other hand a blur, dropping bombs, cymbal smashes, rim shots, one foot working the bass drum, the other working the high hat, the amber light reddening, Smoky blowing wilder and wilder solos on the A theme, then swaying in tempo, riffing behind you in a series of descending figures, all flatted thirds, fifths, sevenths, each starting on a higher note, and you, you work toward that manic key change and Dizzy's famous lick, biddleyadip, biddleyadip, biddleya deeeEEE, explosions in the brain above high C, the climax. Hoo boy. Then a quick diminuendo and out.

The credits fade and the lights come on. The Reboppers are playing on a portable platform in a skanky high school gym. A double handful of students applaud without enthusiasm.

Enough daydreaming! Still, I wouldn't want to get too puritanical about it. The adaptive function of fantasy is to give us in our imaginations what we can't get in the flesh but need for life to be worth living. That is also what literature is for.

On Thursday night, Hector Suarez and I were settled comfortably in my study, he on one side of the desk, me on the other, he with a cigar, that cop affectation, me with a cigarette, and he said, "Got anything to eat?" So I went into the kitchen and found my chub of bologna amid Julie's containers of tabouli and grape leaves and pesto and kumquats. While I was slicing the bologna, Julie came up silently and put a hand on my bicep, and damn me if I didn't nearly lop off a thumb, for my interview with Kay had left me jumpy. "Let me make the sandwiches," she said. "I want to."

"This Irenaus von Blinky was queer, right?" said Hector.

"We never discussed his sexual orientation," I said.

"This whole place is queer," he said. "You got a guy in your own department teaching a course in the Fag Hag, did you know that?"

"Try to rope Ziggy in, and he'll leave for the coast in a minute," I said. "He can get a job wherever he wants."

"I understand there's a whodunit out with a guy a lot like you in it who's queer," he said. "That's what's *good* about him."

"The author doesn't like heterosexual men," I said.

"I haven't got time to horse around, Slim," he said. "Who was Blinky fucking?"

There was not much point in trying to protect Blinky's memory. He would not thank me for waffling about his sexual bent, which he considered superior to the usual thing, more aristocratic-like, you know. "My understanding is that Professor von Hartmann was celibate during the school year," I said, "but flew to Morocco the minute we had a break of more than a few days."

At that moment Julie came in, holding twin little fancy trays Belinda had not bothered to take with her. On each tray were a napkin, a bottle of beer, and a mug, nice of Julie to frost the mugs up for us. And on the trays were two arriviste party plates, cost Belinda seventy bucks apiece, and I can't imagine where Julie found them, for I once spent an hour looking for them myself, wanting to take them to Fern Hill Farm, for target practice. On each plate was an artistically arranged sandwich, cut in three, the pieces interspersed with a pickle, two radishes, an orange slice, and in the center a sprig of parsley.

"Listen to me, Cousin Julie," Hector said, taking his tray, "if he doesn't treat you right, get in touch with me. I'll bust him for criminal stupidity." Julie looked at me as though expecting something.

"Beautiful," I said. "Why is it, the better food looks, the better it tastes?" From the satisfied look on Julie's face, I gather that I had said the right thing.

"Synesthesia," she said, over her shoulder, as she left, a knockout punch line, but she had skimped on the mayonnaise and the bologna.

"Don't be shy now," said Hector, "just tell me everything you know about Blinky."

You have to visualize the man, Joel, to feel the pathos of his death: short, pear-shaped, sixtyish, pink (especially between the stray tufts of blond hair), round-lensed glasses, always a three-piece suit, hands in pockets, rocking on his heels and toes, a stern manner. He was called "Blinky," but not to his face, because of a mannerism or twitch. He would open his mouth into an oval on its side, open his eyes so wide that the balls looked ready to roll out, hold the position for two beats, then clamp his eyes and mouth shut, the latter now about the size of a bullet hole.

Felicia Zhang, laughing, tolerant, not meaning to be a snitch but to share the fun, once told me about a class (Religion UC3232x: Medieval Schismatics) she took with Blinky. His teaching method, which he announced in a now-hear-this voice on the first day of class, was "strictly Socratic," a method we all use when hung over or otherwise derelict, for it takes less effort to ask questions, or even answer them, than to prepare a lecture. He would walk up and down the aisles, one hand in a pocket, stopping now and then to rest a hand on an athlete's shoulder, all the while answering the question not quite asked him. When, by and by, inspired by his own words, an out-of-the-way question occurred to him, he would draw himself up, interrupt himself in mid-sentence, and pose his stumper in an achtung voice, looking around, challenge in his eye, lower lip outthrust, until some student entered into the spirit of the thing by answering a question Blinky had not quite asked.

If he liked the answer (or the student) he would say, "Give that man a ten!" even if the student was a woman, blink, point with the hand that wasn't in his pocket to his "Recorder," the best-looking male student in the class (in this case named "Alistair"), who would put a "ten" next to the answerer's name in a roll book. If he didn't like the answer, he would say, "Give the dummkopf a four." Felicia was convinced that Blinky never glanced at the roll book when entering grades at the term's end. Male students who handed in their term papers received an A; females an A-minus; the Recorder an A-plus, no matter who answered what questions how. It was generally suspected that Blinky never read the term papers, which he did not return, his office crowded with thirty years' worth of them, to prevent future plagiarism, he said.

I've been on a few orals examinations and dissertation defenses with Blinky. On orals he always asks the same questions, whatever the student's field. And he always interrupts my questions about *Ulysses* with the same stumper: "Why in the 'Circe' episode does Bloom's mother carry a bicycle pump?" (The fact is that she doesn't.) On dissertations he always asks a question or two about the footnotes or bibliography, not having read the rest, thus enhancing a reputation for a hard-nosed scholarly severity that exists only in his own mind. Mostly his colleagues treat him as a dog-lover would treat his wife's sick cat when the wife was present. But I have never heard anyone express a strong animus toward him—except maybe Angel Terrasco.

Blinky once wrote a defense of the Spanish Inquisition that lingered too long, in my opinion, on the instruments of interrogation. Angel, who usually gets the words right but the melody wrong, missed both the campy overtones and the salacious undertones; she wrote him a fan letter. His snotty return note implied that her scholarship was unequal to the occasion.

"Someone felt enough animus," said Hector, "to drive a Ka-Bar through the crown of his skull, through the roof of his mouth, through his tongue, and out that ticklish spot under your chin, nailed his mouth shut, you might say."

"Those who live by the word die by the sword," I said.

"You sure about Morocco?" he said.

"There was a near-scandal about a dozen years ago, when these things could still be hushed up," I said. "Some student complained to the College dean that Blinky molested him. The story I heard is that Blinky called the student over to his apartment for a conference, but wound up spritzing Reddi-wip along the student's posterior buccal rift and then licking it out. The triumvirate of deans from SAS, GAS, and YOOK put it to him: one more incident with a student and he's unemployed and unemployable. So Blinky goes to Morocco."

"They had to do something," Hector said: "that Reddi-wip is

nasty stuff. We found something in Blinky's posterior buccal rift, but it wasn't spritz."

Well, I asked Hector about that and he asked me about this and I asked him about the other thing and from the back-and-forth I got a sketchy picture of what the police think happened. The Departmental Administrator over in Religion there was not worried when Blinky failed to appear for his classes on Tuesday, for Blinky had similarly failed before, for Blinky had chronic and debilitating heartburn, and she was not worried when Blinky failed to answer the telephone, for Blinky never answered the telephone on those days when he skipped classes. She was not worried when Blinky failed to appear on Wednesday, for Blinky never appeared on Wednesdays, even if summoned to an important meeting by his chairman. But when Blinky failed to appear for his classes on Thursday, the Administrator thought she better do something, if only to cover her ass, just in case, you know. So she sends her work-study underling over to Blinky's apartment with an official note to the super, for Blinky was not important enough to live in a building with a doorman. What the work-study slavey saw when the super let him in nearly soiled his posterior buccal rift.

The way the police worked it out, Blinky had come to the door in response to a knock or a buzz. He recognized the perp, let him in, turned around to lead him into the living room, at which point he was Ka-Barred. According to the M.E., Blinky would certainly have twitched a bit, would quite likely have thrashed about in convulsions, before dying. The perp then dragged Blinky into the living room, the Ka-Bar still in his head, for there were only a few scattered drops of blood. He then removed Blinky's pants and briefs, and very pretty briefs they were, red, yellow and blue paisley on a heliotrope background, but he did not remove Blinky's undershirt, shirt, tie, vest, or suit jacket, the shirt, now decorated with blood from the exit wound under Blinky's chin. Did I get the picture? I would be particularly interested in what happened next, according to Hector.

The murderer looped an electric cord he had ripped from a lamp around Blinky's neck; he tied one end of the cord with a slip knot around Blinky's right ankle and drew it tight; he then tied the other end of the cord around Blinky's left ankle and drew it tight, thus folding him like a jackknife, his feet by his ears. He then yanked the Ka-Bar out of Blinky's skull, blood oozing, rather than spurting, placed the briefs over Blinky's face, so he wouldn't have to look at him, and fucked him up his posterior buccal rift, poetic justice, in Hector's opinion.

There's a touch of the artist about our perp. He apparently did not think Blinky looked his best, too much blank space, if I knew what Hector meant. So he did some cosmetic surgery. With the Ka-Bar he cut lines radiating out from Blinky's anus—like a sunburst in a cartoon.

"Like a cat's whiskers?" I said.

"You could say that," Hector said.

Like a mouth with wrinkled lips, I said to myself.

That had to be the way it went down, for there were dried traces of the same kind of gunk that the crime scene guys had swabbed out of Terry. The swabs from Terry, when analyzed, proved to be the kind of lubricant you get with condoms. What kind of condom no one could say, for there were few suppliers of lubricant, but many makes of condom. Because Blinky had a conversation on the telephone with his mother and her caretaker, the police knew that he was still alive on Saturday night. He had spoken of being in his pajamas, pouring himself a glass of edelweiss, getting ready to watch a video cassette of an old Joan Crawford movie. From a cursory look at Blinky's maggots, what stage they were at in their life cycle, the M.E. figures Blinky died Sunday, maybe Monday. Hector was leaning toward Sunday, for it was well known that Blinky always wore a black three-piece suit, a white shirt, and a homburg to church. Did Blinky ever make it to church? That's easy to find out.

"Where were *you* Sunday?" Hector said.

"Right here," I said.

"Just you and Cousin Julie," he said.

"She went to Jones Beach," I said. "What have you learned about the Ka-Bar that killed Terry?"

It turns out that when all the metalwork on a Ka-Bar is finished, an inspector looks it over, and if satisfied, scratches his mark on the tang under the handle leather. The mark on the first Ka-Bar was made by an inspector who retired nearly ten years ago, after thirty years with the company. But the company historian, Norman Bates there, says that over the years the molecular structure of the metal and the method of processing the leather have changed. He'll pin down when the knife was made and who was the distributor, if not the retailer, yet. Hector surmised that the company historian did not have enough to do.

"Did Blinky ever spritz Terry, do you think?" he said.

"Their sexual inclinations, I would say, were neither parallel nor complementary," I said.

"Isn't there this female professor of English," he said, "goes around giving lectures on the pleasure of taking it up the ass from queers?"

"There is," I said. "Sometimes, Heck, this whole rigmarole of sex gets tedious."

"You see what I'm after," he said. "What did they have in common that made the killer go after *them*, rather than say you, or nobody?"

"Blinky and Terry had about the minimum musculature required to keep you upright and ambulatory," I said.

"Might be something there," Hector said. "We know the perp is chickenshit already, cause he only buggers his victims after they're dead."

"Both were of a certain age," I said.

"Might figure in," said Hector. "You think maybe they're the age of the perp's parents?"

"Both professors, both tenured professors, both tenured professors at this university, both—" I said.

"Queer," said Hector.

"Medievalists," I said.

"They have the same shtick?" he said.

"You've got to know more than I do to get this right," I said. "But loosely, Terry was interested in the craziness that underlies orthodoxy, the culture of convents and monasteries. Blinky was interested in what he considered the higher sanity of heterodoxy, Cathars, Beghards, Fifth Monarchy Men, Brethren of the Free Spirit, flagellants, and other such crazies."

"So what does that mean," he said, "they broke off diplomatic relations?"

"They couldn't," I said. "Their world was too small. They worked mostly with the same few graduate students, worked on the same orals and dissertation defenses, attended the same professional conferences, read the same journals, were probably on the same editorial boards, no matter that Terry thought Blinky was a fraud and Blinky thought Terry lacked intellectual discipline, being a woman."

"They ever fuck over the same student?" he said. "I'm speaking figuratively, of course."

"You have those lists Irene gave you," I said. "See if they were ever together on an orals or defense that failed someone. It doesn't happen often, but it happens."

"That's how many years down the drain?" he said.

"In the case of a defense," I said, "six to ten, sometimes more."

"Could piss you off," he said.

"It's not down the drain," I said. "The student could get a degree of M. Phil. by way of consolation."

"What's it good for?" he said.

"A part-time job as an adjunct, maybe," I said, "at two thousand dollars per course."

"Those lists don't tell me the outcomes of the exams," he said.

"I imagine Monika told Irene to hold them back," I said. "Monika's a stickler for confidentiality."

"Goes with being queer," he said.

"Let's see the poem," I said. "Maybe I can still get in a nightcap with my date."

Hector put down his cigar, reached for his gun, as I thought, but pulled out a sheet of paper, on which, in his neat hand, were written the following winged words:

The Ploys of Autumn

If your rump dump a lump of clay
Do not go humble into that great fright:
Young rage should curse and kill at time to pray.
I am the wight to right this blight.

Hi, ho, the jism and the jolly,
For they are full and foreign in the pouch.
I am the dark denier where I crouch
And drifting doomward in my folly.

They divide the night and day with fairy thumbs
And break a kiss in no love's quarry.
We punch black holes in radiant suns
Like lightless Lucifers, but are we?

Man in his maggot's barren.
For roadkill, send the raven.

"Who put a bug up his ass?" Hector said when I looked up.

"It's an irregular sonnet," I said.

"Is that so?" he said.

"It used to be a sonnet was typically a love poem," I said. "But this one is a dark denier.... The final couplet ... with its lame rhythm ... the missing feet ... the off-rhyme ... it's like ending 'Pop Goes the Weasel' with a flatted fifth."

"Spare me the poetry," he said. "What does it say?"

"You have to understand that it's a pastiche of three poems by Dylan Thomas, mainly 'The Boys of Summer,'" I said.

"Thank you, Professor O'Leary," he said.

"In Thomas' poem, an old-timer, apparently, accuses the boys of being profligate and perverse," I said. "They answer him back. Then the boys and the oldster exchange one-liners. 'Oh see the poles are kissing as they cross.' They exchange positions, for every position contains its own contradiction."

"Who are these boys may I ask?" he said.

"Probably sperm," I said.

"Just give me the fucking original, and I'll work it out myself," he said.

I pulled the *Collected Poems* off the shelf, found "The Boys," handed the volume over to Hector.

"Why doesn't he just spit it out?" Hector said, reading.

"He's trying to say a lot of things at once," I said. "His words are fully loaded, like, too often, the poet himself."

"So he was a souse," he said. "Maybe that explains it. Wasn't he a Welshman?"

"He was," I said.

"And Yeats was Irish," he said, "like your father."

"All too Irish," I said.

"That doesn't necessarily make him a bad person," he said. "And Blake."

"Well, at least Yeats tried to claim him for Ireland," I said.

"You know anyone but you who's Welsh-Irish around here?" he said.

"I'm in a majority of one," I said.

"In a sentence, and no fucking around, what does this pistachio as you called it say?" he said.

"The speaker describes himself as a scourge who is part of the blight he wants to wipe out," I said.

"Then he too breaks a kiss—" Hector said.

"—instead of a fart—" I said.

"—in no love's quarry," he said. "Typical. What about the other two masterpieces this hard-on pistachioed?"

"The killer's first line is a send-up of 'If my head hurt a hair's foot,' in which a fetus tells his mother that if he is interfering with her sex life, she should abort him," I said. "She nixes that. She goes for the pain of life over the peace of death. The next three lines are a take-off on 'Do Not Go Gentle into That Good Night,' in which Thomas tells his dying father not to die without making a fuss."

"Much good it would do you," Hector said.

"You recover any sperm?" I said. "Maybe this guy's a secretor."

"Not a molecule, not a pubic hair," he said. "The FBI have a guy in their files who shaved his bush. One thing we did is, we stuck a cantaloupe on a broomstick, and had one of the squad hold it so it was exactly Blinky's height. It turns out a tall guy standing back a bit comes in with a Ka-Bar the same angle as a short guy standing up close."

Julie knocked on the open door. When I looked up and Hector corkscrewed in his chair, she took a step in, waving her hand before her face, letting out two fake coughs, ack, ack. "I just wanted to remind you," she said to me, "we have homework to do."

"I've got to go anyway," Hector said, standing, as Julie left the room. "You want to be careful you don't overtax yourself, Slim—homework with Cousin Julie and nightcaps with Big Blonde. If you got any strength left write me a close reading of the poem. Try to picture the guy behind it. I'll be by tomorrow, around suppertime, to pick it up."

"I'm heading north for the weekend tomorrow," I said.

"You could have let me know," he said. "Did it ever occur to you I might like a weekend in the country? How far are you from Hylas Cutlery?"

"Maybe forty miles," I said.

"I ought to make you take the second Ka-Bar to my man there," he said.

"Come on, I'll walk you to your car, get some fresh air," I said, and the air was worth breathing, thin and cool. East Harlem was bright and surreal on the far side of the park, under a layer of clouds illuminated from below by the electric city. The streets and sidewalks were deserted, except for a derelict asleep on a bench along the park wall and a rollerblader, macho in her pads, gloves, helmet, moving fast on scissor legs. The leaves rustled and showed their pale undersides.

"You know that crackpot walks her dogs along here?" Hector said. "She's maybe five feet tall, skinny, earmuffs and sunglasses the year round."

"She takes in strays from the park, 'orphans' she calls them."

"So you know," he said. "To give her credit, she feeds the mutts, housebreaks them if necessary, takes them to the vet if they need it, cleans them up, you know, with a bath and brushing, then poses them for snapshots, I mean it. Then she goes door to door with the Polaroids, and if you don't take in one of the mutts, she lays a curse on you. Well, she was over to the precinct the other day, raising the dust. She says there's guys across the park catch strays and throw them to their pit bulls for sparring partners."

"She's got an overheated imagination," I said, "popping her brain cells. She once told me she'd like to go through East Harlem, house by house, with a flamethrower."

"I've noticed myself," Hector said, "that the more you're an animal lover, the less you like humans."

"Unless you're like me," I said, "and it's the animal in humans you like best about them."

"The reason the dogwoman was at the precinct is she found this stray bitch and four pups with their heads cut off," he said, "nice dogs, mostly golden retriever, she said. She wanted us to do something about it, put them together again I think. The guys we radioed to go over and look said the mutts were all killed by a single stab with a big knife between the ribs and into the heart."

"Did they find a poem?" I said.

"They were killed somewhere else—we could only backtrack so far—then dragged to where the dogwoman found them," he said. "Then they were relieved of their heads."

"But not buggered, I hope," I said.

"Someone got rid of the carcasses before I thought to go over and look-see," he said.

"Next you're going to tell me the retriever had a reputation for going both ways," I said.

"I'm telling you that if the word's around that you're queer, this guy could come after you," he said.

"He might get to me, but Julie would flatten him with her wok," I said, as Hector unlocked his car door, and right then I decided to go for the homework, rather than for the nightcap. Facing Kay would be complicated, whereas nuzzling Julie would be comforting, foreplay without consummation, like life itself. Besides, as it suddenly came to me, during our first session I had not by a long shot done justice to Julie's long lean latissimus dorsi, as they ran in two elegant lines from under her arms to the small of her back.

"While you're up there among the vegetables," Hector said, getting into his car, "do me an *explication de texte*—that's what you guys call it, isn't it?"

"It used to be," I said.

Julie was waiting for me when I got home, and we spent a long time together in the shower, soaping each other, as though putting something off, and I kept telling myself that my habit of anxious watchfulness was the enemy, although it's what made me a good enough linebacker to get my tuition paid. (Have you ever noticed how when you try to talk yourself out of a mood you intensify it?) While she put on her finishing touches, I slipped "Funky Blues" into the boombox, something romantic. I would have been content to wrap myself around Julie and breathe her in for an hour or two, but she got me right to work, demystifying the female body, as I think she thought we were doing. It took me a while to get to her latissimus dorsi, for on the way I discovered her triceps, which, and I know this is hard to believe, I had completely neglected the first time around.

I regret to inform you that while Julie was doing me, I broke Rule One: I let my mind wander—to Kay's proposition. 1) Did I love

Kay? 2) Did Kay love me? 3) What is this thing called love? 4) Who cares? 5) Kay is a feminist. 6) What about my little problem? 6) Join the Foreign Legion? 7) A father is not a superfluous man. 8) Kay's flesh. With the concept of flesh came a picture, for I am a visile, as you are an audile, and with the picture came a pang of guilt, as though I were being unfaithful to Julie, whose flesh was there in the flesh, so to speak, and with the pang came a return of my thoughts to the here and now, where a miracle was in progress, for I was erect within Julie's lightly stroking fist, the first time in nine years that my treacherous go-between had held its head up when surrounded by alien flesh. The instant I became aware of this miracle, it ended, as though it had never occurred, for a miracle in retrospect is hard to distinguish from a mirage. I did, however, receive a consolatory kiss on the drooping head of my ex-miracle.

When I was once again stretched out on my belly and she was stretched out on my back, I initiated our post-coital chat, for it was time I stopped playing the churl with Julie: "Do you still feel that *The Odyssey* was written by a woman?"

"I can't talk to you about *The Odyssey* anymore, you being an expert and all," she said. "It would be cheating."

"Right now you probably know more about *The Odyssey* than I do," I said, for if you can't do the gallant with a naked woman reposing on your back, when can you?

"I'm thinking of doing my term paper on *The Odyssey*," she said.

"It's early," I said. "At least wait until you've read *The Oresteia*."

"I want to get my term paper out of the way, so I can concentrate on finding a career," she said.

"You've got lots of time for that," I said.

"I've been spending some time every day at the placement office," she said. "They've got piles and piles of books, brochures, government handouts, job descriptions from corporations and the FBI. You can learn what you need to study, how to get started, how to do an interview, write your resume, do your makeup, how much you can make—it's very interesting."

"Anything turn you on?" I said.

"SAS has this new program in food services," she said.

Damn it Joel, in spite of myself I let out a groan. It happened before I knew it was happening.

"What's the matter?" she said: "feeding people is a useful occupation."

"The secret of life is to find a paying job that also satisfies some need," I said, and I can't help it, it's not so easy to stop being a professor just because a naked woman is stretched out on your back.

"You can be a chef, a nutritionist, a dietician, a caterer," she said. "If I work on my prose, I could even be a food critic. You could help—"

"Don't be a critic," I said.

"This SAS program gives you points for field work," she said, "not just chopping vegetables, and there's an affiliated summer program with Cornell."

Another groan escaped me.

"Would you miss me?" she said, her voice sexy, her lips against my ear.

Well, there was my opportunity. Am I mistaken in believing that Julie was asking for some kind of commitment? Maybe I'm missing something, but I can't think of anything that happened suddenly to make me decisive. "You know I would," I said, a response that, while not exactly churlish, would not have impressed Sir Walter Raleigh.

"Anyhow I haven't decided anything yet, except what I'm going to say about *The Odyssey*," she said. "Professor Confalone will love it. You know, I think he's a little soft on me."

I did not say a word, for I was on my good behavior. Julie slid halfway off my back, so that she was resting on her side, pulled the sheet up over us, and in roughly three seconds fell asleep. I lay still, for I could not toss and turn without dislodging Julie, trying to decide whether I could decide anything until I drifted off, undecided.

Remember that song, "Saturday Night Is the Loneliest Night in the Week?" Well, it's not for me anymore, now that I have you to talk to. I'm off to bed. Tomorrow morning, over coffee, for there are no spare ribs left, I shall try to tease out the latent content of the killer's poem, if there is any. There's not much poetry in the poem, outside of what the killer pilfered from Dylan Thomas, except maybe the last line, "For roadkill, send the raven," almost as good as "And no birds sing."

I'm a-coming, quoth the raven.

12

Julie was uncharacteristically silent and withdrawn on our way back to the city. "How did it go with your parents?" I said.

"Good," she said.

Turning off the air conditioner, pulling out my tape of the set Dizzy did with Sonny Rollins and Sonny Stitt, winding down the window, I modulated off the Henry Hudson onto 125th Street, and man, that rich Harlem air, thick with river and ocean, with exhaust and rap and barbecue and blowing scraps of paper, with scents from the nearby sewage treatment and meat-packing plants, the mixture of styles, Baptists dolled up for church, amazing hats, nihilists dressed down in tank tops and shorts looking to score, sharpies in neo-zootsuits, dead cats, death-defying pigeons, dying whores at work in tractor-trailers, jaywalkers moving slow with a fuck-you glare to piss off honking cabbies, the El crashing down like a rusty avalanche, the pigeon-toed kid with the sweatshirt rapping on my windshield when I stopped for the light on funky Broadway, tipping me a nod, the reality principle saying Give me some skin, Pops, and I returned the greeting by scat-vocalling a few bars of "Anthropology," Julie falling in with my mood, hunching over an air guitar, a shearsman of sorts, clanging out cords.

It's Sunday, just getting dark, for we had an early dinner, spinach salad, with chopped scallions and big pieces of raw mushrooms, oven-ready sourdough rolls ("You ever think of getting a microwave, Cuz?"), just enough to whet my appetite, and we had an early treatment for my little problem, during which I was allowed to touch the hot spots, but not to bring Julie off, and damn all saints and sinners alike, there goes the telephone.

"It's a student," said Julie, handing me the phone in such a way that the right pectoral muscle lifted her breast prettily.

"It is, is it?" I said.

"You will forgive me for disturbing you at home," said the voice of Teddy Nakatani.

"Not likely," I said, then remembered that I had resolved to be friendly.

"I am not calling about myself," he said.

"You can tell Ms. Zhang—" I said.

"I am calling about Irene Howland," he said.

I groaned.

"Last night I accompanied Irene Howland to the piano recital," he said.

"Good for you," I said.

"During a throbbing adaptation of 'Death and the Maiden' she began to cry, quietly at first," he said.

"It's not my kind of music either," I said.

"People began to look at us," he said. "There were murmurs. Professor Zutkin of Sociology, whom I always thought of as a coarse person, told Irene to shush."

"His breakthrough into intelligibility," I said.

"She only began to cry more noisily," he said. "I felt compelled to escort her out of the auditorium."

"That's right," I said. "Get her away from those pianos."

"I tried to extract some statement from her as to what was

wrong," he said, "but her words were so mingled with sobs and wails and a kind of high-pitched mewling that could not make them out. It was most distressing."

"Now, now," I said.

"I will not be an object on show for the idle curiosity of passersby," he said. "You can imagine the speculative glances."

"Well, if you want to be a teacher. . . ."

"Irene was in no condition to be left alone," he said.

"I'm afraid she never has been," I said.

"You have never been to my apartment, for dinner," he said. "I assure you that I am a skillful cook."

"You are omnicompetent," I said.

"My 'apartment' consists of a single room nine feet wide," he said. "At one end is a kitchenette, and next to it, in what was surely once a closet, a toilet bowl and a shower stall. At the other end, from wall to wall, is a length of plywood that serves as my desk and the table on which I eat my Spartan but nourishing meals."

"In legendary times the scholar's calling was always to monkish asceticism and dyspepsia," I said.

"Along one wall is a couch that opens into a bed," he said. "I coaxed Irene into it."

"Was that wise?" I said.

"She declined the soothing drink I made of green tea, sugar, lemon, and brandy," he said. "I am a teetotaler, but I have spirits for my guests."

"Irene was not herself," I said. "It is not like her to be an ungracious guest."

"All night long, while I tried to write a dissertation proposal for your evaluation, Irene mumbled, giggled, sighed, and cried, and occasionally dozed off," he said.

Teddy does not ask for sympathy in a way that makes offering it easy. "Where's Irene now?" I said.

"There was sunlight in the airshaft," he said, "and I was whipping up a cheese omelette for her—a proper omelette has no brown scorch on it, so you must attend—when I heard her distinctly say 'there's hair on the moon.' She then slept for six hours without moving or making a sound. The whole time I sat at my desk, scarcely moving. I did not even get up to relieve myself of the tea I had been drinking. Imagine!"

"I could have managed six minutes, maybe," I said.

"I have great faith in the restorative powers of sleep."

"Was your faith justified?" I said.

"When Irene awoke she was coherent," he said. "She asked whether I had slept with her. I was able to assure her that I had not."

"Was that what she wanted to hear?" I said.

"She immediately put on her shoes, which I had removed," he said, "and smoothed out her dress, which I had not . . . removed."

"Of course not," I said.

"She said she had to do something," he said, "and that no one could help her."

"I don't like the sound of that," I said.

"My attempts to detain her were of no avail," he said. "She did not want to talk. She did not want to eat. From personal experience I can say that a sauna or a long soak in a hot tub will often cast out tormenting demons. But I have no sauna or tub, no sauna or tub."

"She never said what was bothering her, I suppose," I said.

"The other day she said something without emphasis, you know, in a wondering kind of voice," he said. "One Christmas morning, she and her brother forgot to put their new toys away. Her father walked back and forth in front of the Christmas tree, crushing the toys along his way. She said it was the type of all her experiences with men. She had an off-center smile on her face that in my opinion was not healthy. In a failed attempt to divert her, I said it was the type of all my experiences with everything. It was then that we decided to attend the recital together. Felicia Zhang was somehow able to get me tickets. . . . But I am not aware of any man in her life."

"I'll call Murray," I said.

"I've already tried to get in touch with Professor Weinrein," he said. "Mrs. Weinrein informed me that he would not be available any time today."

"What do you recommend?" I said, for one of Teddy's many fields of expertise might well have included affairs of the heart.

"I tried to interest Irene in a therapist friend of mine, a remarkable woman," he said, "not the usual thing. I was then I learned that Irene is already under treatment, for depression apparently."

"I'll have Monika track down the therapist first thing tomorrow morning," I said.

"I was hoping you would call Irene yourself, this very evening," he said. "I gather that you have never stepped on her toys."

"Listen, Mr. Nakatani: in forty years I have never yet said anything that made a troubled woman feel better," I said. "It must be a missing gene."

"I am lightheaded from lack of sleep," he said. "Important business I was unable to sumconnate because of Irene weighs on my spirits. Yet I am determined to dit at my sesk until I have written you a dissertation proposal that will compel your enthusiastic participation."

"Take the night off," I said. "Drink some of that brandy. Watch Sunday night football to take your mind off your mind. Report to me tomorrow morning. You'll find me ditting at my sesk."

Scratch the surface of anyone who has survived puberty and you'll uncover at least one layer of misery. The point is that it's bad form to let the misery become visible. Tell it to St. Ursula, if you can't keep a wrap on it. I suppose that somewhere in the back of my mind I had hoped that these two waifs would find a haven in each other's arms. Let them go to California and raise artichokes for Teddy's father, where I wouldn't have to look at their doleful mugs. I can sympathize with everything except suffering, says a character in Oscar Wilde, whose superficialities run deep. I have my own weedy garden to tend. To each his own weeds to pull, or hers, yes hers, and by the dark of the moon, for the signal moon is zero in the void.

Okay, I know. I don't mean that, not entirely. After all, what is

Julie doing, if not yanking my weed? As I was about to tell you when Teddy interrupted, there are signs of progress. I was lying on my back, my eyes closed, trying out waffling phrases to use on Kay tomorrow, when I felt a sensation compared to which Marcel's experience with the petite madeleine was a twinge of heartburn. I opened my eyes and lifted my head, making all those unattractive wrinkles under my chin, to see that Julie had taken my weed into her mouth damn near to the root. I must say she had never looked prettier. (As you can see, I'm trying to recover some of that old male brutality.) I immediately went limp. You can judge the quality of the woman when I tell you that Julie did not act insulted. Nor did she wallow in sympathy.

"What goes up must come down," she said.

While Julie tinkled, for my effect on her seems to be diuretic, I assumed the position, for I am easily trained, give me your paw, sit, roll over. Julie climbed aboard, made herself comfortable, and the feel of her cheek on my shoulder blade was more stirring than our whole session of stroking and poking. I felt the anxiety float off me into the silence like protoplasm from a medium, but Julie finally spoke. "My father shrank," she said.

"As you get older the intervertebral disks—" I said.

"I mean he was like . . . diminished," she said. "He was, you know, *deferring* to me, like I was this big success from the big city and he was a poor relation. He seemed afraid to touch me even. When he opened the door and saw me, he didn't know what to do with himself, so he shook my hand. Can you imagine? And there were tears in his eyes when I told him I was going to college. You remember what he used to be like."

"Maybe he felt that when he started touching you he wouldn't be able to stop," I said.

"For God's sake, Cuz, he's my father," she said.

"Female beauty can be intimidating," I said.

"What's that you said?" she said.

"You're very beautiful," I said.

"I can't believe it," she said. "That's the first time you've paid me a compliment."

"Not everything has to be said," I said. "That's the first law of cohabitation."

"Nice things have to be said," she said, "or how would you know? 'Cohabitation...' that's a good one. Mom and dad were impressed when I told them we were cohabiting."

"You didn't—" I said.

"Tell them you were debauching me?" she said. "No. Not everything has to be said, right? I said you were putting me up until I get settled."

"Did you try to sell them the Yankee Stadium while you were at it?" I said.

"They want to believe something is going on between us," she said. "I could see it in their eyes. I think they hope you will save me from myself. Besides, my father thinks you're an OK guy. He says, no disrespect to your mother, but you can't be a real O'Leary."

"He doesn't know anything about me," I said. "It's just because I played football."

"It's because you're so educated," she said. "He never made it to high school himself. He gave me such a slap once when I offered to teach him how to read a little better. I was just in the eighth grade. It was only a couple of years after that I started to go wild.... They couldn't control me.... It's a miracle I finished high school myself.... Now, because I've had a couple of weeks of college, they ask my advice about things."

"They can see that you're a woman of the world," I said.

"They want me to speak to my sisters," she said. "My mother thinks they're throwing their lives away. They think my younger sister, Jacky, is into drugs.... We used to sleep together."

"My ex-wife has two sisters," I said, just to say something, for I was three-quarters asleep. "If you have influence with your sister, use it. My own brother..."

"You can understand why I have to succeed in college," she said.

"Do it for yourself," I said; "familial responsibility is a bottomless pit."

"He used to seem so big to me," she said. "But he's lost weight. I don't know, something about his liver, ulcers, and he gets out of breath easily. He only works a few hours a week, at a garage—he used to be a first-class mechanic. My mother brings in most of the money now, from her job at a home for old people. They could get food stamps if they weren't so proud."

"No more," I said.

"What I mean to say is," she said, "it's a funny feeling. I always had this idea, without really thinking about it, that if everything, you know, fell apart, I could go home, eat crow, and they would take care of me. But now I feel cut loose for good."

"Before you were in revolt, which is a form of dependency," I said. "Sounds to me like this weekend you grew up," and look who's talking about being grown up.

"What I am is in between," she said, "cut loose but still at sea. After all, I'm still dependent on you," she said, and she slid her arms under me, gave me a hug, "my big papa bear."

"Don't make me feel incestuous," I said.

"I've got to go and revise my paper for Style and Substance," she said. "By the way, how come you don't have a computer? That typewriter of yours is an antique."

"I can't get any heft or color into words even with a typewriter," I said. "I lose my sense of rhythm."

"If you had a computer I could do up in a flash whatever it is you're always writing," she said. "What is it, anyway?"

I must have stiffened.

"Just curious," she said. "Professor Confalone told me you're writing a book called *Studies in Skepticism,* about William Conrad, James Joyce, and T. S. Eliot."

"Joseph Conrad," I said. "What's your paper about?"

"We're supposed to argue the question whether or not the speaker in 'The Garden' is androgynous."

I groaned.

"The other choice is to rewrite 'To His Coy Mistress' as though the speaker was a woman," she said.

"Can't be done," I said.

"Pfoo," she said.

What do you think, Joel, could you call these letters Studies in Skepticism? That's the book I was supposed to have finished this summer. My argument about T. S. Eliot is that even after his conversion, he had faith, but not belief. He wanted to believe, he acted and wrote as though he believed, but he couldn't, a transparent attempt on my part to rescue him from the believers. As for Joyce and Conrad, their skepticism was shot with gullibility. There's also a chapter on Yeats, whose superstitions may hide, may depend on, the most relentless skepticism of the whole modern era.

No more shop talk. I sometimes envy those higher civilizations that allow polygyny. What would be so wrong with that, so long as we allowed polyandry too? Yeah, but then suppose you had a polygynous man married to a polyandrous woman? And then suppose that the spouses of that man and that woman were also pollied up? Your head it simply swurls. I'm not talking about that universal male fantasy of two women at once. To hell with that. You wouldn't be able to concentrate on either one of them, where it's at, bat. I'm talking about being a serial lover, sleeping with Kay for a few nights, then switching to Julie for a few nights, then back to Kay, or to Felicia Zhang, say. And I'm not talking about a sequence of affairs. I'm talking about living together, watching Kay rub the red welt left on her hip bone by the elastic waistband of her panties, discarding my Bic razor because Julie blunted it shaving her legs, buttoning up the back of Felicia's party dress, putting caps back on four tubes of toothpaste each morning, for screwing the caps back on tubes of toothpaste is uncongenial to women, bringing back little presents of overpriced soaps and the season's first bing cherries, editing their prose, though Felicia's doesn't need it (and I still haven't read "Footman Beware"), picnicking together by a riverbank, the three of them collapsing on each other in laughter when I have to dive in the water to escape a honeybee, posting a schedule on the refrigerator: Monday, Felicia makes the beds, Julie polices the johns, I do the floors, Kay does the kitchen, we shop and cook together (a roast pork shoulder), pulling their hairs out of clogged drains with a fish-hooked clothes hanger, thinking up nice things to say that are true, different ones for each of them, surprising one of them with an urgent hard-on while she is talking on the phone to her mother.... That's a good one. Who's kidding whom? It must be that my little problem is making me goopy. My fantasies used to have a lot more salt in them.

It's time I dragged Julie away from her homework and into bed, for her felt presence makes sleep come easier, for I have caught one of her dependencies, for two million years ago protohumans huddled together for protection against cold and dark that have nothing to do with temperature or time of day. I don't want to wrestle myself to sleep thinking about tomorrow. What I'm going to tell Kay is this: the truth, last resort of a coward. Believe me, if I could think of an evasion that was not in effect an insult, I'd use it. Kay is too good a practical psychologist to make a show of pity, but she might feel compelled to come on sympathetic. "Poor Wynn," and a hand on the cheek. Save it for the Armenians.

Say Joel, do you guys up there sleep alone?

13

When I opened the door

to my sanctuary this morning, whistling Miles' solo on "Walking," what did I find behind it but Monika Wright ditting at my sesk, and man, I was so surprised I dropped my keys and let out a note never before heard by man or mule.

"I couldn't take it anymore," she said, tilting her head toward the main office. "Give me a cigarette, quick."

"Murray's got the rag on?" I said, sitting in the chair usually reserved for petitioners, lighting us up.

"For the past hour I've been trying to extract Irene from Murray's chair," she said. "I think she's been there all night, weeping and moaning. You're the vice-chair: do something about it. But I warn you, the woman's popped her cork."

I was still too discombobulated to catch all that Monika was throwing at me, distracted by the chair-there rhyme. "She's got a shrink apparently," I said.

"I already called her," Monika said. "This sweet little voice. I switched her over to Murray's line so she could talk to Irene, at probably two hundred dollars an hour of Daddy's money. I didn't listen in, but before long I hear Irene shout, 'If you care that much about me you can drag your satchel ass up here where I need you,' and she slams down the receiver."

"When's she coming?" I said.

"Are you kidding?" she said. "I called that twerp before she could hide from the sound of her telephone. She says she can't go out, she's got Achilles tendonitis from her Stairmaster."

"I'll call Murray," I said.

"You think Murray's going to allow himself to get involved in this?" she said.

"There ought to be someone at University Health Services—" I said.

"They said call EMS," she said.

"We could call Teddy," I said. "Maybe he can schmooze her into, ah, you know."

"So I get this Rasta voice at EMS tells me this is no job for amateurs," she said. "He tells me to handle Irene like she's standing on the windowsill threatening to jump."

"We don't want guys in white coats storming up the stairs and wrestling Irene into a straitjacket," I said.

"They won't come into a campus building without authorization from a responsible officer of the University, meaning you," she said.

"Surely this requires a woman's touch," I said.

"No you don't," she said. "You get right in there and talk her down. When she's ready to come out, I'll call EMS. They'll be waiting downstairs."

"Maybe I should call Kay," I said.

Monika got out of my chair, took me by the hand, pulled me to my feet, turned me around, pushed me from behind to the door of Murray's office, said, "First let me have another cigarette."

I lit us up and walked in. Irene's face looked as though someone had sharpened it with a whetstone, the skin pulled tight, her eyes dark and deep, could keep the crows out of your cornfield. " 'Lo, Rene," I said.

"I'm sitting in the catbird seat and you can't get me out," she said.

"Let me tell you about the origin of that expression," I said. She swiveled one full circle in Murray's chair and then rested her heels on his desk, showing lots of leg. "Pretty nice, aren't they?" she said, slapping herself on a thigh.

"Very," I said, watching the red silhouette of her hand fade to pink.

"Come on over here and lean back against the desk," she said. "I'll give you a blow job. That's what men like, isn't it?"

"That's one of the things some men like," I said, sitting in the chair on the other side of the desk from her, the petitioner's chair. "Come on, Irene, don't talk dirty, it's not like you."

"Sex *is* dirty," she said, brooding. "Mucilage."

"It was Woody Allen, I believe, who said, 'If it's done right,' " I said.

"Here's another quotation for your collection, from Alice Walker: 'We offer them love and they give us babies.' "

"Is that it?" I said. "Are you pregnant?"

"I'm full of it," she said.

Did I see the faintest glimmer of a rueful smile? If so, it was evidence that Irene might still be sane enough to allow herself to be reached. I'm one of those pains in the ass who believe there is a certain willed quality about nervous breakdowns.

"You need to get away for a while," I said. "You need to talk to someone who can give you a new slant on things."

"It's not his fault," she said. "No one forced me. That's what's so mordid." Her teeth began to chatter.

Mordid? I stood up and started to take off my jacket to put around her shoulders.

"Stay where you are!" she said, leaning forward and pointing a finger at arm's length. "Don't you dare take off your clothes!" all the while the click-click of her teeth breaking up her words.

"I thought you might be cold," I said.

"Frigid," she said.

"On my authority as vice-chairman, I order you to take the rest of today off," I said. "Come on, I'll walk you home."

"The messages on my e-mail know all about me," she said. "Bless this tool to his use and us to thigh service."

I knew it would happen: tears began to roll down her cheeks. I offered her the bandanna I use as a handkerchief. She snatched it out of my hand and stuffed it up her skirt, between her legs.

"Forslive us whore tristesses as we forlove hose youse twistass inside us," she said. "We ask it in his shame, a man."

"That tears it, Irene," I said. "That was rehearsed—it's all an act. And don't think we can't all see that this play for sympathy is a sneak's mode of aggression." Sometimes I wonder what is wrong with me. I have made a career of keeping the barrier between what I say to myself and what I say out loud as closed as a Marxist's imagination. Letting it open a crack, in a moment of self-indulgence, was an act of irresponsible stupidity.

With animal agility, with a speed and ferocity that froze me in terror, Irene coiled in Murray's chair, leapt out of it onto the desk, and leapt onto me. She landed on all fours on my chest, like a cougar landing on the slow-moving and slow-thinking yak. I tipped over onto the petitioner's chair, which tipped over onto the floor, which banged into my head, in back, while Irene's forehead banged into my head, in front. She then sank her teeth into my left superorbital ridge, down to the gums, so it felt.

I would like to have a large studio photo, suitable for framing, of that scene, your brother on his back, knees hooked over the seat of the chair, his secretary kneeling on his chest, teeth in his brow, growling, a conversation piece. I want right quick to assert that I did not panic, for a purely physical pain, of mere skin or muscle or bone, is an old friend of mine. I twisted her ear, to no avail. I gripped the hinges of her jaw with a forefinger and thumb, then squeezed. She opened like a guppy. I pushed her head back, got my legs under me, and stood, lifting Irene by her jaw. I was about to twist her head off when I saw the blood on her lower lip and the panic and horror in her eyes.

I lowered her until her feet touched the ground and then released my grip. She sagged. I caught her, laid her out on Murray's desk. She drummed her heels, in six-eight time I believe it was, and howled.

I bent down, and we big guys don't bend easily, to pick up my bandanna, for it had fallen from under Irene's dress when I jacked her up. This will tug at you, Joel: I caught a whiff of lily-of-the-valley, Mom's scent. Poor Irene had perfumed her crotch. By now I don't have to tell you that pathos is one of my least favorite literary emotions. I like it even less in life. Irene's howl became a wail. I was working toward a world-class howl of my own, when there was a knock at the door.

The knocker was an elderly black gentleman in campus security blues. His nametag said "Julius Hall." There were deep lines of chastening experience, humor, and tolerance on his face. "You just step outside, professor," he said. "I have some little experience in these matters." He leaned in the doorway and said, "Hidee, little lady," at the same time giving a gentle backhand push to one relieved fat professor, who closed the door behind him.

Kay Pesky, Monika Wright, Teddy Nakatani, and a young strong-looking security officer were tightly grouped in the open area of the main office. Two work-studies were at their desks pretending to be busy.

Looking at my eye, Monika said, "I didn't know Mike Tyson was paroled."

Looking at my eye, Teddy said, "A chain saw makes a gash like that. My father one summer —"

Looking at my eye, the guard said, "You gotta watch those bites. The human mouth is full of germs. Lookit here," and he started to roll up his sleeve.

Looking at my eye, Kay said, "What did you do to earn that?"

"I said the wrong thing," I said.

"Again?" she said, leading me to a chair, pushing me down. "Let me look," and she took my bandanna to the kitchenette, wet it, came back, wiped the blood out of my eye socket. "Your blood clots quickly, probably loaded with cholesterol. You're going to need stitches." She stood back, assumed the pose of a connoisseur. "Yes, I definitely think the scar will add something. Cosmetically speaking, the one under your chin is a waste." She folded her own fragrant handkerchief into a small rectangle and strapped it tight to my brow with packing tape. "What do you think, Monika?"

"Something about that man makes people want to bite," Monika said.

I leaned forward and rested the good side of my face against Kay's surprisingly firm belly, not because I felt faint, but because of the soundness radiating out of her. She massaged my neck. "Who do I thank for calling security?" I said.

"The Rasta at EMS called Clark Eight, which called security," Monika said. "They were afraid Irene might be a danger . . . to herself." I should explain that Clark Eight is the psychiatric ward at St. Luke's. I have often visited students and colleagues there. I wonder, does the academy draw crazies or produce them?

The door to Murray's office opened, and out came Irene and Mr. Hall arm in arm, Irene holding on tight, looking down demurely, on the way to the prom. Kay walked over, stood looking at Irene for a moment, then suddenly gave her a big, long, full-bodied hug. Irene first stiffened, then gradually relaxed, rested her head on Kay's shoulder, where mine should have been. As Kay released, she said, "I'll stick with you until you're settled." Irene looked at Kay without recognition.

"The ambulance is waiting downstairs," said Monika.

"What say we walk over, Missy?" said Mr. Hall. "I've often found that a little stroll is salubrious. Come on, now." He led her out, followed by Kay, who said over her shoulder, "Teddy, walk Professor O'Leary over to Emergency. He looks a little pale." You have to admire the way she took charge, without fuss, as though it were unthinkable that anyone would challenge her right. Not me, certainly.

Not too long ago Norman Grantz released an album made up mainly of outtakes of "Chicken Wing," that blues Dizzy did with

Freddy Hubbard, Clark Terry, and the Oscar Peterson Quartet. It's some of Dizzy's best blowing since bop died in the fifties and became its admirers. The dissonances are life-giving, discoveries of new harmonics in a meta-diatonic scale. Dizzy redirected his considerable store of violence and aggression in various ways, by humor, by the put-on, by using a mute, by pointing the bell of his horn upward, out of his listeners' faces, by (late in his career) pinching off his raucous tone, but it all comes out in his musical subversions, his rapid runs, his high notes, his unexpected rhythms, his funk, his dissonances, his harsh beauty. I'm listening to this album as I write, by way of restorative.

I want you to know I would have been just as shaky if Irene had bitten someone else. I speak as a man who has had a broken jaw, a thrice-busted nose, a fractured clavicle, bone chips in the left ankle, a ruptured muscle sheath in the right calf, a hyperextended elbow, dislocated digits, bruises so deep they near came out the other side. None of that bothered me so much as a spot of spaghetti sauce on a new ten-dollar necktie. What bothers me is what Irene saw in herself when her eyes went wide in panic and horror. I have a phobia not so much of the physical act as of what sets it off. I always backed off from guys who in a fit of psychopathy were trying to start a fight, even when on a purely physical level I had the advantage. Pa once told me that if I didn't fight I would have to learn to run or talk fast. No doubt that is how I became a professor, by diverting the other guy's rage with words, or by sublimating my own, although in fact I get just as shook up by unrestrained verbal violence as by the other kind.

On my way back to the office from Emergency, I stopped at a pushcart for a hot sausage with sauerkraut, a complete meal. Teddy declined. ("Do you know what they put in those things?") He pulled me by the arm. ("I have a bag of Fritos in my desk.") I did not return to my office in the hopes that people would make a fuss over me, for of the two kinds of people, those who like others to make a fuss over them, and those who don't, I belong to the second, for the first brings out the worst in himself and in the fussers. For one thing, Hector would be by for my analysis of the murderer's poem, and for another, I meant to tell Kay about my little problem.

Kay was on the phone in the main office, so I worked at my desk for a while, designing a curriculum for next year: a skeleton of historical courses; courses in themes, genres, and figures to flesh it out; fashionable courses, such as "Juissance and G-Strings" or "Postmodernism and Epistemic Subversion" or "Crossing Borders: The Spy and Gender Transgression" to trick it up. Poor Willie Yeats was always seeking Unity of Being, which he imagined as "a perfectly proportioned human body." Chapter by chapter, Joyce's masterpiece, *Ulysses.* puts together a complete human body. We Irishers, when faced by obliterating disorder, try to preserve ourselves by pretending it has a human form.

By and by, Kay walked in, shaking her head, and just sort of collapsed into the chair across my desk, legs spread out, arms hanging, practically supine, uncharacteristically slack. I took her unguarded attitude as a sign of trust, rather than as an invitation to leap onto the desk and then onto her chest, pulling an Irene. "I just got off the phone with Irene's father," she said. "Ever meet him? No? Take it from me, he's an asshole."

"Cigarette?" I said.

"Can't," she said.

"You can get back on schedule tomorrow," I said.

"I'll give in to anything, except temptation," she said, and a faint smile flickered across her lips. "You ought to stop too."

"What did the Reverend Howland have to say?" I said, lighting up.

"The whole time I was telling him about Irene, he went 'a-hunh' and 'a-hunh,'" she said. "When I was finished, he said 'Well, keep me informed.'"

"My father says the way to lose your soul entirely is sell it to God, not the Devil," I said.

"I told Howland that if he was not down here by tomorrow morning, I was going to call in a shrink friend of mine, the one who specializes in getting her patients to recall repressed memories of parental molestation," she said.

"You wouldn't!" I said, properly aghast.

"I may do it anyhow," she said. "Something made Irene the way she is."

"What way is that, exactly?" I said.

"When we got over to Emergency, there was a resident waiting for us," she said. "He got Irene to lie down. The minute her head hit the gurney, her eyes rolled up and she went rigid, gnashing her teeth, making this noise like a high-pitched hum."

"No more," I said. "You're giving me the creeps."

She gave me a look, seeing something I don't know is there, no doubt. "They kept me hanging around filling out forms," she said, "but they wouldn't let me see Irene. I did peep into the cubicle where they were stitching you up. I thought you might want someone to hold your hand."

"Teddy had already offered," I said.

"He had a funny look on his face," she said. "Let's see: it was both exalted and stoic."

"Sympathy pains," I said.

"He said you refused anesthetic," she said.

"I was punishing myself," I said, "or proving something."

"He said you refused a prescription for painkillers," she said.

"I've got an addictive personality," I said, "like my brother."

"Well, you've got yourself another admirer," she said.

"And here I thought you already admired me for my prose style," I said.

"I did, I do," she said. "By another admirer, I meant Teddy, you big dope."

"Let's go someplace where you can hold my hand," I said. "We can talk about your . . . proposal."

" 'Proposal' is it?" she said. "I want the setting to be romantic. How about dinner this Thursday? On me."

"On me," I said.

"On me," she said. "This is my show. I'll pick you up at seven."

"We'll go Dutch," I said.

"For Christ's sake, Wynn," she said, standing.

"Thursday at seven," I said, quickly.

"I'll bring you a corsage," she said, smiling. "And simmer down: no one's out to usurp your precious masculine prerogatives."

Kay stopped at the door, turned suddenly, as though she had just thought of something, smiled seductively, blew me a kiss, turned, and looking back over her shoulder, walked toward the elevator. The buttons on the back of her dress, along her spine, were awry, the first button in the second buttonhole, the second button in the third buttonhole, and so on, to the last button, which had no hole to go in, no hole to go in. A sweet disorder in the dress kindles in clothes a wantonness, which is what it kindles in me, as does a complete perfection in the dress—not to mention no dress whatsoever.

Do you like kissing, Joel? I love it, although blown kisses do less for me than the other kind. I ask because recent research has shown that the nervous system continues to develop after we are born. Neurons grow in this direction or that, connect in this way rather than that, depending on our sustained experiences. It follows that someone who has played a wind instrument all his life has more intelligent lips than the rest of us. His kiss would be more finely discriminating, receptive to a greater range of sensations. Or is it that a trumpet player's lips are just one big callus?

It was only after I noticed that I was seeing through only one eye, the other closed by swollen flesh, that I stopped moving around the pieces of my curriculum. I stood up for a stroll into the main office, to stretch my legs, clear my head, allow any newcomers to admire my wound, but somehow, while sitting, I had gained five hundred pounds, so it felt. My legs wouldn't hold me. I sagged, held onto the desk. Obviously, I needed something to eat.

At that moment the Academy Market, two blocks away, seemed as far from my office as Newark, New Jersey, the other side of the world. I called the main office and asked Teddy to send a work-study out to get me a couple of sandwiches, a brisket on rye with horseradish and a sausage and jalapeno on a hero, a quart of any kind of orange juice not from concentrate. Then I called right back and told Teddy to hold the sausage and jalapeno, for I liked that new feeling of a slight relaxation of pressure against my waistband.

Then, gingerly at first, I tried to get the vital juices flowing. I bounced up and down on my toes, swung my arms, twisted to the sounds of a phantom Chubby Checker, jumped in place, shaking the building, pressed against the doorjamb like Samson, jumped ropeless rope, threw a short left hook, followed with another unexpected hook to the rib cage and when my opponent lowered his guard looped a right cross over it and when he raised his guard followed with a couple of devastating uppercuts, take that motherfucker, when Teddy walked in holding one of those flimsy plastic shopping bags. I danced in on him, backing him up with feints and jabs, following with ferocious hooks and crosses that stopped maybe two inches short of his face.

"I warn you," he said, "were this not in play, your life would be in danger." He reached the shopping bag onto the library table, as I continued to throw punches, and in a motion I never saw, though I was looking right at him, caught my right fist and twisted my arm so that I had to lean forward, my nose one foot from the floor. "Leverage and surprise," he said, "will always take the laurel from mere strength."

I bunched the muscles in my arm and began to revolve it backwards, at the same time slowly straightening, moving from a question mark toward an exclamation point. Halfway up, both of us shaking with the strain, it came to me that in a real fight Teddy would have released his grip by now and kicked me in the face. I relaxed. He relaxed and let go. I straightened up. He bowed, almost smiling. I bowed.

"Neither of the work-studies was free," he said. "I am friendly with the countermen: you will find your sandwich thicker than usual."

"Would you like half?" I said, for I did not believe he would accept.

"I do indeed eat some meat," he said, "for the sake of the protein. Dairy products and beans, otherwise so different, are alike in that they produce volcanic activity in my stomach, as do artichokes." He placed bills and change on the table. "That is the change from a ten-dollar bill," he said.

I pulled out the folding money from my pocket, for it is nerdish and wimpish and all-around bad form to keep your money in a wallet, and slipped Teddy a tenner.

"I am on my way to Clark Eight," he said. "Shall I wait for you to finish eating?"

"I am going home," I said, picking up the money, packing my briefcase, heading for the door. "Give Irene my love."

"It is not likely that I will be allowed to see her," he said. "But one of the residents in Clark Eight is an old friend. I will see to it that she sees to it that Irene is given more treatment than a massive dose of Haldol, a nasty drug believe me, and a quick ticket of leave."

As we walked down the stairs, for Teddy and I are alike in normally eschewing the neurasthenic elevator in Hancock Hall, it occurred to me that as a career student he might have developed sources outside my ken. "What's your take on the murder of Blinky Hartmann?" I said.

"Though I have heard you disparage it, our calling is a noble one," he said. "Surely it is as venerable as that of the warrior."

"I disparage everything I value, so as not to bring bad luck down on it," I said.

"We are not birds," he said. "We are not born with all the knowledge we need to get by planted in our genes. The teaching scholar is no mere ornament. The survival of the species depends on him."

"Tell that to whomever it is controls the exchequer," I said.

"I cannot find it in me to regret the death of a man who brought dishonor to our profession," he said.

"Who do you think killed him?" I said, as we crossed Amsterdam Avenue.

"Imagine an inexperienced young man unsure of his sexual identity," he said. "Imagine overtures from someone with a professor's power and prestige. Imagine the Serpent whispering in your ear that *he* is one and you are another. Imagine after the Fall, your guilt and revulsion and murderous rage. You see it in the accusers of priests just now stepping forward."

We stopped to face each other on the southeast corner of 116th and Amsterdam, he to go south and I to go east. "And am I to imagine a similarly inexperienced young woman as Terry's killer?" I said.

"I have heard you praise the operations of the sympathetic imagination," he said. "Perhaps it is time to deploy it. Why, for example, have you withheld your sympathy for Irene's suffering?"

"If I spent my time sympathizing with everyone I knew who deserved it, there'd be no time for anything else," I said. "Consider the callus: its natural function is to protect us from abrasion. Ever take a course from Blinky?"

"Every other year Professor von Hartmann offered a seminar entitled 'The Religions of the Oppressed: From Jesus Christ to Charles Manson.'"

"Yes," I said, "but it's their religion that oppresses the oppressed."

"When he let drop, in the tone of a brag, that all the charismatic leaders of oppositional cults, not just Christ and Manson, but all the others from Thomas of Munster to Jim Jones, were homosexuals, whether or not they admitted it, even to themselves, I decided that the course was not for me," he said. "It was as though you were to imply greatness for yourself by noting that Buddha and David Hume were also stout."

"I had forgotten about Buddha," I said. "You down on homosexuals?"

"No more than any straight male," he said, and he gave me a look. "What I felt then, and what I feel now, is that the professor as special pleader is a self-contradiction. The professor with an ulterior motive or hidden agenda, whether it be political, religious, or erotic, is an abomination."

"I don't see how he's any better if he lets it all hang out," I said.

"Your multivalent skepticism is heroic," he said. "But its rigors are not for everyone. Belief requires less effort than doubt. And some people cannot do without it. But a professor must be able to stand back from his belief and see it as one among many of equal interest."

"Yes, if you believe in something," I said, "the only decent thing to do is keep quiet about it."

"Perhaps we can continue this conversation at another time," he said. "I shall then give you instances of people whose belief in what is strictly speaking a fiction saved them from dissolution and despair."

"There are things a man must not do, even to save his sanity," I said, misquoting Yeats's hero, John O'Leary, who said "country" where I said "sanity."

"We are not speaking of matters that are under one's conscious control," he said.

What do you think, Joel: is Teddy's inability to get started on a dissertation the result of some kind of cock-eyed integrity; is my little problem the erotic equivalent to my skepticism? In any case I am nowhere near as skeptical as I pretend to be or people take me to be or for that matter I want to be. But your true believer is just another species of hard-on.

I had scarcely gotten settled behind my desk, the sandwich unwrapped on a plate, a mug of coffee beside it, instead of the orange juice, for with Irene off-duty, the office coffee-making operation went into decline, for there were symptoms of withdrawal, some Ellington on the boombox, and I had forgotten how hard the section-work swings on "Perdido" or how lovely is Betty Roche's vocal on "A Train," when the doorbell rang, or more precisely, buzzed. It was Hector Suarez.

"Umm," he said, sitting in the chair facing my desk, looking at the sandwich. I took the wax paper that the sandwich had come in out of the wastepaper basket, put half the sandwich on it and pushed the plate with the other half to Hector. "You got any pickles?" he said.

So we went into the kitchen, where I filled one little wooden salad bowl with pickles and one with cherry peppers. "I can help myself," he said, taking out a bottle of beer, for I prefer not to drink beer out of a can, and a mug to pour it in.

When we were once again seated, he said, "I see you've got a new letter opener," referring to Uncle Alf's Ka-Bar, now mine, lying on the ink blotter.

"Yes," I said.

"Looks like it's seen active duty," he said.

"It's got to be older than we are," I said.

"The one that killed Terry Jones is ten to twelve years old," he said, "what I hear from my man in Hylas Cutlery."

"So where's it been all these years?" I said.

"Could be it was part of a batch packed in these cute little wooden crates, twelve to the crate, stencils all over the outside so as to look military," he said.

"What would you do with twelve Ka-Bars?" I said.

"There's these clubs," he said, "assholes dress up in camouflage and shoot paintballs at each other."

"They stab each other, too?" I said.

"What they do with the Ka-Bars is anybody's guess," he said.

"They wear them for show," I said.

"The way a bald guy wears a beard," he said.

"How about the Ka-Bar that decorated Blinky's tush?" I said.

"I sent Jimmy Walsh up to Hylas with it," he said. "Called me this morning. Right about now Norman Bates and his technical people should be conducting an autopsy on it."

I placed three cherry peppers on the wax paper, sliced them into halves with the Ka-Bar, dislodged the seeds and stem into my ashtray, opened the sandwich, pressed the peppers into the horseradish sauce, closed the sandwich, took a big bite, for nature has kindly arranged things so that it is pleasurable to do what is good for us. Then why do some people find it pleasurable to inject heroin? It must be that injecting heroin is so close to something that is in fact good for us, like getting laid, say, that the body cannot discriminate. Hector ate first a bite of pickle, then of sandwich, then puffed on his cigar, then drank a mouthful of beer, then ate a cherry pepper, seeds, stem, and all. "You write up that poem?" he said.

"I did, much good it will do you," I said, rummaging around in my briefcase.

"The NYPD's got its own 'criminal assessment and profiling unit,' " he said. "It's headed by a woman been a cop for twenty years, so she's got her feet on the ground. Knows how to get on with the Feebs, too. The thing is, she gets lost in that 'forest of symbols,' you know, what you said about the first poem. You got to be my pathfinder," and he batted his eyes seductively.

"There's no path through a forest of symbols," I said, in my pain-in-the-ass mode, "otherwise known as a 'wilderness of mirrors.' " I handed him a sheaf of papers.

"You couldn't have typed it?" he said.

We heard the door to the landing open and Julie sing out "Cuz, you home?"

"In here," I sang back.

Julie walked into the study, saw Hector, said "You!" an accusation, walked to my chair, said "What happened to your eye?" bent over to look, one hand on my shoulder, Hector's watchful eyes taking everything in.

"I was going to ask that myself," Hector said, "but I didn't want to pry, case it was a lovers' quarrel."

"Poor Cuz," said Julie.

"Far be it for me to linger where I'm not wanted," said Hector.

"The reason you cops smoke cigars," Julie said, waving imaginary smoke away from her face, "is you know everybody else hates the smell." I have not myself, Joel, discovered the law behind Julie's wide fluctuations of timidity and audacity.

"A symbol!" he said, holding up his cigar and looking at it. "Did you know, Cousin Julie, that man wanders in a forest of symbols?" He crushed out his cigar in the cherry pepper seeds, which hissed, wrapping the remains of his sandwich half and a pickle in his handkerchief, putting it in his briefcase.

"Do you know what Samuel Beckett said about that?" I said.

"What's this you're eating?" said Julie, taking a good bite out of my sandwich.

"Never heard of him," said Hector.

"Yow!" said Julie, holding her mouth, running from the room.

" 'No symbols where none intended,' " I said.

"My sentiments entirely," he said. "What you playing at with that Ka-Bar on your desk?"

"Self-defense," I said.

"I been trying to keep track of the queers I know about who work in this funny farm," he said. "Last I heard they're all intact. Don't think I didn't notice that when you go upstate for a weekend no one gets killed."

This time I did not walk Hector to his car. Julie came out of the bathroom with toothpaste on her breath. "Who's cooking tonight?" she said.

"Me," I said.

"Good," she said. "I want to watch the 5-to-7 news. How come you're not interested in this election coming up? There's a lot at stake."

"Interest follows knowledge," I said. "I don't know enough about who's running or what they stand for to get interested."

"Well, find out," she said. "Watch the news with me, come on, Cuz."

Julie sat in the chair I think of as my chair, although they are all mine, a big maroon leather mission-style chair (with footrest) that you could rent out to a family of four. I sat slightly behind her and to the right, in a straight-up ninety-year-old Sears chair Uncle Alf bought for three dollars at a garage sale and refinished, from where I could look at Julie's face in three-quarter's profile while pretending to watch TV, on which there was first an ad for Pepcid AC, then for Orudis KT, and then for Axid. I went to the kitchen and cut four large onions into the bacon fat heating in my Dutch oven and returned to Julie and the TV, on which there was an ad for Tagamet HB. Julie's complexion? Take a glass of milk and drop a teaspoon of coffee in it. As erogenous zones go, and all of Julie's zones are erogenous, I find the brow to be of relatively low voltage. Too carefully considered, Julie's brow is on the low side, rather than high, faintly convex, rather than straight, smooth, rather sagaciously wrinkled. (An ad for Zantac 75 came on.) In that respect it is unlike her nose, which is faintly concave and fuller on the tip than on the bridge, feels good against your neck. When an ad for Motrin IB came on, I went to the kitchen, stirred the onions, and returned to the TV, on which there was an ad for Maalox. There's this heroine in an eighteenth-century novel, whose lower lip, says the author, looked as though a bee had stung it. Bees, as you know, hang around honey. (An ad for Dulcolax came on.) Both of Julie's lips look as though a bee had stung them. I went into the kitchen, removed the onions from the Dutch oven, replaced them with the short ribs, so they would brown, and returned to the TV, on which there was an ad for Melatonex. Julie's chin, in my opinion, is a masterpiece. It is different from the O'Leary chins in this: it is not shaped like the business end of a spade, nor are her teeth like tombstones. When the ad for Tylenol came on, I went to the kitchen, turned over the ribs, returned to the TV, on which there was an ad for Advil. I am not a man to write rapturous prose. There will be no attempt to do justice to Julie's cheeks. (An ad for Aleve came on the TV.) I will only say this: to the eye they are lean, even hollow, under the cheekbones: to the touch they are of unequalled softness and warmth. Julie's neck. Ah yes, Julie's neck. The fact is, that as the ad for Anacin came on, I kissed Julie's neck. "Um," she said. I went into the kitchen, removed the ribs from the Dutch oven, sprinkled flour onto the residual fat, stirred the flour and fat into an emulsion, slowly adding water, stirring all the while, until I had lots of thick gravy. I added a dose of Gravy Master, a squirt of soy sauce, a sprinkle of vinegar, a pinch of sage, two pinches of thyme, a fair amount of salt and too much pepper. I dropped the ribs and onions into the gravy and on second thought diluted the gravy before putting on the lid and sliding the dutch oven into the gas oven at 300 degrees and returning to Julie, who was watching an ad for Excedrin PM. I kissed her brow, her nose, her cheeks, her chin. "Ummmm," she said, turning her head, so that as the ad for Selsun Silver came on, I could kiss her lips. Oh. Joel, I kissed her lips all through the ad for Ensure! I pressed the button that releases the lock that holds up the back of Julie's chair, I mean the chair in which Julie was sitting. The back suddenly tilted over to form a flat surface with the rest of the chair. "Oops," said Julie, our lips disengaging. I stood, put one arm under Julie's knees, one under her shoulders, lifted, sat, lay back, stretched Julie out on me, chest to breast and all the rest, and kissed her, or she kissed me, who cares which, this was no time for niggling distinctions, while the ad for Jouvex came on, and who needs it? I reached down, lifted her dress, slid my hands inside her panties, and Julie's lower cheeks are like her upper cheeks in this: they are of unequalled softness and warmth. She began to rotate her pelvis clockwise, with a double tuck at six o'clock, while we kissed, and man, something was building, and before my mind had time to play a dirty trick on my body, I had passed the point of no return, Julie rotating and tucking, me kissing and thrusting, so that as the ad for Depends began, I came in my pants.

"Kids' stuff," you say? Nothing to brag about? It is true that during my senior year in high school, on days when there was no football practice, Peggy McNif and I would walk home together, ascend to the O'Leary apartment, and neck on Ma's pristine couch until I came in my pants, but no longer than that, for Peggy's attitude was that enough is enough. Did Peggy get anything out of it? I think she did, but not the same thing I got. When Peggy realized that I was going to college, she finally let me inside her. I was at the point of no return when I realized that what Peggy wanted was to get pregnant, so I would have to marry her, for as you will remember, in that neighborhood, at that time, if you knocked up a girl, you married the girl, or moved away, never to return, or joined the army. I therefore pulled out and came on Peggy's belly. Oh, the ignominy of sexual desire! The question is this: how come just now I came? Did I unconsciously regress to those afternoons with Peggy McNif? Was it the clothes between Julie's privates and mine? Or was it the smell of short ribs cooking in the oven?

Julie, as usual, would not let me bring her off by artificial means. "I'm waiting for the real thing," she said. There's a character named Shrike in a novel called *Miss Lonelyhearts* who describes himself with unqualified contempt as a "grateful lover." That's what I am. I can't help it. I've loved every woman who allowed me to make love to her. I want to do something for any woman who bestows on me the immense boon of access to her body. Julie knows all this about me (and everything else) through some unthinking process that is very close to instinct. Can you beat this? The woman is trying to blackmail me into solving my little problem.

Just the same and because of the kids' stuff, I was given the night off. No sex therapy until tomorrow. Thus it is that I had the whole evening to write you this letter, even if with only one eye open. Julie's taking her shower (I took mine before supper, right after the kids' stuff): soon we'll be in bed together. I intend to force everything else out of mind—my little problem, Kay, Irene, Teddy, Departmental doings, the murders—but the class I have to give tomorrow. Putting a class together in my head is one of the things I can do without generating insomniacal anxiety. Here's hoping we can get through tomorrow without anyone finding another Ka-Barred corpse of a queer professor.

14

There was no Irene

when I got to my office yesterday morning, Tuesday morning, for this is Wednesday morning right now as I dance my Scripto over these pages, for in a minute I'll tell you why I didn't write last night. Therefore there was no coffee. I have keys to the main office. I used them. I made the coffee, made it à la Irene: half again the recommended dose of grounds, a tablespoonful of chicory. You have got to preempt the work-studies from making coffee. They are fully capable of adding coconut flavoring, or cinnamon, or amaretto, or some other perfume.

"Smells good," said a voice behind me.

I whirled around and bumped into Felicia Zhang, and why had she sneaked up on me like that, close enough to slip a Ka-Bar under my ribs?

"Join me in a cup?" I said.

"If there's room," she said.

"That's an old joke," I said, pouring.

"The best kind," she said.

"What are you doing prowling these halls so early?" I said, as we walked to my office, a few feet away.

"I was looking for Irene Rowland," she said. "She has a collection of materials relating to graduate programs in English around the country. I want to look at them. I also wanted her to put me down for an appointment to see you."

"I thought you were going to law school," I said, and we sat, she on one, and me on the other side, of my desk. I lit up, for Felicia is too smart to be taken in by the superstition that smoke filtered through someone else's lungs is bad for you. Some day I'll have to write to you about the neo-puritanical religiosity that is sweeping provincial America. The idea is that if it feels good, you have to pay for it. If you screw, you have to pay for it by bearing a child, one reason neo-puritans like to spank their children. If you smoke, you die, and kill someone else in the bargain.

"That's what my parents want," she said. "The idea is that I specialize in law relating to international trade and become rich. I speak Chinese, you know, and China is slowly shedding its communist cocoon. That's over a billion people getting ready to join the rest of the world in its addiction to Coca-Cola and blue jeans and gangsta rap and Pall Malls."

"You'd be like those missionaries who destroyed the People of the Kilakang," I said.

"My parents believe that financial security comes first," she said: "it's what makes everything else possible."

"Wise parents," I said: "whatever you do, the missionaries are already on their way."

"Their unwise daughter wants to be a professor of English," she said. "I want to be like you. I want an office like yours. I want this office, in fact."

"If it were mine to give . . . ," I said.

"Being that you're my advisor, I have come for your advice," she said.

"Apply to law schools," I said. "Take the LSATs."

"I'll apply, all right, just in case," she said. "I've already taken the LSATs."

"How'd you do?" I said.

"I got a perfect score," she said, smiling in self-deprecation.

"Well, look over Irene's materials—I'll fetch them for you in a minute—then we'll have a talk," I said, for the idea is to have Felicia come round as often as possible, so I can tan myself in the sunshine of her personality.

"Will you write me a letter of recommendation?" she said, pulling out the form from Career Services that I fill out maybe forty times a year, differently each time, of course.

"It will be the easiest I ever wrote," I said. "I'll simply inform whomever it may concern that if they don't admit you I'll come after them with my Kilakang."

"That reminds me, what did you think of my Kilakang piece?" she said. "You didn't write any commentary. That's what I wrote it out for."

"I seem to remember some marginalia," I said.

"You circled the word 'this' and wrote *loose ref* in the margin," she said.

"A fuzzy reference is a fuzzy thought," I said.

"You underlined 'different than' and wrote *illiterate* in the margin," she said.

"And so it is," I said.

"They say it all the time on television," she said.

I glared at her.

"Sorry," she said. "You circled the word 'since' and wrote *temporal not causal.*"

"It's what I'm paid to do," I said.

"You added the second 'n' to millennium," she said.

"The word, and therefore the concept, looked shrunken without it," I said. "Would you really, in the circumstances I described, have become a serial killer of missionaries?"

"I would probably have become a convert, or pretend convert anyhow," she said. "I am that much my parents' daughter," and my respect for Felicia, already way up there, rose a notch. "But it's more fun to think about being a killer."

"Only if you're not thinking clearly," I said. "Picture it: you come in too low; the tip of the knife snags on the victim's belt; he struggles frantically; the knife slips off and gashes him, blood on your hands and clothes, the insane terror in his eyes, blood everywhere, on your face as you stab and stab, an awful smell when you perforate his gut, the sounds . . ."

"Who said anything about a knife?" she said. "We are not speaking here of gratuitous slaughter, but of significant murder. Only a Kilakang would have the right kind of meaning." I can't understand it, Joel: some men don't like intelligent women. Well, intelligence in a woman turns me on, from which you are not to assume I have never come across a case of fetching stupidity.

"Besides," she said, "you're the one who said that literature allows us to do in our imaginations what we can't or won't do in the flesh. I wrote it down."

"I wish people wouldn't use against me what I say in the classroom," I said.

"Professor Arno agrees with you," she said. "You know me, the first day of her class on detective fiction, I asked her why people like to read about murder. She said it's because we all want to kill someone. She said reading about it is the next best thing."

"Then why do we also like to see the killer get caught?" I said.

"That's to assuage the reader's guilt," she said: "the private self wants to kill; the social self wants to make the private self feel guilty, just for thinking about killing someone. The killer gets caught to appease the public self. And it helps that the killer is presented as a bad guy. Some day I'm going to write a *noir* in which the killer is a good guy."

"Maybe you ought to be a defense attorney," I said, "specialize in hit men."

"In women who kill abusive husbands," she said, "or missionaries. You want to go out on a date?"

She giggled at what must have been a stunned expression on my face. "Every month my sorority has a favored professor over for dinner," she said. When Felicia sat, the straps of her jumper relaxed, so that the low-cut top could lean forward. Felicia is not only plump of calf, but also of bosom. "You'll be sitting at the large table, with eleven admiring females, including me." A picture flashed across my mind: we are standing on the stoop of her sorority house saying goodnight. She looks up at me. I lean over and kiss her on the lips. Well, why not? Felicia is a senior, twenty or twenty-one or even twenty-two years old, a grown woman. "Will you come?"

I doubt that Felicia intended a pun, so I gave her a straight answer. "Of course," I said.

See what I mean: it's only since I became a gelding that there are these women making overtures.

I went to lunch early, for Leonard was always the first to arrive, for I was worried about him, for even his physical prowess was no defense against a sneak attack, from behind, with a Ka-Bar. There he was, in his usual chair, wearing a safari jacket, a white shirt with a long pointed collar worn outside the jacket, so you could see the gold chain around his neck, whipcord breeks, highly polished chukkas. "See here," he said as I sat, handing me a sheet of paper. It was a teletype from the Feuerback financial news service:

6699 Corp
BBN

1299 BBN 11:00 2 Men Injured During Bizarre Sexual Practice

Loon City, FL Sept. 20 (UPI) -- Two men were seriously injured today during what authorities say is a deviate, dangerous and illegal sexual practice. Toto Indelicato, 37, sustained second-degree burns to his face and scalp, while Bebe Salazar, 34, suffered first- and second-degree burns to his anus and lower colon.

The act which caused the injuries to Indelicato and Salazar is known in the gay community as "fetching" or "rat-running." Fetching begins with the insertion of a cardboard tube into the rectum of the person to be "fetched." After injection of the tube a live rodent, typically a gerbil, is inserted in the tube and forced into the person's colon. The movement of the rodent in the colon allegedly intensifies one's sexual orgasm.

The problems started when Indelicato could not retrieve the gerbil from Salazar's anus.

Salazar had orgasmed and demanded the removal of the rodent. Indelicate, unable to see up the tube to retrieve the rodent, lit a cigarette lighter in order to provide some illumination. The flame from the lighter, however, ignited some intestinal gas which escaped from Salazar's rectum. The flame apparently traveled up the tube, igniting the fur of the rodent, which then detonated a larger pocket of intestinal gas behind the hapless animal.

The ensuing explosion shot the flaming gerbil down the cardboard tube and into the face of Indelicato, causing the burns.

Sheriff Grant Tuber commented to reporters, "It serves the faggots right."

When I looked up, Leonard said, "You know any orgasms that are not sexual?"

"Joyce plays with the notion that when you hang a guy. . . ." I said.

"I'd like to hang Sheriff Grant Tuber," Leonard said.

"By his tuber?" I said.

"By his red neck," he said. "The Christian right is making homophobia acceptable again."

"They are not exactly champions of duty-free heterophilia either," I said. "And not a word of sympathy from you for 'the hapless animal': you're not a speciesist, are you?"

"It was sacrificed in a worthy cause," he said.

Marshall Grice arrived just as the bells tolled twelve (the silver circles brightened the air). "What are you two talking about?" he said.

"Sex," I said.

"Good for you," he said. Leonard folded the teletype and slid it into an inner pocket of his safari jacket. "What does Sanchez have to say about the murder of Blinky Hartmann?" said Marshall, looking at me, sitting, taking the food off his tray: a bagel, a packet of cream cheese, a side order of mashed potatoes, a glass of milk.

"Suarez," I said.

"M'dears," said Lizzie, sitting (grilled cheese and bacon, fries, some kind of cola, brown betty mit schlag).

Zeno, his arm hooked into Kay's, approached, Serena a step behind them. (They had not yet been through the food line.)

"That purplish-green around your eye is a color hitherto unknown to medical science," said Zeno.

"It's so garish," said Serena.

"He needed something," said Leonard. "The man dresses so drab."

Kay bent over and kissed me at the corner of my eye. "Make it all better," she said.

"Has anyone tested Irene for rabies?" said Serena.

"I believe you have to cut off the head," said Leonard.

"Irene and violence?" said Lizzie. "They don't go together. A character structure such as hers is not easily disinhibited."

"If the meek inherit the earth," Marshall said, "it will be because someone has released the violence their meekness was designed to cover and control."

"Wynn rejected her advances," said Zeno. "What's a poor girl to do? She should have come to me."

"Her father is in the hospital right now, trying to get her released into his custody, against medical advice," said Kay.

"In such cases, as I recall, the patient or concerned parties can request a hearing before a judge," said Marshall. "To keep Irene in, the doctors would have to satisfy the judge that she's a danger to herself or others."

"Teddy Nakatani tells me she's calmed down," said Kay. "But she's still a little paranoid. She thinks Vanna White is parodying her style."

"What does Nunez say about Irene?" said Marshall.

"Suarez," I said. "He says she keeps better records than her counterpart in Religion."

"Let's get something to eat," said Kay, standing.

I stood up to follow her. So did Serena. "Get me a large coffee, will you?" Zeno said to Kay. "Black."

Shorts are in style among the students this year, Joel, even among guys whose knees look like sacks full of golf balls. "Why, do you think, do men like women's legs?" I said to Kay, as we wound our way through tables full of students.

"All fetishes are socially constructed," she said. And that's that.

"Because of where they go, if you follow them upward," said Serena. "Men are pigs: that's what's good about them."

It occurred to me that I should ask whether Malcolm Tetrault had been piggy enough for her.

I don't know, Joel: as we made our way through all those bare legs, it occurred to me that the best indicator of structural soundness throughout a woman's soma is the kind of legs men like. If the legs are good, so usually is the rest, good bones, properly distributed sinew, muscles with tone. You can gather plants and seeds and roots and firewood all day, the papoose strapped to your back, no bother. And your papoose, when grown, is more likely to be fast of foot, able to outrun the cave bear sow whose cub he killed, unlike the bow-legged guy who was run down by a Neanderthal out for revenge, waving his ur-Kilakang. Never, but never, will I succumb to that Lysenkoist propaganda, now sweeping the academy, to the effect that the human sense of beauty is a mere by-product of how we bring home the bacon. Think how vulgar it is to say that economics is all, the bourgeois left imitating in theory what the bourgeois right does in practice. Against the Führer, Big Brother, and Big Nurse I assert that I am what I am because I am an animal. The animal in humans is the human component in humans, as distinct from the individual and social components. And to the extent that you deny the animal in me you are my enemy. In biology lies not destiny, but freedom.

Yes, I know about the counter-evidence. I can see the holes in my logic. Give me a little credit. I just believe it is richer and deeper to think of myself as the product of a billion years of evolution than of two hundred years of capitalism.

Nevertheless, I did not, as the animal in me urged, place my hand on Kay's hip where it swelled under her chino skirt and in such a way as to suggest the good bones and the distribution of sinew, muscle, and fat that evolution has programmed men to admire—although a less scrupulous man than me might have taken the rip along the zipper, the exposed oval of panties, as an invitation.

Serena had Salisbury steak smothered in onions, mashed potatoes, and greens, all of it submerged in a pint of gravy, that bitch. Kay had spinach salad, which would have been all right, had it not been contaminated by raisins, walnuts, and shreds of coconut. I had breast of chicken product, in texture somewhere between styrofoam and particle board, for I had promised Julie to eat a low-cholesterol lunch, for she lit into me last night over the short ribs, succulently fat, for she threatened, not seriously I believe, to cut off treatments unless I cut down on cigarettes and cholesterol. That the new killjoyism has gotten even to someone like Julie will show you how pervasive it is.

"Someone's been following me," said Leonard as we sat down, "I'm setting a trap for him."

"It's probably a cop," I said. "Suarez tells me he's watching over all the potential victims of the Ka-Bar killer that he can identify."

"And why am I in particular a potential victim?" said Leonard.

"Because you're queer, you dummy," said Zeno.

"I forgot," Leonard said.

"I forgot!" said Kay. "That wretched book of Amabelle Bloor's! If the killer knows how to read, you could be in danger, Wynn," and she put her hand on my bicep.

"Neither of the victims so far have been physically imposing," said Marshall Grice, "quite the contrary."

"Get his head in the crook of your arm and crack it open like a walnut," said Kay, squeezing my bicep.

"Malcolm Tetrault's arms are skinny *and* soft," said Serena, "give you the creeps."

"Did he win you over to Angel's cause?" said Marshall.

"He tried to talk me into a number of things," said Serena. "But I am not going to put in a good word for him with Wynn. I am not going to support Angel just because a female chair will make us look good. As for sucking his dick. . . ."

"No!" said Zeno. "Malcolm? Will wonders never cease?"

"The bum," said Lizzie.

"Maybe he's not an alien, after all," said Leonard.

"And he pretends to be a feminist sympathizer," said Kay.

"It is eagerness in men that produces reluctance in women," said Marshall.

"As long as he only asked . . . ," I said.

"After the piano music, we sat on a bench along Riverside Park," said Serena. "The air was full of water, but it wasn't raining right then, although I got my bottom wet sitting on that bench. He was going on about the concept of the sublime among the German Romantics when I felt this hand on the back of my neck pushing my face toward his lap. His other hand was unzipping his fly."

"What did you do?" said Marshall.

"I jumped up, I was so surprised," Serena said. "Then I unstuck the wet part of my skirt from my behind. Then I said if he pulled out his thing, I'd pull out my Shrade Folding Hunter."

"Good for you," said Lizzie.

"What did he say to that?" said Kay.

" 'What thing?' he said in this meek little voice, playing the innocent," said Serena. "I declined his invitation to go up to his place for a nightcap." She shook a Salem out of her pack, offered one to Kay, who shook her head, lit up.

As Kay, Leonard, and I walked out, Leonard said, "I've got my granddaddy's fine old Parker side-by-side hidden behind an umbrella in my foyer, in that antique pickle crock you gave me that I use as an umbrella stand, better than an elephant's foot. It's loaded with turkey shot, put a hole in you the size of a grapefruit. In my study, on a stand, lies a Webster's unabridged second edition. Under it is the Government Model 1911-A1 I brought back from Vietnam, loaded with the Black Hills 230 grain JHP, a man-stopper. In the kitchen, in the broom closet, is my new Ruger sporting clays over-and-under. I have shot the three-inch double-aught load at a telephone book: instant confetti. In my living room, under a couch cushion. . . ."

"Wouldn't it be better to just have one man-stopper and keep it with you?" said Kay.

"And wherever I go I carry this," Leonard said, and in a move that for swiftness and dexterity was worthy of Teddy Nakatani, he pulled out a switchblade from a pouch sewn on the inside of his jacket and flicked it open. "You'd have to be pretty slick to get to me before I got to you."

"Do you think you could really stab someone?" she said.

"If he was coming at me," said Leonard, "I could stab him, quick as you can say 'knife.' "

"Could you?" she said to me.

"That's what I don't know," I said. "I would look for an alternative."

"I played some football, too, remember," he said. "The guys who had fast reaction times were the ones who never missed practice, one; and two, rehearsed in their minds every possible situation that could come up, again and again. It's a mistake to believe that when crunch time comes you'll automatically do the right thing, just out of the blue. There's always an initial moment of fluster. That's when the Ka-Bar gets introduced to your liver."

"That's gruesome," said Kay.

"Like Malcolm's arms, 'skinny *and* soft,' " I said, "that Serena is a hoot."

"I told you," said Kay.

"Let me lend you my S & W Model 642 in .38 special," Leonard said; "it's the best concealed-carry handgun ever built. I'm never without it when I go south."

I remembered Dizzy saying in his autobiography that when the band traveled south all the musicians carried handguns. And I remember his cutting Cab Calloway with the blade he always carried. You've got to be willing to odysseus someone and to risk getting odysseused in return, lest you get calypsoed.

"Let me think about it," I said to Leonard.

By the statue of Benjamin Franklin, with his look of having the inside dope on everything, we split up to go our separate ways, Kay to her class, Leonard to his, me to mine. The class went well, thank you. Felicia Zhang asked a question that if written up and padded out would go a long way toward getting her tenure. She had counted the number of times women's hair is mentioned in *The Wind Among the Reeds* (for we have moved from Pater to Wilde to early Yeats): twenty-nine times, she said. She then compared the associations of the hair in those mentions to the associations of the women's hair in paintings by the pre-Raphaelites Yeats mentions in his autobiography, for starters. She demonstrated a tangle of meanings, some regressive, some demonic, some fairly ethereal, some downright funky. Then she asked her question: was there any reason why at that time and that place men should have been in such a state about women's hair? Head hair was the only part of women you could see to build a pipe dream upon, I said (and without a second's hesitation), except for the face and hands, which were too socialized to be arousing. And Leonard says I can't think fast upon my feet.

All right, wise guy, what *is* the answer to Felicia's question, in either its historical or universal form?—for it is not just nineteenth-century men who have gotten themselves into a state over women's hair, for modern men can also get themselves into a state over women's hair, which is why so many modern women cut theirs short, to dis them. I have explained to you why men like the kind of legs on a woman they like. I believe I can also explain why the buttocks of human females, unique among mammals for their roundness, are sexual releasers. Way back then, before humans were entirely upright, females in heat "presented," as do number of female mammals still, primarily primates. Did I ever mention to you my theory that no sexual impulse is ever lost through evolution? (although some are inhibited by later developments). I don't see that there is much room for discussion, unless you want to argue that God put allure into the buttocks of women for the express purpose of teaching humility to men.

Now we are getting somewhere. Next I suppose you want to know what evolutionary goal put allure into the human female breasts, for you never see a bull fondling the cow's udder. That the human female breast is of great evolutionary significance no one can doubt. It is the only breast in nature that is distended around the seasonal clock, whether or not the possessor is lactating. That gives men something to like the year round, to the benefit of women, for in the good old days women needed men as protectors and providers. But that does not explain why men like what is there to like, for they are seldom aroused by the elbow, which is always there. Theories are not lacking, including some that imply an aroused male is essentially a big baby. The one I like best comes from Wolfgang Stutt-Wormgarten of the Max-Planck-Institute fur Verhaltensphysiologie, Seewiesen. He argues that as humans gradually became upright, the female breasts evolved in imitation of, and as a substitute for, the buttocks. Although Wolfgang doesn't say so, the consequence is that women arouse men no matter which way they are facing.

We are now in a position to address Felicia's question in its proper form: what evolutionary goal is served by the attractiveness to men of the hair on women? I haven't the foggiest. Maybe there was a time when women's behinds were hairy.

For supper Julie served eggplant parmesan artistically arranged on a platter of gnocchi garnished around the edges with parsley, black olives, and little rolls of anchovy, for Julie belongs to the school of vegetarianism that does not consider fish to be meat. We had a nice talk during dinner, although I did not get a word in myself, about Julie's new interest, institutional cookery. Did I know that in some of those awful jails down south the prisoners had to eat pork every day? The thought of getting myself a cell in one of those prisons by tickling Jerry Falwell with a Ka-Bar flashed across my mind. In Julie's opinion, attached to every prison should be a farm, on which the prisoners could work, keep them out of trouble, all those rapes and stabbings, and provide themselves with fresh vegetables instead of all that fatty meat, save the state some money, too, millions in fact.

"I've been thinking a lot about this stuff," she said.

"Urn," I said, for my mouth was full, for Julie's tomato sauce was thick and oniony and garlicky, and just think if she had used pork chops with the bone off instead of eggplant. Hey Joel, is there pork chop parmesan in heaven?

She knew that people didn't like to think this way anymore, she said, but suppose the government put up these retreats for people with AIDS all over the country. You know, put them up in places like where her parents live, where there's not much work. No one would have to go to these sanitaria, though we wouldn't call them that, but anyone with AIDS who wanted could go—and *for free*. She knew it would cost a lot to begin with, but it would save money in the long run. For one thing, everybody would have to work as long as they were able, you know, in the kitchen, following the dietician's orders, in the laundry, changing beds, mopping floors, on the farm. It would be a kind of cooperative. There would be a loving atmosphere, the patients taking care of each other, and they would be more kind than those snippy nurses when she had to go into the hospital with that antibiotic-resistant strain of clap. There would be a clinic right on the spot 'cause lots of gay doctors would be willing to work there, and people who were doing research on AIDS. You would have to go along with the research, you know, the kind that doesn't hurt you, telling your life, giving test tubes of blood, doing randomized double-blind experiments, and she looked up at me to see if I was digging it.

"What are you smiling at?" she said, a Ka-Bar in her voice. What did I do now? "You are always laughing at me," she said, getting up from the table.

"No, I'm—" I said.

"You think I'm just a dumb cunt," she said, sliding the platter of leftover eggplant into the refrig, slamming the door. "And it's only my dumb cunt that you're interested in," dumping dishes into the sink.

"Now, that's not—" I said.

"You don't care enough about my ideas to argue with me, even," she said, washing with exaggerated motions of her arms, her back to me. " 'Condescension,' that's the word I was looking for." How come women's tears lie so close to the surface, Joel? It's recently become the style for men to cry in public, especially politicos and athletes. I have to admit I'm not big on men who cry in public, or in private, for that matter. I got up, went over to Julie, put my arms around her, nested my chin on her head, rocked her from side to side.

"I don't think you're dumb," I said. "I know you're not dumb. I was smiling in admiration."

"Tell it to the marines," she said.

"You're smart," I said. "And you've got the gumption to apply your smarts to problems that no one else can solve."

"Don't try to soft-soap me," she said.

"Look, Julie," I said. "You can be stupid, you can be ignorant, or you can be crazy. You're not stupid and you're not crazy. That puts you at least one up on most of my colleagues."

"But I'm ignorant," she said, scornfully.

"Compared to my colleagues, since I mentioned them, you're short on book-learning," I said. "That you can get, you're getting it, and I love to see you using it. But if you haven't got smarts and sanity, book-learning won't get it for you."

"Just don't touch me, OK," she said. And when I gave her a squeeze, she said, "Get your fucking hands off me!" in a voice that everybody across the airshaft could have heard.

I went into my study and sat at the desk in a jangled funk, as when Belinda and I had spats. Legend has it that there are men who browbeat their women into submission. Have you ever met one? I haven't. And women are surprised when men sock them, not that I've ever socked a woman myself. When reason, explanation, conciliation, cajolery, pleading fail, what else is there? (A man who would use moral blackmail on a woman is not a man.) A man's natural mode of expression is an exertion of physical force, just as a woman's natural mode of expression is a deployment of words. That's why men who live by the word, especially professors of English, seem faggy to other men—and why writers like Hemingway, James Jones, and Norman Mailer are always exposing their hairy chests (morally speaking).

I was itchy and I was twitchy. I wanted to do something, but had no idea what. My calves tingled, my head buzzed, my shoulders hunched and bunched. I noticed with scientific detachment that the fingers of my right hand were clenched into a fist; as I watched they hooked open into claws. My face was hot; a sharp pang spasmed through my rectum. What I wanted clearly was to smash something, or somebody. No, I don't have any pacifying drugs in the house, no drugs of any kind, the ten-year-old bottle of aspirin still unopened. So I put on a cassette entitled *Basie Plays the Blues,* experience having convinced me that the rhythm section of Doctors Basie, Page, Green, and Jones would do a better job of regulating my neurotransmitters than anything a pill-peddler could prescribe. But when Jimmie Rushing sang "How long, baby, how long, how long?" I felt tears come to my eyes, and here I hadn't cried since I learned how to talk. How long, Joel, how long, how long.

There was nothing for it but go to the gym, knock myself out on the machines, better yet, take a long walk, down to Battery Park, at least, maybe stop in a Banana Republic, get myself one of those barn jackets everyone was wearing, for a Banana Republic XL was sometimes long enough and loose enough to fit, but I couldn't get out of my chair. You'd think Julie would have the consideration to fetch me a stiff drink, after all I've done for her. Then I remembered that Julie was pissed off at me.

I'll tell you, Joel, there is nothing more eerie than to see one of your thoughts, especially a secret thought, a shameful thought, make something happen in the material world, for when I looked up, there was Julie standing in the doorway. She was holding a small tray, on which there was a plate (on which there was something I couldn't see) and a big brandy snifter. Now where did she get that snifter? I know for a fact that I didn't have one in the house. Then I noticed what she was wearing: a black satin dress that came down to maybe two inches below her crotch; black mesh stockings; black leather high-heeled shoes; a little white apron, even shorter than the dress; something that looked like a starched doily worn in her hair like a tiara.

"Perhaps sir will take some refreshment," she said, eyes cast downward.

Catching on, I gave her a severe look, as though she were the Person from Porlock. "Yes, yes, come in, come in, can't you see I'm busy?" I said in a bad imitation of a fussy, snooty, upper-class voice.

"Yes, sir," she said meekly, "thank you, sir," with a curtsy. She walked in, little steps, eyes down, but instead of placing the tray on the desk from her side, she came over to my side and bent over, straight-legged, from the waist, her bottom so close to my face that it was slightly out of focus. She held her position, while I tilted back my head, for my eyes are permanently in focus for objects as far away as you would hold a book. I was pleased to note that Julie was not wearing pantyhose, never mind panties. Her stockings were held up by black satin garters that plumped out the flesh just above them nicely. But she needn't have gone through the trouble of perfuming herself, reminding me of Irene.

Zeno says they're all alike in the dark (the attitude of all successful seducers), but that only illustrates the unsoundness of the man. One: they are not all alike. Two: it's the differences under a strong light that count. Julie's labia majora are very attractive, which by no means goes without saying. They are plump, elastic, compact, snugly closed, lightly furred. From the angle at which I was observing them they were shaped like a little football wedged up high between her legs, a slightly irregular seam running down the middle (which I licked. "Oh, sir," she said). Her perineum was clean, a pale rose, her rosebud a shade rosier. It is the back of a woman's thighs that above all brings out their vulnerability, my desire to protect them (from what? from guys like me), essential womanhood, how they're alike in the dark after all, evocative of something human, not merely individual.

The trouble is that bending over at a ninety-degree angle like that took the plump out of her rump. I leaned forward, so that we were cheek to cheek, grasped her on either side of her rib cage, and lifted, until her upper body was at an angle of forty-five degrees to the perpendicular. That's better. The cheeks relaxed, came together and formed those lines that have driven men to acts of abysmal love, madness, ferocity, and self-sacrifice for a million years. Socially-constructed fetish, my ass! I was about to stand up, drop my pants, see what I could do, when Julie dropped back onto my lap and began to grind, lightly, sweetly, prettily.

She fed me a cucumber sandwich, what was on the plate. I pulled down her bodice and released a breast, which I then proceeded to kiss. She daubed the nipple and areola with brandy, gilding the lily. I fed her a cucumber sandwich and helped myself to some brandy-flavored breast. And so on. Talk about never being satisfied, but we were not making effective contact below, because my stomach was in the way, and right then I resolved to lose some weight, a lot of it. I put one arm under Julie's knees, one under her back, stood up, and carried her out of the study, as you would carry your new bride over the threshold, and into the den.

In the den and via the remote control, I turned on the TV, for the ten o'clock news was in progress, except that what blinked on instead was an ad for Fibercon. I pressed the button that released the lock on the back of my big chair, lowered the back, stretched myself out, face up, sat Julie on my now unencumbered lap, face toward the TV, so she could watch it, something to occupy her hyperactive mind, so I could lift her dress and watch the play of muscle and fat on either side of that necromantic cleft, as she began to move. For the occasion she had sophisticated her motion, the clockwise rotation integrated with a back-and-forth rocking of the pelvis. Contact was effective and the outcome, during an ad for Mylanta, as expected. I am not a groaner, even less a screamer, but Julie knew the minute I began to erupt, ceased her motions and bore down until the flow stopped, then leaned back, rolled over, and spread herself out on top of me. I was pleased to see that her face was flushed and her lips swollen, for in the sexual realm it is almost as blessed to give as to receive, although even I have experienced the keen pleasure of a cold, heartless, impersonal fuck. I reached a hand down and slid my middle finger between her well-lubricated lower lips. She rocked on it a few times, then stopped, said "No," pulled my hand away, "not until you can get it in. It's an incentive." I put my middle finger in my mouth.

"You're silly," she said.

"What was that maid routine in behalf of?" I said.

"I was thinking about our therapy sessions," she said, "—you know how you can only keep on working at something if you see signs of progress—when it struck me that you're a literary man, you deal in fantasy. So I thought that if I could take you away from yourself, I mean come on like one of your fantasies, sort of, it could, well, distract you from your spectatoring, you know, standing back from yourself to see how you're doing. 'Performance anxiety,' it's called. Well, we're making progress: there was only one layer of clothes between us today."

"The fantasies I deal in don't take you away from yourself, but equip you for living," I said.

"What's your favorite fantasy?" she said.

An image flashed across my mind:

> Belly, shoulder, bum
> Flash fishlike; nymphs and satyrs
> Copulate in the foam:

Yeats's pornutopia. "I have several favorites," I said, "but it would be too embarrassing to talk about them."

"How come, after all we've been through together, you still don't trust me not to laugh at you?" she said.

"It's myself I don't trust not to laugh at me," I said.

"And how come I practically have to throw a tantrum to get you to say something nice to me?" she said.

My guess at the time was that Julie asked me about my favorite fantasy because she wanted me to ask her about hers. Sometimes I'm slow on the uptake. "What's *your* favorite fantasy?" I said.

"We both come home from our jobs to a cozy little place we just bought in the suburbs," she said, ". . . that I decorated myself . . . we kiss, have a drink, make supper together . . . trying out a new recipe for seitan . . . and during supper we make plans for this long weekend we're going to spend at a swank Catskill resort, where the tennis pro has a crush on me, lots of educated people around. Like that: or I'm in a tailored business suit at the head of a conference table and everybody is looking at me to hear what I'll say. I tell them. . . . You're right, it *is* embarrassing."

But not shameful, unlike certain fantasies I could tell you about, pathetic maybe, or bathetic, or just sad. But then what's the use of having a fantasy about something that can actually happen? (Unless it really is true that in dreams begin responsibilities.) That's why I had resolved never to get tangled up with a woman again. Somehow you always let them down, even if you don't have a little problem like mine. And you can't help feeling for or with their sadness, imaginative sympathy again. *Post coitum, homo tristis,* they say. It's not just that I felt I was using Julie. After all, what's a lover for, if not to use her, or him? It's the suspicion, to put it mildly, that I was degrading her, although if our positions were reversed, I would not myself feel degraded, that much you can bet your precious Martin Committee Model on. But can you speak of someone as being degraded if she doesn't feel that way? Maybe Julie doesn't feel degraded. Maybe she feels relief at being able to do something for me in return for my taking her in, for some people find it intolerable to owe anything to anybody, as though you could get through life without accumulating debts. Maybe she feels exalted like some dumb Christian martyr. Your head it simply swurls.

"It doesn't have to be you in that cozy little house, you know," she said. "I don't want you to think.... It's because you're handy, if you know what I mean."

Anyhow, those were the thoughts that were swirling through my mind, for you could not say I was entertaining them, as I sat at my desk last night, not writing this letter, for my growing suspicion was that the person who was being degraded, or at least humiliated, nothing new in that, was me. And the source of my humiliation is sexual desire. And the sad fact is that it would be no less humiliating if I could satisfy it. The guy who gets laid every night makes just as big a buffoon of himself. Think of what we go through and give up to put our peckers in a pucker!

Fuck Mother Nature. Fuck the force that through the green fuse drives the flower. Fuck the evolutionary pressure to sow our seed and make it prevail. Fuck the desire that makes us comb our hair, brush our teeth, scrape our cheeks, jump through hoops, flex our muscles, preen our feathers, crawl on our bellies, sneak around corners, kick up our heels, clutch at straws, chase after rainbows, lie through our teeth, betray our friends, wear shit-eating grins. At one remove or another all wars are over Helen of Troy. Enough, no more, I've had it!

Easy for me to say? If you don't think what Julie and I have been doing is sex, it must be the thin air you're breathing. Right there, last night in my study, I made the historic decision to swear off sex. On behalf of human dignity I renounce the thing. When tomorrow night, or what yesterday was tomorrow night, Julie comes to the door of my study to claim me for a session of therapy, I'll say Nothing doing. Of course I'll say it in a nice way, so as not to hurt her feelings. I'll sit her on my lap, put an arm around her, look into her eyes.... And if she starts to rotate? I was asking myself that question when Julie appeared at the door in the flesh, rather than in my imagination.

"Come on, Cuz, let's go to bed," she said. "You look like you're going under for the third time," coming over to the desk, pulling me to my feet. "That job of yours takes too much out of you," resting a hand on my shoulder. "You're losing weight too fast, especially your face," guiding me into the hall. "Who knows what's going on with your body better than me?" and as we walked down the hall she rested her head against my upper arm, hand still on my shoulder. "I like big men because they give me a sense of security. They're more calm and stable and even-tempered. You can rely on them not to be flighty and fickle. Little men can be so excitable. I had a boyfriend once, was only five foot six, but well-formed, you know. Well, he . . . ," chatter, chatter, music to my ears, until we both were abed.

It's nearly twelve noon, but instead of joining the gang for lunch, I am going to the University gym, for it is also humiliating to be fat. Talk to you later.

15

I was not surprised

that I could lift, push, and pull more weight than your run-of-the-mill collegiate gym-fly. All summer I worked like a man possessed, extending the lawn, some of those white pines three feet in diameter, some of those rocks the size of a microbus, for when I could teach my son how to catch a long pass. He hooks and flies for the post, looking back over his left shoulder, and snares the ball neatly, left hand up, right hand down, without breaking stride, and crosses the goal line, drops the ball nonchalantly for the official to fetch, no spike, no cakewalk, no high fives, just a light pat on the can from the center, who is captain of the team. What surprised me is that I am not as fat as I thought.

The only full-length mirror in my apartment is on the door to the closet in Julie's room (as I now think of it). I never look in the other, smaller, mirrors unless I have clothes on. I even put on a tee shirt after I shower, before I shave. But you can't avoid all the full-length mirrors in the gym, for they are everywhere. If I were to lose thirty-five pounds and retain all the muscle I would look all right. It would no longer be humiliating to undress before a woman, although I am finished with all that, although no woman has ever surveyed my gut with a look of withering disdain, draw your scrotum up to your adenoids. I've been lucky that way, or women are too considerate, or too aware of their own imperfections, which everyone has, while we are still in the flesh. Just now I had a vision of thirty-five pounds of steak. That's a lot of meat to lose. Well, if you can put it on, you can take it off, spare me the bullshit about slow metabolism, and hyper- or hypoactive hormones, or what runs in your family.

None of that means I had a container of yogurt for lunch. Can you imagine? I was in my office, unwrapping a Philly cheese steak hero, but only one, with quick fingers, in case Hector was on his way, when a voice said, "May I come in?"

"Come in of your own free will," I said, in my best Bela Lugosi voice, for you have to enter Dracula's domain on your own volition, or invite him into yours, before he will kiss you on the neck.

Serena's neck is short and thick, for a woman's. I lit up our cigarettes. She was wearing a waist-length black cape, the high collar open, a brown dress hanging loosely below. My belief is that Serena wears shapeless dark clothes because she is self-conscious of being overweight, nothing to speak of, by my standards. "Could you go for half a sandwich?" I said, tipping my head toward the Philly cheese.

"I better not," she said. Good girl. "But it was nice of you to ask. You missed a good conversation at lunch. We were trying to figure out what kind of person could kill Terry Jones and Blinky Hartmann—that's what everyone called him, right?"

"That kind of person doesn't know himself what kind of person he is," I said, living up to the reputation I have in some circles of being a pain in the ass. I took a bite of Philly cheese steak.

"Marshall says every one of us has it in us to have done it," she said.

"No doubt," I said, chewing. "But you'd need an irresistible motive to go through all that trouble and risk. Which of us has one?"

"That kind of person's motives are not the ones he thinks he has," she said, as though to prove she too could be a pain in the ass.

"In that respect he is like the rest of us," I said.

"Marshall thinks that Gonzalez is telling you things you don't tell us," she said.

"Suarez," I said. I held up a slice of pickle, which she accepted.

"How would you like to write an essay?" she said.

"I have written several already," I said, picking some escaped shreds of steak off the wax paper.

"Kay and I are editing a volume called *Postmodernist Marriage: Gays and Lesbians Together,*" she said. "We want you to write an essay on Carrington and Lytton Strachey as modernist precursors." And here I bit off a piece of sandwich the size of a bull's nose.

"It's not a subject . . . ," I said, for my mouth was full.

"You'll be in good company," she said. "Kay knows everybody."

"She goes to a lot of conferences," I said, putting the sandwich down, giving up for now.

"Don't you?" she said.

"Conferences are for people on the make—in both senses," I said.

"Well, I'm on the make," she said.

"So long as you're on the make with style . . . ," I said.

"If you're not on the make, in either sense, what is there to live for?" she said.

Has someone told this woman about my little problem? "I'll think about doing the essay," I said, although I'm as likely to become a Presley imitator as write about that nest of ninnies they call Bloomsbury.

"We want your name to help us pry a contract out of Routledge," she said.

"Tomorrow at lunch," I said, or was I going to the gym? For it was nice to feel that heaviness and burn in my muscles again.

"There's one more thing," she said, as I lifted my sandwich. "I want to make my spring course on the turn to postmodernism as good as possible."

"We all have confidence in you," I said, for I had only taken a nibble of my sandwich.

"My problem is strategic," she said. "How do I make clear to the students what postmodernism turned away from, turned against, superseded, negated, namely modernism, without wasting half the course on it?"

"You could work from those parallel columns in Hassan and in Harvey," I said. I needed a drink, for some fool had cut all the fat off the beef.

"They're too—" she said.

"Do you know how to work the office coffee machine?" I said.

"I'm good at figuring out that sort of thing," she said. "Give me a gadget. . . ."

"Why don't you make us some coffee," I said— "use one and a half packages of grounds—while I lay down some chords you can take off on."

"Key of B-flat," she said, getting up and going out.

Chomping big clumps of sandwich, I wrote out the following:

MODERNISM	POSTMODERNISM
short-haired women	long-haired men
irony	camp
the parricide	the serial killer
flapper	fag hag
relativity	entropy
the artist	the critic
Daedalus	Erostratus
nostalgia	amnesia
spiral	Mobius strip
absinthe	bottled water
impersonality	anonymity
Dali	Warhol
Stravinsky	Sex Pistols
archetype	kitsch
exile	immersion

Lost Generation	Baby Boomers
blighted womb	polyphiloprogenitive
asshole	
labyrinth	shopping mall
correspondence	heterogeneity
Odysseus	Calypso
Hamlet	Caliban
decircumferencing	decentering
making the familiar strange	making the strange familiar
radical individualism	dispersion of the subject
the museum	the graffito
politics psychologized	psychology politicized
an approach to the condition of music	white noise
Krazy Kat	*Cats*
Bop	Pop
Dizzy Gillespie	Michael Jackson

I had the last pair in mind from the beginning, but saved them for the climax, wrote them down only as Serena walked into the office, sipping from one cup of coffee, holding out another for me to take. "Dark, no sugar, right?" she said.

"Right," I said.

We sat, sipped, smoked, sized each other up. "What have you got for me?" she said. I handed her the sheet of paper with the two columns on it. I could see her eyes shuttling as she scanned the thing in thirty seconds, a speed reader, snickering once.

"I always thought it was fruitless to grump because things are no longer the way they were," she said.

"You can only criticize, only see, your own historical fix from a point outside it," I said, "either from an imagined future or from a point on the margin, or from a moment in the past. You've got to dislocate your mind."

"Why do you have to *criticize* at all?" she said.

"It's what intellectuals do," I said.

"Why not just open yourself to whatever winds of change are blowing?" she said. "The criticism I like best is a kind of celebration."

"Unlike Christians and Marxists, birds of a feather and therefore rivals, I can't predict the future," I said; "the margin, of late, has become overcrowded; but I am comfortable with the culture of modernism, its point in history."

"And I am comfortable with the culture of postmodernism," she said, dipping her cigarette in the last of her coffee, abruptly standing. "Does that mean a fight to the finish?"

"Not at all," I said, "We would both be superseded by something neither of us can predict before either of us could win."

"What I mean is, sometimes I feel that besides disapproving of me in general, you resent my friendship with Kay," she said.

What brought this on? Her face had gone blotchy and her lower lip was trembling. "Easy now," I said. "Take a deep breath."

"We don't have to be rivals, you know," she said. "I'm not going to seduce her away from you. Men always think—"

"You're not taking out your Shrade Folding Hunter, are you?" I said, for she was fumbling with her handbag.

"I'm looking for a handkerchief," she said, sitting. Mumbling, looking down, she said, "On the first page of his autobiography, Miles Davis talks about the greatest feeling he ever had in his life (with his clothes on)," and she shot me a glance. "It was when he heard Dizzy Gillespie and Charlie Parker in person for the first time. 'Man, that shit was so terrible it was scary,' he says." She sniffled, began to speak clearly. "They were in Billy Eckstein's band, with guys like Gene Ammons, Lucky Thompson, and Art Blakey. Then he uses an odd phrase: 'Man, that shit was all up in my body.' But the climax comes when he says, 'And me up there playing with them.' That's some of what I felt that first day when Leonard gave me a cigarette and Zeno lit it," she dabbed at her eyes with a tie-dyed bandanna the size of a tablecloth.

"None of us are of that stature," I said. What do you think is the selective advantage in women having a gene for making men feel like shits?

"Anybody who wants to work on Dr. Johnson has to come through Marshall," she said. "Anyone who wants to work on African American poetry has to build on Leonard. Anyone who wants to do feminist criticism of eighteenth-century culture has to deal with Kay. A whole industry has grown around your concept of the minor poet in the age of modernism. Your essay on Edith Sitwell has been reprinted what, a dozen times?"

"Twenty-three times," I said.

"When Miles Davis first came to New York, Dizzy Gillespie took him around everywhere, opening doors," she said. "That's what Kay is doing for me."

"What are you doing reading Miles Davis' autobiography?" I said.

"I read it because I assumed you read it," she said, standing, putting her bandanna away. "Who was Erostratus?" Her face was blank, as though she had already given too much away.

"He said that if he couldn't win immortal fame by an act of creation he would achieve it by an act of destruction," I said, "so he burnt down the temple to Artemis."

"Well, it was a start," she said. "You ought to look into Carrington and Strachey, expand your sympathies. When he died, she committed suicide, did you know that? It's pretty good proof she wasn't just playing a part. You can't judge the quality of a love by its object." And she walked out before I could even stand in one my fuddy-duddy shows of courtesy.

If she had waited a minute, I would have told her that there were theatrical ways of committing suicide, too. I don't see how a postmodernist can get away with Serena's touching faith in the possibility of sincerity. Damn the woman: there she was again, standing in the doorway.

"What's more," she said, waggling her pointer finger, "I believe we have not only a right, but a moral obligation to get what pleasure there is to get in things as they are before we scratch around with a ten-foot pole for something to criticize." She did an about-face and marched off before I had a chance to say that that depends on how things as they are *are*, doesn't it? Still, she had a point. Criticism as an act of celebration—there's a revolutionary idea for you.

Poor old Sam Coleridge, a junkie like you, Joel, used to say that an arresting object in your field of view will call up the opposite in your imagination. A withered gaffer, for instance, might call up a nymphet gymnast; a faculty meeting might call up a primal scream (these examples are not Coleridge's); and Serena's ambitions called up a vision: I am sitting at the kitchen table, watching Julie bend over the stove, listening to her explain how her seventy-eight recipes for tempeh will turn the wayward denizens of Riker's Island into solid citizens.

I threw books and lecture notes into an old gym bag, for Julie was still using my carryall, and headed for the door—where Murray barred the way.

"Whoa, big fella," he said, the palm of a hand on my chest. "I have come expressly to charge you with dereliction of duty."

"I don't remember signing on to spearhead your campaign," I said, removing his hand.

"It doesn't look as though I'll need a spearhead," he said. "Angel hasn't learned what every street hustler knows: that if you squeeze a fish too hard, he'll slip out of your grasp. The emerging consensus seems to be that old Murray's not so bad, after all."

"I get the feeling I'm about to be squeezed," I said, moving to sidle out the door.

He took a step sidewise to block me. "Monika tells me that you have not yet gotten your field committees operational," a hand on my chest.

I ought to explain: when an assistant professor comes up for a third- or fifth- or seventh-year review, the vice-chair appoints a committee, for a change. This committee will consist of three senior professors in the assistant professor's field, except that there are few fields in which we still have three tenured professors, for the policy of our administration is to increase the number of students, who pay tuition, and to decrease the number of faculty, who get paid salaries. So the vice-chair will raid an adjacent field, thus making an enemy for life. Fine. These three field committee members read, or if they are like Blinky Hartmann, pretend to read, everything the candidate has written, look up the students' course evaluation protocols, which can throw a conscientious teacher into terminal despair, smooch around to see whether the candidate is accessible to students, has not recently molested one of them, takes on committee work, fits in, knows how to buy a round of drinks. They then write separate reports, or on the rare occasion when they agree, a joint report, to the vice-chair. So far so good. The vice-chair then distributes copies of the report or reports to the Administrative Committee, which after the members have done some reading and smooching around of their own, is called to a meeting by the vice-chair. The Administrative Committee is made up of the chair, the vice-chair, and the three DD's or divisional directors of College English, Graduate English, and SAS English, for which they do instructional housekeeping. Their charge is to take the larger view: will the candidate's writing have an impact on the profession, thereby bringing honor to the University and the Department, thereby attracting good students and promising new Ph.D.s and alumni money. Do we need someone with the candidate's special expertise, or do we already have all the experts on Rhonda Fleming we can handle? The Administrative Committee debates these matters until fatigue or boredom or disgust sets in, whereupon the vice-chair calls a meeting of the Executive Committee. This august body is made up of all the tenured members of the Department, some of whom will have read the candidate's prose (for assistant professors of English seldom write poetry) or done their own smooching around. To the Executive Committee the vice-chair reads a judicious report on the wranglings of the field committee and the Administrative Committee, so that the Executive Committee can wrangle in an informed manner. In the case of the third-year review, the members of the Executive Committee, after having spent as much time in each other's company as they can bear, will instruct the chair and vice-chair to tell the candidate, say, that he or she better get his or her ass in gear, either that or apply to law school, where a goof-off won't be noticed, or apply to that junior college in East Houston with a job in her or his field. In the case of a fifth-year review, the Executive Committee, after displays of eloquence equal to that of Milton's fallen angels, will instruct the chair and vice-chair to tell the candidate that he (or she) better get a second book written in the next two years or look into that job up north in St. Lawrence County, which has the nation's highest rate of incest, for the winters are cold, teaching five sections of freshman composition each term. In the case of a seventh-year review, the Executive Committee, after unspeakable pomposities, sinister silences, and on good days, a fist fight, votes, in a secret ballot, either to recommend the candidate for tenure or to pauperize her (or him), for s/he or it will be nearing forty and maybe sixty thousand in debt. Should the majority share the candidate's politics, the chair writes a brief, though Murray got Terry Jones to do it, arguing the candidate's qualifications for tenure. The brief is then forwarded to the triumvirate of deans of University College (or UC, familiarly known as YOOK), Graduate Arts and Sciences (GAS), and SAS (or School of Advanced Studies), who, if the candidate has not rocked the boat, will forward it to the Provost of the University. The Provost, if he has not got it in for the Department, will appoint an Ad-Hoc Committee of tenured professors from different departments (to forestall nepotism) but related fields. If the Provost has not stacked the Committee against the candidate, for provosts are by nature conservative and assistant professors are by nature progressive, the Ad-Hoc Committee is likely to let the candidate through, for they are busy people, and it takes less effort to nod sleepily in agreement than to dream up a counter-brief. The

Provost then sends a heavily edited report of the Ad-Hoc Committee's deliberations to the President of the University, who may say, "Fuck this shit, there are too many Hungarians in this hellhole already. Send him to Princeton." Or he may say, "If those assholes in English want this turkey now, they better not come crying to me later on for a purge." He will then get the Trustees, also busy people, to rubber-stamp his whim. You can see why even a dedicated vice-chair might hesitate to set this process in motion.

"There have been personal . . . uh . . . complications," I said, removing Murray's hand from my chest.

"We want to do Nina on the third Tuesday in October, Francine on the second Tuesday in November, and Malcolm on the first Tuesday in December," he said, for tenured professors do not schedule classes on Tuesdays from 12 to 2, when the Executive Committee has its brown-bag meetings. "That way we can avoid the end-of-the-term crunch."

"Can't be done," I said.

"You could at least wish me luck," he said.

"What do you need it for?" I said.

"This weekend, at a conference center in Bear Mountain, I present my benefits plan to the Trustees," he said. "Irene was putting together a video when she . . . flipped. She could have waited two weeks."

"I don't suppose you've seen her," I said.

"I was going to," he said, "but she's getting out this Friday. Her father twisted arms. The deal is, she lives with her parents; she never leaves home unescorted; she visits a designated shrink daily. Have you?"

"I was going to, but something always comes up. I thought I'd drop by when I went in to have my stitches checked this Friday," I said, further proof that I can think on my feet.

"Better get there before noon," he said. "Teddy says she feels terrible about biting you, but Oprah Winfrey made her do it. That damn woman squirreled away some charts I need. . . . Monika and I have been turning the office upside down . . ." and he walked away waving an arm against the injustice of it all.

I don't think a man in my position should have to sneak around. Just the same, I took our neurasthenic elevator down to the subbasement, so I could walk crouched over along an ancient tunnel lined with pipes that rumbled and hissed. I exited a block away from my office, for I was not in a mood to encounter Hector Suarez.

Good old Julie was in fact bending over the stove. "I'm making black bean and spinach burritos, Cuz," she said, over her shoulder. I sat down at the kitchen table and fanned out the mail, so that I could see at a glance whether there were any love letters or checks (there were not). "I know you like lots of onions," she said. When Julie looked back to talk, I dropped my eyes to an Eddie Bauer catalogue, for some women consider it rude of men to study their asses. Damn if there wasn't a Gore-Tex parka with a zip-out fleece lining, color of bottle-green, just what I needed. I bless Eddie Bauer, for their talls are truly tall and their XL's are ample. And I curse L.L. Bean for the short sleeves of their Talls and the narrow shoulders of their XL's. "There's some pesto I made in the icebox," Julie said, "if you want to try it. You may not think it goes well with Mexican food because it's, you know, Italian and all but—" An invisible hand pulled me out of my chair and pushed me over to the stove, where I wrapped my arms around Julie in a chaste hug, my chin on her head, hands off the hot spots. She kindly backed into me, with a wiggle.

"You're under arrest," said the unmistakable voice of Hector Suarez, "for contributing to the delinquency of a minor."

"Where did you come from?" I said.

"Your study," he said. "I wanted to see whether your versions of the list Ms. Howland gave me might not be a bit more forthcoming. By the way, when she gets out of the loony bin you ought to have her over to straighten out your files."

"Where's your search warrant?" I said.

"My mother used to say I had a Spanish nose, smell burritos cooking from the other side of Central Park," he said. "Still, if you want an authentic burrito, you start with diced cat and build it up from there. I already told Cousin Julie."

"Suppose you two get out of my kitchen," Julie said. "We eat in forty minutes."

Once we settled into our usual places, Hector on one side of my desk, me on the other, he with a cigar, me with a cigarette, both of us with beers, Hector said, "I got some names here I want to run by you. These are graduate students who were flunked in something or another by Terry or Blinky or both."

"Shoot," I said.

"Trafalgar Oursly-Hatch," he said.

"Oh yes," I said: "she took my course in the novel of empire."

"She flunked her pre-oral," he said, "administered, it says here, by Terry Jones. Is that a big deal?"

"No," I said: "you can keep on taking it until your sponsor is satisfied. Then you move on to the Orals."

"Sounds vaguely obscene," he said.

"The pre-oral is written," I said; "its function is to see if the student has the facts. The function of the Orals is to see what he, in this case she, can do with them."

"Well, she finally passed her Orals," he said.

"Passed her dissertation defense, too," I said.

"What was she defending?" he said.

"Her claim that the Crusaders were not only mean to the Saracens, but that they went on to *inscribe* them, the dirty rats," I said.

"Are we talking tattoos here?" he said.

"The Crusaders wrote about the Saracens in such a way as to justify being mean to them," I said.

"Could make you ashamed to be a Christian," he said. "What did the Saracens have to say?" he said.

"My guess is that they inscribed the Crusaders," I said, "but Ms. Oursly-Hatch didn't even guess."

"What happened to her?" he said.

"She's up for tenure at Yale," I said.

"I don't see her killing Terry and Blinky," he said. "Bernard Schwartz."

"One of my favorite students." I said.

"Yeah, well he flunked something or another," he said, "but this form. . . ."

"When you take your Orals," I said, "two professors whipsaw you for an hour in your major field. Then three professors work you over for a half hour each in two minor fields and a major author."

"But in a nice way, right?" he said.

"If you fail your major field, you've had it. You look for another line of work. If you fail a minor field and the examining committee thinks you're worth salvaging, you get six months to retake that part of the exam, but in written form. Blinky failed Schwartz in a minor field for not doing justice to the Cathars."

"But then it's so seldom that anyone does do justice to the Cathars, whoever the fuck *they* were," he said.

"I worked with Bernie on his dissertation from before he knew what he was going to write about," I said, "but only unofficially. We thought it best for his career that his advisors of record be medievalists."

"Terry Jones and Bertil Lund," Hector said.

"They had their heads elsewhere," I said. "Bernie began by examining the relation between the hero and his king in classical literature, Achilles and Agamemnon, for starters."

" 'Great Achilles, whom we knew,' " said Hector, who is nowhere near as ignorant as he pretends.

"Then in two long middle sections, he does the same for medieval epic and romance, Beowolf and Hrothgar, Roland and Charlemagne, Tristan and Mark, the knights around the table and Arthur, Cuchulain and Conchubar, Siegfried and whatshisname—"

"Moishe, I believe it was," he said.

"Then in his last section, Bernie stands back for a sweeping glance at recent American popular culture," I said: "how MacArthur looked at himself in relation to Truman, how his fans looked at Patton in relation to Eisenhower: the western hero as opposed to the town bigwigs, the banker, the mayor, the preacher, the sheriff; Dirty Harry and his precinct captain."

"Spare me," Hector said.

"In each case you have on one side a representative of merely institutional authority: his power comes from his position, not from something in himself. He needs the hero to defeat their common enemy, a threat to their society's existence. But the very force in the hero that makes him heroic resists socialization, can't be controlled, flies beyond good and—"

"You don't come across guys like this in real life," Hector said, "good thing probably."

"Think of Lawrence Taylor," I said.

"I can tell you there are no Dirty Harries in the NYPD," he said. "IAD has made us all Hamlets."

"That's why we need him in literature," I said.

"Movies are not literature," he said. "I'm surprised at you. What's Bernie doing now?"

"He's freezing his ass in Wisconsin writing catalogue copy for Land's End," I said.

"He decided to go straight?" he said.

"He couldn't get a job in academe," I said.

"What, no one went to bat for him?" he said.

"When I saw that Bernie wasn't getting any interviews, I asked the Placement Office to send me his dossier," I said. "The letters of recommendation from Terry Jones and Bertil Lund praised Bernie in general, but pointed out, with what I consider misplaced scrupulosity, that he had not entirely mastered the new feminist criticism of medieval literature."

"What is this Bertil Lund?" he said.

"The French call guys like him a vaginard," I said.

"A cunt!" he said.

"Blinky's letter was the same one he wrote for everyone," I said. "My own letter was a rave, but I'm not a medievalist, so it didn't count for much."

"This dissertation you wish you had written yourself, it didn't count for anything?" he said.

"Lisbet Arno and I sent the manuscript with a cover letter to every university press where we had an in," I said. "The letters we got back were all more or less the same: for one thing, the essay was old-fashioned; for another, it was too well written."

"You got to get out of this, Slim," he said; "maybe you could write catalogue copy for J. Crew. I think probably I ought to have a word with Bernie Schwartz. You got his address?"

"It's probably in Irene's computer," I said.

"Ms. Wright won't give me the password," he said.

"Try the Alumni Office," I said.

"The last address they have is Convent Avenue," he said. "Christopher North."

"I never knew him," I said.

"He flunked his dissertation defense," he said.

"That's not supposed to happen," I said. "Your sponsor is supposed to make sure your dissertation is up to snuff before he lets you defend."

"I only got four signatures on this form," he said.

"Professors get sick, too," I said. "Their sainted mothers also die suddenly. If you miss a defense, and it had better be for a good reason, you write a letter saying whether you vote Pass or Fail, and why. It should be stapled to the grade form."

"What I got is a Xerox of the grade form, and that's it," he said.

"Whose signatures are on it?" I said.

"Terry Jones, Bertil Lund, Marshall Grice, and some name I can't make out, only it ends in 'elli,'" he said.

"Fran Vocatelli," I said, "art history. Our medievalists use her on weak dissertations, because she's got a soft heart. Our students like her because in her enthusiasm for everything she answers her own questions in the process of asking them. A canny student just says enough to egg her on. If she failed this dissertation, it must have been truly awful."

"In fact, she voted Pass; but the other three voted Fail," he said.

"Who was the sponsor?" I said.

"Under Terry Jones's name it says 'Co-sponsor,'" he said.

"Here's what we know," I said: "Chris North had to be in the English Department, given the three examiners from English: Jones, Lund, Grice. His dissertation subject had to be interdisciplinary, because the other cosponsor came from another department, because you can't have more than three examiners from the student's home department. His subject had to be one that stretches from the medieval period to the eighteenth century, in that Marshall Grice is an expert in the eighteenth century with disdain for what precedes it and contempt for what followed."

"As far as the Alumni Office is concerned, Christopher North doesn't exist," Hector said.

"Try Teddy Nakatani," I said. "He's been around a long time, too long, and he somehow gets to know everyone. When was this defense?"

"May 22, nineteen ninety-something," he said, "it's smudged."

"Classes are over . . . ," I said: "some of us are still reading final exams and term papers . . . others are already on their annual diaspora . . . graduate students are—wait! Some time back there Terry was on leave for whole academic year, out there in Santa Fe, some old nunnery. Two hundred years ago a bunch of nuns began to raise hell, said they were possessed by the devil."

"And you know better, right?" he said. "What are you, one of these mush-brain liberals, thinks the devil doesn't exist?"

"I am," I said. "I forgot you went to school with the nuns."

"That's right," he said. "All you got to work with is prejudice, but

I got personal experience. I wouldn't say all nuns is possessed by the devil. Some may be possessed by aliens."

"Around the same time Marshall Grice was the acting vice-chair," I said. "He created a kind of era of good feeling, even curriculum committee meetings.... His memos read like pages torn out of Gibbon."

"I can see that everything to do with this Chistopher North is going to be a pain in the ass," he said. "Shana Plotkin."

"Oh, her," I said.

"Let's see," he said. "She defended in 1987, got her degree in 1988...."

"If your dissertation is punk," I said, "and the committee is too fainthearted to fail you, they can vote 'Pass with Major Revisions.' That means you've got a year to rewrite."

"So Ms. Plotkin rewrote," he said.

"So I rewrote," I said. "She came to me for help. Besides being stupid, she had a jones for words like 'addressivity' and 'performality.' At the end the dissertation was still punk, but the prose scanned."

"In other words, because of you Ms. Plotkin is out there shoveling bullshit on students at $3,000 a load," he said. "Where's your professional ethics?"

"She's teaching at Duke, where no one will notice," I said.

"What's her schtick?" he said.

"There was a twelfth-century writer of romances," I said, "name of Chretien de Troyes. Shana Plotkin said he stole all his stuff from the writings of court ladies."

"Did he?" he said.

"She also said that in a patriarchal culture, then as now, the writings of and by women are first discouraged, then disparaged, then destroyed, expunged from memory," I said.

"My sister is big on Mary Baker Eddy," he said. "How come she was never expunged?"

"Come and get it," Julie said, her voice echoing down the hall, and you gets no bread with one meatball.

There were four immense burritos on a platter garnished with parsley and radishes cut to look like flowers. I prophesied accurately who was going to wind up with two of them, and it wasn't me. There was the famous pesto, a tureen of yellow rice, a small bowl of sour cream, a small bowl of chopped onions, two small bowls of salsa, one of which, to my gratification, was hot enough to make the roof of your mouth hang in shreds. From the freezer Julie took beer mugs encrusted with ice.

"I think I'll have a beer myself tonight," she said, sitting down, surveying us with that look of modest but complacent expectancy anybody whose mother knew how to cook will remember.

Chewing judiciously, eyes closed, nose in the air, then opening his eyes, looking at Julie, Hector said, "Will you marry me?"

"Well, a woman does like to be appreciated," she said.

"The best burrito ever," I said, too late to do me any good.

"You haven't even tasted it yet," Julie said.

I walked Hector to his car, for Julie insisted on cleaning up herself, for she didn't want me getting in her way, for she did not want to share, as I saw it, in any way whatsoever, the credit for dinner.

We paused for a cigarette on the parapet diagonally across from the site of Terry's demise. Side by side we rested our forearms on the wall and looked out over Morningside Park. A full, fat, sulfurous moon loomed over East Harlem, soliciting us to madness and sin. It cast a yellow glow into the haze rising out of the huddled tenements, like steam from overheated bodies. I tipped back my head and howled.

"That's the way it is with professors," Hector said. "They always know what to say. Right now, on one of those rooftops a guy with AIDS is passing his needle to someone who hasn't got it yet."

"At a kitchen table, some kid, his legs intertwined with a chair leg, is doing his homework," I said.

"On another rooftop, some kid with a stutter, an I.Q. of eighty, and no hope of ever finding a job, is getting a fourteen-year-old girl pregnant," he said.

"On another kitchen table, mom and pop are using pencil and paper to figure out whether they can afford cable TV," I said.

"On the street below two kids are using a hacksaw to cut a piece out of the steering wheel of a Cherokee, so they can remove the Club," he said. "Some wiseguy will give them 200 dollars for the ten thousand dollars worth of parts."

"At a big old-fashioned kitchen sink, the kind that is also the wash tub and bathtub, Grandma sponges the back of little Altagracia," I said.

"Grandma thinks little Altagracia is possessed by the devil," he said. "Grandma is getting ready to drop Altagracia into a tub of scalding water."

Below us, in the brush, a dog, I assumed it was a dog, let loose with a howl that began in a growl and ended in a moan. Hector lifted his face to the moon and howled. I joined him. We howled and howled, my howl beginning before his ended, his beginning again before mine ended. Uptown in the park, where nobody ventures, a dog, it had to be a dog, answered. Below us there was a yelp, a ki-yi-yi, a thrashing in the brush. Further down the slope, further east, a black shape burst out of the brush and lumbered onto the walk. It was a dog, a big dog, a black dog, a Labrador mix, I'd say, with a limp. It stopped under a lamp and looked back, showing its teeth in what were it human, you might call a shit-eating grin, something you see a lot of nowadays.

I looked at Hector and Hector looked at me. I saw movement over Hector's shoulder, a luminous blob. It was floating three or four feet above the steps leading from the park onto the parapet. Steadily it ascended toward us, grew legs, resolved itself into a man in a white shirt, into Teddy Nakatani, who stepped onto the parapet. "Gentlemen," he said, for it is the custom in these parts, when at night you come upon someone, to greet him so as 1) to show that you mean no harm and 2) to show that you expect no harm, for there are local people whose sensibilities have been rubbed so raw they take any sign that you fear them as an insult.

HECK. The fuck is this? You got a death wish, Bub?

WYN. What art thou that usurpist this time of night?

TED. Friend to this ground and liegeman to the Chair.

WYN. Be thou a spirit of health or a goblin damned
Thou com'st in such a questionable shape
That I will speak to thee. I'll call thee Tedsuo
Jug, Teddy, what you will. O answer me.

TED. I am thy older ergo,
Doomed for a certain term to walk the night
Until the foul crimes done in your days of nature
Are burned and purged away.

WYN. Alas, poor ghost
Who op'd his pond'rous but mobile jaws to no avail.

TED. O my prophetic soul!
Thus lust, though to a radiant angel link'd
Will sate itself in a celestial bed
And prey on garbage.

HECK. That's because
The signal moon is zero in his void.

WYN. Yon park is chock-a-block with errant spirits:
Suppose one tempt you with razor-slick tongue
To where the dreadful summit of the wall
Beetles o'er his base into the brush
And there assume some other horrible form.

TED. I'd cut off his prick and shove it up his ass.

WYN. Why air your quiff in the thick and poxy night
And not in the thin and healthful rays of the sun?

TED. I prefer my constitutional to take
When no need there is to return the hostile
Gaze of passers-by, you see.

HECK. A likely story, Peter Lorre.

TED. That don't rhyme, Frankenstein.

HECK. Yes it do, Fu Manchu.

"You must learn to make distinctions among your Orientals," Teddy said. "We Japanese are as different from the Chinese as Swabians are from Saudis."

"Did you know a graduate student named Christopher North?" said Hector.

"I knew him, yes," said Teddy. "You will excuse me. I promised myself a brisk circuit of the park before returning to my books," and he pushed off, moving uptown.

"Those foul crimes done in your days of nature," Hector said, "they weren't done with Teddy there, were they?"

Before I knew it was happening, my arms shot forward, the heels of my hands thumping into the front of Hector's shoulders. He lurched backward, bounced off the wall and onto one knee. The look on his face, of shocked surprise and yes, damn it, of fear, gave me a lift. "You can move for your gun if you want, motherfucker, but I'll throw you over the wall before you get it out, guaranteed," I said.

He got up deliberately, no sudden moves, an evil smile on his face. We stood facing each other, our shoulders hunched. If either of us had blinked, the other would have been on him. I, for one, was ready to do some serious damage. Then he relaxed, leaned back against the wall, a look of genuine amusement on his face. "Well, well," he said.

"Yes," I said, for we had both grown up in an environment where there were certain things you could not let pass. We lit up. Nothing more of interest occurred between Hector and me on that occasion.

But the night's adventures were not yet over. I was sitting in my study, minding my own business, trying to think of something at once interesting and true to say about Sue Bridehead, for after aestheticism I move to some state-of-the-nation novels, *Jude the Obscure, The Secret Agent, Tono-Bungav, Howard's End,* before colliding with full-blown modernism, when Julie appeared at the door. On my right hand, from the cigarette in the ashtray rose a thin line of smoke that ended in a squiggle. On my left hand, from a brandy snifter, ascended the fragrance of Armagnac. All around my head were the opening phrases of Flip Phillips doing "Perdido" for Jazz at the Phil, the greatest rabble-rousing solo ever. Man, when he gets into that repeated phrase, dah du DAH, dah du DAH, the crowd erupts, and you can almost smell the spermy drawers and sticky panties.

Julie was leaning against the door frame, head tilted forward, sucking on her thumb. She was wearing maryjanes, one foot crossed on top of the other. One white sock was limp around an ankle: the other aspired to her calf. Her pleated, black watch plaid skirt was short. I do not believe I have ever seen a skirt shorter. Her white blouse was demure, chaste, buttoned up to her neck. She removed her thumb from her mouth, said, "Father, I've been a bad girl again," simpering nymphet-like.

"You mustn't go around saying 'Jesus sucks,' my child," I said.

"Sister Ambrosia sent me up for punishment," she said.

"There are times when a priest's burdens are too heavy to bear." I said.

She walked on pigeon toes to the right side of my desk, about-faced, bent over. As I had suspected, hoped, something, she was not wearing anything under her skirt, which now covered only that subtle expanse from waist to coccyx, so I folded it over her belt. Even now, just thinking about it, the beauty of Julie's derriere gives me a pang. I had meant to slap-stroke her, effectively a caress, but some demon took possession of my arm and delivered a roundhouse smack that nearly knocked her over. "Yipes," she said.

I was aghast. How could I have abused that delicate, tender, trembly thing!? It was the act of a vandal. I leaned my right cheek against the side of her left cheek, over the reddening palm print, which felt hot. That's when Julie farted.

I am not depraved, you know: I consider it a good thing that my face was not in the line of fire. We are not talking here of some chthonic explosion, some horrible BROUCH! that makes the knickknacks on your shelf jingle. It was more like a purr: frrt, prrf, fnrit, fif.

"It's the beans," she said.

We were still cheek to cheek, so I could feel her shaking. Well, given what she was wearing, there was no surprise in her being cold, although she didn't feel cold. "Piffft," she went. I then realized that Julie was quaking with suppressed laughter, which finally erupted in a hair-raising whoop, then a howl.

"It's, ha, ha, your own fault, huh, huh, huh, if you hadn't hit me so haaard," which last word turned into a wail. She straightened up, so that her skirt fell over my head, and she turned around, so that my face was against her lower abdomen, which I kissed, although it was bucking with belly laughs. "Frrupp," she went, "fup." I pulled my head out from under her skirt and leaned back. She was bent over, one hand on my desk for support, weak with laughter, trying to say something—which finally came out as, "Good job you weren't kissing me on my ass," half the words strangled.

Well, I began to laugh myself, at what exactly I couldn't say, until CARUMP, man, I let go of a fart that lifted me two inches off my chair. Julie was bent over, one hand holding her stomach, laughing just about silently, gig gig gig gig, a look on her face of someone about to cry, finally catching a breath, collapsing in the chair opposite my desk. Maybe she's right, maybe the fart is like the yawn, that is, contagious, for by then I was also laughing entirely out of control, letting go of the occasional brrrrip, pip.

We subsided together, as in a legendary fuck. Julie's mind must have been running along parallel rails: "You have to admit, Cuz, a hard laugh is as good as getting laid," she said.

"Except I've forgotten what it's like to get laid," I said, a boorish remark, under the circumstances.

"Lighten up, Cuz," she said. "What you always got to remember is that sex is funny."

"Not if the joke's always at your own expense," I said, and here I'm a person who says he hates self-pity.

Julie got up, walked around the desk, put her hands on my shoulders, bent over, kissed me, said, "It's not you I was laughing at; I was laughing at us. *All* of us."

I pushed her back until she was leaning against the desk, lifted her skirt, said, "How would you like me to go down on you?"

"I think we've had enough sex therapy for tonight," she said. "Tomorrow's another day."

The window in my study faces west, but just the same I can see the sky turning a lighter shade of black, premonition of dawn. I think I'll turn in, curl up to Julie for a few hours. I don't want to be dimwitted from lack of sleep on my date with Kay tonight.

16

I have been writing these letters to help you pass the time. There may be other reasons, of course, for every human utterance, written or oral, is overdetermined. I wanted you to see what a life is like, my life, for you can see a life more clearly when you read about it than when you merely observe it, or live it. My initial impression, on reading my life as I write it, is that, like history, it meanders here or there with no goal, whirled without aim, to quote Jimmy Joyce, nudged this way or that by an intersection of causes too numerous, overlapping, and inside each other to be unraveled.

I am now beginning to see, dimly, disconnected, interrupted, as though through four layers of palimpsest, the indicia of a goal: to get laid. It is the instinctive and ineluctable goal of every male animal, after all (I am forbidden by feminists to speak of women), to make his genes prevail. The method is sexual intercourse, as often as possible, with as many females as possible. All other goals are supererogatory. Everything a man does is to attract women or to provide for his women (and children) or to serve as a substitute for copulating with them. The rest is garnish.

I know, I know, I'm holding forth, professor that I am. The point is that all day long I was uptight about my date with Kay. There was a lot at stake. Providing for Kay and a child, I don't mean providing money, for Kay already has too much of that, but with every other kind of support, would give my mammalian-specific goal a local habitation and a name, a consummation devoutly to be wished, to wax Shakespearean for once. All day long this goal coexisted in my mind with the knowledge that it was unachievable, by me at least, not for any reason you would call tragical, but for a reason you might appropriately call comical, better yet, farcical, my little problem. I was in a fifty percent state of denial. Over breakfast, that is coffee for me and for Julie a bowl of sugar-frosted, oven-toasted, fat-free, sodium-rein, sans-cholesterol, vitamin-enriched something that looked as though it had been cut from the bottom of a broom, I told her that I would be eating dinner out. "Why don't you do the same," I said, "my treat, here, take a pal," and I put two twenties and a ten by her bowl.

"Who are you taking?" she said.

"I'm eating with a colleague," I said.

"A female?" she said.

"Well, yes, in fact," I said.

"Who?" she said.

"It's, um, you met her in my office, Kay Pesky," I said.

"You watch your step, Wynn O'Leary," she said. "That woman has eyes for you."

"Come off it, will you? Don't you think that's something I would have noticed? Nobody has eyes for a fat man." Do you think that Julie, for the instant, forgot about my little problem? After all, it's something I do.

"I've got to stay home and write a paper—that Crashaw was a nutcase—but I can use the money," she said, pocketing it.

After a couple of hours of vice-chairmanly paper-shuffling, I went to the gym for three hours, instead of to lunch, got myself stiff, hard, surcharged with blood, gave my class, returned home, napped out, showered, dressed. "You smell good," Julie said, straightening my tie, "that Torrie never used aftershave or deodorant or anything." When Kay arrived, *a punto,* Julie had to let her in, for I was at the other end of the apartment, in the kitchen, pouring myself a glass of Armagnac (for courage): "It's for you," Julie shouted down the hall, in an "all aboard" voice. When I got to the foyer, drink in hand, Kay and Julie were looking past each other. Kay was wearing a tubular, slenderizing black coat that Julie had not offered to take.

"Time for a drink?" I said.

"No," said Kay.

Kay took me (by cab) to a place called La Grotte, Cro-Magnon style art on the faux-stone walls and ceilings. The light was encouragingly low. But I can't say I liked the look of the stalactite that hung over our table. On the wall behind Kay's luminous shoulders, for she was wearing Zeno's gift, a wild-eyed medicine man was shaking a snake at me.

"I hope you like it," Kay said, looking around. "I thought it might be your kind of place."

I have long known that I am not refined or delicate of aspect. I have, for example, big superorbital ridges and a thick neck. Does that make me a caveman?

The waiter handed me the wine list, which I passed on to Kay, for I consider it unseemly for a man to know a lot about wine. She ordered something in what to my unrefined ear seemed impeccable French, for I also have a prejudice against men whose French is impeccable, unless, of course, they are French, in which case the word "prejudice" scarcely gets the job done.

As the waiter, one of those who affect a look of lofty disdain, stalked off, Kay said, "You owe me something."

"I owe you many things," I said, and I braced myself for a question about how I liked "Footman Beware."

"I'll settle for a two-page synopsis of your essay on Carrington and Strachey," she said.

I groaned.

"I'm pushing for a contract from Routledge," she said.

"I can't write about those people," I said.

"Why not?" she said. "You're not a secret homophobe, are you?"

"I can't think my way into those ninnies," I said. "They're on the other side of the moon from me, and not because they're queer."

"Carrington loved Strachey," she said. "What's so unimaginable about that? You've been in love, haven't you?"

"I've loved every woman who ever let me make love to her," I said.

"Like other men, you don't know the difference between loving a woman and fucking her," she said.

The waiter materialized by Kay's shoulder, visibly struggling to keep his eyebrows level. Having learned his lesson, he poured a sample of wine into Kay's glass, waited for her nod, filled our glasses, and when Kay said, "We'll order in a minute," departed.

We clinked glasses, drank. She looked at me. "Delicious," I said, for I am finding that there are fewer and fewer occasions on which honesty is the best policy.

"I took the liberty of assuming that a mesomorphic red would be your style," she said.

"Look here, Kay," I said; "you're a thorough-going social constructionist, aren't you?" for I was irritated by her complacent put-down of men.

"I try not to be half-assed about anything," she said.

"Then you believe that gender is socially constructed," I said.

"That's where we begin," she said.

"Then you've got to believe that love is socially constructed, too," I said.

"Well . . . ," she said. "I can guess where you're going with this, but sure: love is constructed. The social medium is thick with instructions about whom to love, how to fall in love, how lovers look and talk and act, how to fall out of love, how to be jealous, how to deal with rivals, what to feel, so forth."

"And these instructions come from where?" I said.

"Come on, you know all this," she said.

"Bear with me," I said.

"So you can play Socrates," she said. "So you can make me play the straight man."

"Straight person," I said.

"The instructions come from the means of production," she said, "in our case late capitalism. Where else?"

"We'll put aside for a moment the long distances the instructions have to travel from the Mexican at her sewing machine to my hard-on," I said. "For your school, then, love is a product of instructions that are a product of the means of production, right? An epiphenomenon, a tertiary characteristic, a mere symptom, by definition unauthentic, in bad faith, right?"

"What else is there?" she said, smiling broadly, the corners of her mouth nooked into folds of her full but firm-looking cheeks. The impulse to slide my tongue in those nooks was not, I believe, a product of late capitalism. Tell me, Joel, did you ever court a woman by arguing with her?

There was that damn waiter again. "Shall I order for both of us?" said Kay.

"Please do," I said.

She ordered something I didn't catch *nicoise* for herself and *porc lascaux* (specialty of the house), for me.

"Sex," I said.

"I beg your pardon," she said.

"You asked what else is there but products of the means of production," I said. "I say sex. Sex is not tertiary, but primary. It is not an epiphenomenon, but the thing itself. It is not a symptom, but the cause of all the others, including the whole cultural superstructure. It is the evolutionary means of producing new humans that drives us to produce all the other means of production."

"Let me have a cigarette," she said, for we were sitting in the three-table smoking section, far from the madding crowd. "I've never heard you wax so eloquent." I lit us up. "I think you've finally found your subject. But I have to tell you, sex is also socially constructed."

"How can that be?" I said. "There was sex before there was any human society to construct it. Among hunters and gatherers, in Oriental despotism, in feudalism, in classical capitalism, whether a theocracy or communism or . . ."

"Yes, yes," she said: "there's always copulation. But from time to time and place to place the meaning people attribute to it varies."

"Now I gotcha," I said.

"If sir will allow me," said the waiter, from behind my left shoulder. I leaned back, and he placed a platter, size of a skateboard, before me. On the platter was what I took to be a whole shank of pork, cooked enough to be hanging loose on the bone, the way I like it, and largely covered with a thin layer of fat, such as makes women tender to the touch (so I once read in Margaret Mead). On the platter were a mound of mashed potatoes and a mound of sauerkraut, both neat enough to have been formed in molds, and pale gravy in a bowl like a coffee cup without the handle. For Kay there was a plate of what looked like glorified tuna salad. I suddenly remembered what the waiter looked like. Remember Victor Borge? Imagine the look on his face were he to discover a dead mouse on his keyboard.

Kay speared a petal of artichoke and I dug in. Was the pork as succulent as I thought or was it just that my mouth was watering?

"Good?" Kay said, and I cut her a slab from where I had not yet put too much pepper on the meat, lifted it onto her plate. "I can't eat all that," she said, digging in, and I could see the pleasure flush through her, a beguiling shine of pork fat on her lower lip.

"What do you mean, now you've got me?" she said, filling our glasses.

"Your school can't distinguish between a thing and the meanings we attribute to it," I said, a chunk of pork languishing at the end of my fork. "Some guy has written a book about the death of nature.

Another dimwit has written one about the end of history. A couple of frogs and their sedulous apes in America write about the death of the author. Periodically there are essays about the death of the novel. Even Yeats wrote an essay about the autumn of the body. But what passed away or is passing is not nature or history, not authors and novels, least of all the body, which lives! but a certain conception of them," and I put the pork in my mouth.

"In all the time I've known you, I don't think you have ever put so many words together at once," Kay said. "Let me have a tiny bit more of that," she said, pointing, so I cut her another slab.

"You've got to distinguish between a thing and our idea of it," I said. "Sex is real, God bless it, before, behind, below, and above all our reconstructions."

She raised her glass in a kind of toast, so I clinked mine against it. We ate and drank in silence, and never before have I eaten pork that did not require one to chew it.

"The moon," Kay said, "is to you what you conceive or perceive it to be. To me the moon is what I think it is. To any society the moon is whatever meanings the members of that society in common attribute to it. There is no moon outside of someone's idea of it. And the various ideas of the moon have all been socially constructed in accordance with the various economic substructures."

I have often noticed that Kay speaks better than she writes. Now why is that? It is possible, of course, that I was attributing to her words the shapeliness of her mouth and shoulders. "Say you think the moon is a goddess," I said. "Say I think it is pure Roquefort. Say Irene thinks it is an outpost of aliens sending her messages. How can one economic base construct such different ideas of it? The moon is what it is, whatever fictions we tell each other about it. So is sex, which is real."

She leaned on her elbows, knife in one hand, fork in the other, her plate empty of pork and tuna, although scraps of flora remained. "All right, then," she said; "suppose you tell me what the moon is outside any idea you have of it. How can you get outside your idea of it? As soon as you say, or even think, the moon is this or that, you are constructing it. There is no moon known to us other than the moon we know. And the moon we know has been socially constructed. A genius may indeed add to our knowledge of the moon, but always by working through concepts that have been socially constructed before he began to work through them. If to you the moon is something in itself unknown to us, that's what it is to you, another construction, and one with a long history. There's no way out of that."

I put down my knife and fork, for my platter, like the shank bone, was as immaculate as a sheet of paper just extracted from the center of a ream. I finished the wine in my glass. The bottle was empty. "Your argument has a certain logical force," I said. "But the equation of the logical with the true is by now an ancient error." The waiter, with his gift for materialization, stood at my elbow.

"Was everything satisfactory?" he said.

"I didn't like mine," I said: "please take it back."

"Monsieur will have his little joke," he said. He handed Kay the dessert menu.

"Not for me," she said.

"Could you go for an Armagnac?" I said.

"Why, yes, I think I could," she said.

"Coffee and Armagnac for two," I said.

"Very good, sir," said the waiter, taking the plates away, masculine honor restored.

Kay gave me a long look, one eyebrow cocked. I reached forward, gripped her bare arm, lightly, just below the elbow, drew my hand toward me, slowly, down to her wrist, barely touching flesh, let go. I was gratified to see gooseflesh, blonde hairs standing on end. "You're not going to tell me that the feeling of my hand on your arm was socially constructed, are you?" I said.

She leaned back in her chair. "Let me have another one of those cigarettes," she said. I lit us up. "Tonight you have revealed to me two sides of yourself that you normally keep concealed," she said, smoke trickling out of her nostrils: "the sophist and the seducer."

That, of course, was the waiter's cue to appear with the coffee and drinks, place them before us, and promptly, discreetly, depart. Sophist? Maybe. Seducer? No: for that you need the killer instinct, which, you will remember, I don't have. We raised our glasses, clinked, sipped.

"I'm woozy already," she said. From behind her gleaming shoulder, the medicine man shook his snake.

We just looked at each other for a while, letting something build. Then she leaned forward, put her right hand on my left. "Have you considered my proposal?" she said.

"No one has ever paid me a greater honor," I said.

"I see," she said, removing her hand, sitting back, her lips severe. "Somehow I had the idea, mistaken I guess, that you . . . I kept waiting for you to make a move, silly me."

I put my right hand on her left. "I can't," I said.

"What is it, moral qualms?" she said.

"Morality is not my bag," I said.

"You don't think I'll be a good mother," she said.

"With breasts like yours?" I said.

"Are you queer?" she said.

"I'm going to kill Amabelle Bloor," I said.

"You're fucking your cousin," she said, removing her hand.

"The sad fact is that I'm not," I said.

She leaned forward, lowered her voice, although no one else was in the smoking section. "Do you have a disease?"

"There's been no opportunity to get one," I said.

Kay's features were getting blurry, but not because my eyes were out of focus, her posture the slightest bit slack.

"Can't git the band up?" she said, and we exchanged smiles over her quotation from *Finnegans Wake,* friends again.

"Oh, I can git it up," I said.

"Can't keep it up?" she said.

"As well as the next guy," I said, "until I try to put it in a woman."

"Aha!" she said, and gulped her drink, and thereby brought on a fit of coughing. I stood, patted her back. She waved me away. I sat.

"Can you go off," she said, "you know, if you pull your own trigger?" Her voice was squashed, her face red, her eyes teary, for it takes restraint to drink Armagnac properly, but there was a premonition of the old amused look she habitually bestowed on me.

"But only then," I said.

She nodded, as though I had confirmed a suspicion. "Men," she said. "For Christ's sake, Wynn, do you think you're the first man whose wife walked out on him? Did you have to verify the wound to your male ego by becoming impotent?"

"No," I said.

"No?" she said.

"That's not what happened," I said.

"No?" she said.

"No," I said.

"Bare your wound to Dr. Pesky," she said.

"Well . . . ," I said, for I had never tried to put this in words before, even to myself. "One night Belinda and I were going at it," I said. "This is long before we broke up, you understand. Well, I was riding home, man, near the point of no return, when she dug her fingernails into my trapezius and said, 'Wait, hold back, wait for me, I'm going to make it.' I tried to hold back, but that's something only men who hate women can do; instead, I drooped, shrank, retracted. Belinda said some things for which she later apologized. I was never able to get it inside a woman again."

"You big dummy," she said. "Your problem has about a ninety-five-percent cure rate. Didn't you know enough to see somebody?"

"I saw a urologist," I said, "who after four thousand dollars worth of tests pronounced me fit, fat, but not diabetic. Then I saw a shrink."

"A shrink!" she said. "Somebody's got to take you in hand." She looked to the side, glanced at me out of the corner of an eye. "I don't like the idea of artificial insemination. It seems so . . ."

"When there's no other way . . . ," I said.

"That's settled, then," she said. "I have a friend, Ruthie Pipkin, who's director of the Sex Therapy Program over at Payne Whitney. She pioneered the 'brief treatment' method for problems like yours."

"You know everybody," I said. The waiter, hovering on the periphery of the smoking section, caught my eye. In pantomime he poured liquid from a bottle into a glass. I nodded.

"Ruthie, as you might expect, is tremendously busy, but as a favor to me she'll somehow fit you in," Kay said.

"I know a little about the 'brief treatment,' " I said, "and I'm not so sure . . ."

"There's one complication," Kay said. "You need a partner." The waiter arrived with two more glasses of Armagnac, departed.

We clinked glasses, drank. "I understand there are trained women you can hire," I said.

"The training, I assume, is less important than a certain rapport," she said. "You could go with your cousin."

"Will you get off my damned cousin, dammit," I said.

"How about me?" she said, meekly. There you have it, Joel: if you want to become a lady's man, get fat, get yourself a little problem. I looked Kay over, her mouth, her sturdy neck, her strong shoulders, her cleavage, her shapely arms.

"You're hesitating," she said.

"You are talking about one of my fantasies becoming flesh, an unsettling experience," I said.

"Now, then," she said: "we both have classes on Tuesday and Thursday; I have my seminar on Monday: I'll try for an appointment on Wednesday."

"Let's just slow down a little," I said.

She slid her hands up and under the sleeves of my jacket and held me by the wrists. "You're a handful, you know," she said. "Listen, Wynn, I haven't had much experience with sex, but we can become experts together. We can get in shape together. You'll love my personal trainer. I want to be built just like her. Our baby will have no choice but to be beautiful. But you'll have to give up smoking."

Kay is not usually a babbler. But I suppose that the prospect of having a baby is a big thing. I wouldn't know. My experience is that women who pin their hopes on me wind up with a punctured balloon. "You've got to understand, Kay," I said: "this problem of mine has turned out to be fairly recalcitrant."

"You leave that to Ruthie and me," she said.

Kay allowed me to leave the tip, which I admit was prodigal, for she is a strict fifteen-percenter, and to hail a cab. I did not think I was out of line, given all that had passed between us, in venturing a kiss, while the driver honked, swerved across lanes, raced to corners, and braked for lights. Remember that blues: *I want to kiss you all over till your toes turn a cherry red.* That's what I had in mind. I slipped my hand down her dress and cupped a breast, which filled my hand, and then some. She did not resist, but neither did she respond. I left off nibbling on her ear (and earrings look better than they taste), to whisper, "Let's stop for a bottle of Armagnac and go up to your place for a nightcap."

She shivered, probably because my breath tickled, and said, "Let's start off with a clean slate with Ruthie, so we won't have to erase any mistakes."

I kissed her again at the door to her brownstone, rubbing my hard-on against her belly, for her pelvis is lower to the ground than mine. She pushed off. "You'll have to be patient with me, Wynn," she said. Well, she isn't so inexperienced that she doesn't know how to make a man feel like a boor and a shit.

Julie was in the kitchen making herself a mug of herbal tea when I got home. She looked over her shoulder at me as I walked in and said, "You taken to wearing lipstick, Cuz?"

"Professor Pesky gave me a collegial kiss goodnight," I said.

"From ear to ear?" she said, and she strolled out of the kitchen, nose in the air, dripping tea on the floor. I gathered there was to be no sex therapy, although the night was young. I did not act on an impulse to remind Julie of her offer to take me round the world while I pulled my own trigger. Instead, I wrote this letter.

I see that it's nearly four a.m., for Julie went to bed without me, without saying goodnight in fact. I have pretty much left behind my old insomnia now that I can feel Julie sleeping beside me. There will be people who believe, mostly women I suppose, that because I find Kay attractive, I should keep my eyes (for starters) off Julie, or vice versa. I'll have to do something nice for Julie, get on her good side again. I wonder, would she like to eat in La Grotte?

17

Julie was gone

when I woke up, elevenish by the clock radio. So I rolled over to her side of the bed, the better to inhale her spoor. But I am too anxious a type to linger in bed. Besides I had to pee. If you can figure you why a professor with tenure should ever be anxious, let me know. On the kitchen table, propped up against my half-quart coffee mug, was a note:

> CUZ —
> I may not be home for dinner.
> —J.

Damn the woman: she was punishing me for going out with Kay. I know, I know: the decent thing would be for me to commit myself wholeheartedly to either Julie or Kay (or to celibacy), leave the other (or both) to hook up with someone else. But decency, when you think of it, is just another social construction. It was that fuddy-duddy Wordsworth, I believe, who said that in pleasure lies the native and naked dignity of man. Well, I need all the dignity I can get. So I decided to waffle, my métier.

By the way, I discovered the secret of Julie's coffee. On the table, next to the container of soy milk, was a can of espresso, a spoon still immersed in it, for Julie does not always remember to put things away. Julie has been spiking the coffee with espresso. I wonder if she's gotten to know Irene. Maybe her half-formed ambition to become an institutional chef is not so harebrained, after all. Even half a bottle of wine is enough to give me a hangover, so I lumped it over to Whipple Hall for lunch with the gang, rather than to the gym. I arrived with Marshall Grice, just as the bells tolled twelve (the silver circles brightened the air). "What's the news from Montez?" he said.

"Suarez," I said. "He's got a profiler on the case."

"This killer has to have a sexual hang-up," said Serena.

"Don't we all," said Leonard.

"Amabelle Bloor is looking for you," said Serena.

"I'm going to take that shillelagh she carries and play Vlad the Impaler with her," I said.

"A zealot might consider that harassment," said Zeno.

"Let's get some food," said Kay, pulling me to my feet.

Walking to the line, we passed a table at which Felicia Zhang was sitting with some callow youth. She smiled and waved, her hand circling by her ear.

"You've got a lot of female admirers for a man who can't git the band up," Kay said.

"I *can* git the band up," I said.

"Ruthie Pipkin thinks she can fit us in on Wednesday," she said. "I'll call you when I know for sure."

I took the halibut steak—at least it was a kind of steak—rather than some real food. Kay had penne marinara (she declined the grated parmesan) and a piece of chocolate layer cake.

"I don't know, Wynn," Kay said as we walked to the table, Felicia's shoulders aglow, the callow youth biting into what looked like a bean sprout and shredded carrot sandwich. "I'm uptight about Wednesday. I know I'm not a very sexy person."

"Kay," I said, but we had arrived at the table.

As we sat, Marshall was saying, "I'm always jittery when Harriet leaves me."

"Harriet is leaving you!" I said.

"She's going to St. Louis for the weekend," he said. "There's a meeting of the American Gloxinia Society, of which august body she is the treasurer-secretary."

"Maybe you could get her to recruit Marta," said Zeno: "she needs something to keep her occupied."

"I thought you said that the worst thing a wife could to do her husband is develop interests of her own," said Kay.

"The worst thing a wife can do to her husband is get fat," said Zeno.

"What's the worst thing a husband can do to his wife?" said Serena.

"Tell her she's getting fat," said Zeno. "Say anything that undercuts her self-esteem."

"As though men were strangers to self-esteem," Kay said.

"Don't say anything," said Lizzie. "He's just trying to get a rise out of us."

"A good marriage survives the vicissitudes of the flesh," said Marshall.

"Nothing survives the vicissitudes of the flesh," said Leonard.

"Let's go to Fern Hill Farm for the weekend," said Marshall. "We can get there in time to warm ourselves around Wynn's cavernous fireplace with some single malt Scotch, which I shall provide. On Saturday, I picture us rising late in the morning, a skeet shoot in the afternoon, a barbecue at dusk. Think of local corn roasted in the husk, civilized conversation over coffee, and as for the evening: it has been too long since we contributed to Lizzie's retirement fund by playing poker with her."

"Yes!" said Serena.

"Can't," said Leonard, "I've got a date."

"Unfortunately, I, too, have a commitment," said Zeno.

"Willi is prostrate with asthma," said Lizzie. "I can't leave him. "

"I've been asked to chair a panel with three lesbian poets from Brazil at a meeting of PEN this Sunday afternoon," said Kay.

"That dashes it," said Marshall. "I thought it would be a good time to rusticate ourselves, given the killer's predilection for weekends—not that I think he is after any of us."

"Let him come after me," said Leonard. "I'll predilect his ass for him good."

"Maybe we can all get clear for next weekend," I said, standing. "I have to go get my stitches removed."

"I'll walk out with you," Kay said, and she took my arm. "Are you going to see Irene?"

"I thought patients were discharged in the morning," I said. That's why I had scheduled my stitch-removal visit for after lunch. I did not want to see Irene, for if I am physically strong, I am also morally weak: I cannot face up to other people's misery.

"Look in on her, just in case," she said. "She wants to apologize for biting you."

The intern ditched the stitches without a hitch, thank you. Irene, I am sorry to say, was still in her room, dressed, packed, sitting on the bed, her head low between her shoulders, very like a monkey, big-eyed.

"My father was supposed to be here three hours ago," she said.

"How are you?" I said, kissing the air by her cheek. She was not wearing makeup, her hair just hanging.

"I'm all right, as long as I don't watch television," she said. "We have this common room where patients can smoke. In the whole hospital only crazy people are allowed to smoke. Did you know that?" and she gave me a pointed look. "Well, the television set is always on. It's a strange thing, Wynn: I know those talk show hosts can't be talking about me, but when I watch them I know they are."

"You are not crazy," I said.

"What do *you* do when you feel on the verge of a breakdown?" she said.

It would have been churlish to say that I never feel that way. "Lift weights," I said, "eat too much, buy myself something I want but don't need, a hundred-dollar stock pot, a fancy cleaning kit for my shotgun."

"I'm sorry I bit you," she said. "You're going to have a scar."

"I've already been thinking up heroic stories I can tell about it," I said.

"Why were you mean to me," she said, "when I most needed sympathy?"

"I guess I thought you were putting on a performance," I said, "as though you could get something by a breakdown that you couldn't get otherwise."

"That's why I bit you," she said. "You don't have much sympathy for other people's weaknesses. Don't you have any of your own?"

"Few emotions are sweeter than self-pity," I said, standing, "or more reprehensible." I went over to the bed to peck her goodbye, but she caught me off-guard by getting to her feet and giving me a big hug and a serious kiss. You can imagine my surprise when her hand slid down to my crotch. In different circumstances . . . I disengaged. "Is there anything I can do," I said, for I was flustered.

"You already asked me that once," she said. "Whatever's got to be done, I've got to do it myself. But I'm under what they call 'supervision.' The condition for my release is that I always have to be with at least one of my parents. I even have to sleep with my mother."

"Well, if you ever come down to the University, I'll serve *in loco parentis*," I said.

"One father is enough," she said, and at that moment he entered, the ponytailed pastor.

"I was just leaving," I said.

"You are . . . ?" he said.

"He's my boss," she said.

"Well, Professor Weinrein, I've heard a lot about you," he said, but I was already walking out through the door.

I did not feel like going to my office or to the gym or even less to the empty apartment, so I walked fifty blocks downtown to Eddie Bauer. There was the bottle-green Gore-Tex parka, size XL Tall. I couldn't resist. On a whim I bought one just like it for Julie, size S Regular. Don't think for a minute I was spending money because I felt on the verge of a breakdown. Then I walked home.

I meandered into the kitchen, expecting to find it empty, but there was Julie, at the stove, and if I had known she was going to evoke strong feelings, I never would have taken her in. I walked over and put my arms around her. She did not back into me. "I've got something for you," I said.

She revolved, pushed me back. "Oh yeah," she said; "what's that?" thinking I meant monkey business apparently.

I unwrapped the parka and held it up for her to see. "Thanks," she said, on the cool side, I thought. "I can use it. I don't know how long it's been since I had a coat that covered my ass." I held up the parka I had bought for myself. "His and hers!" she said, and flew into my arms, as the writers of romances write. "It's neat," she said, looking her parka over. "How did you know my favorite color?" (I didn't). "With the lining out I can wear it as a raincoat right now. Then when it gets cold . . . I've got a surprise for you too."

"Gimme," I said.

"Later," she said, turning to the stove.

"What's for dinner?" I said.

"Vegetarian shepherd's pie," she said.

I did not groan. I poured us each a beer into the mugs she had frosting over in the freezer. We clinked mugs.

"Salut," she said.

"Slainte," I said.

"You know," she said, as I set the table, "cooking for you has been a learning experience. Torrie didn't like me to experiment. Besides, we hardly ever sat down to eat together. It was always catch as catch can," the chatter a sign that she had forgotten to be mad at me. "Do you think I will make a good dietician?"

"Far as I know, you're good at everything you do," I said.

"Thank you," she said.

For three hours after dinner I sat at my desk writing this nowhere letter about the nothing that had happened—so far. For I had lifted my pencil, paused over paper, waiting for that great dirty lick of Bird's on "Now's the Time," when Julie appeared in the doorway. She was wearing a middie, a white sailor's cap, and snug bell-bottoms with all those buttons in front. "Hi, Sailor," she said.

That tore it! How many insults did she think a man could take? These good-looking women think they can get away with anything. It didn't help that she looked so fetching in that stupid sailor suit. The room darkened, as from a sudden eclipse, for I'll bet that half the blood in my body rushed to my face and neck.

When I came to I was charging her, the scared look on her face for some reason enraging me further. With one hand I held her by the back of the neck; with the other I twisted an arm behind her; then I quick-stepped her down the hall to the bedroom. She tripped once or twice, but I didn't. "Easy, Cuz," she said. "I don't like rough stuff."

I threw her down on the bed, rolled her over so that she was face up, got a good grip on the waistband of her bell-bottoms, and ripped them down and off, panties and all, buttons flying in all directions. "Listen, Cuz," she said; "none of my books say that this is the way to go."

I manacled her ankles into my left hand and held them high, so that she was bent into an L, her bottom at the edge of the bed. With my right hand I dropped my pants and placed my hard-on, into which by now the rest of my blood had surged, against her rosebud, there at the bottom of the nook formed by her cheeks. If she was going to pretend I was queer (such was my thought, not that I was thinking), so could I. "Don't," she said, and I thrust home with all my might.

The look on her face went from worried to wide-eyed. I glanced down. In thrusting home I had slipped up a notch (for Julie was well lubricated, in spite of the rough stuff), from her bottom to her bower. But I was in her, Joel, all the way. For the first time in nine years, I was in a woman, in Julie. As soon as the realization hit me, of course, the blood ran out of my softening hard-on and out of my head. Where to? To my big fat stomach, no doubt. "Wait," she said. "Don't pull out. All I need is a limp dick. *Will you let my legs down, dammit!*" So I did, and she began to rotate. "Lean forward," she said; so I did.

She began to rotate more decisively, with a double tuck at six o'-clock, mashing our pelvic bones together. Soon her breathing became regular and audible. Then she began to sigh, three, four, five times. Then her sighs became voiced, three, four, five. Then she came, prettily. She smiled dreamily. The thing is, Joel: I was hard again.

Whereas Julie moves in a circle, I move in a spiral, like one of Yeats's gyres, the shape of all that is past, passing, or to come. She caught my rhythm and began to move contrapuntally. "Slow down, Cuz, and enjoy it," she said. But I couldn't, wouldn't. Just the same, like Eliot's Magus talking about the coming of Christ, I can tell you that it was (you might say) satisfactory.

I collapsed onto her. I wrapped myself around tight enough to crack her ribs, had she been pressed against something harder than my stomach. I snuggled my cheek against her damp cheek, her hair around my face soft as a cloud. "Julie, Julie, Julie, Julie, Julie, Julie, Julie," I said.

"There, there, there," she said, massaging the back of my neck. "I knew that together we could do it." She was moving, just perceptibly. I lifted my head, kissed her nose, the corners of her mouth, her eyes. She was now moving more decisively. I got up on my elbows. She began to rotate with the double tuck at six o'clock. Soon she began to breathe regularly and audibly. Then she began to sigh, three, four, five times. Then her sighs became voiced, three, four, five. Then she came, endearingly. "Oh, my," she said, her smile dreamy.

You may not want to believe this, Joel, but I was hard again. Womanish, you say: no real man gets his pleasure from giving it? Next thing you'll accuse me of being sensitive. Sorry, it won't wash. This time I held my rhythm, in the tempo of "Funky Blues," not rushing the beat, Julie moving contrapuntally, and there is no feeling, none, like the feeling of being inside a woman for whom you have a feeling. It was (you might say) most satisfactory.

I rolled off Julie, onto my stomach. She rolled onto my back. "See how things work out, Cuz? When I saw you this afternoon arm-in-arm with that Kay Pesky, I said to myself, 'No more sex therapy for him. He can go fuck himself.' I was going to take the sailor suit back to this place where you can buy or rent costumes. But I changed my mind when I saw those matching coats. Right away I knew they were symbolic."

"Kay was steering me to the hospital," I said; "there was someone she wanted me to visit."

"Your departmental secretary, right?" she said. "Professor Confalone told me she went bonkers."

"He did, did he?" I said.

"After class, he invited my friend Fawn and me to the Other End for a beer," she said.

"He did, did he?" I said.

"He says the most outrageous things," she said.

"I have heard him," I said.

"He asked Fawn and me to go out with him tomorrow night," she said. "YOOKA is playing at CBGB's."

"What is a YOOKA?" I said. "For that matter, what is a CBGB?"

"YOOKA is a rock group made up of ex-students," she said. "They all met right here. CBGB's is a famous dive."

"Are you going?" I said.

"Fawn is," she said. "I said I'd let him know."

"Call him up, quick, tell him you are otherwise engaged," I said. "The cure for a condition like mine requires lots of follow-up; positive reinforcement is the technical name for it."

"Fawn's lucky," she said.

"I'll take you to heebie jeebies, for Christ's sweet sake," I said.

"I don't mean that," she said. "Fawn knows what she wants to do. She's graduating this January. Then she's going to the New Mexico School of Natural Therapeutics. She's going to be a massage therapist."

I groaned.

"I think that might be my kind of profession," she said. "I like the idea of being a healer."

"You already are one," I said, reaching for the pack of cigarettes on the night table.

"I think a woman should have a career," she said, "even if she gets married. Don't you?"

I lit up, blew smoke.

"Don't you?" she said. The woman was pulling my head back, hand across my forehead, teeth closing lightly on a deltoid.

"Only if she wants one," I said, twisting my head, blowing smoke her way.

"I'll tell you what, Cuz," she said. "Let's make a deal. If you give up cigarettes, every time you feel a craving, I'll give you a French kiss."

I've heard worse ideas. "Suppose you're in class and I'm in a meeting?" I said.

"Buy cellular phones," she said. "Call me anywhere and I'll be right over."

I had to laugh at that, Julie bouncing on my back. Picture a dozen professors around a conference table, waiting politely for Julie and me to disengage, Angel Terrasco looking for a bucket of water to throw over us.

"I mean it," Julie said, joining in the laugh, the two of us bouncing on the bed.

I have been writing the second part of this letter since shortly after Julie made me whole. I don't feel as different as I would have thought— a little lighter maybe, a little less clenched, but not all that sure I'll still be functioning tomorrow. Just now Julie shouted down the hall, "Time for bed, Cuz." I answered that I wanted to write just a few more sentences. So that's what I did.

I wonder if, from your new location, you would verify something for me. From my fallen perspective it seems true, but I'm not sure. St. Flaubert said, *"le bon dieu est dans le detail."* Was he right?

18

Dear Joel,

I'm sorry that I did not write to you this past weekend, but you will have to admit that I never promised to write every day. The fact is that I felt used up, nothing left over. Julie and I cleaned house all day Saturday, except when I imposed my gross flesh upon her subtle contours. Julie was as accommodating as a pipe dream. She had an air of being pleased, or even flattered, by my desire, but as though it was her due. I cooked the spare ribs for supper, and she even ate a couple, for sex is fueled by protein.

On Sunday morning, she and I woke up about the same time. When she looked over at me and said "Morning, Cuz," with the dreamy smile that I am just now beginning to appreciate, I rolled up against her. Even in my days of impotence, I pretty much always awoke erect. "Let me go to the bathroom first," she said. So while she tinkled and brushed her teeth in her bathroom, I did the same in mine. Have you ever noticed that when you make love first thing in the morning, you take a long time a-coming. From my limited experience, I would say it is unusual for the woman to come first. You will perhaps think better of me when I tell you that I brought Julie breakfast in bed, scrambled eggs, toast, grapefruit juice ("Why do you only like things that are harsh?" she said), coffee with chicory. I held her close to me until she said "Let's do something," which is what I thought we were doing.

It was cool and clear, so I suggested that we stroll down Broadway, which is what I would have suggested had it been hot and muggy. We walked even further than to Eddie Bauer, stopping on the way for falafel, for when a woman has done for you what Julie did for me, you humor her whims. At Barnes and Noble I bought her a classy edition of *Jane Eyre*, which her friend Fawn told her she would love. On Fifty-seventh Street I bought her two pairs of Levi 501s and two pairs for myself, a size smaller than I had been wearing, for the evidence is unmistakable that I have been losing weight, in spite of the *porc lascaux*. Julie likes jeans cut for men, for like all decent people she wears her jeans low on the hip. I splurged for a cab home.

While she was taking her bedtime shower, I stole into her bathroom, stepped into the tub, and joined her under the water. "Oh no," she said: "not again." But when it came down to it, she was accommodating—oh, the blessings of the quotidian! Oh, the glory of the ordinary!

Monday, today, has been something else.

I have been looking for music to fit the occasion. But classic bop, unlike the modernist poetry I teach, lacks the elegiac note. You can find that note in Coltrane, all right, but I don't have much of his stuff around, just a cassette called *Blue Trane*. And there's a note in Miles, especially after the mid-fifties, that you might call "plangent," if you allowed yourself to use that word, which I do not, any more than I allow myself to use the word "poignant." I could play "Blues for Bird," but Diz is too tough, ironic, and finally affirmative for my mood. So I'm making do with a cassette of blues by Miles that I had Julie put together for me (her boombox can record from one cassette to another or from a compact disc to a cassette): the two takes of "Bag's Groove" and "Walking" and "Blue and Boogie."

There go the opening phrases of Miles' solo on "Walking," with that brilliant timbre he was so proud of. Miles and Diz together prove that it is as possible for a genius to be a stinker as it is for him to be a great human being. I went into the office early, carrying a little sandwich bag of chicory, for the departmental coffee has lacked bite since Irene became incapacitated.

After you unlock the double doors to the English Department office, you step into a kind of corridor. On your left is a counter, behind which is first a cubicle for the "undergraduate coordinator" (a secretary) and beyond that a cubicle for the chair's secretary, namely Irene. On your right is also a counter, behind which is first a cubicle for the "graduate coordinator," namely Teddy, and beyond that a cubicle for a work-study. At the end of the corridor is the chair's office. The door was closed. Against the bottom of the door was what I took to be a roll of clothes. When I got closer, I saw that the clothes were occupied. When I got closer still, I saw that the occupant was Irene.

She was lying on her side, facing me, her knees drawn up, her head on a pillow. She was in a dress I had seen at only a couple of formal departmental functions, her best dress, black, old-fashioned, full-skirted, high collar buttoned up to her neck, around the collar a string of pearls. In her hand was a business envelope, slightly crumpled. Near her head was a nearly empty bottle of mineral water and four plastic vials of the kind that hold pills, three empty, one half full. Her lips were drawn back, her teeth parted and angling forward, scary looking. In front of her mouth, on the pillow, was a spread of dried, clear vomitus. The one eye I could see was slightly open, a gleam between the lids. I had no doubt she was dead.

I came pretty close to fainting, Joel. Whether it was the pillow or the pearls is hard to say. Maybe it was the mineral water. You can imagine how I felt, for Irene had reached out to me and I had stepped back. But how I felt is not the story. The story is that this poor woman, this valuable person, handsome, intelligent, capable Irene, had thrown her life away, the only life she would ever have.

I was leaning against the counter, the inside of my head warm, black, and tingling, when Monika burst in. She saw the roll of clothes, looked at me, and sidled along the opposite counter, crouched, hesitant, shifting her glance from me to what was on the floor and back, ready to flee on the instant, as though that wild Irisher had finally gone berserk and killed someone, to no one's surprise. When she got close enough to see clearly what was on the floor, she said, "Oh, fuck," leaned back against the counter, and slid down, until her bottom was resting on her heels. I slid down the counter on my side, reached out to Irene, and closed my hand over her ankle, which was cold and semi-rigid.

Monika and I were still squatting there, looking at each other, not saying a word, when Teddy arrived. He bent over Irene for a closer look, felt first her neck, then her wrist, went over to her desk, opened a drawer, removed a makeup mirror, held it before Irene's mouth, replaced the mirror, removed a card from his wallet, moved his lips while reading something on it, went over to his desk, dialed a number, said, "Detective Suarez?" He then described what was on the floor, sparing Hector the details.

Teddy pulled Monika to her feet and herded us into my study. I sat at my desk and lit up. "Let me have one of those," said Monika, sitting, extending her hand. I lit her up. "I wonder if I might have a cigarette," said Teddy. I lit him up. He went out and paced in front of the door, on guard.

As the office staff arrived, one by one, Teddy directed them to the conference room at the end of the hall, where we held oral exams, dissertation defenses, and meetings of the Executive Committee. "And stay put," he said. Then, in mid-stride, he made a right-angle turn into my office, extended his arm, aimed his pointer finger at my sternum, and said, "I hope you're satisfied." I jumped to my feet, the room darkening. "I find that I have become inured to your displays of lunatic rage," he said. "They may have impressed Irene. . . ."

"This is the limit," Monika said, standing.

"Did you have to prove to yourself that you're a man on Irene's body?" he said, scratching his armpit.

"I ain't got the strength to ride herd on one more colicky calf," she said, putting a hand on his chest. "Go make us some coffee."

I found that I was still holding the bag of chicory. "And add two tablespoonsful of this," I said.

Teddy went out.

"What was that all about?" said Monika.

"He obviously thinks I've been having an affair with Irene," I said.

"I warned you," she said.

"She'd still be alive," I said.

"Sure, and after a half hour in bed with you I'd forget all about Terry," she said. "Don't kid yourself."

As Teddy arrived with two mugs of coffee—he remembered that I liked mine dark, no sugar—so did Hector and a partner.

"Where?" he said.

"This way," said Teddy and led Hector into the Departmental office.

After a while Hector strolled in, wearing rubber gloves, holding an envelope in one hand, by a corner, and in the other hand holding a sheet of Departmental stationery, by a corner. "I need to talk to the big professor alone," he said. Exit Monika, toward the conference room.

"A poem?" I said.

He held the sheet of stationery so I could read it. Written in longhand, slanting downward, were these words:

Teddy says that if you kill yourself on somebody's doorstep he will have to propitiate your ghost through all eternity.

The rest of the afternoon was given over to questions, questions, questions, to which you know my answers, for mostly I told the truth. I did not tell Hector that Murray had been screwing Irene until recently. Crime scene guys arrived and took over the main office, although they allowed Monika to man, so to speak, her phone. At one point she came into my office to say that Irene's father was on the line. He wanted to know if Irene was here.

"I didn't tell him what happened," she said.

"So tell him," I said.

"You tell him," she said.

"I'll tell him," Hector said.

I happened to look up as, around noon, Irene was wheeled into the elevator, and I was overcome, once again, by the finality of death, you dumb bastard. I busied myself with paperwork, including a letter to Felicia Zhang's candidate for the job of adjunct to teach Asian-American literature. Monika, of course, had notified Murray, who did not arrive, however, until late in the afternoon, when everyone else was gone.

He sat in the petitioner's chair, waving imaginary smoke away from his face.

"I've had a talk with your friend Suarez," he said.

"So have we all," I said.

"He recited, from memory, Irene's final words," he said. "Do you know what she said?"

"It may be that you and I are the only civilians who do know," I said.

"He wanted to see how I would react," he said. "I'm sure of it."

"And how did you react?" I said.

"With blank incomprehension," he said. He gave me a long speculative look.

"It is my firm belief that relations between a man and a maid are of no one's business but their own," I said.

He sat back, crossed one thin ankle over a skinny knee. "I was hoping you would take that attitude," he said. "How did you know?"

"People tell me things," I said.

"You're like a big fat spider," he said. "Everything falls in your web."

I deliberately picked up my pack of cigarettes, removed one, lit it, turned my head to the side, blew smoke into a corner.

He waved imaginary smoke away from his face anyway. "Including the chair."

"I'm not a candidate," I said.

"I have been meeting with my sponsors in the Administration," he said. "They instructed me to step down."

"I don't see why," I said. "If the police keep quiet about the letter. . . ."

"Suarez will have to tell the family," he said. "That nitwit father of Irene's—there's no telling how much noise he will make."

"Yes, he will want to blame someone other than himself," I said.

"I have already consulted the University counsel," he said. "I don't have to say anything to anyone. You will have to handle the press."

"This is not a matter of public interest," I said.

He removed an envelope from his inside breast pocket and handed it to me. "This is my letter of resignation," he said. "In accordance with the bylaws, as of this moment you are interim Chairman of the Department of English. Congratulations."

I was barely into the foyer of my apartment, when Julie came rushing out of her room at me, a concerned look on her face. "I heard about your secretary. You must feel terrible," she said.

"Well yes . . . of course," I said. "Exactly what the fuck are you talking about?"

"What I keep hearing is that she had a crush on you but that you wouldn't give her a tumble," she said. "That's why she committed suicide."

I shouldn't have gotten mad, I suppose. After all, I make my living off the human hunger for tall tales. "You listen to me," I said. "Irene had a condition, clinical depression, something out of whack with her neurotransmitters."

"The other story I hear is that you two had an affair," she said, "but that you dumped her, you know, that now you were acting like there was never anything between you."

"For the love of Mike, you could have cleared that up from your own firsthand experience," I said.

"Well, you know, Cuz, you never talk to me much about your past love life," she said. "And when you do, I'm never sure you're telling the truth." It would be a very, very serious mistake to underestimate Julie. "Anyhow, you look like someone who feels terrible," she said.

"Mostly, I feel an immense weariness," I said.

"Come on, then, and lie down for a while," she said, pulling me to the bedroom. "I didn't bring home anything to cook for supper, because I was going to make you take me out. Then I heard about Irene. But I can throw something together. A good cook knows how to improvise."

She removed my jacket, sat me on the bed, removed my tie, pushed me onto my back, began to unbutton my shirt. "I don't need to undress for a few minutes' nap," I said.

"Yes you do," she said.

When she had us both naked—and I must say, Joel, that she undressed in the most provocative manner imaginable—she climbed aboard and rested on her elbows, reversing our usual positions. She gave me a quick kiss and jerked her head back, a teasing smile on her face, three, four times. Then she gave me light, tickling kisses on my neck, raising gooseflesh, my chest, my belly. When she took into her mouth the organ with which men are alleged to think, the thought occurred to me that Julie truly knew how to comfort a man. She had absolute confidence in the efficacy of her flesh—entirely justified, I might add. In a lovely gesture—I wish I had a large trompe l'oeil painting of it—she reached behind her, lifted a hip, and slid me inside her. She sat back and rocked once or twice, then leaned forward, moving just perceptibly, just enough to keep me hard. Whether her smile was the outward sign of inward laughter at my expense or of pleasure in her own power, I couldn't say and didn't care.

What the thinking part of me was thinking was that at one time this power of women had the survival function of keeping men around to provide protection and meat for the woman and her babes. This thought does not in my mind diminish the value of that power, not by a long shot. I scarcely moved, careful not to approach the point of no return. My paltry woes evaporated. I felt light enough to float. Here I was inside a good-looking woman, functional, tenured, solvent, in a low-rent apartment, my health adequate and potentially excellent, once I began to take care of it, which I then resolved to do. Not all of these feelings were an elaboration of that hateful lift you get when someone you know dies—that "better you than me" effect. Then Julie gave me a long kiss more nourishing and mouthwatering than *porc lascaux*. That kiss proved that Hopkins' "no worst, there is none" is only half the story. The other half is "no best, there is none," for if things can always get worse, they can also always get better. I put my hand on the back of her neck to keep her lips where they were. Then the phone rang. Can you believe it?

Julie sat back, and when she nodded to the phone, the look on her face, which had a fair amount of mischief in it, signified "Go on, answer it."

"Hello," I said.

"Wynn," said Kay. "Isn't it awful about Irene?"

"Oh, hiya Kay," I said. When Julie heard the name, she began to rock with purpose, a devil in her smile.

"I can't help feeling we are all to blame," said Kay.

"Her neurotransmitters are to blame," I said.

"Was she carrying a torch for you?" she said.

"Uh, Kay, right now I'm in the middle of something," I said. Julie put a hand over her mouth, as though suppressing a laugh. "Can I call you back later?"

"Is someone there with you?" said Kay. Julie leaned forward and began to give me a hickey. In panic, I felt a laugh trickle up my esophagus.

"Julie's doing her homework, and I'm, ha, ha," I said.

"I just wanted to tell you that we're on for two o'clock on Wednesday," Kay said. "But if you feel because of Irene—"

"No, no, that's terrific, hah!" I said. "Let's talk before the others arrive for lunch tomorrow."

"See you then," Kay said, and hung up.

Julie disengaged and sat back, moving just perceptibly again. "You're going to have to choose between us," she said.

"Here's what I choose," I said, rolling us over until I was on top. I spiralled into her. She circled, different strokes for different folks, the two of us meeting at six o'clock to mash our pelvic bones together. She required a dozen more turns than I did. I'm one of those people who sweat a lot. I have always sweated a lot. That urologist said I had a high rate of metabolism. Then why did I get fat? Julie was slick with my sweat, but she didn't seem to mind.

She put a finger on the hickey. "I've left my mark on you," she said. I turned her over and bit her on the ass, right next to her butterfly tattoo.

"Hey," she said.

"Now I've left my mark on you," I said, and I used her bottom as a pillow.

"You made the right choice, Cuz," she said. "A woman who's a good cook and a good fuck—what more could a man want?"

What more, indeed?

Julie fixed me a grilled Spam and cheese sandwich in pita bread, for I always have a few cans of Spam around the house, for when you run out of pickled ham hocks or salami rolled in black pepper. Julie dipped her pita bread in some kind of mashed Arab substance, chatting all the while about *Paradise Lost*, which she was reading for Style and Substance. She was not of Satan's party, but she did not think much of Milton's God either. "I mean, if He's omnipotent and omniscient then we have a right to blame Him for what happens," she said, looking up to see if I dug the big words. "Like it's His fault that you and I have been living in sin together."

Then I went to my study to write this letter, some of the glooms returning. Did you know that Freud was only pretending to quote someone when he wrote *omni animal post coitum triste*? He seems to have thought that one up himself. I'm going to call Julie to bed, snuggle up next to her.

Give Irene a warm welcome, will you, Joel?

19

I did not this morning,

Tuesday morning, want to see anybody connected to the departmental office. So, wearing a turtleneck jersey under my sport jacket (to hide the hickey), I snuck into my own office and closed the door, nor did I turn on the light. My plan was to drop off the books and notes I needed for my class later on, pick up my bag of workout gear, and beat it to the gym. You can imagine my annoyance when I heard a knock on the door. I swung open the door with what some might say was excessive force. Seeing the expression on my face, Teddy Nakatani said, "I shall not occupy much of your time. May I come in?"

I stood aside to let him in. "If we could sit down and have a cigarette together," he said. So I sat and lit us up. "I should like to apologize for my intemperate words yesterday," he said.

"I have told you before that sometimes you presume," I said.

"I was not myself," he said.

"When are you ever?" I said.

"I felt a special affinity with Irene," he said. "My own thoughts have on occasion turned to suicide."

"It seems to me you have a shaky sense of self, Mr. Nakatani," I said. "You are always seeing yourself in other people."

"Not always," he said, "but selectively, very selectively. Are you of the opinion that we are all completely sealed off from each other?"

"Outside of sexual intercourse, yes," I said. "Anything else?" and I stood.

"I am completely dependent upon your good will," he said. "Without your sponsorship I shall never achieve a Ph.D."

It occurred to me right then that the condition of true blessedness is one in which you have no obligations to anyone or anything. Or is that the condition of damnation? "I'll be here for you," I said.

"Thank you," he said, standing. "Oh, Pierre Howland has been trying to get in touch with you."

"Who the fuck is Pierre Howland?" I said.

"Irene's father," he said. "He says that if you don't call him back, he'll come looking for you."

I felt my neck swell and my shoulders hunch. Man I was a-tingle with a zest for combat. "I'd like that," I said.

"I said yesterday that I have become inured to your displays of anger," Teddy said. "I lied."

"I'm off to the gym," I said.

"Professor Lund has also been trying to reach you," he said.

"I'll be here after my class," I said, pushing Teddy out the door, "in case he calls back."

Man, I worked out in the gym for two hours, as though making the team, or a good-looking woman, depended on it, not just bulk-building routines, but lots of repetitions with light weights, a two-mile jog around the track, jumping 3,000 times in place, for I hate skinny calves. At the end I weighed six pounds less than when I began, and don't tell me it was all water.

I arrived for my talk with Kay feeling as lean, clean, and resilient as a new hacksaw blade. She arrived promptly at 11:30. She seemed to have settled on the French braid, to the greater glory of her cheekbones. She was wearing a pink cardigan open over a tight pink sweater, to the glory of her prominences, as though otherwise you wouldn't notice them.

"I hope I didn't interrupt anything last night," she said.

"Kay, about my problem," I said, "I've been thinking ... well, it occurred to me—"

"They say that the big thing is to get beyond performance anxiety," she said.

"Yes, so I've heard," I said.

"Women suffer from it too, you know," she said.

"Let's get some coffee," I said.

As we walked to the coffee counter, Kay said, "I'm trying to arrange a memorial service for Irene—over her father's objections. I made him a courtesy call. He raved about us all being con-artists and atheists."

"Kay, I swear to you that I never..." I said.

"With your problem—how could you?" she said.

"Right," I said.

Kay took an oatmeal cookie, size of a dessert plate, to go with her coffee.

"I wanted something intimate, you know," she said, "just for her friends at the University. You'll have to say something."

"What could I say?" I said.

"You'll think of something," she said, as we sat; "you always do."

"What I was going to say about my problem," I said, "is ... those women I tried to make it with—maybe they were part of the problem. I think I could make it with you." I know, I know you don't have to say anything. I will only point out that the world's folk literature is full of tricksters. Even great Odysseus was a trickster. Everywhere before the Fall, which is how I think of the Neolithic Revolution, heroes won honor by cunning, treachery, lies. In works like *Felix Krull* and *Lafcadio's Adventure* my modernists had begun to recover some of this ethos—before the second Fall, into postmodernism.

I do not believe I had ever seen Kay blush before. Man, you couldn't tell where she ended and the sweaters began.

"Wynn . . . ," she said.

"If you are willing, I could come over to your apartment this evening," I said. "I'll bring a bottle of Armagnac."

"I have to be at a meeting of the Gender Institute," she said. "I'm presenting a preliminary report on my research into the evolution of the dildo. Since ancient times it has provided women with a means of taking matters into their own hands."

"I'm free tomorrow morning," I said, and Joel, I want you to know that this was the first time in ten years that I had taken the initiative with a woman. Who knows—next thing I may develop the killer instinct.

"I don't know: this is all so sudden," said Kay, uncharacteristically resorting to a cliche.

"Lovemaking is good for you," I said, "burns off calories too."

"How about our appointment?" she said.

"You'll still have time to call Pippa there and tell her we pass . . . if everything works out," I said.

"Ruthie Pipkin," she said. "I'm not used to this show of ardor from you."

I put my hand on hers.

"Well . . . OK," she said.

"I'll be there at ten," I said.

"Perks of the chair?" said Leonard Sistrunk, nodding to our hands, sitting.

"I forgot," said Kay. "When I came in this morning, Murray was cleaning out his office. Are you moving in there?"

Lizzie and Serena joined us.

"No," I said. "I'll just be chair for the interim, until I get a few things done," and I gave Lizzie a significant look. Zeno joined us.

"You'll be a good chair," said Lizzie.

"I'll give you a list of hardworking senior African Americanists we can choose from," said Leonard. "They're rare as ticks on a snake."

"We need a senior feminist more," said Kay.

"This would be a joyous occasion were it not for poor Irene," said Lizzie.

"Why did she do it?" said Serena.

"She died for love of our chairman," Leonard said. "No one ever did that for me."

"She did not," I said.

"I must admit that I never admired the Dido syndrome myself," said Zeno. "It's blackmail."

"Where would Italian opera be without it?" I said.

"Ah, but the music . . . ," said Lizzie.

"On this occasion, mingling a smile with a tear, I should like to name Professor Kay Pesky as my vice-chair," I said. "Confirmation by the committee as a whole should be pro forma."

There were exclamations of bravo, *gesundheit,* hooray, and right on.

"We should see what Angel—" Kay said, when Monika rushed up to the table, panting, eyes wild, a trickle of sweat on one temple.

"Marshall missed his ten o'clock class," she said.

"Maybe his ulcer —" said Kay.

"I called his apartment," Monika said. "I called and called."

"So he—" said Zeno.

"I called the super," Monika said. "He called back to say he pounded on the door: no answer, not a sound."

"He's probably at the airport, picking up—" I said.

"I called Harriet's hotel in St. Louis," Monika said. "She decided to stay over for a few days. She hasn't heard from Marshall since Sunday morning."

Everybody around the table was taking on Monika's expression, eyes wide, lips compressed, a pinched look around the nostrils.

"The super must have a key," I said. "Tell him—"

"He won't enter the apartment without someone in authority there as a witness or something," Monika said.

"Call Murray," I said.

"You're the chairman," Monika said.

"Call Suarez," I said. They all just looked at me, so I got to my feet.

"I'll go with you," said Kay, who is intrepid.

Leonard pressed her back into her seat with a hand on her shoulder. "If this is what we all fear it is, you won't want to see it," he said. "Remember, I'm the grandson of an undertaker."

When we got to Marshall's house, over on Riverside Drive, the super was waiting for us, reminded me of Joey Buttafucco, plenty of attitude, noisily chewing gum, ostentatiously bored. "I'll open the door," he said, studying my I.D. "But I ain't going in there. Anything's missing, people blame the super."

The door to Marshall's apartment opens into the usual foyer. If you walk though it into the hall, straight ahead, and keep going, you pass first a small bedroom on the right, then a window to the air shaft on the left, a large bedroom on the right, a bathroom on the left, the kitchen on the right, and "You better walk along the side, off the carpet," said Leonard.

"Why's that?" I said.

"You've been walking on what look like little drops of blood to me," he said.

I hopped to the side. It must be that the sudden chill you feel under such circumstances results from the rush of blood to the center of your body, so you won't bleed to death from a wound that's only skin deep.

After the kitchen you pass a medium-sized bedroom on the left; ahead is the living room, with which the dining room to the right forms the crossbar of an irregular T on the stem of the hall. Marshall was in the dining room.

I stumbled down the hall, along the side, off the rug, to the door, where I told the Joey Buttafucco type whom to call. In my excitement, I may have been a wee bit peremptory.

"The fuck you think you are, telling me what to do," he said. Before I knew what was happening, my arms shot out, the heels of my hands punching him on either side in the pectoralis major. This was getting to be a habit. He sat on the floor. You will be relieved to hear that he was not hurt, for this super is the kind of guy who puts on weight around his hips and thighs, as I am the sort who puts in on around his middle.

"Who I am is a daymare you are about to have," I said, moving toward him.

"The fuck?" he said. "You crazy or something?"

Well, Joel, I sagged inside. I was chastened and I was contrite. You will remember that even in the days when my muscles had muscles, I was not a bully. The truth is that I was feeling not so much grief for Marshall as anger at his killer. Thinking about it now, I wonder if Julie, in solving my sexual problem—no, that's going too far, for no one's sexual problem is ever solved entirely—has not released the berserker in me that I never knew was there, or rather, that I knew was there theoretically, but never had the pleasure of meeting.

I pulled Joey to his feet. I explained that Professor Grice had been murdered, that he was a close friend. "Why take it out on me?" he said. I said that I would very much appreciate it were he to call the number on the card I had given him. I said that I would be grateful, should Suarez himself not answer the phone, were he, the super, please to inform whoever did answer the phone that a murder had been committed; that it was one of a series; that Detective Hector Suarez was the principal; that he should be paged immediately. "Do you think you can do that, motherfucker?" I said, and as he opened his mouth, "one word," poking his chest with a finger, "one word and I'll screw your head off and shove it up your ass."

Marshall was bent at the waist, his torso spread out on the dining room table, his feet on the floor. Those feet, by the way, were in lime-green mules with pompons. His legs were in celadon nylons. Holding up the stockings was a black garter belt. Rolled up to his shoulders was a flesh-colored peignoir with a feathered boa, for Marshall, in the privacy of his home, liked to relax in women's clothes. Something in Harriet, Marshall once told me, approved of this eccentricity.

The Ka-Bar was in Marshall's spine, almost up to the hilt, a little below his shoulders. Blood had run down the inside of his legs to form a pool of coagulated blood, into which the mules were stuck, for the killer had cut off Marshall's genitals, which were in a pathetic little pile on the table. On his left side, just below the rib cage, was a wound that without poetic license could be described as "gaping." Inserted into the wound was a rolled-up sheet of paper.

"Marshall opens the door," said Leonard, "lets the killer in, and turns around so that his guest can follow him down the hall. That's when this lowlife stabbed Marshall in the back."

"I'm going to get this guy," I said.

"You understand that the stopping power of a knife or bullet—or harpoon, for that matter—is dependent upon the interior dimensions of the wound it makes," he said. "A knife like that makes a bigger hole than a bullet, especially if you work it from side to side."

"First I'll cut off his fingers, one per hour," I said.

"You saw the way Oswald crumpled when Ruby shot him?" he said. "That's what happened to Marshall. He went down face first or there would be a splotch of blood in the foyer or on the hall runner."

"Then I'll nip off his toes," I said, "taking the whole day to get the job done."

"I see our man taking Marshall under the armpits and dragging him down the hall, walking backwards," said Leonard.

"Then I'll cut off his ears," I said, "his nose."

"Marshall would have sagged in the middle," said Leonard. "The flesh on his back would have pressed against the knife blade from either side, allowing for only a trickle of blood. You saw those parallel lines on the carpet, where the nap is pressed down?"

"No," I said.

"They were made by Marshall's toes," he said.

"Would you advise I go for the eyes next?" I said, "or the tongue?"

"Those slippers must have fallen off," said Leonard, "but our man replaced them once Marshall was laid out on the table."

"High heels give the leg so much more elegant a line," I said.

"He then pulled out the knife and cut off Marshall's balls and dick," he said.

"Getting blood all over himself," I said.

"I think not," he said, squatting, peering under the table, closer to the body than I wanted to get, although it was just poor old Marshall. "There are no blood splatters anywhere. By that time Marshall was dead."

"How about all the blood that ran down his legs?" I said. "When the heart stops pumping—"

"Why do you think we hang deer by the horns, heads up?" he said. "To drain them out. You may have noticed that blood, like any other liquid, runs downhill."

"Then I'll puncture his eardrums," I said.

"Next I see him pushing that roll of paper into Marshall's wound," said Leonard. "From that bitty rubber band around it, I'd say he brought it as is, rolled up, ready for insertion. Last thing he brings the knife down with all his strength into Marshall's spine."

"Then I'd leave him to die at his own pace," I said, "you know, with plenty of time to think things over."

"Is this our gentle giant I hear talking," he said. "Let him have life without parole. This is the kind of squirt does the hardest time there is."

"Look to see if Marshall was buggered," I said.

"Say what?" he said.

"Just do it," I said.

"I don't want to touch him to spread his cheeks," he said. "I don't remember those true crime books I sometimes read saying whether you can lift fingerprints from flesh."

First two uniforms arrived, Joey standing on his toes to see over their shoulders. I escorted him down the side of the hall with no more force than was necessary, for I did not want him to see what Marshall was wearing. I sent him downstairs to direct traffic. When I turned back Leonard was showing the uniforms what was on the rug. They herded Leonard and me into the kitchen, one staying to keep us company, the other going to stand guard at the door. Then two detectives from Homicide North arrived, then Hector and his partner, then the coroner and crime scene people, then cops from the Two-Six precinct, then brass, for we were well within the turf of the Major Crimes Unit.

Sitting there in Marshall's kitchen, I felt first queasy, then shivery. Without asking anyone's permission, Leonard made a big pot of strong tea, first scalding the pot, for the only coffee he could find was instant. The only cups he could find looked delicate, expensive, and useless, too small to justify the effort of pouring anything into them. So he served the three of us our tea in beer mugs. Without asking anyone's permission, into my mug he spooned sugar, squirted lemon, and added a jigger of rum. I was no longer shivery when Hector put his head in the door and said, "Anyone know where the wife is at?"

"Call Monika Wright," I said. "And she can tell you how it is that Professor Sistrunk and I discovered the body."

"Should be interesting," he said, turning, pushing buttons on his cellular phone, for by now he had memorized the number of the Departmental office.

I fell into a kind of trance. I don't want to be icky about this, but snapshots of Marshall flashed before my inner eye. He was most himself, I believe, not before a class, in tweeds, nor in the woods, wearing hunter orange, but sitting at the kitchen table at Fern Hill Farm, in one of my old flannel shirts, the parts of an electric iron (for I have learned how to use one) or something else that needed fixing spread out on an old issue of *The New York Review of Books.* A leaky faucet, a short-circuited toaster, a recalcitrant chain saw, a sagging door—Marshall could fix anything wounded, so long as it was inanimate. What was not flashing before my mind was a picture of how

I learned that he liked to put on that uncomfortable stuff women wear, for this kink was by no means generally known. It was because of this kink, I believe, that he was killed. The killer, as it then came over me, had it in for anybody whose sexual dispositions are interesting. In that respect he is in sympathy with the punitive and puritan hysteria that is once again sweeping the country.

Writing that sentence made me realize that I have not in these letters provided you with a context. I began with the assumption that you would be more interested in my private affairs than in public affairs, if that's the word for them. I know I am, for of the two categories of egoist, those who are immersed in the self and those who wish to impose on the world, I belong to the first. Are you spirits aware of everything that goes on or only of what those of us still in the flesh tell you? If the latter, and if like our most prestigious academic critics you believe that individual subjects are constructed by impersonal processes, I may not be the informant you need. I only hear of the outside realm in which big things happen from the eleven o'clock news and rumor, neither of which is known for an exacting standard of veracity. It is true that during the football season I usually read the sport pages, but not recently. Julie says I am remiss, it's an election year, the stakes are high, I should climb down and out of my ivory tower. Ivory tower my ass!

Yet you don't have to be an anchorperson to note how the old American puritanism that, like herpes simplex, hides in cells for a while and then erupts around the mouth and genitals, is once again spreading its pus and vinegar. Everywhere puritans are demanding more punishment and less sex. American prisons have never been so full. Mandated minimum sentences prevent judges from taking into account mitigating circumstances, especially for sex crimes and drug possession (drugs are like sex in that you don't have to labor or deny yourself something else in order to reap pleasure, thus refuting the Protestant ethic). The death penalty is once again in fashion. District attorneys (who are elected officials) are pressured by voters to treat juveniles like adults, so they will become liable to capital punishment. People who wail like banshees over every penny of public money spent on the environment are prodigal when it comes to building new prisons. All over the place local busybodies picket pornography shops and topless bars—they lean on local pols to close them down or to rezone them, which means putting them where no one wants to go. Streetwalkers who have long had understandings with the police, who service the police, are driven into even more desolate areas, where it is easier for maniacs to kill them. The names of johns are published. Times Square, our old funky Broadway, has been Disneyfied. There is a new crime, called "sexual harassment" (pronounced with an accent on the first syllable, so that no one will hear her-*ass*-ment). Ask a coworker out to lunch and you can be cited for "inappropriate" behavior and canned. Firemen and garbagemen are subjected to sensitivity training, from which they learn that the pinups on their locker doors are "inappropriate." Public figures are spied on for evidence of trysts; when no evidence is forthcoming they are set up and caught on hidden cameras. Bimbos, with celebrity sugar daddies, are paid fabulous sums for telling all. Even the President...

There is a move to put warning stickers on CDs when the rap is randy. (Do you know about rap? Don't get me started. Oh, that the music of Diz and Bird and Oscar should devolve to this?) Ratings are to appear at the beginning of TV shows to warn you against bare flesh and bad language. There's talk of a gizmo you can put into your set that will filter out tits and ass. Hand-wringers talk of censoring the internet (which I won't explain because I can't).

All this is justified in behalf of "family values." We have to protect the kids, don't we? Especially from themselves, for kids from six to sixteen are looked at as horn-mad monsters of lust, bless them. Soon there will be federal and state money available for the teaching of sexual abstinence to schoolkids, who unless they have changed since my day will become all the more eager to explore that *terra,* the mysteries of which will always remain largely *incognita,* thus its endless allure. In suburb after suburb, PTAs are empowering teachers to "discipline" the kids, on the principle that they shouldn't be deprived in school of what they can't get enough of at home. In these same suburbs kids are forced to wear uniforms to school, the attire of their choice being too sexy. Every month some congressman (or -woman) comes up with a new dodge to sneak prayer into the schools, at the expense of the Constitution. Puritans would rather have fourteen year olds become pregnant than tell them about contraception. Puritans would rather have fourteen-year-olds become mothers than tell them about abortion. The result is that fourteen-year-olds deliver their babies in the lavatory of a McDonald's and dump them in the garbage. The opposition to abortion boils down to this: if you have the pleasure of sex, you should pay for it with the anxiety and expense of bringing up a child, as though there were not too many people in the world already.

Do you watch television? I have seen the people who shoot abortion doctors, bomb clinics, and screech at women arriving for treatment: frigid females with permanents and pinched mouths, thwarted males who close their eyes and grit their teeth while covering their wives, who patiently endure the indignity, relieved that it's over so quickly. There are calls to end funding for the National Endowment for the Arts, the arts being notoriously naughty. Every week the food commissars hold a press conference to announce that another favorite dish, Mexican or Chinese or dineresque, is no good for you. As for the anti-smoking campaign—I have to stop before I get a heart attack.

Forgive the outburst. It's what happens when an apolitical man pratfalls into politics. My apologies. I am not myself, to quote Teddy, though I would be hard put to say who I've become.

The death of Marshall has shaken me up—as has the death of Irene, whose congenital instability was further destabilized by the murders of Terry and Blinky. It's time I got involved, time I showed this egomaniac what it is like to be pursued by someone with the instincts of a linebacker. He is an egomaniac in that he thinks his transcendent goal is more important than the fleshly individual human, another instance of the similarity between religion and psychopathy.

Before I make a start on the documents Irene put together, I'll just say that Hector let me off easy, with a promise to stop by tomorrow night, around dinnertime, for my reading of the killer's latest poem (which I have not yet seen). I may yet become the first literary critic in history to have an effect on the real world. Julie greeted me with sympathy, a tension-melting hug, and an oven-stuffer chicken roasted to perfection, chestnuts in the dressing. Am I any less a man for being enamored of hugs? You wedge your face between the woman's neck and shoulder, where you can smell her hair. You press her eternal contours into your own. You may even let your hands slip down to cup her bottom rounds. (I don' t remember whether I ever told you that I am a great admirer of women's necks.) How did Julie get to hear of Marshall's death so quickly? Well, she's a gregarious person.

"Reporters have been calling," she said. "Some television babe dropped by with her cameraman. I've got their numbers written down. I want to be there if you give an interview. One thing I've always wanted was to be on television."

I have just now come back from the kitchen, where I cut off a drumstick and thigh, scooped out stuffing, for a little snack. Good thing I did, too, for while I was there, having myself some cold mashed potatoes (well-peppered) for an appetizer, Kay called. "I got it," I shouted down the hall, at the other end of which Julie was writing a paper in defense of Milton's Eve.

"Hi there," I said. "You OK?"

"I was so upset I bought a pack of cigarettes," Kay said. "I've smoked nearly the whole pack."

"How did your presentation go?" I said.

"The response was gratifying," she said, "but I could hardly keep my mind on what I was saying."

"Do Lizzie and Zeno know about Marshall?" I said.

"Leonard's been calling around," she said. "He said he can't divulge any details—that's the word he used, 'divulge.'"

"We were told to keep mum," I said.

"I told Leonard to sleep over in my guest room," she said, "but I think he's got the idea he can ambush this killer. It's so foolish. It's a man's answer to violence: more violence. There: I just shivered again. It's been happening all evening."

"Would you like me to come over?" I said.

"You're sweet," she said. "But no, I'm going to have a glass of wine, maybe two, and the last of my cigarettes and watch the eleven o'clock news."

"Try hot tea with rum," I said.

"About tomorrow morning," she said.

"We'll comfort each other," I said.

"I couldn't," she said; "I just can't. Not after—"

"We've got to assert Eros against Death, that bully," I said. "We need to affirm—"

"I can't," she said.

"Marshall would—" I said.

"Please, Wynn," she said.

Could you have insisted? Well, I couldn't. Chalk up another score for wimpery against the big professor. And now this wretch with the Ka-Bars has interfered with my love life. Murder I could forgive but now he's gone too far.

Julie walked into the kitchen just as I was hanging up.

"Are you going to do an interview?" she said.

"I'll answer any question you ask," I said.

"Milton divorced his wife, right?" she said.

"There's a poet named Robert Graves who said Milton was a trichomaniac," I said.

"What's that?" she said.

"A hair fetishist," I said.

"Do you like hair?" she said.

"I love all your hair," I said, "the little goat's beards under your arms, the sun-bleached hair on your forearms, the —"

"Don't get piggy," she said.

I have decided to leave the documents for tomorrow, now that the Ka-Bar killer has emptied out my morning for me, that cocksucking, motherfucking, cunt-lapping, blue-balled bitching bastard. Instead, I'm going to ask Julie if she wants to go to bed early, so that we can affirm life and love in defiance of fear and death.

20

I woke up with a sense of mission. Naturally, my impulse was to wonder if I was coming down with something. I trudged over to my office with a knapsack full of documents after only a single cup of coffee.

For three hours, drinking coffee (with chicory), smoking half a pack of cigarettes, my mind in focus, my zeal already sagging, I went through grade forms, evaluation cards, records of oral examinations and dissertation defenses, lists of students who had filed complaints against professors (there were few, for it is amazing what students put up with from us), lists of students who had taken psychiatric leaves (there were many), the rosters of all courses given by Terry and Blinky during the last ten years, and decided I needed the rosters for Marshall's courses, the names and fates of students he had examined on orals and defenses, see if there was a match, so forth.

The office staff was unnaturally subdued, all of them peering into computers, eyestrain and brain drain. I walked over to Teddy. "There's something I want you to do for me," I said.

"Yes, well, we begin interviewing candidates for Irene's job on Friday," he said. "Monika asked me to sit in, a gesture of confidence that —"

"I want *you* to do it," I said.

He stood up. "I am honored, of course," he said.

"I want you to go fishing in Irene's computer," I said, giving him a list of the lists I wanted.

"You can't be expected to know," he said, scanning the list. "Irene's relation to her computer, hum . . . was not entirely sound. She treated it, you might say, as if it were a portion of her personality that she wanted to keep hidden not only from others, but from herself. Of late she complained that it was talking back to her. The point is that all her files are hidden behind passwords, even when the data are easily available elsewhere."

"They can't be very arcane," I said. "If anyone can figure them out, it's you. Besides, aren't there ways . . . ?"

"There are," he said. "This will amuse you: in an office such as ours, scissors, staplers, tape dispensers rotate from desk to desk. But Irene jealously maintained her own, each with a label reading 'Howland' neatly taped to it. On the day you became vice-chairman, and after Irene had departed for a class, I went over to her desk in search of a staple remover. There I found a sheet of paper on which she had been trying out possible passwords for your new correspondence file. The first word was 'slim,' with a line through it."

"One doesn't think of Irene as given to irony," I said.

"She had heard from Monika, who had heard from Suarez, that 'Slim' was once your nickname," he said. "The second try was 'high and mighty,' also with a line through it. The reference was, I surmised, as much to your physique as to your aloofness."

"Me? Aloof?" I said.

"Under 'high and mighty,' again with a line through it, was the word 'norther,' which is, I believe, a cold wind."

"I see," I said.

"Then there was the word 'Northman,' but she had crossed that out too," he said.

"I don't get it," I said.

"Irene associated you with the north because of your coldness, especially to underlings."

"This is gross calumny," I said.

"On that unforgettable night of the musicale, Irene confided to me that you had once used the word 'berserker' in her presence," he said. "It reminded her of her theory that you labored under the weight of severe repression, that someday you would try to throw it off in a violent rage. There you have it: berserker, Viking, Norseman, Northman."

"You're making this up," I said. "This is the way you think, not Irene."

"I think the way you think," he said.

"My father's people," I said, "who came from the north, were more likely to have been victims of Norse berserkers than victimizers," I said.

"I exclude you, of course," he said; "but the Irish sometimes act as though they were the world's only victims."

"Did you say the other night that you knew Christopher North?" I said.

For a moment he looked blank. Then he began to scratch his armpit. "I knew him," he said.

"What was he like?" I said.

"He was a wispy, wistful, wasted WASP," he said.

"And?" I said.

"He disappeared shortly after failing his defense," he said.

"And?" I said.

"We were not intimate," he said. "My impression was that he had no close friends—of either sex. One pitied him."

"Did no faculty member take pity on him?" I said.

"As I recall, he was working with Professor Jones—until she went on leave," she said. "For the duration, she turned him over to Professor von Hartmann."

"Any personality conflicts?" I said.

"If pressed, I would venture to say that Christopher, like Irene, turned his aggressions inward," he said. "One often observes this syndrome among graduate students in English."

"Get busy on those lists," I said, turning—right into Monika.

"You messing with my staff?" she said.

"That's the way," I said: "it's much healthier not to turn your aggressions inward."

"Something wrong with your phone?" she said.

"It's taking messages," I said.

"Well, we've been getting all these calls from people who want to interview you," she said, "disrupting business."

"Direct them to the University Information Office," I said.

I spent three hours at the gym turning my aggressions outward, returned all a-tingle to the office, wrote no-nonsense letters to the three deans who had it in their power to renew Lizzie's contract, delivered them, sat down with Monika till closing time working up separate curriculum letters for each member of the teaching staff, so no one could doubt what I wanted him or her to teach, graded a makeup exam from a student who had not spent the summer hitting the books, decided against listening to my phone messages, and I'll tell you, Joel, there is nothing so energizing as an active sex life, went home.

Hector Suarez was sitting at my chair at the table, watching Julie cook, looking through my mail.

"Hi Cuz," she said.

"I must say, Cuz," said Hector, "your mail is even more boring than mine—except for the catalogues. Some of these I never heard of."

"They'll be my undoing," I said, "now that they're starting to stock talls."

"Your old student Bernie Schwartz, over there at Land's End, sends his regards," said Hector.

"How's he doing?" I said, pouring us each a Dos Equis.

"Good," Hector said, "now that he's used to the weather. He's moving up the ladder. He says you give him a call, he'll send you anything from the catalogue. He says he owes you."

"They have a fisherman's sweater in tall sizes, Cuz," Julie said, "in dark green, my favorite color. You'd look terrific."

"I'd look like a prize-winning watermelon," I said.

"They have matching sweaters for women," she said.

"I take it that Bernie is not our man," I said.

"Not a chance," said Hector.

"What do you hear from Christopher North?" I said.

"Let's save our business for after we eat," he said. "I can't think with those smells coming from the oven."

For supper we had peppers stuffed with rice and beans and in a bed of chunky, garlic-laden tomato sauce, crusty tops of bread crumbs and parmesan, and on the side were little carrots buttered and bechived, a salad with anchovies, warm, crusty French bread. Julie's learning how to cook. Now if I could only cure her carnephobia.

For dessert we had melon, but I would have preferred a big hug and a long kiss from Julie. A good host, of course, does not engage in activities that exclude a guest, make him feel like a fifth wheel. "Let's have our coffee in my study," I said, and as Hector started down the hall, I went over to Julie and whispered, "I'll order the sweaters as soon as I get rid of Suarez."

"You don't have to," she said.

"I want to," I said.

"They'll match our jackets," she said.

When we were settled in my study, Hector on one side of the desk, me on the other, him with a cigar, me with a cigarette, my stomach no longer rumbling, for I had forgotten to eat lunch, Hector said, "Let's get this over with," and passed over to me a folded sheet of paper.

As I unfolded it, he said, "It's the perp's latest," and it was copied out in Hector's neat hand. "The way it was sticking out of your colleague there, it looked like he was stabbed with it. I used to be just indifferent to poetry, now I hate it. What's it for?"

"Equipment for living," I said, reading.

"Our profiler's full of ideas about this poem, but she don't know if there's another one behind it," he said. "Did our asshole rip this one off too?"

"All right," I said: "In 1873 a man named Walter Pater published a book entitled *The Renaissance.* It was very influential, especially the Conclusion, which some guy, I forget who, called 'the breviary of the Decadence.'"

"What was this Walter Pater?" he said.

"A limp dick," I said.

"Figures," he said.

"In the chapter on Leonardo da Vinci he describes the Mona Lisa. Wait a minute," I said, fetching a book from my shelves. "Here it is," and I read:

> The presence that rose thus so strangely beside the waters, is expressive of what in the ways of a thousand years men had come to desire. Hers is the head upon which all "the ends of the world are come," and the eyelids are a little weary. It is a beauty wrought out from within upon the flesh, the deposit, little cell by cell, of strange thoughts and fantastic reveries and exquisite passions.

"Bah," Hector said. "What's an exquisite passion anyhow?"

"The kind serious Christians refuse to admit they have," I said.

"What, like sucking your girlfriend's toes?" he said. "None of that you read is anything like the poem."

"Wait," I said, and skipping a few lines, I read this:

> She is older than the rocks among which she sits; like the vampire, she has been dead many times, and learned the secrets of

> the grave; and has been a diver in deep seas, and keeps their fallen day about her; and trafficked for strange webs with Eastern merchants; and, as Leda, was the mother of Helen of Troy, and, as Saint Anne, the mother of Mary; and all this has been to her but as the sound of lyres and flutes, and lives only in the delicacy with which it has moulded the changing lineaments, and tinged the eyelids and the hands.

"A fag hag!" Hector said.

"Joan Crawford's lineaments, as I recall, were not delicate, but angular," I said.

"In any case, we got a change," he said. "The first two were rewrites of other poems. Here we got a rewrite of some purple prose."

"It's to correct mistakes like that we scholars exist," I said. "In the mid-thirties our old friend W. B. Yeats brought out an anthology of poems. The first item was the passage I just read arranged as free verse," and I fetched *The Oxford Book of Modern Verse 1892–1935*.

"Why'd he do that?" he said.

"Because he felt that's where the modern movement began; because he thought Pater's prose was poetic; because he thought free verse was prosy; because he was a genius," I said.

"Show me," he said. So I showed him:

> She is older than the rocks among which she sits;
> Like the vampire,
> She has been dead many times,
> And learned the secrets of the grave;
> And has been a diver in deep seas,
> And keeps their fallen day about her;
> And trafficked for strange webs with Eastern merchants;
> And, as Leda,
> Was the mother of Helen of Troy,
> And, as Saint Anne,

Was the mother of Mary;
And all this has been to her as the sound of lyres and flutes,
And lives
Only in the delicacy
With which it has moulded the changing lineaments,
And tinged the eyelids and the hands.

Hector let out a big sigh. "Arranged like that, the words feel different," he said, looking up from the page, letting down his Philistine facade. "There's some of all that in every woman worth more than a three-minute boff. So what the killer did was paint a mustache on the Mona Lisa."

"That puts him on the cutting edge of current academic criticism," I said.

"Yeah?" he said. "Well, what has academic criticism got to say about the perversion version that a college dropout can't figure out for himself?"

I reread through the killer's traduction of Yeats's rearrangement of Pater's words:

She is colder than the wrack on which she shits.
Like the vampire,
She has been dead many times,
And sucks the life from the living,
And has been a diver in deep seas,
And keeps their fishy murks about her,
And traded for the evil eye her sulphurous flesh,
And, as Lilith,
Was the mother of Morrigan,
And, as Pasiphae,
Was the mother of a monster,
And all of this has been to her as the sound of silent screams,
And lives

Only in the confusion
She has moulded into his changeling lineaments,
And tinged his sulphurous flesh.

"Like, for example," Hector said, "what do you make of 'sulphurous flesh'?"

"Well, sulphur burns and it's associated with hellfire," I said. "His flesh torments him, and he fears it will consign him to damnation."

"How does that make him different from anyone else?" he said. "Who's Morrigan? Pasiphae I remember—from the old neighborhood."

"Morrigan was the ancient Irish Queen of Demons," I said. "She was the goddess of fate and death. One description of her, as I remember, has her as 'big-mouthed, swarty, swift, sooty, lame, with a cast in her left eye.' "

"What are you, a lookist?" he said. "We men have to get over judging a woman by her looks."

"In fact, she appears in Yeats's valedictory play, *The Death of Cuchulain*, with whom he identified," I said.

"What else?" said Hector wearily.

"The lady in the poem, like Helen Reddy, could sing 'I Am Woman,' " I said, "as you already intimated. She made the guy a monster and bequeathed him her sulphurous flesh. She is both seductive and frigid. She confused him and wrecked him and then disdained him for being on the rack. She lives in the life she has stolen from him."

"These guys always blame their mothers," he said. "Then when we look into it, a lot of the mothers aren't much different from the usual pains in the ass."

"A guy like this lives in a condition of sustained horror that began before he was old enough to have done anything to deserve it," I said. "He's got to blame someone, and momma's handy."

"We' re going to get this guy—I don't want you thinking otherwise," he said. "If he survives it, you can be a character witness."

"The evil eye, by the way, is a paranoid delusion," I said. "The paranoid has a secret about himself that he doesn't want to know he knows—the secret being, according to Freud, that he's queer. He projects that knowledge onto someone else, whom he then says torments him by getting inside his head."

"Does academic criticism tell you who this paranoid's about to kill next?" he said. "We got another weekend coming up."

"The poem doesn't say."

"Then what good are you?" he said, standing. "I want to borrow these books. And where' s a copy of that play?" So I fetched Yeats's *Collected Plays.* "I've got to stretch my legs. After a meal like that in civilized countries people take a siesta, or they eat it just before going to bed, no aspersions on Cousin Julie's cooking."

"Do you remember Christopher North?" I said, as we moved out.

"Does a hound dog know how to lick his balls?" he said, turning, so that he was in the hall and I was still in the study.

"I dug up a little tidbit for you to chew on," I said.

"Now what might that be?" he said.

"Blinky was the co-sponsor of North's dissertation," I said. "It means that Terry, Blinky, and Marshall Grice were on his committee. The other two are Bertil Lund and Fran—"

"I know who the fuck the other two are," he said.

"Well, maybe you ought to be looking for Christopher North," I said.

"Maybe you ought to do it yourself, smart guy," he said. "But to save you some time, I'll tell you this: He doesn't live in New York or California, where he grew up, around Anaheim. Would you even know how to start getting that kind of information? A sweep of death records shows he hasn't died in New York or California. His parents and younger brother haven't heard from him since he flunked his dissertation, but they say they believe he left the country. Then how come no passport was ever issued in his name? State Department has no record of him leaving the country and the Treasury Enforcement Communication System has no record of him trying to reenter. Just to be sure, we're checking out every phone number his parents or brother call regularly and every number they get calls from. He has no credit rating, far as we can tell, no major credit cards. Social Security and IRS haven't heard from him in years. Not the New York, not the California, not the fifty-state DMV know his name. The same for NADDIS, the secret drug enforcement system; and for the U.S. Marshalls; and for ARJIS, the Automated Regional Justice Information System; and for the National Crime Information databank; and for the New York and California Department of Law Enforcement Data Processing Systems. He hasn't been in any of the armed services. He hasn't given the power of attorney to anyone in New York or southern California. He hasn't been divorced in New York or California. We got his fingerprints because he did grand jury duty, but they don't match up with any others we got. The graduate students in his class and the class before his and the class after his are mostly out of here, but the ones we located don't hear from Christopher North. You can start from there. Maybe you're better at this than we are."

"Why are you so pissed?" I said.

"You understand that some of those databanks are off-limits," he said, "because there're no criminal charges against North. Our FBI Liaison Officer and me, we're going to be paying back favors for the rest of our careers, if they survive this case. And so on. Maybe my disposition isn't as sweet as usual. Now you'll excuse me while I use the facilities."

I poked my head into Julie's room. She was at the desk, poised over my old portable typewriter. "May I come in?" I said.

"Don't kid around, Cuz," she said; "this is the toughest paper I ever wrote. You've got to get the tone just right. I don't want to sound like some nasty bitch, defensive like. Usually I just type these papers right out, the way you would talk."

I came into the room, put my hands on her shoulders, kissed her on the head, on the clean part in her hair. "Above all, eschew righteous indignation," I said. "A maxim for all occasions."

"That's what I mean," she said.

"I'm going to walk Suarez to his car," I said. "When I get back, we can order those sweaters."

"Don't you want to wait until tomorrow, so you can call your student?" she said. "Maybe you won't have to pay for them."

"Then yours wouldn't be a true present," I said.

"I'll have a nice present for you when you get back," she said, turning to face me. I pulled her to her feet and gave her a hug, salve for the sting of Hector's putdown, and how did I manage to survive all those years without a woman? "Could you order those sweaters express mail, so I can have mine for the weekend?"

The night was chilled and clear, like a good martini. Across southeast Harlem the lights strung along the Triboro Bridge sparkled. A pale, thin, half-moon, looking transparent, shone down on us all impartially. There was no wind. No birds sang.

"Any doubt that Irene killed herself?" I said.

"Not in my mind," he said. "We're still waiting on toxicology."

"Could she have killed Marshall Grice?" I said.

"We got various ways of figuring the time of death," he said, "including the life cycle of maggots, my favorite. Nearest we can tell they both died between dusk and midnight on Sunday."

"Theoretically, then, she would have had time," I said.

"She was a hardbody," he said: "I can see her pulling Grice down the hall. But I can't see her lifting him onto the table, his arms flopping around. Besides, far as anyone can remember, she never had anything to do with Blinky; the word used by two of your colleagues for the way Grice treated her is 'avuncular'; Terry Jones and Howland respected each other as fellow pros. Naw, the Ka-Bar Killer is someone who has it in for queer professors."

"Ka-Bar Killer!" I said.

"Don't you read the papers?" he said. "Don't you watch television? I got a leak on my team, and when I find it I'm going to plug it good. And if some TV babe makes googoo eyes at you I don't want you saying anything about poems or Christopher North or Professor Grice's panties."

We walked out onto the parapet diagonally across the street from Terry's apartment, rested our arms on the wall. "Marshall wasn't queer," I said.

"You saw the way he was dressed," he said. "Lots of queers get married."

"Lots of cross-dressers aren't queer," I said.

"I forgot you was a liberal," he said. "How many people knew he had a thing for frillies?"

"Hard to say," I said. "Couldn't be many."

"You knew?" he said.

"Yep," I said.

"How?" he said.

"Each year there's a meeting of the Modern Language Association," I said. "Maybe nine thousand professors and would-be professors attend."

"God," he said.

"Some people read papers, and from what I hear, some people listen to them," I said. "And departments looking to hire interview new Ph.D.s looking for jobs. All right: when we have openings we rent a suite, so-called, a bedroom and a sitting room, maybe a bar. At night, the chairman sleeps in the bedroom; during the day, the hiring committee, led by the vice-chairman, conducts interviews in the sitting room; at the same time, the placement officer sets up shop in the bedroom. Our students looking for jobs can drop in, rest their feet, exchange horror stories, get a cup of coffee and a sticky bun, use the phone, pick up leads, and solicit advice or sympathy from the placement officer, as indicated."

"Get to Professor Grice and Victoria's Secret," he said. "I see that's one of the catalogues you get."

"This time I was thinking of, maybe eight years ago, Derwood Bobbie was chairman; Marshall Grice was vice-chairman; and I was the placement officer. But Derwood wasn't using the suite bedroom. He had a separate room with his wife. She never lets him go anywhere alone, for fear he might have some fun."

"I met this Derwood Bobbie," he said. "Like the Mona Lisa, he has been dead many times."

"The second night of the meeting," I said, "I was having drinks with five graduate students—they weren't much different from me in age—two couples and a singleton, one of our interviewees. I could tell she was beginning to think it might be a good idea to make it with a professor then thought to be a comer, maybe could help her chances. (At that time I wasn' t fat.) But she wasn't my type."

"What does that have to do with it?" Hector said. "Tell me straight, Slim, are you queer?"

"Ask your sister, motherfucker," I said.

"I asked you in a nice way," he said. "I have reasons for wanting to know."

"I've got a rule against talking about my sex life," I said. "But I'll tell you to put an end to this shit: I am not queer. The mere idea of going at it with another man, makes me feel sickish, like handling a dead rat."

"Better than a live one," he said. "That's all I wanted to know, not that I give a fuck one way or the other. Now get to the punch line."

"The couples were getting ready to go, and I didn't want to be left alone with the aspiring singleton." (The real reason, Joel, is that I didn't want anyone to know I was nonfunctional.) "So I suggested we go up to the suite for a nightcap. I told them that Marshall never went anywhere without a bottle of single malt Scotch. Instead of knocking, like a fool I used my key. And there was Marshall wearing a satiny negligee, looking like Bette Davis in a forties film noir."

"And the graduate students blabbed," he said.

"I swore them to silence," I said. "But they probably told a few close friends, who were sworn to silence, of course. I haven't heard it mentioned in years, but there have to be old-timers among students and faculty who know."

We stood silent, smoking, the moonlight casting shadows into nooks that hid our secret fears and desires, for if you are human, you have them, the park below us shaggy and silver-tipped as a werewolf.

"Speaking of dead rats, you smell something?" I said.

"I been wondering would you notice," he said.

I leaned out over the wall and looked down. "That's where it's coming from. FWOO," I said, "Wow, man. . . ."

"Doesn't take a big animal to make a big smell," he said.

"Maybe we should take a look," I said.

"This is New York," he said. "There's a dead cat on every block, if you know how to look for it."

"Is there a flashlight in your car?" I said.

"No," he said.

"No?" I said.

He gave me his evil smile, corners of his mouth up, center down. "My plate is full," he said. "You understand?"

We walked in silence to his car. As he unlocked the door and removed the Club, I asked him what he had heard from Hylas Cutlery. He gave me a lecture, no match, however, for his lecture on Christopher North. It turns out that changes in processing and in the suppliers of steel show up in metallurgy. The leather used on the handles, the dye used on the leather, the cut of the leather rings, have changed over the years. They have moved from bluing to Parkerizing to their own patented process. People in the know can tell whether the cutting edges on two blades have been ground by the same guy. Add stuff like this together, and what you got is that the knives used by the Ka-Bar Killer were manufactured between 1977 and 1981.

"Climbing the Matterhorn for a sprig of edelweiss," I said.

Not so bad as that, in Hector's opinion. We know, for example, that you can't just go in a store and buy two Hylas Ka-Bars ground by the same cutter around the same time. Too many have been made over too long a time by too many hands. Even if you buy in bulk, like distributors and the military and catalogue companies, you get mixed lots. If the third knife matches up, and it will, we can be sure all three were sent out in a little wooden presentation case of twelve matching Ka-Bars, military-looking stencils all over the outside.

"Who would want twelve matching Ka-Bars?" I said.

"Assholes playing soldier," he said, and he drove off.

I suppose that made me an asshole playing detective, but I persisted. I went home and rummaged around in the stuff I brought to the city from Fern Hill Farm until I found my three-battery Mag-Lite, also good as a cosh. I stood there undecided as to whether I should strap on my own Ka-Bar or even Uncle Alf's .45 Colt Government Model, but Julie walked into the room.

"What's up?" she said.

"There's something in Morningside Park I want to check out," I said.

"Can I come?" she said, and when I hesitated, "Yes, I'm coming."

"Come along, then," I said, for I had just pictured myself walking down into the park alone, and maybe the essential fact about me, after all, is that I'm chickenshit. "But put something on: it's getting cold."

What she put on was the liner to her new parka, which liner, to my surprise, made a very presentable jacket, pockets, decorative trim, and all. She handed me mine, which I put on. "We're like the Bobbsey Twins," she said.

"We are *not* like the Bobbsey Twins," I said.

Hand in hand we walked down the very stairs Hector and I had seen Teddy floating up, the stench thickening. There must be an adaptive reason for the human revulsion from that smell. After all, it doesn't bother animals. The stairs were treacherous, broken, chunks missing, dead leaves, fallen branches, creeping vines, dissolving paper. The brush at the bottom was thick, pathless, so far as I could see. "Let's have the flashlight a mo," said Julie. "Come on," she said, leading the way.

There was space enough between the turret and the brush for us to follow around, hugging the wall, sure-footed Julie leading the way, that abysmal smell making my eyes water. On the side facing the moon we came to a chamber cut into the turret, a nightmare out of the West's collective unconscious. The wrought-iron gate was off one hinge, but secured to the frame on either side by two big new padlocks. Julie directed the flashlight toward the interior: cut stone walls, a kind of nest of rotting burlap, a spade, the long handle broken off halfway up.

Julie redirected my Mag-Lite to the small clearing in front of the chamber, branches embracing overhead, dapples of moonlight shining through. Something big and black was stretched out on the leaves and weeds. Julie approached; I hung back. "It's a dog, Cuz," she said, squatting. "Someone bashed in its head. And there's an iggy wound here, behind its shoulder, all crusty and crawly. Can you see? Looks like it was stabbed." She stood up and shone the light on my face. "You OK? It's just a dead dog. When you grow up in the country, you get used to dead animals."

"Let's get out of here," I said. All right, I admit it, I wilt and wimp out in the face of death, whether it's death in the abstract or death in an instance. All these deaths around here have crumbled my resistance, already low to begin with. In a letter, Jimmie Joyce writes: "How I hate God and death; how I like Nora," one of the reasons I venerate him. That's the thing: hate those bullying and blackmailing abstractions; like (Joyce thought the word "love" was a con) the individual fleshly human. I couldn't wait to love a certain individual fleshly human so I hustled Julie into the shower, where we could wash off the smell of death, a metaphysical more than a material entity, and then into bed, where I could nose her fragrances, for starters.

I think I'm changing for the better, Joel. I was looking through earlier letters for the Ka-Bar Killer's first two poems when it came over me that my prose style has changed. I now waffle more decisively. And I've come not only to endure but to enjoy my post-coital conversations with Julie. While she tinkled, I rolled over onto my stomach, so she could climb aboard, which she did.

"Do you think women are temptresses?" she said, nibbling my ear.

"That's what's good about them," I said.

"I want a straight answer," she said, biting my ear.

"Ow," I said. "Sure, they're temptresses. But it's not anything they have to do. It's how they are, what they have."

"Like what?" she said.

"Pussies," I said, "tits, asses, soft skin. You want more?"

"You know, you don't always have to pretend to be so low-minded," she said. "But suppose you're right: how are we to blame? We can't help the way we are, what we have. It's not fair."

"Sexual desires are sinful," I said. "Women arouse sexual desires. Therefore they have to be punished. That's how the puritan thinks."

"And Milton was a puritan," she said.

"His God was, anyhow," I said.

"Well, if He didn't want men to sin, He could have made women different," she said. "Better yet, He could have made men different."

"The way I understand it, free will is so great a value that we were made free to choose sin, even if the consequence for the vast majority is an eternity of exquisite torment."

"Well, God can do anything," she said. "He could still have made us free, but without sexual desires."

"That's too mean, even for Him," I said.

"It's still not fair," she said.

"Exchange evolution for God and the problem disappears," I said.

"Oh yeah," she said: "does evolution explain why men blame women for their own sinfulness?"

"Have I ever blamed you for turning me on?" I said.

"No, that's one dirty trick you never tried to pull," she said.

"In fact, I honor a woman precisely for the sin she commits with me," I said.

"That's not exactly a compliment," she said.

"There's a story by Somerset Maugham called 'Rain'," I said. "In it a very strict Reverend Dickerson hounds a floozie mercilessly, nearly gets her sent to jail, ostensibly to cure her of her sinful ways. At the end it turns out he had a hard-on for her."

" '*Davidson*' " was his name," she said. "That's an interesting mistake, Cuz. But you can't use a modern story to interpret an old poem."

"Sure, you can," I said. "There's an Argentine writer named Borges who speaks of Kafka as Hawthorne's predecessor."

"Who was Hawthorne?" she said.

"A nineteenth-century American who wrote eerie stories," I said. "Borges meant that after reading Kafka, we read Hawthorne differently, we notice things we might otherwise have missed."

"You want me to use Maugham and Borges to interpret Milton?" she said.

"We always interpret the past through the present," I said. "There's no other way. Blinky Hartmann read Jesus Christ through Charles Manson and Jim Jones."

"If we lived in Plato's time—that's who I'm reading for Professor Confalone, Plato—you would be made to drink hemlock for corrupting the morals of the young," she said.

I squeezed out from under her, so that I could turn to give her a kiss.

"You've had enough sin," she said, pushing me back. "Where's a copy of 'Rain' and that Borges? I should never have broken my rule not to talk to you about what I'm studying."

"Zapping puritans is a big part of the struggle for human dignity," I said, leading her by the hand to the bookshelf.

"What's so dignified about screwing?" she said.

I began this letter last night while Julie worked on her paper. I picked it up first thing this morning, over coffee, and I'm still at the kitchen table, in my pajamas. But I'll have to break off now, if I'm going to make it for lunch with the guys. I didn't say this before because I don't want to be a scold, but part of what is behind my morbid fear and hatred of death is you. Were you there in spirit, looking on, when I stumbled over your body?

21

From atop the many steps that fall from the administrative building down to College Walk you get a panoramic view of the campus. On cool bright glittering days like this, eyesight is a pleasure separate from anything you see. It was almost enough just to be alive—you hear? I took in a deep breath, displacing old cigarette smoke, and nearly lost my pants, for already my new jeans are loose around the waist. I surveyed the scene before me for someone to dis, for cigarettes affect me mainly as pacifiers, for Julie had gotten me to promise putting off my first cigarette until lunch.

There was Leonard going into Whipple Hall, where I would soon join him for lunch. There was the guy in the Norfolk jacket feeding squirrels, don't ask me why. There was Amabelle Bloor sunning herself before the statue of Nathan Hale, which faces south. And there was Molly O'Toole, chair of the History Department, one of my favorites, trucking on down College Walk, crossing my field of view from right to left. Molly is fifty-fivish, full-bodied, as though there was something stingy about being slim, big of breast and bum, no makeup, freckled face, loose auburn-gray hair, some spring in it, always a slight disorder in her dress. She was one of the examiners on my dissertation defense, and man, did she give me a ride. Years later, she said that once it was clear I would pass, she just decided to have some fun with me. Our conversations have a flirtatious undercurrent that is not intended to sweep either of us away.

I started down the stairs to intercept her, digging her vigorous stride, for there is no getting too much of congenial women. I could see right away what was going to happen, but I was too far away to do anything about it, so I stopped to watch. The pigeon-toed kid in the big sneakers and hooded sweatshirt was walking fast a half block behind Molly. Then he broke into a run and slapped her bottom as he whizzed by. She threw her book at him, but he outran it.

When I arrived, Molly was standing in the middle of the walk, legs spread, fists on hips, fuming. I fetched her book. As I approached, she unstiffened, broke into a rueful smile. "Usually, when someone lays a hand on my ass, I like it to linger," she said.

"You ought to be ashamed of yourself," I said, "rolling your buns before that poor child. I wonder, is that harassment or molestation?"

"From what I hear, he only goes after women of a certain age," she said. "Does that make sense? I ask you as a well-known connoisseur of women's bodies."

"He's doing something symbolic," I said. "He—"

"Oh God, you literary types!" she said. "Everything is something else."

"Everything *is* something else," I said.

"I remember when on your defense I asked you a question of plain historical fact, you began to sweat and shiver at once," she said. "I had never seen that before."

"I assumed you were out to get me," I said. "And that plain question was to compare Parnell in Yeats and Joyce, a maze of complications."

"You could have started off by noting that Yeats was a Protestant," she said. "But you recovered when I asked what in the world around him fed into Yeats's notion of the intelligent body."

"He's not the first man to have a thing for dancers," I said.

"I hear the most amazing rumors about you," she said: "that you drove Irene to suicide; that you're shacked up with a student; that you're Leonard Sistrunk's latest conquest; that you're a suspect in the Ka-Bar killings; that you're a tyrant of a chairman."

"I'm an unrepentant smoker, too," I said

"Where are you going?" she said, taking my arm.

"To lunch," I said.

"I'll walk you," she said. "I want to pick your brain about a move I'm making into your professional turf."

"You'll have to give up the notion that things are only what they are," I said.

"I'm writing a paper I think I'll call 'Poetry *Did* Make Something Happen.' It's about the literature leading up to the Easter 1916 insurrection."

"The insurrectionists died, Molly," I said. "That's no advertisement for poetry."

"They died so that a country could be born," she said.

And so we walked along, arm in arm, talking, not saying anything important, enjoying the sounds of our own voices, for we are professors (and Irish), nodding to Amabelle Bloor as we walked by, catching her fake smile, for she does not like to see men and women enjoying each other, right to the Smokers Club's private table, but Molly would not join us for lunch. "It took me three years to break my habit," she said. "Lunch with you guys and I'd be addicted all over again."

Before going through the food line, I sat down to have my first cigarette of the day. There are people who will tell you that cigarettes don't taste good. They are wrong. Julie says I should go around saying "smoking is for losers" under my breath: that's the way to conquer my addiction. I suppose, except that there are certain victories that make you a loser, as there are ways of losing that make you a winner, for of the four kinds of people, those who lose when they win, and those who win when they lose, and those who win when they win, and those who lose when they lose, I belong to the first and aspire to the second.

"We all had a present from you in our boxes this morning," said Zeno: "your now-hear-this curriculum letter."

"Yeah, well," I said, "I thought it was time we offered the students some meat and potatoes along with the arugula and kiwi."

"You really want me to teach 'Women Writers of the American South,'" said Leonard, "turn my brain to mush."

"Yes," I said.

"There's no mush in Flannery O'Connor," said Kay.

"You don't know what *mean* is until you've spent some time up close to a white high-toned old Christian lady of the south," said Leonard.

"What does Valdez have to say?" said Lizzie.

I was about to say "Suarez" when I saw the look on her face, the watery eyes.

"Poor Marshall," said Zeno.

"I'm sworn to silence," I said.

"Me, too," said Leonard.

"I spent a couple of hours with Harriet yesterday," said Kay.

"How's she holding up?" said Zeno.

"She was already tippling when I arrived," she said, "vodka on the rocks. I just let her ramble, how Marshall said this, how Marshall did that, her tone as satirical as it was affectionate. But one thing she said, with nothing leading up to it, stuck with me. She said, 'Who will lay an old broad like me now?'"

Some note in her tone made a wisecrack impossible, so we all sat there in silence, thinking maybe what it would be like to believe you would never get laid again, something I could tell them, but didn't. Instead, I stood up to go for food. I passed a table at which Felicia Zhang sat with three callow youths who otherwise had the look of spaniels at a feast begging for a scrap. As I was about to step on line, a hand closed over my arm in a particular way I recognized as Lizzie's. She pulled me aside.

"Katie Campbell called this morning," she said.

"Good," I said.

"She called to ask if I really wanted a contract renewal or if it was something you dreamed up," she said.

"What did you say?" I said.

"I don't have to put on airs with Katie," she said.

"So it's settled?" I said.

"The other two deans will not act until you have been elected chair by the department," she said. "Until then in their eyes you are only pro-tem."

I did not say anything, but I may well have let out a big sigh.

"Poor Wynn," she said.

"I'll send out a notice after my class," I said. "We can have an election two weeks from tomorrow."

"Give yourself another week," she said, "so we have more time to offset Angel's campaign."

"Come on, walk me through the line," I said.

"Try the Salisbury steak," she said. "Schmeckt gut."

"I promised my cousin to eat a low-cholesterol lunch," I said.

"Do you know a single educated young person with a devil-may-care attitude?" she said.

"No one comes to mind," I said, pointing, so the counterman (a student of mine) could see, to the scalloped potatoes, for I am Irish, to the baked lima beans, and Julie didn't have to know about the bacon bits, and to the broccoli, for she didn't have to know about the melted cheese, either.

"What happened to make them so self-preserving?" she said. "Try the bread pudding mit schlag. What are they afraid of?"

"I think that they believe that between soy milk and the Stairmaster they will live forever," I said. She did not speak. I looked at her while the coffee poured from the urn. To my surprise, her head was down, her face squinching. I had no idea she and Marshall had been so close.

"Willi's dying," she said in a whisper.

I checked the impulse to drop the tray and run. Enough of this dying crap! In fact, I paid the cashier with a semi-steady hand. When we got to a clear area between tables I said, "Is it sure?"

"He has cancer of the liver," she said. "The doctors have tried one thing after the other."

"I can't believe it," I said.

"He also thought he would live forever," she said. "There's no life insurance. Willi is not a worldly man."

"He's the last Christian humanist," I said.

"There's Derwood Bobbie," she said, and would you believe that she managed a little smile?

"We'll get you that renewal," I said.

"I couldn't tell you," she said, "but it is above all for the medical benefits I wanted a renewal. You can't imagine how expensive it is to get sick nowadays. All our lives Willi and I acted as though it was beneath us to think about money."

"I didn't know that adjuncts qualified for the university health plan," I said.

"It cost Murray months of heroic maneuvering," she said. "He took it as a challenge. Come on, or your forage will get cold. I don't believe it is natural for a man to be a vegetarian."

So we moved on toward the table, until Lizzie yanked me by the arm to a halt, and my tray nearly spilled onto one of Felicia's suitors. Felicia waved, her hand circling by her head.

"Hi, Professor O'Leary," she said.

"Ms. Zhang," I said.

"What a dumbhead I am!" said Lizzie in a hoarse whisper. "My contract is good until July. By then Willi will be dead. I don't need the damned renewal or the double-damned health plan."

"It is we who need you," I said.

"Dear Wynn," she said, pulling me toward the table, full of energy. "I hate to destroy your touching faith in human nature, but the thought of being without a husband or a job hit me in the pleasure center like a jolt of lightning. Compared to it, the shock that brought the Frankenstein monster to life was as stimulating as a kiss from a dachshund."

"You'll need something to do," I said, as we arrived at the table.

"I am not the sort of person who needs a job to keep busy," she said, "or, for that matter, needs more than Social Security and a small pension to live on. The things I never let myself do! The things I never allowed myself to say—or think!"

We sat, and I removed the forage from my tray, my touching faith in human nature undiminished. After all, Lizzie had been married to that complacent old fraud for forty-some years. Yes, he had resisted Hitler; yes, he had helped Lizzie and her family escape the Third Reich; but he had been living on the moral income ever since, self-congratulatory talks to Jewish groups and Christian socialists. My job was to get Lizzie's term appointment converted to a full professorship, another jolt to her pleasure center.

"Anybody here know Christopher North?" I said. There was a shaking of heads, except for Leonard's.

"I knew him," Leonard said, "just my type, reminds me of Alistair in fact. I tried to bring him out of the closet, but he wouldn't budge."

"What happened to him?" I said.

"No idea," Leonard said; "one day he just wasn't around any more."

"Terry, Blinky, and Marshall were all on his dissertation defense," I said, "which North failed."

"Oh, oh," said Zeno.

"Who else was on it?" said Kay.

"Bertil Lund and Fran Vocatelli," I said.

"Someone ought to warn them," Kay said.

"My impression is that Suarez already has them under surveillance," I said.

"Are we going to Fern Hill Farm?" said Zeno. "I need a change of scenery."

"Yesss!" said Serena.

"I'm free," said Kay.

"Let's do it," said Leonard. "I need to get myself ready to kill something, the way this term's been going."

"Babs and Derwood Bobbie have kindly offered to spend a weekend with Willi," said Lizzie, "so I can get out of the house. The unstated fact is that they would rather play pinochle without me: they all talk too much to remember which cards have been played."

Everybody else had finished eating, but I hadn't started, and I needed to get going if I was going to make class on time, so I lit up instead. One last time, as we filed out, Lizzie pulled me to a halt.

"You have remarkable arms," she said.

"Compared to my stomach, they scarcely exist," I said.

"You and Kay are beginning to show symptoms of the pandemic fitness virus," she said.

"Lizzie, I've got—"

"Willi wants to see you before he dies," she said.

"Well, of course, if—"

"He says that he would rather confess to an atheist than to an official of any established religion," she said.

My class was not inspired. By way of compensation I dumped loads of facts on the students' defenseless heads. My habit is to glance toward Felicia Zhang when I think I have said something smart, for she will smile or look thoughtful, as appropriate, when she thinks so too. Today all I saw was the top of her head, she was so busy taking notes. The upshot is I was grumpy when I arrived at my office to draft a letter announcing the date for an election. I became grumpier (for there is no grumpiest) when I saw that my office was already occupied by Angel Terrasco, Amabelle Bloor, and Bertil Lund.

"Monika let us in," said Angel. "We are witnesses to that curious solicitude you inspire in others: Teddy Nakatani refused to unlock the door for us."

"Good for him," I said.

"We have not come here to waste your time," Angel said.

"Yes, you have a hassled look, so to speak, if I may say so," said Bertil Lund.

"It must be stressful for a noncombatant such as yourself to hold the chair," said Amabelle.

"I have decided to put my name forward," said Angel.

"Good for you," I said.

"Our informal poll, strictly unscientific you understand, has convinced us that absent your opposition, Angel will be a shoo-in, not to mince words," said Bertil.

"Suppose my opposition is not absent?" I said.

"In the prevailing atmosphere of moral degeneracy, the department is like the whole country," Angel said: "it would prefer to be led by a pansexual waffler."

"Pansexual!" I said.

"Pedophilia and incest with your cousin, sodomy with Leonard Sistrunk, and God knows what with Kay Pesky," said Angel. "And I always thought that Molly O'Toole had something of the dominatrix about her."

"Angel," said Amabelle Bloor.

"In fact," I said, "I always thought that you—"

"Wynn," said Amabelle.

"All right," I said: "but the department elected Murray twice, and he is no waffler."

"Murray Weinrein is a murderer," said Angel. "I called Pierre Howland to offer my sympathy and confirm a suspicion. He finally read me Irene's suicide note. He said that it was only with extreme difficulty that the night before her death he had extracted from Irene a confession of her affair with Murray."

"Committing suicide to get out of that father's clutches begins to look like a rational decision," I said.

"Don't blame the victim," Angel said: "Pierre Howland did what any good Christian would do. You cannot have forgotten my warning about the dangers of unleashed male lust on young women unfortified by religion."

"It was not so much Murray's unleashing of his lust as his leashing of it that got Irene down," I said.

"To return to the point, and I hope you won't take this the wrong way," said Bertil, "because we mean it as a compliment you understand, but the three of us, with all due respect, believe that you are temperamentally unsuited for the chair, not to put too fine a point on it."

I wish I could bring this guy before you, Joel, but he is too nondescript. Amabelle, as usual, looked like two sacks of potatoes in a flowered slipcover. Angel was striking in a black double-breasted, broad-shouldered linen jacket, black blouse with high lacy collar, the thin gold chain and cross, pale fleshless face and dark red lipstick, sitting very straight. But Bertil . . . well, he is not short, nor (by my standards) tall, an inch or so under six feet. He is not thin, nor (by my standards) fat, but tending toward plump. His hair is of a color that might be described as light yellow or dark white, parted on the right side and always neat. His face is oval approaching round, his teeth large and healthy. His eyes are the color of faded denim.

Can you see him? Maybe this will help: he always wears a blue blazer. He always wears a white shirt with a button-down collar. He always wears a striped tie, gray slacks, and gleaming black loafers with tassels. But one of his blazers (I believe he owns two) has a badly sewn hole over his left pocket; the other is shiny under the sleeves and over the tail. At least one of his shirts is frayed around the collar. Beneath the polish on his loafers are fine wrinkles and cracks.

I would like to believe that this air of genteel poverty is a consequence of some expensive vice, but I doubt it. Bertil does not visibly gamble, drink, smoke, abuse controlled substances, or pursue wild women, more's the pity. He is not a degenerate record-collector or depraved feinschmecker of any sort. He does not go to musical comedies. The vegetables he eats and cooks himself probably cost him less than my coffee, beer, and cigarettes cost me. He keeps his daughter on a tight leash. He does not send money to the old folks at home in Sverige, for they are, in Bertil's phrase, "no more than pagans." It's a mystery. Maybe he's just cheap. No, I'll bet he thinks the seediness testifies to an absence of vanity, which is a sin. I'll bet the son of a bitch plugs every spare cent into the stock market, never mind that he's a socialist. I'll bet he sees his accumulating cash as a sign of God's favor.

It was seven, maybe eight, years ago his wife left him. She took off (with her dentist!) to a commune in Mexico, leaving her daughter behind. Oh, there were signs that something was amiss from the time we hired him. (Terry Jones said that either he comes, or she goes.) At faculty parties, after a few drinks, Viveca would put him down, Bertil nodding in agreement, and there were innuendoes of sexual inadequacy: "Anything he does for me, I can do for myself, unless they cut my hands off." Bertil did not take her departure well. He went to his bed and refused to get out of it. There was a brief institutionalization; there were antidepressants, shrinks, urologists, social workers, therapists for his limp psyche and limp dick, but to no avail: he would not get out of bed unless pulled out of it by one of his professional hand-holders.

Angel, we all agree, rescued Bertil from terminal funk. She hauled him to church daily. She, a priest, and a variety of spiritual advisors spent hours with him dispensing comfort, uplift, and the inside dope about Christ's boundless love (especially for the meek, weak, and cast-off) and God's mysterious ways. Bertil, who had been born into the Lutheran church, converted. He became an evangel of good causes.

Conversion magnified the bumper-sticker component of his personality—"testifying Lund" Zeno calls him. He wears immense buttons urging us to save the whale, the spotted owl, rain forests, the ozone layer, and pre-postmodernist buildings. He is a champion of native Americans, forest folk everywhere, the rural poor, the urban poor, neglected oldsters, abused children, working women, and abandoned pets. He has marched for prostitutes and paraplegics. He has renounced his tenure as elitist, although as far as the university is concerned he still has it. He has denounced the SATs and GREs as racist. To offset the hegemony of the white male West he wants the Humanities reading list to include the Mahabharata, the holy Koran, and the plays of Hrosvitha. When one of the university unions goes on strike, he joins the picket line. He has called for an end to big cars and breast cancer. He is against abortion and overpopulation, his remedy for both being abstinence. He organized an on-campus lecture by a woman who advocated parthenogenesis, all sexual congress between men and women being a species of rape. He once told me he admired me for having renounced sex.

Bertil is cheerful of demeanor and reasonable in manner. He is entirely without rancor or a sense of humor. His militancy, in fact, has something oddly docile about it. Ask him for any kind of help and you will get more than you want. To see him with his daughter, to whom he has been both a sustaining father and a nurturing mother, is to make you wonder whether your touching faith in human nature is not, after all, justified. Bertil Lund is a saint, but he is not much liked. Even Angel will sometimes look at him with narrowed eyes. Amabelle puts up with him as one of her few allies. My own feeling is that his selflessness is among the less admirable of the many forms that egotism can take. And don't give me any of that *mon semblable, mon frere* bullshit just because we were once victims of the same little problem. I am not distancing myself—I repeat *not* distancing myself from him in an attempt to deny that deep down we are alike. It's just that I have an allergic reaction to victims—especially when they rise above their victimage in a kind of exaltation. What do you think, Joel, has Bertil got the makings of a serial killer?

"I couldn't agree with you more," I said to Bertil.

"Given that moral sloth in which the department wallows—" said Angel.

"Your passivity, your tolerance, your sympathy for the wayward, otherwise so admirable—" said Amabelle.

"Extremism in behalf of virtue is no vice, as the man said," said Bertil.

"The situation calls for a hard hitter," said Angel.

"Especially a woman," said Bertil. "Das Ewig-Weibliche Zieht uns—"

"Under certain conditions I could be talked into stepping aside," I said.

There was a pause, Amabelle sitting hunched over, her cane between her knees, her hands folded over the brain-crusher knob, her chin on her hands, Bertil absolutely still, an alert expression on his face.

"Let me have one of those," said Angel, pulling a cigarette out of the pack on my desk.

"I would see to it that Kay is promoted," said Angel. "You know my word is good."

"Won't require much doing," I said.

"I would send a letter to the triumvirate recommending that Lizzie's contract be renewed," said Angel. "You can draft it."

"After much thought, I have decided that Lizzie should be put up for a regular line professorship," I said. "She has earned it: her work is read throughout Christendom, if not always by Christians."

"Why Lisbet Arno is no more than a journalist," said Amabelle, as though her own book on Jacqueline Susann were a triumph of the historical imagination and philosophic rigor. (She argues that Saul Bellow won a Nobel Prize and Jacqueline Susann is forgotten because he is a man and she was a woman.)

"I don't want to be pejorative, if that's the word, but frankly, to put the matter in a nutshell, Lizzie is no scholar, not that there are no higher callings," said Bertil, as though his own book, *Negotiating Gender: Women in Old High German Epic* had not been slam-dunked by every scholarly reviewer (except Terry Jones).

Angel, narrowing her eyes, studied my face, then looked over to Bertil, who looked over to Amabelle, who raised her chin high enough to nod, once.

"You can present her case to the Executive Committee," said Angel. "I will guarantee our neutrality."

"You can be neutral during the discussion," I said. "But I don't want any negative votes or abstentions. I don't want to give the administration any grounds for turning us down."

"This is not like you," said Angel.

"I've been learning from a master," I said, "or should I say 'mistress?' " Amabelle let out a snort. But Angel had a point: under her tutelage I might have become a no-holds-barred pro linebacker.

"All right, then," said Angel. "I want your support when I put Amabelle up for an appointment to a full professorship in our department."

"I guarantee my neutrality," I said.

"No you don't," said Angel. "Don't you play the sly boots with me. You can be neutral during the discussion." And here she allowed herself a thin smile. "But I want your vote."

I put out my cigarette and lit a new one, giving myself time to think. Amabelle is not a member of our Executive Committee: she would not be able to vote for herself. A reasonable guess, then, is that the vote would go something like twenty-five to two against her, if I abstained. I couldn't see that my vote would make much difference. "You've got it," I said.

"I knew you would do the right thing," said Amabelle, smiling sweetly. "In my latest mystery there's a character inspired by you who is very favorably treated. Have you read it?" And reaching into her big leather handbag, looked like a collapsed octopus, she said, "I just happen to have —"

"It's on my must-read list," I said.

"That's settled then," said Angel, standing.

"There's a couple odds and ends," I said.

Angel sat down, pulled out a cigarette, put it between her lips, and leaned forward for me to light it. She sucked in enough smoke to lay a fog all over London, then let it slowly drift out of her nose and mouth in a cirrus cloud. "Go on," she said.

"Really, Wynn," said Bertil. "I know that life isn't fair, as the man said, but you—"

"Spit it out," said Angel.

"I want to be in charge of the curriculum," I said. "You can create a new post, Director of the Curriculum, with me as the inaugural director." I didn't know they were all holding their breath until I heard them let it out in a collective sigh of relief.

"Well, Bertil will be my vice-chair . . . ," said Angel.

"Please, please," he said, "that is an obligation I shall gladly relinquish; help yourself, if you have an appetite for it, figuratively speaking."

"I thought the curriculum pretty much took care of itself," said Amabelle.

"Only because of the moral sloth in which the department has been wallowing," I said.

"What else?" said Angel.

And here I was hit by an inspiration, like a depth charge from chthonic powers. "I mean to send out a memo announcing a meeting of the Executive Committee for a week from Tuesday, so we can vote on Kay's promotion and Lizzie's appointment," I said.

"I think I liked you better when you waffled," said Angel. "We will scarcely have time to read—"

"A week from Tuesday," I said.

Angel looked at Bertil, who looked at Amabelle, who lifted her chin to nod, once. "This is a nonissue," said Amabelle. "Everyone respects Kay, aside from some of the company she keeps," and she stretched her wrinkled lips in what she thought was a smile.

"Not to beat around the bush," said Bertil, "in this department a feminist like Kay is a rara avis, if you know what I mean."

My "inspiration" was this, Joel: once Kay became a full professor she would qualify for election to the chair. Yes, of course, I would stay on as vice-chair to make sure she had enough time for mothering. Oh, I know, I had promised to step aside. But by what shyster's interpretation of "step aside" was campaigning for someone else a breach of contract? Machiavellianism in behalf of virtue is no vice.

You know, Joel, I think I am learning to live by the ethos of our old neighborhood: when pushed, push back. Amabelle got up (in about seven stages), the lumps shifting and settling inside her tent of a dress, the others following her cue.

"Bertil, hang on a minute," I said. "Remember Christopher North?"

"That detective has been pestering me about him," he said.

"He flunked his defense," I said.

"Yes he did," he said. "It was very sad. *Qui haec vidabaut flabaut.*"

"How come he was allowed to fail?" I said.

"Well, the dissertation was very bad," he said. "*Res ioqa loquitur.*"

"Don't bullshit me, Bertil," I said. "How come he was allowed to defend?"

He put a roguish look on his face and waggled a finger. "*Wavon Mann nicht sprechen kann, daruber muss Mann schweigen,*" he said, turning to leave. I put my left hand on his right shoulder and spun him around with enough force to send him ass forward into the bookshelves. Damn, that woman moves fast: Angel was between us before I could take a single step toward Bertil, in effect hugging me.

"Have you lost your mind?" she said.

"What did you say, Bertil dear, to make him so mad?" said Amabelle.

"He said if it's ineffable, forget about effing it," I said.

"I don't get it," Amabelle said.

"If you can joke about it, you're not really that mad," said Angel. She took my face in her hand, chin in the web, forefinger on one side of my jaw, thumb on the other, and shook my head from side to side. "Am I right?" she said, and I was thinking that's a nice firm body of Angel's pressed up against me. You know, there's something special about tall strong women (as there is, of course, about short, weak ones). She twisted around toward Bertil, rotating her hip against my belly.

"Bertil," she said.

His face was red and his eyes were blinking rapidly. "Go on, beat me up," he said. "Bertil," Angel said.

"Detective Suarez asked me not to talk about this matter," Bertil said.

"Dear God," said Amabelle. "Wynn won't tell on you."

"Terry was the sponsor," said Bertil, "to take the bull by the horns. Baldly put, the dissertation began as a study of Chaucer's Pardoner in the context of contemporary discourse about homosexuality. Terry didn't want to be bothered while she was on leave. To make a long story short, she turned North over to Blinky von Hartmann as cosponsor, any port in a storm. Blinky pressured North into adding two new sections. If memory serves me, the final title was *Some Versions of the Sissy: From the Pardoner Through Osric to Blifil: Homophobia and Historical Change.*"

"Blifil!" I said.

"All during the academic year—and the summer before, to be precise—North submitted completed sections of the dissertation to Blinky for approval. I believed, we all believed, that Blinky approved them without reading them, *subdolus soiritus.* To slide down the slippery slope of speculation a level further, we believe that the day before, Blinky skimmed the dissertation, as was his wont, saw it was impossible, and absented himself from the defense. He sent over a student named Alistair something-or-other with a message that he was laid up with severe heartburn."

"Under the circumstances, couldn't you have cut North some slack?" I said.

"This is not an eleemosynary institution, as the man said," he said.

Can you beat this pip-squeak? If anyone had a motive for revenge, it was Christopher North.

I walked home feeling that I had made up for that flat-footed class by dancing around the moral minority there, for whether Kay or Angel took the chair, I was out of it and Kay would be promoted and Lizzie would get her regular-line appointment, looking forward to a beer, to my seat at the table, from which I could watch Julie cook, to her chatter, for one of the good things about talking to Julie is that you don't have to say much, to food, even if it is health food, for people who gripe about domestic routine have never lived for a long time without it. Julie met me in the foyer while I was hanging up my new parka, for absent the liner it fit over a sport jacket. She was without lipstick or that green eye shadow, her hair like Uncle Alf's knitting when the red squirrel got onto it.

"I'm really into that paper about Eve, Cuz," she said. "It's my masterpiece. Now I know why you're always writing. It's, like, absorbing. But you never told me how hard it is to write, you know, transitions."

"Leave them out," I said, "makes you sound uncompromising."

"Compromising is just how I want to sound," she said. "That story by Somerset Maugham? It doesn't hold up so well. Where did he *get* his idea of how Americans talk?"

"Convincing dialogue is even harder to write than transitions," I said.

"What I wanted to say is, are you cooking?" she said. "I've got to hand this paper in tomorrow morning."

The cupboard was bare, the refrigerator naked. I could have made potatoes, sides of rice and spaghetti (without sauce), but somehow that seemed too.... An omelette? No, we only had two eggs. We also had one carrot, two baby dill pickles, and three black olives. A sensible person would have ordered out, but not the new me, the ex-waffler, the former easy-way-out O'Leary. While the spaghetti cooked, I hard-boiled and deviled the eggs. I sauteed slices of garlic cloves in olive oil and then dumped the spaghetti (al dente) into the oil, stirred. I placed the eggs on a little plate with the carrot (sliced), the pickles (sliced), and the olives (whole). I slid the spaghetti onto a platter, garnished it with parsley flakes, set it on the table next to a canister of grated parmesan cheese, and called Julie to the table.

"It's good to see you becoming more sensible about food," she said, pretending to dig in.

It seemed to me . . . yes, there were a couple of jalapenos in a jar behind the ketchup. I minced them, sprinkled them over my spaghetti.

"You're going to get ulcers," Julie said. She twirled spaghetti around her fork, then untwirled it, the fork scraping on the plate, for I had not provided a spoon, for I consider the twirling of spaghetti with the fork held against the belly of a spoon an abomination. Then she retwirled and untwirled. "I've been thinking about this for days, but I was . . . well, shy about asking you. I want to invite some of your friends over for dinner, you know, six or eight of them."

I did not answer immediately, for my mouth was full. "You're not ashamed of me, are you?" she said, damn the woman.

"Ninety-eight percent of male humanity would consider you a trophy girlfriend," I said.

"That's not what I mean," she said. "It's that they're so smart. I promise to keep my mouth shut."

I got up out of my chair, walked over to hers, pulled her to her feet, hugged her. "Some of us are driving to my country place for the weekend," I said into her hair. "You come too, see how you get along with them where everything's loosey-goosey."

"You mean it?" she said, disengaging, pushing me back. "Thanks, Cuz."

"We leave at noon," I said.

"It won't be awkward for you?" she said, sitting.

"No one has to know we're lovers—yet." I said.

"I see," she said.

"We'll come on strictly as cousins," I said, taking my chair.

"OK," she said, looking down at her plate. "This is good," and she buried her spaghetti under parmesan cheese.

"I've got it!" she said. "I'll pack a lunch to eat in the car. That reminds me: we used up all the household expense money."

I have been keeping the money for quotidian domestic expenditures in a copy of *The Intelligent Woman's Guide to Socialism.* (My own walking-around money I keep in a copy of *Hard Times.*)

"How much do you need?" I said.

"It just occurred to me!" she said. "Tomorrow's the week anniversary of the time we first made it together. I was planning a celebration. I've already bought a bottle of champagne."

Oh, Joel! I can't bear it when people are nice to me. Think how much easier my life would be if Julie were a heartless (but lascivious) bitch! Why can't I be like Zeno?

"We'll make a night of it some time next week," I said. "There's a restaurant I want to take you to." (I was thinking of *porc lascaux.)* "Afterwards we can go to Heebie Jeebies."

"CBGB's," she said. "You know, Cuz," and she looked up. "You may be right," talking herself into it. "Maybe it's best your friends get used to me being with you little by little. That way, after a while, without remembering how they got there, they'll take our relationship for granted. It'll be, what do they call it, a *fait accompli,* without anybody having a chance to be scandalized."

"Just what I was thinking," I said.

"I'm going to have fun this weekend," she said. "I'm going to pretend you treat me like a poor relation. I'm going to be meek and obedient, like I was terrified."

"Don't overdo it," I said.

"Do you mind cleaning up?" she said. "I want to get back to that paper."

I cleaned up and worked on this letter until I happened to look up and there was Julie slouching in the doorway. "I'm saving my concluding paragraphs for tomorrow morning," she said, "when my mind is fresh. Come on, let's drink that champagne."

Man, we fooled around in the shower for a half hour, reaching out of the curtain now and again for the glass of champagne we were sharing. Then, in bed, she showed me some stuff that had never occurred to me. It's true that, in gross, the sexual variations are limited, but not in fine. Afterward, we just lay there on our backs, replete, not moving, and I for one could not think of any change in anything that would be an improvement. "Whooee," she said.

I couldn't say I loved her. I haven't sunk that low. Instead I improvised a blues. You'll remember my voice. It's only gotten more so. The requisite gravel is there. Phrasing I learned from you. But I haven't gotten any better at singing on pitch since Ma used to give me a look when we all sang "Happy Birthday." Nevertheless, I belted out the following with enough volume to peel the paint from the walls.

My baby's rowdy,
Green stone in her nose.
My baby is raucous,
Green paint on her toes.
My baby's rambunctious,
When I touch her right she explodes.

"You're bragging," she said. Then I sang:

She's got green on her eyelids,
Tattoo on her duff.
That butterfly flutters by
When she shows me her stuff.
She's my rock-and-roll baby,
Someday she'll be my death.
She's my rock-and-roll baby,
Won't let me catch my breath.

"Who won't let who catch whose breath?" she said. Then I sang:

My baby's randy,
Makes me want to sin.
My baby is raunchy,

Feel my abs getting trim.
My baby's resourceful,
Her sailor suit makes my poor head swim.

"Well, no one ever put me in a song before," she said. "I suppose I should be grateful. But couldn't you have been more romantic?"

I slid an arm under her back and rolled her on top of me. In a clear low voice, every note right on the button, she sang the following into my ear:

My baby's grumpy,
All I do is sigh.
My baby is grouchy.
Someday I think I'll cry.
My baby's a gourmet,
He can't get his fill of hair pie.

And I thought if I married her this gaiety would be mine all day and then I thought that in thinking that I was quoting someone I did not like and I saw a silver plane flash across a blue sky smiling at me for I was no longer what you would call awake.

I wrote a lot of this letter last night, between the food and the foreplay. I'm going to break off in a minute or two, so we can get rolling. Julie got up early, finished her paper, ("All about Eve"), dropped it off, shopped for food, packed sandwiches and beer in the cooler, parboiled two slabs of corned beef for supper, stood in the doorway of the study saying, "Look, Cuz," for she was wearing her new dark green fisherman's sweater (which UPS had just delivered), looking good. I'm looking forward to this trip. It's funny how a change of position in space can feel like a change in the condition of your substance. Do you agree?

22

I hate to say this,

Joel, but I don't see you as clearly as when I began to write these letters. You're fading—into a new dimension, I hope. Willie Yeats, on the other hand, found that the more he communicated with his spirits, the more vivid they became (until, at the end, he had terrified doubts as to whether they existed at all). In fact, Yeats, in one corner of his mind, believed that he brought his spirits into existence, or at least made them conscious, by communicating with them. If you faded into nonexistence, would it be good for me and bad for you or the reverse, or good for both of us or bad for both of us or of no consequence to either of us? In any case, the compulsion to write these letters has gotten far less urgent. That's why you haven't heard from me for a while.

It's early Wednesday morning: I spent the last two days catching up on paperwork and class preparation, so I can write all day long if I want, daydreaming between sentences. On one side, faint steam rises from a mug of coffee; on the other, smoke curls up from a cigarette. Behind me, Diz and Bird are blowing up storm clouds, thunder and lightning, a night on Bald Mountain. Man, members of the audience who just a few years earlier had relaxed in those same Carnegie Hall seats, comfortable with Benny Goodman, must have felt they were under assault by demons released to destroy all civilization, the cold ferocity of it. You wouldn't think that such dissonances, such riptide rhythms, could be so beautiful. I suppose it's possible that I love bop because opposites attract, me being so tame. It's not important to know: I'm sitting here, comfortable with Diz and Bird, to tell you about my weekend, during which something momentous (considering the miniaturized scale of my existence) occurred.

There they were, all gathered on the corner of Claremont and 116th as Julie and I drove up. She jumped out to help the others stow their gear, while Kay pulled herself into the bucket seat up front, next to the driver (me), her usual seat, in which Julie had been sitting. We boppity bopped off in the spirit of kids playing hooky, Leonard leaning out a window to say "Later, suckers," as we turned onto 125th Street, heading for the West Side Highway and deliverance. In the rearview mirror I could see Julie sitting between Serena and Lizzie, the three of them talking and laughing like long separated childhood chums recently reunited. There were trees still strutting their stuff for the first hundred miles or so, but after that the trees had pretty much stepped out of their finery. Then Julie strutted her stuff, each half sandwich wrapped separately, neatly labeled, turkey and Swiss on sourdough with Russian dressing, liverwurst on pumpernickel with hot mustard and cole slaw, Cheddar and tomatoes on nine-grain bread with mustard and mayo, for examples, beer or iced tea or orange juice not made from concentrate. Leonard leaned forward, for in a Vanagon Carat the second row of seats is back to front, picked up Julie's hand and kissed it, at which she batted her eyes, preened, and put her hand to her breast, parodying the generic heroine of those old melodramas that shamelessly aroused fantasies of domination in the male, and I saw it all in the rearview mirror.

It was dusking and it was cold by the time we arrived at Fern Hill Farm, colder inside the house than out, our breath visible. Zeno, by long established tradition, started the fires, although he is no good at it, smoke leaking from the kitchen stove and backing out of the fireplace. Leonard and I, designated donkeys, emptied the car, carried in firewood. Kay and Serena fetched the sleeping bags from upstairs, spread them out to air on the couch before the fireplace, Serena inheriting Marshall's. Julie took charge of the kitchen, putting the two slabs of corned beef into the water (brought along in canning jars) in which she had parboiled the beef that morning. Lizzie joined Julie in the kitchen to whip up her famous German potato salad, and one of the many things I love about Lizzie is that she does not make it sweet. Then Leonard joined the two women to make tea with rum. Pretty soon we were all in the kitchen, crowded around the stove, drinking rum and gabbling a mile a minute, getting in the way of Julie and Lizzie, and Serena, who was trying to set the table.

We lingered a long time over food, Lizzie and Zeno and Kay exchanging yarns about their first days as immigrants to the States, Lizzie's *gymnasium* English brought to its knees by a sign painted on a wall that read "Post No Bills." And it occurred to me that, except for Leonard, all of us seniors were immigrants or children of immigrants, and I don't care, even when the president is a Republican, this is still the best place on earth. It took a long time to clean up the kitchen, for everyone insisted on helping Julie, until Leonard took charge and assigned us each one job and one job only—"You hear?"—my job being to put things away, all of us a little weak with laughter and giddy with drink. Then *Lizzie,* European-style, insisted we take a postprandial walk, an aid to digestion, for the air was clear and the moon was on the wax. So we walked along the road, carrying flashlights, Zeno taking Julie's arm, which was inside her new parka. By the time we were gathered around the fireplace in the now-warm living room, in our hands glasses of single malt Scotch (at sixty bucks a fifth), in honor of Marshall, we were all pretty much talked out and droopy around the eyes.

In fact, I was only technically awake, hypnogogic images flashing across my inner eye, when Julie's clear voice said, "Let's tell ghost stories," making me jump, her first words in my hearing since we arrived.

There was a silence that suggested no one much liked the idea, until Leonard said, "You'll have to lead off, Hon: ain't no one else in a condition to hang one sentence on another," the idea being, I suppose, that Julie's telling a story would no more pull the others out of their own thoughts than eight bars of Muzak.

"Well, I don't know," she said, "you guys being professional critics, and all."

"We became critics out of a craving for stories," said Zeno.

"Can't keep our hands off them," said Leonard.

"Story-molesters, that's us," said Serena.

"How about the storyteller?" said Julie.

"If we like the story, we make her tell another," said Kay. "And another. And another, 'til she drops."

"If we don't like the story, we stone her to death," said Serena.

"And eat her heart out," said Zeno.

"A feeding frenzy," said Leonard.

"Enough!" said Lizzie. "Pay them no mind, child: we would love to hear your story, if you have one."

"It is true, Julie," I said, coming on like Auntie Wynn, "that critics mainly kill the things they love. But we left our critical faculties at home."

"Suppose the storyteller throws the first stone," Julie said, but with a disarming smile. "Suppose she's got better aim," a flush on the skin over her cheekbones, "hits the monocular monster" (Zeno's phrase) "right in the eye."

"Then her stories become the stones we throw at other storytellers," said Zeno.

"Well, I don't have a story, exactly," Julie said, "but I was sitting here daydreaming like, about a rock group I used to know, four guys and a girl." I can't reproduce her story verbatim, Joel. Too much depended on her fake-naive and wondering tone, her choice of the most common words, the words that constitute us without our noticing them.

It seems that this rock group, "Meth," was not doing well. Their rare gigs were in upstate dives or New Jersey roadhouses, where the denizens would have preferred Vic Damone or Bobby Darrin, white noise. They had no money for payola. The few critics that noticed them dismissed them. The female member, who sang, played the guitar, and writhed, sacrificed a big black dog to the powers of darkness, for the powers of light were not coming through. Sure enough, demons soon took up residence in the instruments—and possessed the musicians while they played them. The demimonde, women with genital warts and rings in their tongues, guys with pale faces and black lipstick, parricides with trust funds, pricked up its ears. Meth changed its name to Meph. They played at CBGB's. They warmed up audiences for more notorious groups. Radio stations began to play their demo. A record company found a way to exploit them. Their video became an instant cult classic. The group members succumbed to hubris: swaggering interviews, an entourage, biker bodyguards, cocaine, teenage groupies freaking out, one found headless in a dumpster, the drummer's wife a suicide, tattoos reading "666" on their skinny shoulders.

An impresario arranged a tour. At the first concert, held in a college auditorium, half the seats empty, a critic tore off his clothes, danced in an aisle, stabbed another critic with his ballpoint pen. At the second concert, held in a movie theater, all sold out, a girl was thrown off the balcony; another dived after her; a dead newborn was found in the ladies'; fans rushed the stage but were beaten back by the bikers. At the third concert, held in a hockey arena, every seat and spot you could stand on occupied, "666" tattooed or painted on foreheads, the fans erupted as soon as Meph began to play its snarling anthem, "Mephistropolis"; ripped off each other's clothes; beat each other with belts; humped on all fours; the bikers rioted;

fires broke out in a dozen places; the squares fled, but were crushed at the fire doors, which were locked, or the front doors, which opened inward; the lead guitarist crushed the skull of the lead singer with his guitar; the rhythm guitarist garrotted the female member with his G string; the drummer poked out his own eyes with his sticks; of the few who escaped, none told what happened, except one, now in an asylum, who told Julie. But the music of Meph lives on, lives on, the music of Meph lives on.

"Egad," said Leonard.

"And the Meph death holds illimitable dominion over all," I said.

"The apocalyptic imagination is very dangerous," said Lizzie.

"I'm going to bed," said Kay, "and pull the covers over my head."

I joined Julie in the kitchen, where she was washing up the glasses and ashtrays, while the others got ready for bed.

"Where did that come from?" I said.

"I swear to God, Cuz, I didn't know what I was going to say until I started saying it," Julie said.

"Something had to be building up inside you, where your inner eye couldn't see it," I said.

"Well, I wouldn't have let it out if it wasn't for those drinks," she said. "I'm not used to drinking any more. Where did I read that alcohol was a disinhibitor?"

"It's what was disinhibited that surprised me," I said.

"Well, this place is spooky, away from everything like it is," she said. "And all these people getting killed around us, makes me jittery. And all this sex we've been having.... I'm not blaming you: I was pretty wild there myself for a long time. But I was raised a good Catholic, you know. It never leaves you entirely."

I put my arms around her and kissed the part in her hair, for the others were out of sight. "Let's go to bed," I said; "tomorrow promises to be a bright, bright sunshiny day."

You'll remember how the upstairs is arranged. In the "new" part (dates from 1960, as I remember), over the living room and mud room, are a john and three bedrooms, a double bunk in each. Leonard and Zeno took one, Lizzie and Kay the second, and Julie and Serena the third. On the landing, between the "new" and old parts, is a door, which I keep shut during the winter, when I heat just the old part. The master bedroom, over the kitchen, pantry, and downstairs john, is where I sleep, and anybody who doesn't like it can go out and sleep with the coyotes, who were yipping. I've put in a new bed, big enough for me, Kay, and Julie to thrash around in. That's not likely to happen, but I put myself to sleep picturing some of the possibilities.

Saturday went pretty much as Marshall had predicted: an early breakfast of waffles, cooked to perfection by your champion waffler, local maple syrup. Then up the hill behind the house, on the plateau, which I had cleared myself, we had a skeet shoot. Kay is a pretty good shot, for her father had taught her. Lizzie's not a bad shot either, but she doesn't hunt, for she has a qualm against killing "innocent" animals. Julie, who won't even *touch* a gun, worked the clay pigeon flinger. Leonard, who has won sporting clays competitions (wearing tweed knickers), showed us how it's done. Zeno and I were, as usual, competent. Serena was, and always will be, helpless: her hand-eye coordination is strictly postmodernist.

We spent the afternoon on a scouting expedition back to the lake: over there we flushed out grouse; there was a new game trail; there was a deer rub; there was a rotten log a bear had pulled apart. We got back so late I had to rig a floodlight out over the grill, so Julie and I could see what we were cooking. She cut potatoes, onions, peppers, and zucchini into chunks about the size of golf balls, soaked them in a marinade, skewered them, laid them out on the grill. This grill, which Marshall and I made one summer, the stones split by me, better than lifting weights, was big enough to hold a T-bone steak for each of us, except for Julie, who got a beanburger (crushed kidney beans flavored with tomato sauce, chili powder, and onion flakes), the others sitting around the deck, drinking, kibitzing, inhaling the savory smoke from the grill.

After dinner, all of us sitting around the fireplace, mellow with food, drink, and fresh air, our legs stiffening from the walk, Leonard poured us each a glass of that mellow-yellow scotch, liquid gold.

"To Marshall," said Zeno.

"Amen," said Leonard.

"He was a nice man, " said Serena, offering a Salem to Kay, who shook her head.

"We've got a lot of brainpower here," said Leonard. "We ought to be able to figure out how to ambush this feral cat who killed Marshall. I'm willing to serve as bait, the tethered goat that nets the man-eater."

"We were looking to Lizzie for guidance," said Kay. "What would Hercule Poirot do?"

"For the past six weeks I have been reading the so-called 'classic' whodunits by those British high-toned old Christian women: Josephine Tey, Dorothy Sayers, Agatha Christie, Ngaio Marsh, Margery Allingham, P. D. James. There is absolutely nothing to learn about either crime or detection from any of them, nothing, nichts," she said, and the vehemence was unusual for Lizzie.

"Why ever do people read them?" said Julie.

"These fairy tales are informed by a consoling delusion," said Lizzie.

"We need all the consoling delusions we can get," said Leonard.

"We do not," said Lizzie. "In the long run, the only consolation is in reality."

"Yes, reality," said Kay: "the biggest delusion of them all."

"These women betrayed the dark knowledge that made detective fiction necessary," said Lizzie. "It's unforgivable."

"Ah, Lizzie, " said Zeno; " we have long known you are guilty of a crime for which there is no parole: for you, if it ain't dark, it ain't knowledge."

Yes, I thought, but did not say, and that's why Lizzie is so kindly. There's a tangled cause-effect relationship between her pessimism and her tenderheartedness—and her good humor—but it would take that book on skepticism (pessimism's fraternal twin) I will never write to unravel it.

"L'Chaim," said Lizzie, holding up her glass for Leonard to fill.

"What is this dark knowledge we're talking about?" said Julie, and it speaks well of the puffaddicts that not one of them gave her the fish eye, speaks well of Julie that she risked it. Her oscillations between diffidence and chutzpah continue to knock me out.

"Poe invented the detective story," said Lizzie, "when, *erstens,* he finally accepted the fact that there is no God to separate the sheep from the goats, or, for that matter, to guarantee poetic justice. In the first whodunit ever written, 'The Murders in the Rue Morgue,' a man named Adolphe Le Bon is falsely accused of the murders. Without Poe's detective, Adolphe the Good would have been guillotined. Never ask a professor a question, child, unless you want a fifty-minute lecture by way of an answer."

"The death of God always seemed like good news to me," said Zeno, "nothing dark about it."

"Und Zweitens?" said Kay.

"Zweitens," said Lizzie, laughing, pointing her cigarette at Julie, "poor Edgar knew from personal experience that the mind unaided cannot save itself. It is the subject of his most notorious tales. Only in America would they be considered children's literature."

"So we are all lost," said Leonard, "what I figured anyhow."

"No: we are found out," said Lizzie. "By C. Auguste Dupin! As his urWatson says, Dupin excels 'in these more important undertakings where mind struggles with mind.' When faced with an adversary, he 'throws himself into the spirit of the mind he is trying to master' and 'identifies himself therewith.' As the great man himself observes, with respect to him, most men 'wore windows in their bosoms.'"

"How about women?" said Zeno.

"And what does he see through these windows?" said Kay.

"In this case, an orangutan," said Lizzie, "something wistful and subhuman in us, something struggling to emerge and ferocious when repressed."

"Otherwise known as a berserker," I said. "I've been trying to get in touch with my own inner berserker. How do you do it?"

"When the sailor who owns the orang comes home," said Lizzie, "it is seated before a mirror, all lathered up, holding a razor, attempting to shave in imitation of its master. The sailor reaches for his whip. The orang flees—into the apartment of two women. It seizes one of the women by the hair, and 'flourishes,' says Poe, 'the razor about her face,' in imitation of a barber. Her screams and struggles—and here only Poe's words will do—'had the effect of changing the probably pacific purposes of the orangutan into those of wrath.' It goes berserk."

"It's an old story, " said Zeno. "Another case of alleged date rape. My sympathies are with the Orang."

"So were Poe's," said Lizzie. "Any other writer would have had the orang killed off, but Poe has it taken in by the Jardin des Plantes."

"Poe was a proto-postmodernist," said Serena. "Whereas Conan Doyle's rip-off of the orang, a certain Andaman Islander, is shot off of a boat, so he can sink into the mud of the Thames, his element."

"Now I remember," said Leonard: "that misshapen little monster is no more like a real Andaman Islander than Poe's orang is like a real monkey—both figments of racist hysteria."

"Nu," said Lizzie. "It's true that Doyle violated Poe's corpus, but he shied away from Poe's spirit."

"He was a man, after all," said Kay.

"In the first of the Sherlock Holmes yarns we read that he has written an article called 'The Book of Life,' no less. It argues that from a drop of water one could deduce the possibility of an Atlantic or a Niagara without any experience of either. 'All of life is a great chain,' he says, 'the nature of which is known whenever we are shown a single link of it.' For Poe, of course, there is no reason in things, but only in the reasoner, except that in the grouselgeschickten, even the reasoners are mad. Poe's universe is as absurd as the one we inhabit outside of literature."

"Where is, that, pray?" said Leonard.

"Nowhere," said Kay.

"Exactly," said Lizzie. "These morality plays written by Doyle's followers slip between life and literature into pure fantasy."

"Fantasies are a part of life, too," said Serena.

"The best part," said Leonard.

"So are consoling delusions," said Julie.

"Is it possible to get a drink around here?" said Lizzie, holding up her glass. Leonard opened a new bottle and poured us each a glass.

"Look!" said Julie, pointing to the picture window. We all went out on the porch, drinks in hand, to watch the big, fat snowflakes fall. Without thinking, I put my hand on Julie's shoulder and pulled her close, so our sides were touching. I wasn't conscious I had done it, until I saw Kay looking at us.

As we took our seats inside, Julie pulling her chair up to mine, the snacks circulating, Lizzie said, "One of the more celebrated of these lumpen theodicies is Agatha Christie's *The ABC Murders*. The denouement occurs in a movie theater, where the killer makes a providential mistake. The name of the theater is the Regal Cinema. The lead actress is named Katherine Roval, who poses next to a window in the Van Schreiner Mansion. And the name of the movie—are you ready for this?—is *Not a Sparrow*."

Zeno and I let out loud groans.

"Wait," said Lizzie, "it gets worse. As Christie's version of Adolphe Le Bon leaves the theater, a quotation flies into his head: 'God's in His heaven. All's right with the world.' A mischiaas, nicht wahr?"

I was about to say that the second sentence of the quotation does not follow from the first, when Zeno shot to his feet and said, "Enough. I can't take any more. I'm going to bed."

"Wait a minute," said Serena, as we one by one got out of our seats. "Popular culture has to use broad strokes. Subtlety isn't everything, you know. And who's hurt by a belief in Providence, that things will work out, that the universe is on our side? In our secret hearts we all believe that anyhow."

"It is because in our hearts we believe in it, that in our minds we must not," said Lizzie.

"Where the heart leads, the mind follows," said Kay.

"I take it that you are not going to tell us how to catch the Ka-Bar Killer," I said.

Lizzie walked over to me, unsteady on her feet, a solemn expression on her face. "If you want to catch a killer," she said, poking me in the chest to accent each word, "learn how to think like one."

"I'm working on it," said Leonard.

Lizzie suddenly put on this terrific smile, like a sunburst on a rainy day, threw her arms around my neck, and gave me a squeeze, something she had never done before. "I don't care what the feminists say," said Lizzie, disengaging, "I like a man to be big and strong."

"Me too," said Kay, sidling between us, a signifying smile on her face, and damned if she didn't give me a big hug—and a kiss to boot.

"I'm next," said Serena, laughing as though the very idea of hugging me were a triumph of comedic extravagance.

"That's the way it is on cold and snowy nights," said Leonard: "fat men are at a premium."

"Stay right where you are," I said.

When we were alone in the kitchen, washing up, I said to Julie, "I never realized this before, but falling snow makes people feel amorous."

"Everything makes you feel amorous," she said. "You want me to sneak into your room tonight?"

"Let's not risk it," I said. "But tomorrow night . . . ," and I put a hand on her ass.

"Sweet dreams," said Kay, her head in the doorway.

Hours later, I was lying on my side reading, looking up from a volume of Poe's tales every now and then to watch the snow fall, when I heard the door open behind me, and I thought, well, since Julie had snuck into my room after all, maybe a quiet quickie. . . . So I rolled over, like a wallowing whale, and there was Kay. She carefully, quietly, pushed the door to, makeup washed off, hair down in loose ringlets, a pink flannel nightgown, ribbons on the breast, and, man, she looked immense, gathering all the room's light about her.

And I must have looked panicked, as though Poe's orang waving a razor had walked in on me, for Kay said, "Easy, big fella, it's just me. Were you expecting someone else?" She walked toward the bed, where I was sitting, the look on my face, I suppose, as though she had told me my hair was on fire, for she said, "Relax. They're all asleep, and there are three doors between us and everybody else."

"How now, fair maiden?" I said.

Standing between my knees, she reached down, arms crossed, took hold of her nightgown with either hand and pulled it up and off over her head. "How like you that, golden lad?" she said.

Man, I began to kiss everything within reach, my hands full of her ass, for although Kay's ass, unlike Julie's, ripples with cellulite, it is still sweet to the touch.

"I thought that maybe surprise would help solve your little problem," she said, "that it would prevent you from building up performance anxiety. And men get a special charge out of sex that is transgressive, thumbing their cocks at propriety, which they see as female."

Yatata, yatata. Still, I couldn't help thinking, my mouth and hands full, that in fact women were bigger risk-takers than men. Those famous outdoor adventures of men who risk life and limb to climb mountains or exterminate native populations are tame compared to the risks women take indoors, where the real dangers lurk, where the risks are to more than mere life or limb. "Ummmhum," I said, for it is impolite to talk with your mouth full.

I pulled her into bed and took my time, doing all the usual things, for I am not an inventive lover, until Kay's face, neck, and chest were flushed, her juices flowing. What riches, Joel, what opulence man, a cornucopia, a general magazine of all necessary things (as Robinson Crusoe said of his cave) is Kay's body! The perfume, the texture, the suave resilience of her flesh! The lines and masses, the warmth and heft of it! But was it greedy of me to wish that she had requited my moves with a few of her own?

"Get on with it," she said.

So I entered her, missionary position, which is more than any missionary deserves. Once again I took my time, for with the sex I'd been getting from Julie, my staying power was heroic, backing off every time I felt myself approach the point of no return, Kay not moving, except to swing her face from side to side. Was it that she couldn't or that she wouldn't? "For God's sake, Wynn," she said; "why are you holding back?"

So I began to move in rhythm, funky blues, spiraling in, for in any case I did not want to risk a repeat of my disastrous failure with Belinda, the charge building from my knees to my sternum and going off decisively, for the longer the lava cooks, the bigger the eruption.

"See," she said, while I was still savoring the after-tremors, "all you needed was the right partner," but her voice was squashed and shaky, for the flesh was responsive, if the spirit was elsewhere. "We did it; I knew we would."

One good turns deserves another, does it not, so I began to give her light kisses all over, a butterfly fluttering by ("that tickles"), my hand moving down to massage her mons, one finger on evolution's answer to penis envy. "No," she said, putting her hand on my hand, although she did not pull me away. I slid the middle finger in and began to work it around. "Let it be, Wynn," she said. "This night's for you." I slid my ring finger into her anus, for the whole area was well-lubricated, and I took a nipple, which was prettily erect, gently between my teeth. "Ooowoo," she said, "will you stop! I just know it's not going to happen."

"You're spectatoring," I said, "overseeing your own performance, standing back from yourself to judge it."

She let out a sigh: "That's supposed to be my line," she said.

I moved down her belly in big sucking kisses, down to her sacred grove, which I began to lick. After a while, she said "Wynn, please, you don't have to do this."

I lifted my head a bit to say, "You're supposed to be selfish for once. You can't worry about me, whether I' m bored or impatient or turned off. Just look to your own pleasure."

"Oh Gawd," she said. I went back down on her, but so far as I could tell, nothing was happening. She put a hand on my head, but didn't try to push me away.

"Lizzie may have to get up to pee," she said, "and see that I'm not there. She drank all that scotch. . . ."

"Don't think about anything else," I said. "Just focus on your sensations. 'Sensate focus,' it's called. Listen to what I say now: just focus on this," and began to lick that succulent knob of erectile tissue again.

After a while I could feel the light pressure of her hand on the back of my head pushing my face into her. "Ah," she said, and I slid my index finger in with my middle finger and I slid my pinkie in with my ring finger and she said oh and I began to rotate my hand clockwise and she said oh with a double tuck at six o'clock and she said oh oh and I reached up to hold her breast my thumb rubbing her nipple and she said yes and she drew up her legs and let them down saying oh yes and drew up her knees and let them fall to one side and said yes and began to move in rhythm into my hand and said yes I'm coming yes I will yes and man she let out this moan groan wail growl ooouhrwoewohrr made my hair stand on end.

I rested my head on her fragrant and sweaty thigh, licking my chops, but did not ask whether it was good for her.

"That was a workout," she said. "You're a strenuous lover."

I suppose it was just the infamous old male vanity that made me wish she had said something more lovey-dovey. "I try to please," I said.

"Well, making a woman come is also a way of controlling her," she said, "of imposing your will on her. Finally, it's a kind of rape."

The ride back to the City on Sunday was uneventful.

23

Dear Joel,

Goddamn women have what men want most in the world and withhold it out of caprice. No they don't. Let's be fair. Let's get this right, for once. 1) Strictly speaking, there is *no* such thing as caprice. 2) All human actions are motivated, multiply motivated. 3) Caprice is an effect in the mind of a perceiver of unrecognized motives. Out of what motives, then dear reader, do women withhold their bodies? I'll answer that one myself.

Fastidiousness, for sex can muss your hair, abrade your skin, and leave you tacky with another person's fluids; privacy, for sex is invasive; repose, for sex is a bother; resentment of male privilege; the silent treatment continued by other means; tomorrow's a busy day; she feels bloated; you were impatient when she wanted sympathy; sex for fun is a sin; she just changed the sheets; you spent too much time over cocktails talking to another woman, Miss Big-Tits there: why don' t you go fuck her instead?; something you said; the phases of the moon; oh Gawd, not again!; power, for what other route to power over the male can a woman travel?; an estrogen deficiency; she's tired of her body being . . . well, just *used* for your pleasure: inside that body is a person, you know; simply, maddeningly, the main cause of brain fever in the male, because you want it so much—and there's the heart of the matter.

I do not claim that this inventory of motives is, strictly speaking, scientific.

Imagine what the world would be like if females liked to fuck as much as males! Imagine the fun of being fifteen again! If when Peggy was fourteen and I was fifteen she had wanted to fuck as much as I did, there is no doubt that I would be a better, saner, serener man today—take my word for it. Ever since we got back from Fern Hill Farm, Julie has been "not in the mood." Kay, whether I suggested we get together in the morning or the afternoon or the evening or the dead of night, has been busy.

Ooooooowowowow! I am down and I am desolate. Never during those nine years before Julie brought me back to life was I as desperate as I've been these last five days, for winter kept us warm, covering me in forgetful snow. . . . On Monday I brought home a present of freshwater pearl earrings; on Tuesday a matching stickpin; on Wednesday a matching bracelet; on Thursday a matching necklace. Julie accepted these presents graciously, but she was still not in the mood. I want to kill someone. Nothing less will do, since I can't change the way sexual desire was allotted between the sexes during two million years of mammalian evolution. It would have to be someone who deserved to die, of course. Rush Limbaugh? The Pope? Kenny G? Oh Joel, I can feel Julie's flesh against me the way an amputee feels his absent leg.

Sure, sure, I can sympathize with women. That famous feminine streak of mine is not for nothing. It must be a pain always to have guys leering (O'Learing?) at you, hitting on you, looking to poke around inside you. Sometimes when I'm all over Julie I get a sudden vision of myself as a big scruffy old bear, face smeared with honey, pawing over an exquisite piece of porcelain. Why, then gentile reader, do women allow men to fuck them at all? I'll tell you.

Caprice; to garner a child; to lure him into marriage; to keep him married; status; money; to punish her husband, who is a stick, with a lover, who turns out to be a rake; to dis her parents, a general thumbing of the nose at propriety; he resembles her father; it's more trouble to resist than comply; she believes she's supposed to like it; duty; pity; boredom; absentmindedness; a tropism toward martyrdom; an itch for intrigue; a lust for adventure; self-hatred; narcissism; she's browbeaten; to snatch his power or mana or arete; he has eyes for another woman; love, for I'm beginning to believe that love may exist after all, for what else is this thing I feel for Julie?

Fine: the question, then, is how to get Julie to love me. I confess to being clueless, for what a particular woman will love in a particular man is a mystery—to me, at least. But it's clear that in general what a woman loves in a man is not what a man loves in a woman. The man loves the bundle of flesh and appetite before him. The woman loves something out of sight, his spirit let's say, to put the best face on it. Now we are getting somewhere. It follows that the crucial question is this: what have I got in spirit to offer Julie equal to what she has to offer me in the flesh? I am not talking about "objective" value (that myth) or quantifiable value or generally agreed-upon value, but value to her and value to me. The answer is Nothing.

Now wait a minute. Let's hold on here. I think I see a crevice I can squeeze through and out of the impasse to which these mazy maunderings have led me, for what a women values, and may come to love, in a man, is not necessarily what a man values in himself, unless she is one of those docile types (and why have I never come across one?) who takes a man at his own self-evaluation. It may be that I'm lovable after all, not in the abstract, but to Julie. My task, therefore, is to discover a pressing need of Julie's that I can satisfy, for need is a constituent of value, as value is a constituent of love. There may be a lapse in logic somewhere along the way here, but I'm not going to look for it.

What does Julie need that I can provide but have not provided? I'm thinking.... Julie needs to be rescued. From what? you ask. Don't say from me, just don't say it. Julie needs to be rescued from fear. You are about to ask, Of what? Don't. It's a chastening experience to realize that I have been taking Julie for granted, that I have not attuned my receptors to her signals of distress. For the moment let's just say that what Julie needs to be rescued from is fear itself, free-floating fear. She needs to feel safe. I have failed at being her Romeo, as Katrina Campbell predicted. I have failed at being her Pygmalion. How do you like the sound of "Perseus"? My course of action, as I now see it, is to awaken the Perseus principle within me, assuming it's there, get Julie to acknowledge it, to recognize it as answering to her need, to realize its value to her, therefore to love it, and for its sake take all of me.

I could have known you would ask that. I should think the answer is obvious. But all right, I'll give you a little list of the male's motives for wanting to bed down women.

To prove he's a man; to garner a trophy; the force that through the green fuse drives the flower; to punish his wife, who is plain, with a lover, who turns out to be a pain; the will to power; competitiveness; narcissism; it's what we are here for; because he thinks he's supposed to; it feels so good; to justify a postcoital smoke; to get back at Momma; to get back in Momma; a horn-mad compulsion to embrace beauty; the illusion of control; he can't fall asleep; trainer dans la boue; what could get more intimate than getting inside another person?; love.

The desks in my study and in my office are clear. This past week instead of writing to you and inscribing myself in Julie, I processed paper and practiced chairmanship. My curriculum proposals have pretty much gone through. I got Ziggy Sensum to teach two courses we require our majors to take (for the good of their inner lives), a triumph, but only by scheduling in return two courses of his own devising: "Homotropisms: An Introduction to Queer Studies" and "Musical Theatre, or, the Philosophy of Camp." Derwood Bobbie came to me with tears of gratitude in his eyes for the courses I had assigned to him: "The Classical Tradition," so he could go on about affirmations of the human spirit, upward and onward, and "Irradiated by the Supernatural: Literature and Transcendence," so that he could try to con undergraduates into believing that you could be a Christian and a humanist at once.

I could not talk Kay out of scheduling a course entitled "The Body as Text." The Body as Text! Sure: something that can be erased. Simon's sores, Joel, of course I believe that the body is a signifier, but I don't believe it can be reduced to what we say about it. In that respect it is like the moon. I finally got around to reading "Footman Beware: The Cult of the Calf, a Study of Class and Gender in Eighteenth-Century Literature and Culture." In a fever-fit of energy as though my Scripto had been possessed by one of Julie's demons, I revised and rewrote, whirling dervishly from sentence to sentence. Kay's prose is not easy to revise, for in spite of the broken glass and rusted tin of her jargon, her sentences always swing—there's always a rhythm, news to her, if you told her. Literature by Kay's school is now said to "inscribe" or "negotiate" or "interrogate" or "contest" the prevailing ideology, in this case phallocentrism. Words like "interpellate" and "imbricate" are big. Such critics, instead of talking about the literature in a work of literature, seek to "situate" it, which means in effect to read it as a symptom of something, of some outrage by white heterosexual males. I translated all that into the written equivalent of the voice Kay uses when she forgets she's a theorist. I'm going to call her up in a while to ask if I can bring the revised text over, in the hopes that out of pity or gratitude or nostalgie de la boue she will ask me to stay for a while, for the law is use it or lose it.

Monika stopped by my office earlier today (it's sundown on Friday) to say that she was glad to see I was beginning to assume the responsibilities of my office and it's about time. Her face was somehow fuller and softer, the corners of her mouth relaxed, her hair restyled a la Diana Ross, with the addition of a blonde streak. "You're looking good," I said.

"Think so?" she said, but as though she was glad to hear it. "I want you to meet someone."

"OK," I said.

"He's Frederick Grantwell, out of the University Counsel's office," she said.

"O.K.," I said.

"He stopped by this summer from time to time to advise Murray on the legal aspects of his benefits plan."

"I'm free—" I said.

"After Irene's suicide, Murray called him in again," she said.

"A wise course," I said.

"I can tell you that he gave Irene's father a talking-to that turned his face a whiter shade of pale. Fred doesn't take any prisoners, man."

"I gotta meet this guy," I said.

"I called him in again two weeks ago when I heard about Malcolm Tetrault."

"What's shitbreeches up to?" I said.

"He told two students, one of whom told me, that if he doesn't get recommended for tenure, he's going to sue you, the Department, and the University."

"On what grounds?" I said.

"Reverse discrimination," she said.

"There's nothing reverse about it," I said.

"The last five people we tenured are women, or minorities, or both," she said.

"They just happened to be better at what they do than any of the white male contenders," I said. "There's an infinite number of people better than Tetrault at what he does. Besides, he's a pip-squeak."

"You don't have to tell me, " she said.

"What does counsel advise?" I said.

"That we play it strictly by the book and back our play with lots of paper, that no one criticizes the little prick within earshot of Angel Terrasco or Bertil Lund."

"You come to the meeting and take minutes. Let me work them over before you send them out," I said. "I'm free to have lunch with Grantwell every day next week but—"

"He's right next door," she said. "Can I bring him in?" Without waiting for an answer, she went to the Department office and came back leading Grantwell by the hand, to my surprise. He was maybe fifty-five, maybe older, balding, looked something like Count Basie. You would not say he was fat; nor would you say he was burly plump; he was just naturally heavy, like the Mafia dons of legend, at home in his body, radiating authority.

"Fred, I'd like you to meet Professor Wynn O'Leary; Wynn, this is Frederick Grantwell," Monika said.

"Professor O'Leary, " he said, as we shook hands.

"Mr. Grantwell," I said.

"You don't look as I expected you would from Ira Lovecraft's latest whodunit," he said.

"I'm glad to hear it," I said.

"On the whole, it's a complimentary portrait," he said.

"The implied bias is regrettable, of course, but you don't compliment a heterosexual by depicting him as a homosexual," I said.

"No, you do not," he said. "Probably you could sue."

"I don't believe in censorship," I said, for I can be a prig with the best of them.

"Good for you," he said.

"Will you sit?" I said.

"No. I've got to move on," he said. "Monsy here will tell you how I think you ought to handle the Tetrault matter," he said, and wrapped an immense hand around Monika's upper arm. Monsy!

"Monika has been my unerring guide through the minefield of Departmental affairs," I said.

"I have to warn you," he said, "I plan to steal your administrator away to the Counsel's office," his hand still around her arm.

"I'll sue," I said.

He smiled at the pleasantry, although his eyes said, "Don't even try to fuck with me, Buster," turned to Monika, said, "I'll pick you up at five," accepted her peck on the cheek, and with a nod to me, departed.

Monika's smile was ironic.

"Well, well," I said.

"My daughter had lunch with us on Monday," she said. "Fred moves fast. Afterward, she said he was 'a neat guy,' the first encouraging word I've had from her in years."

"He doesn't mind about you and Terry?" I said.

"Fred is the kind of sexist who believes that female desire is nonspecific in its object," she said. "He says we're all 'polymorphously normal.' I like that in a man."

Begad, we had a laugh together at that one. I complimented her on the words she spoke at the memorial service for Irene: the sympathy was all the more moving for the tough-mindedness and restraint. Kay spoke too, getting in a couple of feminist licks. Murray announced that henceforth, on all future documents, his master plan would be called the "Weinrein-Howland Comprehensive Benefits Coordination." He was also pleased to announce that during a recent meeting at Bear Mountain the Trustees had provisionally accepted the plan (there were still a few wrinkles to be ironed out).

Hector stopped by Thursday afternoon: No sign of Christopher North; the Ka-Bar that killed Marshall is of the same vintage as the other two; Hector thought it interesting that when I go away for a weekend, no new bodies turn up. He was scarcely out the doorway when I saw Teddy Nakatani standing in it.

"May I come in?" he said.

"Come, then," I said.

"Why have you led me astray?" he said, standing stiffly on the other side of my desk, scratching his armpit.

"That's what professors do," I said.

"The dissertation you suggested I write has already been written," he said.

"That so?" I said. "By whom?"

"There is a book entitled *The Double Perspective of Yeats's Aesthetic* by Okifumi Komesu," he said.

"It is not a book on Yeats and things Japanese," I said, "although there is a fifty-page discussion of Yeats and the Noh. I gather that you haven't read it."

"You will perhaps have noticed that whatever book one wants to take out of the library has been stolen or is moldering on some professor's desk," he said. "I naturally assumed from the name. . . ."

"Bulgarian critics do not write solely about Bulgarian literature," I said.

"The note you heard in my voice was not truly anger, but disappointment," he said.

"You are old enough to have developed a tolerance for disappointment," I said. "You will have come across Yeats's remark to the effect that all life is but a preparation for something that never happens."

"We have not developed the relationship I anticipated," he said. "It seems that I must make all the overtures."

"That's the way it is between faculty and students," I said. "Anything else is sexual harassment."

He gave me the long look of someone trying to get behind a mask. My own look, if I brought it off, was essentially poker-faced, mildly expectant.

"I was counting on certain affinities between —" he said.

I stood up, my stomach nearly tipping the desk over.

"Your neck is swelling," he said.

"Go home," I said. "Take the rest of the afternoon off. Do not leave your apartment until you have written at least a rough draft of your dissertation proposal. I want to see it next week."

"Your humble servant," he said, bowing, "as always," and walked out.

I'm home alone myself. Julie and her friend Fawn took off on their bicycles this morning, up Route 9W to a summer camp ("Clover Brook Camp") given over for the next ten days to the Rainbow Gathering, ad hoc bread ovens made of local clay, everybody calling everybody else "brother" or "sister," at night a "sister circle" howling at the moon, discussions of Thich Nhat Hanh, whose motto is "smile and breathe," performances on the mbira and djembe (instruments out of Zimbabwe), lots of companionate sex I suppose, aging hippies conning young women into their sleeping bags with a line about the Spirit.

I'm so unhappy, Joel. I remember bragging that of the two categories of people, those who get depressed and those who get anxious, I belong to the second. It's becoming clear to me that I also belong to the first, and at the same time. I'm overcome with yearning. I want, I want, I want. Mainly I want to make love to Julie. I know it's a mistake to feel that lovemaking will save me from middle age, mediocrity, the unbridgeable gap between what we need and what we get, but that's how I feel. Look who's talking: the hypocrite who told Teddy Nakatani that by now he should have developed a tolerance for disappointment. Stephen's stones, it's only been five days. But it feels longer, a lifetime and another one in purgatory. I'm going out to the kitchen to call Kay, see if I can bring the revised "Footman Beware" over to her.

Here I am again. Kay had forgotten she ever gave me a copy of the essay, so she says, getting back at me for taking so long to read it. The thing has already been accepted for publication, for Kay's name alone can boost the readership of a scholarly journal by fifty percent, to, say, a good two dozen, or even twenty-five. She will, however, consider my revisions when she gets proof. No, I can't come over to see her tonight: she's busy. But—and here my heart did a three and a half gainer—was I free for dinner tomorrow night? We have to talk. How about I take you to La Grotte? I said. If you like, she said.

Oh Joel, life suddenly seems worth living again. I'm anticipating that after dinner we will retire to Kay's place for some baby-making. It is true that Kay is not Julie, but the sumptuousness of her body compensates for any deficiencies in my feelings for her, for her uneasiness about sex. Besides, when I'm not near the woman I love, I love the woman I'm near.

24

Dear Joel,

Julie is still not in the mood. Right now she's in her room reading a book by Thich Nhat Hanh entitled *Peace Is Every Step,* although for my money peace is about the last thing a young person should be after. "You ought to read it, Cuz," she said. For myself, I can't imagine any way of achieving inner peace short of cutting my balls off.

Kay did not wear her black sheath dress to La Grotte. That contrary woman hid her luminous skin under a lot of gray tweed, made her look itchy. The French braid, however, was in place, as were the cheekbones. The *porc lascaux*, the waiter, the medicine man, were as before.

A clink of glasses, a sip of Armagnac, and Kay said, "Zeno has agreed to be the father of my baby."

If I give the impression of imperturbability, to Murray at least, it is the result of a partition between my chronic inner agitation and my ponderous outward inertia. I did not overturn the table, throw crockery at the walls, dash myself head first against the medicine man, or roar cocksucking, motherfucking, cunt-lapping, blue-balled bitching bastard of a whoremonger. "I thought you had me in mind to ply that pert, uuh, play that part," I said.

"But I do want you to be the child's godfather," she said.

"What did I do wrong?" I said.

"You're not going to poke your masculine vanity into this, are you?"

"Can you count on Zeno to be there for you when you need him?" I said.

"I can count on you to be there for me when I need someone," she said.

"But—" I said.

"Zeno is not as muscle-bound as you and Leonard, but you can tell he has good genes," she said. "For all his neglect, he's never sick. He once told me that he didn't have his first cavity until he was thirty-five."

"I have to think my genes are as good as Zeno's," I said, with a sniff, for there is no way a lovelorn man can preserve his self-respect.

"All right, then: I wasn't going to say this: but Zeno knows how to leave a girl some room," she said. "You're too . . . what is the word?. . . importunate, *demanding* a lover."

"What have I ever demanded?" I said.

"Even before you began rooting around among my innards, you worked me over like a laundry mangle. Then you kept holding back and holding back, something men always say women do. While you were coming you pressed me so tight up against you I couldn't move a muscle, I couldn't breathe. I felt the panic of a trapped animal. And after, you still wouldn't relent, although I asked you to, again and again. I couldn't sit down for two days afterward."

"I was trying to bring you off," I said.

"For your own satisfaction," she said. "You're greedy, Wynn O'Leary. You're just a big appetite. You're greedy for food, cigarettes, coffee, and women."

"For life," I said. "How do you know Zeno will be any less greedy a lover?"

She pulled out one of my cigarettes, lit up, and looked me in the eyes, for hours it seemed, a serious expression on her face.

"It's been years since I first kept expecting you to make a move on me," she said, "kept hoping you would make a move on me—everybody expected you to make a move on me—but you didn't. On the rebound, I suppose, I had a brief affair with Zeno. We still see each other now and then for an evening of companionate sex."

"Ursula's urchins," I said. "You're a feminist! Why didn't you make a move on me?"

"I have my pride," she said.

"It seems I misread the signals . . . for a change," I said. "Besides, there was my little problem."

"If you had trusted me not to laugh at you, I would have solved your little problem for you way back then," she said.

"I didn't think you'd laugh . . . exactly," I said.

"How can you have lived so long and learned so little about women?" she said. "A woman likes a man to need her, wants a man she can do something for. That's how we're brought up, practically from birth: to be of service."

"I need you to go to bed with me," I said in a little voice.

"That's not a need," she said.

"Give me another chance," I said.

"Don't beg," she said. "It's unmanly."

Kay did not return the pressure when I kissed her goodnight.

I spent most of yesterday, Sunday, reading your tattered copy of *To Be or Not to Bop* to see if I could learn from Dizzy's autobiography how to live. Diz knew but he never said.

Dear Joel,

Kay's promotion went through as a torpedo goes through water. On a motion from Zeno, we voted her into the tight circle of full professors by acclamation. I admit to laying a ghetto felon's stare on anyone who looked ready to ask for a secret ballot, in particular Hannah Wetstone, our poet-in-residence, who has a low tolerance for words like *narrativize, topicality, knowism,* which Kay has been known to use. Derwood Bobbie was very lucky that Leonard, Zeno, or I did not jump out of our chairs, leap across the conference table, growling horribly, and fall on him, so as to turn him into steak tartare. During Derwood's interminable tribute to Lizzie, you could see from their attitudes that the others were turning against her. Then Ziggy Sensum had the nerve to wonder aloud whether the world needed another book on detective fiction. Oh Ziggy, reason not the need! It's not so sure that the world needs one more paean to Maria Callas either.

Kay, who of course was not present, saved the day with a letter she had given me to read. You have to understand, Joel, that only a few of those present had actually bothered to read any of Lizzie's writings. The rest could assume that if Kay was for Lizzie, Lizzie could not be retrograde, and that was that: the vote was 24 to 4 in her favor. When, after the meeting, I called Lizzie (who was babysitting Willi) to tell her the news, she refused to play Andromeda to my Perseus, for it is seldom that a woman whom a man has a fantasy of rescuing has a fantasy of being rescued.

"After all you've done, I may show my gratitude by retiring," she said. "'Retirement looks better every day. One can never have enough freedom."

"Your income will triple if you stay on," I said. "If money enslaves some of those who possess it, it liberates others."

"I foresee you taking Marshall's place as our aphorist-in-residence," she said. "Willi's condition has made me think of aging . . . of mortality . . . of how little time I have."

"Something is coming to an end," I said, no idea what I was talking about.

"The end of something must be the beginning of something else," she said, "for nature abhors a vacuum."

"Lizzie, Lizzie," I said, "you're not shallow enough to be an aphorist."

"Wynn, dear Wynn," she said, "if I were thirty years younger I'd know how to cure you of that melancholy you hide even from yourself. You wouldn't believe it to look at me now, but I used to be quite a dish."

I am not melancholy, for melancholy is a side effect of self-pity, for it is always Margaret you mourn for.

I dropped into Kay's office to tell her how the vote had gone. She did not seem impressed, although I can't remember another occasion on which the Department voted unanimously for anything. Her hair was mostly hanging in loose waves, but divided into segments, like a peeled grapefruit, by a half-dozen dreadlocks that ran down from her crown. She was wearing a black velvet jumpsuit over a white silk blouse that would be smooth and soft against your cheek. Her lipstick was pink, about the color, as I remember, of her nipples, equally kissable. As for her office, it was a mess, one of those plants with big, shiny, spear-shaped leaves dying in a pot.

"How're they hanging, big boy?" she said with a mixture of satire and sympathy hitherto outside the narrow corridor of my experience with women. "Sit down, and don't look so hangdog."

"Once the Administration acts, you'll qualify for the chair," I said. "I want your permission to get the word out that you're willing."

"You are already getting a taste for manipulation," she said. "But no: I'm counting on you to give me a two-day schedule and to exempt me from committee work. That way I'll have five full days a week to learn the craft of mothering. After next year, we'll see."

"Have you, are you?"

"Not according to my handy little home testing kit," she said.

"Well," I said, sitting back, lighting up, "you'll have to count on Angel. I already promised not to run against her."

"Why ever did you do that?" she said.

"I don't want the fucking job," I said.

She gave me a longish look. "You're not cutting off your nose to spite your face, are you?" she said.

"Fuck the chair," I said. "Fuck the Department. Fuck everything."

She leaned forward, took a cigarette out of the pack, accepted my light, sat back, said, "For old times' sake" with a smile that someone whose brain was not stewing in backed-up semen would have taken as conciliatory. She playfully blew smoke into my face. "You'll have time to finish your book."

"Fuck the book," I said.

"Don't be such a baby," she said. "You can't always get what you want."

"Or what you need," I said.

"What's more," she said, flaring up. "I saw you put your arm around that lollipop, that all-day sucker of yours, when we were on the porch."

"That was just—" I said.

"It's half the reason I humbled myself to come into your bedroom. And what do you greet me with? A fading hickey on your neck, that's what. You weren't wearing one of those dumb turtlenecks in bed, if you remember. Let Miss Hot Lips," and she stabbed at me with the cigarette, "your cradle-snatch," another stab, "your French tickler," a third stab, "deal with your little problem. Why do you need me?"

"I don't," I said, getting up, stalking out, hearing Kay sigh and say, "Oh, for God's sake," just before I slammed the door.

The good news is that Julie was cooking when I came home, evidence that she was coming around, or so I chose to believe. The bad news is that she was cooking a roast pork shoulder and red cabbage, the first meal we had together, a valedictory gesture and a sign that she no longer cared about my cholesterol, so I couldn't help believing. But as she chatted, setting the table while I went through the mail, going on about Thich Nhat Hanh and the importance of breathing and the art of mindful living, about this tall, gaunt guy with deep-set, hypnotic eyes who gave her a lesson on the mbira, I felt my snit dissolve, the blood flowing back into my arms, legs, and head. Julie forgot to make crackling. The pork was undercooked, but I managed to carve off enough from around the edges to make a respectable serving, for my appetite is not what it used to be.

"If you want to know, I got an A on my paper about Eve," she said.

"Congratulations," I said.

"The professor wrote on the paper that my use of Maugham and Borges was inspired," she said.

"You see," I said.

"What I see is that you're the one who should have gotten the A," she said.

"Don't be silly," I said. "Any fool can pick up ideas. I've never met a fool who wasn't full of ideas. It's what you do with them that counts. You obviously did something worth doing with that bit of an idea I passed on to you."

"You really mean that?" she said, brightening. "I'm trying to accomplish something on my own. I want to be what you call 'self-directed' instead of being so dependent."

"Of course I mean it. Besides," I said, playing the fool with an idea that had just come to me, "all comment on literature is collaborative. Just the other day, when I was teaching D. H. Lawrence's *The Rainbow,* I used stuff I learned from you. I was trying to explain what an education could mean to a young woman who didn't fall into it as effortlessly as snow falls in Antarctica. And there's this wood carving of Adam and Eve—"

"I don't believe you," she said, a laugh in her voice.

"Why not?" I said: "when have I ever deceived you?"

"All the time," she said, her good humor growing.

"Give me a for instance," I said, her mood spilling over into mine, and some day, probably not in this lifetime, I will learn to let sleeping dogs lie.

"You sure you want to hear this?" she said, suddenly serious.

"I don't want there to be anything between us," I said, not speaking figuratively.

"That last night in your country place I had to get up to pee, you know, cause I'm not used to hard liquor. Besides, that Serena snores something awful. When I came out of the bathroom I looked through the glass door that divides the two parts of the upstairs, like. Well, I saw a light under the door to your bedroom. So I decided to visit you, you know, sort of to put one over on your know-it-all friends, and the way you're always hot for me makes me feel I don't know, like I count for something, and maybe this will make you think less of me, but I wanted to have sex with you, I wanted to be with you because I spooked myself with my own ghost story and you're so strong . . ." and she dabbed her eyes with a napkin.

"You count for everything," I said.

"You shouldn't say things like that unless you mean it," she said. "I had my hand on the doorknob when I heard this ungodly noise, like a grunt mixed with the yowl of a soul in hell." She blew her nose in the tattered paper napkin. "I guess that's the sound of a Valkyrie in love. . . . I thought I was giving you all the lovemaking any normal man could desire. I thought we had an understanding, Cuz. . . . Don't: stay where you are," she said, for I had gotten up, arms extended to hug her.

You can imagine the excuses, too humiliating to repeat. Julie wasn't having any. Why is it that my relations with women always end up putting me in the wrong? Oh, woe!

Dear Joel,

Something interesting happened yesterday, something weird and violent enough to take my mind off Julie. I've been mooning over her like a newly-made steer separated from his mother. Walking to lunch the other day, I heard myself let out a groan, scared the pigeons into flight. I swear to you, Joel, there has not been a half hour this past week that I haven't thought of her, with regret, with remorse, with rage, with abysmal longings, with fantasies too sentimental for my acidulous pencil to pen.

Of course I've tried to re-route my thoughts—onto my work for instance, but everything I read reminds me of Julie, for if literature is about any one thing, it is about love. The result is that I've been faking my classes, on which my self-esteem depends, last year's stuff warmed over lightly. And I've tried to darken the theater of my mind with fatigue, running three miles in twenty minutes, then lifting weights until all systems augured collapse, but fatigue only makes the light more lurid. Everything I think or do reminds me of Julie, her brawny foot, her wondering voice, all she has done for me, all I could do for her, a long trip together cross-country for the hell of it, stopping in the afternoon at a motel, taking a long walk through the desert behind the motel, a long swim in the pool, a long supper (of spare ribs) a long evening of lovemaking. Don't talk to me about Freud's "The Prevalent Form of Degradation in Erotic Life," namely overestimation of the object. Haven't I described Julie to you with meticulous fidelity? There's no overestimation going on here. If this is love, you can have it, although an infection of love is like catching the flu in this: there is nothing you can do but wait it out.

Here's what happened: I was standing atop the many steps—and some day I will have to count them—that descend from the administration building to College Walk, under the delusion, not quite conscious, that what you can look down on, you can control. Man, the day was tumescent, swollen gray clouds trying to discharge, but not making it. The air, heavy, wet, cold, hit you like a blunt instrument. Naked twigs quivered in the breeze. A twitchy squirrel, cloud-colored, looked ready to leap for my jugular. I looked away and sighted along a descending hypotenuse to College Walk, maybe a hundred yards away, till my eye hit on Angel Terrasco and Amabelle Bloor (with my 30.06 I'd aim two inches low), arm in arm, moving slowly from right to left, on their way to the Faculty Club, where professors who don't like to be around students eat lunch.

Angel, in a black sheath of a coat, looked especially tall and stiff, her shoulders high, as though she needed someone to massage her trapeziuses, shortening her stride to accommodate Amabelle, whose legs are maybe eight inches long, and in any case gimpy, her feet in high white sneakers, holes cut in them, to let her bunions breathe. Over a flowered dress that reached to her sneaker tops, she wore a trench coat, the shifting lumps and knobs inside it, as she scuttled forward, at variance with all known mammalian anatomy.

I refocused my gaze, so that it included the pigeon-toed kid in the hooded sweatshirt, a big puffy black parka over it, walking fast, maybe forty yards behind Angel and Amabelle. I may have allowed myself a smile when he started to run; I know I allowed myself a smile; I probably allowed myself a snicker. As he came even with them, he slowed down, and reaching across and behind Angel, slapped Amabelle on the can. In a movement so fast I never saw it, Angel got a hold, with her left hand, on the hood of the kid's sweatshirt, as he passed by her. His legs ran out from under his body, so that he came down on the flat of his back, hard, his head protected by the hood of his sweatshirt, on which Angel still had a grip. She went down on one knee and began to shake a finger at the kid, giving him a lecture. When I saw Amabelle unscrew the knob of her cane and begin to withdraw something long and shiny, I shouted "No!" and began to run.

I was halfway there (you will remember that in my freshman year, before I put on all that muscle, I could do 100 yards in under ten seconds), when Amabelle raised her arms, both hands around the knob—a blur moving toward her from the left, Angel all oblivious, still giving the kid what for—and brought the sword down with all her might, running the kid through, a priestess of some nefarious sect sacrificing the infidel who had defiled her holy of holies. His upper body and legs contracted, forming a V, then dropped. Angel fell back, onto her behind. Amabelle levered the sword from side to side to release it, pulled it out, started to raise it again, when the blur resolved itself into Julius Hall, the security guard who had taken Irene for a salubrious walk to the hospital and who now pinioned Amabelle from behind. She was struggling to break free, the two of them lurching this way and that, when I came up and twisted the sword out of Amabelle's hands.

Amabelle just stood there blinking, her arms half extended,

dumbfounded by the disappearance of her blade. Mr. Hall, careful about where he touched her, pulled her over to the sundial, sat her down, the look on her face at once defiant, exalted, and totally insane. "You stay there, hear?" he said.

"Call EMS and Frederick Grantwell at the Council's Office," I said.

"I've had dealings with Mr. Grantwell," he said, "a most persuasive man. It's just that I happen to be, um, momentarily embarrassed." I gave him two quarters and he hurried over to the bank of pay phones outside Witherspoon Hall, fifty yards away.

I knelt down beside the kid, Angel still sitting on the walk, her face in her hands, unzipped his parka, and pushed up his sweatshirt. His abs were sharply articulated, a hole the size of a nickel in his right external oblique, a worm-like loop of muscle protruding. I pulled the folded bandanna I used for a handkerchief out of my back pocket and pressed it into the exit wound, which was leaking blood. I pulled out a shirttail, cut it off with my pocketknife, for like a male character in Virginia Woolf, I always carry one, folded the shirttail, and pressed it onto the entrance wound, which was welling up and overflowing. He was not wearing a belt, so I slid my own out of the loops and cinched it tight over the ad hoc dressings.

"Why she do that?" he said.

"You pissed her off," I said.

"Am I gonna die?" he said.

"You're going to have a thumb hole in your love handle," I said.

"Ain't got no love handles," he said.

"Lie still until the medics come," I said, "and maybe you'll live to grow them." I stood and pulled Angel to her feet. She fell into my arms, as they say, her stiff hair sanding down the scar on my chin.

"Help me, Wynn," she said. "Please. I can't go to jail." As you have no doubt surmised by now, I am silly putty in the hands of any woman who puts her arms around me.

"There, there," I said, patting her on the back as though I was Clark Gable or someone.

"Please," she said.

"I'll do what I can," I said.

"Please," she said.

"It all hangs on what the other witnesses think they saw," I said.

"Please, please," she said.

"Just keep your distance from Amabelle," I said, disengaging, for I saw Mr. Hall carefully threading his way through the ring of onlookers. I pulled him aside.

"They're on the way," he said.

"You saw what happened?" I said.

"Yes, indeed," he said.

"What exactly did you see?" I said.

"Depends," he said.

"Depends on what?" I said.

"On what Mr. Grantwell tells me I saw," he said.

"Professor Terrasco never meant for the boy to be hurt," I said, for I did not want to cloud his clear sense of duty by mentioning that Angel had once wanted the kid's hands cut off. I looked over to where she was standing, not having moved from where I left her, dazed, leaning to one side, catching herself, leaning to the other side, catching herself, as if unable to decide which way to keel over.

"She's one of ours," he said. "The other one is none of my responsibility."

The cops arrived first and began to question everyone who claimed to be a witness. Then EMS arrived with a siren and ambulance and before anything else undid my admittedly amateurish first aid, checking out the damage.

"That's mine," I said, for the buckle on the belt was silver, southwest style, from my college days. The broad-beamed EMS broad reached the belt back and up without turning away from her patient.

"Hey mister," said the kid, "call my momma? She's Adelaide Thigpen, cleans up over at Carter Braxton Labs."

"I know Adie," said Mr. Hall.

"How about calling her?" I said.

"You got a quarter, Sonny?" he said.

The kid reached, grimacing, for his pocket, but I got a quarter out first, which I passed to Mr. Hall, who left for the phone. A hand, size of a catcher's mitt, closed over my bicep and began to drag me back. Good thing I didn't throw a punch at the owner, who turned out to be Frederick Grantwell.

"Don't spare me the details," he said, when we were outside the ring of onlookers.

So I didn't, telling him what I told you, minus the flourishes, watching over his left shoulder, as two plainclothes cops sidled over to Amabelle where she was sitting, suddenly pulled her arms behind her, cuffed her, pulled out a card, read her the Miranda cautions. She affected a sly little Son-of-Sam smile.

"That's right," he said; "you tell it like that. Emphasize that Terrasco didn't see Bloor draw her blade, that the stabbing took her by surprise, that she just about fainted."

"What can happen to her?" I said.

"I'm not a criminal lawyer, you understand," he said. "But this is the kind of case that can get an assistant DA on the evening news. The bigger the charges, the more respectable the accused, the better the photo ops. You ever see an ambitious assistant DA go to work?"

"What charges, for example?" I said.

"Offhand, I'd say anything from simple assault to criminal facilitation to attempted murder." Over his right shoulder, I saw two plainclothes cops approach Angel where she was sitting on the steps below us, one helping her to her feet, the other taking out his handcuffs. "Whatever happens, she won't be your next chairman. The Administration won't allow it. Professor Angel Terrasco is tarnished."

"Wynn," Angel said, but so faintly that I couldn't hear the word, though I could read her lips.

"Monsy will be relieved," said Frederick Grantwell, University counsel. "She has the idea that Terrasco is out to get her," and his smile was worthy of Hector Suarez.

"The DA is an alumnus," I said. "You ought to get someone here to talk to him."

He looked me over, taking his time, the insolent S.O.B. "Suppose you leave strategy to me, Professor," he said. "This is not exactly your field of expertise."

"You better get over there," I said, nodding in Angel's direction, "before she says something that can be used against her."

He turned, looked, and hurried over to Angel and the cops, one of whom was holding her arms behind her. "That won't be necessary, my man," Grantwell said.

"Yes, it will," said the cop, cuffing her.

The kid was being slid into the ambulance by the time I got back to him. He raised a hand, weakly, to wave goodbye, and the pang that gripped me was distinguishable in feeling though not by word from the pang that grips me when I think of Julie. My guess is that even hermits are not immune to all these pangs. They have memories, after all, imaginations. You can't escape from feeling, as I tried all these years. I climbed in, while the attendants strapped him down, put my hand around his skinny ankle, where I could feel a pulse.

"I'll come see you tomorrow," I said. "You want something to read?" Professorial self-absorption, you say. I can't help it: I'm committed to the belief that reading is good for you, though sometimes when I consider my colleagues, I wonder.

"Can you get *The Jungle Book*, by Mr. Rudyard Kipling?" he said. "I already read Kim." What do you think, Joel? Are ass-men more likely to be readers than tit-men? "You got it," I said, standing, for Hector Suarez was out there, behind the ambulance crooking a finger at me.

"I hear you prevented Professor Bloor from exercising her legitimate right to self-defense," he said.

"You think she'll play it that way?" I said.

"It won't be up to her," he said. "There's interest groups out there will want to make this an issue of race or class or sex."

"It's all three," I said, "when you think about it."

"You think about it," he said. "I got other things on my mind."

"Can you see her as the Ka-Bar Killer?" I said.

"Not a chance," he said. "She hasn't got the muscle." Sure her arms, when I wrested the sword away from her, had no feel of muscle in them, or bone either. The thought of how she would look in the nude brought on a spasm of queasiness.

"Now her companion in crime there," he said, "Professor Angel Terrasco—she's got what it takes. What I hear, she used to be a fencer."

"She may have the muscle for it," I said, "but not the stomach. She nearly passed out when she saw the kid's blood."

"She never married, right?" he said. "My FBI liaison keeps telling me that one kind of mutt who kills queers is all torn up inside about being queer himself . . . or herself."

"Angel's not queer," I said.

"She another one of your conquests?" he said.

"Forget it," I said. "When it comes to affairs of the heart I'm a perennial loser." All this time, without me noticing it, he had been steering me to his car.

"Get in," he said. "You're better off writing out your statement. That way down the road you'll know exactly what you said, case someone tried to put a backspin on your words. Besides, I want you to tell me all about Leonard Sistrunk on the way."

"No one was ever less torn up inside about being queer than Leonard Sistrunk," I said, "unless it's Ziggy Sensum."

"I got my eye on him too," he said.

As we drove along College Walk toward Broadway, I saw Amabelle sitting in the back of one police car, Angel and Grantwell in another. The ambulance was gone.

By the time I got back to the empty apartment, it was dark, late enough for Julie to have arrived at the Rainbow Gathering, howl at the moon. She had taken household money to buy an answering machine ("A man in your position ought to have one, Cuz"). I erased the messages from people who wanted to interview me about Angel. And I erased a message from Kay suggesting that we get together for a drink, for I remembered that Dashiell Hammett, after Lillian Hellman once refused to go to bed with him, never, never made love to her again, never made love to her again.

25

Dear Joel,

John Birks Gillespie was born on October 21, 1917 in Cheraw, South Carolina. "The pictures show me as a very beautiful baby," he said, "but I was the last of nine children and my arrival probably didn't excite anybody."

"Mean" was the way Dizzy's siblings described their father. "Every Sunday morning Papa would whip us," Dizzy said, the other half of the "us" being his brother Wesley. "He treated us that way because he wanted us to be tough and he turned me into a tough little rebel, very early, against everyone but him." Is there a lesson to be learned here? Beatings that were recurrent yet arbitrary (shorthand for human life) turned Diz against everyone but the man who beat him, identification with the aggressor. There are times, it appears, when it is more healthy to identify with the beater than the beaten, unless you are among these Puritan megalomaniacs who by the beater means God. Identifying with the beater is especially healthy if you are one of the beaten, for it multiplies your personalities and counters self-pity, the source of all secular sin.

It was these beatings, I believe, that gave Diz his drive (for Victorian Papas have driven sons), a drive toward restitution and retribution, as I see it, a drive that energized him to odysseus whatever was in his way, rather than succumb to the Calypso of drugs, say, or submit to the Polyphemous of racial prejudice, for starters.

You could not have guessed from Dizzy's school days of wrath that he would become the guiding intelligence of bebop, and is there any other form of music that is at once as visceral and as cerebral as bebop? "I didn't study much," said Diz: "I'd fight every day." Accounts by family and friends are of a familiar kind of future hardcase, a danger to himself and everyone around him. ("I'd pick a fight over anything.") Nor was the hostility and anger buried with his father, who died young: "instead of grieving I became real mean and used to do all kinds of devilish things." He nearly killed a kid who said Papa was going to hell. He kept on taking a shortcut through a neighbor's cotton patch, trampling the crop, until the guy threw a pitchfork at him. He kept on stealing another neighbor's watermelons until the farmer, one more hardcase, let loose with his shotgun. Because the vines grow close to the ground, "never try to hide your head under a watermelon vine with buckshot flying around your ass." Once, when "playing African," he put a sharpened stick, a make-believe spear, through his cousin's nose. "I was dangerous even in playing." Violence was so much his métier that he signified his first crush by assaulting its object. "I used to throw rocks at her to express my affection. She looked so pretty and brown, but I acted too wild."

He took his killer instinct with him when he dropped out of high school. He took it with him to the Laurinburg Technical Institute, which gave him an all-expenses paid scholarship so he could play trumpet on the school band, for in between fights he had taught himself to play on a neighbor's horn. He also played football, like me, chased the girls (and by all accounts caught them, too, unlike me), and taught himself music, trumpet, piano, the logic of chords, often from breakfast to lights out. The band's bass drummer, who weighed about 240, a descendant of Polyphemous, often goofed; Gillespie, who weighed about 140, as often corrected him, not always with tact. Finally, big Blue, the drummer, had enough; he started for Diz with the clear intention of redistributing his embouchere. "Before he could get from behind his drum, my knife was open. When he saw I was advancing on him, his big blue ass turned around and ran." The best part of this story is how it turned out. The principal, seeing that Dizzy acted "seriously and in self-defense," says Diz, "didn't even whip me; he was a very understanding man" and a positive reinforcer of Dizzy's killer instinct.

After Laurinburg, Dizzy moved to Philadelphia with the family. He had to walk home from his job at a club, trumpet under his arm in a paper bag, through a rough section of South Philly. Local white hoods, for the fun of it, used to drive up and "grab little guys, little colored guys, off the street and beat them up and throw them out in the woods half dead." One night one of these clowns reached out of his car to grab Diz, who was walking along with a knife open in his pocket. "I tried to saw his hand off . . . like if you've ever seen somebody cut a chicken leg where the joint goes together, and the meat is left there hanging." The young man who walks with a sense of menace always beside him, like a baleful familiar, tries to exorcise it by becoming a threat himself. ("It was still dangerous to mess with me.") Dizzy was maybe eighteen. So far as the written record is concerned, the last person he cut with a knife was Cab Calloway.

In 1940, Dizzy Gillespie, who on the whole was as sane as you can get without grave consequences to your health, was given a 4F because the Selective Service medical examiners thought he acted crazy: he appeared before them naked, as required, but holding his trumpet, and, when questioned, said that the white men who wanted to give him a gun and ran a Jim Crow army were more likely to have treated him as an enemy than the Germans he was supposed to shoot, whom in any case he had never met. It could lead to a certain confusion on the battlefield.

Instead, he was recruited by Cab Calloway. One night, the band's small group, the Cab Jivers, was out front, finishing its turn, the curtain descending. A big gloppy spitball flew out of the trumpet section and came down, splat in the circle of light around the Cab Jivers. Calloway, watching from the wings, naturally suspected Diz, who in his own words was "acting wiggy" in mockery of Calloway's flimflam and to razz the hostile "moldy figs" on the band. (The real culprit was Thad Jones.) Backstage, Calloway confronted Diz, whose denials infuriated Calloway all the more: how dare this nobody backtalk Cab Calloway, famous bandleader, hepcat favorite, rich, wearing a white suit and beautiful teeth, two fine, healthy young women waiting for him? Calloway slapped Diz, got himself ready to throw a punch. "He didn't know I was getting ready to kill him," Diz said later. Milt Hinton deflected the blade, so that it went into Calloway's thigh or rear end, depending on who tells the story, rather than under his ribs. In the upshot, Calloway's "pretty white suit was stained completely red," according to Hinton; two fine young women were kept waiting; and Dizzy was out of a job.

It's no use multiplying instances: the fact is that as Dizzy grew older, whatever was behind his violence found other ways of expressing itself. By the way, how would you describe that "whatever," the motive power of Dizzy's violence? It was a drive, as I said, in the Freudian sense maybe, a reservoir of energy that required periodic venting, a force of some kind—I've got it, the Life Force! Let's not get mystical. Testosterone? Let's not get vapid either. I am going to call this unknown and unknowable force *Das Etwas,* The Something, on the analogy of Georg Groddeck's *Das Es.* It is in all of us, in every cell, possesses us, *lives us,* makes us do what we do, become what we become. Most of us fight it with weapons drawn from the social arsenal. We resist its promptings, deaden our senses against its solicitations, become rigid and awkward in character armor, distort it and contort ourselves into monstrosities, puritans, limp dicks, true believers, serial killers, cultists of all sorts, charismatics, Republicans, the guy who wants to put his boot in your face and the guy who wants to lick said boot. The more you fight your *Etwas,* the more you approach the condition of Richard Nixon or Amabelle Bloor. But Dizzy's *Etwas,* miraculously, remained natural, a kind of general exuberance that more and more discharged into life-giving alternatives to violence.

Even all those boyhood fights look, in retrospect, more like the effects of high spirits than psychopathy. There seems always to have been a smile in them, partly at Dizzy's own expense, something impish and larking, something playful and rueful, as later there was usually a punch in his famous humor, the pranks and pratfalls, the put-ons and put-downs. Miles Davis describes the young Dizzy walking down Broadway with him, sticking his tongue out at sniffy white women. "I'm from St. Louis and he's doing that to a white person, a white *woman*. . . . He used to love to ride elevators and make fun of everyone, act crazy, scare white people to death." Or he would go to where the Dave Garroway show was being broadcast behind a big plate glass window at street level, so passersby could stop to watch for a while. Through this window Gillespie would make faces at J. Fred Muggs, the chimpanzee. Muggs "would be screaming, jumping up and down and showing his teeth, and everybody on the show would be wondering what the fuck got into him. Every time that chimpanzee laid eyes on Dizzy, he'd go crazy."

But Davis, who has few kind words for anyone else, ends his account of Dizzy's youthful pranks by saying that "Dizzy was also very, very beautiful and I loved him and still do today." That note of affection is there in the remembrances of Dizzy's long-suffering brother James, who concludes that "John was a devil all his life"; and in the remembrances of his sister Eugenia (who in exasperation once pushed Dizzy out of a second-story window), whose ladylike summing up was that "John was always mischievous"; and, more surprisingly, in Cab Calloway's account of the knifing: "Dizzy was a devil, a playful devil, you know." A playful devil . . . is there any other kind? Angels, not Christian angels anyhow, don't play, you know. All fun, all art, comes from the devil's party. (I'll bet there is no note of affection in his voice when Thorwald talks about the guy who broke his wrist.)

Accounts from all periods of his life, including his youthful days of wrath, testify to his playfulness and good humor. "He was always full of fun" (but also "a real show-off") said his grade school teacher. On his first trip to Europe, with Teddy Hill's band, when he was only twenty, the youngest member of the band, "he was just like he is now, always jolly," said the guitarist. Becoming the leader of his own band did not change him: "Dizzy was always in a good mood . . . he was always funny," said the baritone saxophonist. Lorraine, Dizzy's wife, suggested that the good humor was an aspect of his self-possession, his keeping his cool: "if he was sad, he didn't let nobody know. You'll never see Dizzy worried or sad. Never." Dizzy himself sometimes implied that his humor was strategic, a means to control others, not just himself:

Comedy is important. "As a performer, when you're trying to establish audience control, the best thing is to make them laugh if you can. That relaxes you more than anything. . . . When you get people relaxed, they're more receptive to what you're trying to get them to do. Sometimes, when you're laying on something over their heads, they'll go along with it if they're relaxed."

There are even times when Dizzy comes close to letting on that his comedy was the continuation of violence by other means: "That's the thing about it: put people on and get away with it. That's a science in itself." But most often he correctly understood it as *Das Etwas* surging irresistibly through him: "I love playing, I love people, I love making people laugh, and I do exactly what I want to do." Dizzy's humor was like Louis Armstrong's grin, an "absolute refusal to let anything, even anger about racism, steal the joy from his life," said Diz. Think of Odysseus defiantly identifying himself to Polyphemous, symbol of everything in the nature of things and in human nature that would bully you, if you let it.

Getting ready to play at some club, Dizzy might walk up to the microphone, his sidemen settling down behind him, and say, "And now, ladies and gentlemen, I should like to introduce the members of my band." Then he would turn around and say, "Sonny Stitt meet John Lewis, John meet Max Roach, Max meet . . ." and so forth, the guys getting up to shake hands with each other. Or having finished a set, the other band waiting to come on, he might walk up to the mike, his eyes slowly surveying the audience, coming to rest on a pretty woman, and say, "And now, ladies and gentlemen, I'd like to turn you over. . . ." Walking down the streets of Edinburgh, he stopped passersby, put on his stuffed-shirt English accent, and said, "Pardon me, my name is Gillespie, and I'm looking for my relatives." In 1958, at a grand old hotel in French Lick, southern Indiana, which was by no means at the forefront of the civil rights movement, the black musicians were leery about using the big beautiful swimming pool, not wanting to precipitate an ugly scene. Bill Crow describes what happened:

> Dizzy Gillespie stepped out of the elevator [into the lobby]. He was wearing bathing trunks from the French Riviera, an embroidered skull-cap from Greece and embroidered slippers with curled-up toes that he'd picked up in Turkey. A Sheraton bath towel draped over his shoulders like a cape was fastened at the neck with a jade scarab pin from Egypt. With a Chinese ivory cigarette holder in his left hand and a powerful German multiband portable radio in his right, he beamed cheerfully through a pair of Italian sunglasses.

"I have come to integrate the pool!" said Diz. After divesting himself of his accoutrements, which can be seen as making the fig at provincialism, he took Jimmy McPartland (who you will remember was white) by the arm and jumped into the pool with him, thus integrating it.

Comedy with punch was not Dizzy's only alternative to violence. He built no barriers against the flow of his *Etwas* into sex, for as the feminists are always yowling and yammering, there is a component of violence in male sexuality. You can get a hard-on when you are pissed off, but not when you are afraid. (If you think I am talking about myself, I am.) It was at Laurinburg that Dizzy became a ladies' man, climbing into the woman's dormitory, romancing a teacher who admired his dancing—"He was always doing something devilish that wasn't music," said a member of an extracurricular jump band Dizzy played on: "Boy, he was rough on them little gals. Boy! . . . if a little gal's there, Doc, and you miss him, you know where he's at." Dicky Wells (the trombonist) was along with Dizzy on his first trip to Europe: "Every time we'd look, Dizzy was coming out of a whorehouse in Paris. So that's Dizzy," yes, and that's a healthy *Etwas*. "Like a typical musician, I moved around among the women," he said, and I'll bet that all those young men who want to become rock musicians are inspired more by a daydream of groupies than a summons from the Muse.

According to Dizzy, jazz groupies are what you might call discriminating:

> There's always a saxophone freak, who comes to see the saxophone player, who just sits there. Only the saxophone player can sleep with her. There are others who only sleep with trumpet players. . . .

It was a couple of trumpet freaks, I suppose, who hit Dizzy with paternity suits, so that for a while he got arrested every time he tried to play in Pennsylvania or Ohio. Lorraine, to whom Dizzy was married for 52 years, who as a dancer had traveled with musicians and knew their ways, did not let his moving around among the women bother her. Her attitude was that "if your husband takes care of you and gives you respect when he's with you and has a decent place for you to stay and you don't have any trouble," it is no use getting yourself into a lather about what he does on the road. "I just say to heck with it. If he doesn't get caught, good." Lorraine, like Dizzy's principal at Laurinburg, was an understanding person.

What takes me out of myself in Dizzy's music, or maybe in fact it gives me back to myself, is a quality that's penultimately sexual (ultimately, it is *Etwaslich*). It is true that Max Roach said of Dizzy that "he uses music as his particular weapon," that "when you look into the music and listen to what he is playing, he is screaming out there." Nor is Max Roach the only one who thinks of Dizzy's music as signifying black rage. And sure it is that his brain-piercing high notes and desugared tone, his sidewinder phrasing, his booby-trap dissonances, his systematic deconstruction of everything implied by singing violins and tinkling pianos and crooning tenors, his relentless and dislocating rhythms, can be heard as constituting a musical equivalent to violence, if like Max Roach you hear, see, and feel everything in black and white. All I can say is that Dizzy's music does not make me feel angry. It does not make me feel defensive or belligerent. It makes me feel good. It makes me tingle all over. It makes me want to dance, shout, hug a woman (for starters), for Dizzy's solos are the musical equivalent of uninhibited sex, not violence, except to the extent that violence adheres in all male sexuality, for the most erotic aspect of music is rhythm, Dizzy's bag.

"I'm a rhythm man, you know," said Diz, and everyone in the know agrees that he was "a rhythmic genius," in Phil Woods' words. You have often said as much yourself, so I am not going to cite all the testimonials I have been collecting these past two days, how he taught bass players where to put their accents, taught drummers when to drop their bombs, taught Afro-Cuban rhythms to North American jazzmen, taught Latin American musicians how to swing, his own polyrhythmics. But you, like numerous others, put the emphasis on Dizzy's virtuosity and disharmonies. Dizzy put it on rhythm; "the basic thing about jazz music is putting notes to rhythm, not the other way around. I think up a rhythm first and then put notes to it to correspond with the chord. You can play very, very beautiful notes, and if it doesn't have any rhythmic form, it doesn't amount to anything." It don't mean a thing if it ain't got that swing—a sentiment behind Dizzy's rare put-downs of other musicians, of cool jazz, of free-form jazz, of Stan Kenton: "They thought he was a master, they thought he was greater than Duke Ellington, and that motherfucker couldn't even keep time."

That Dizzy could dance, man. No one who has ever seen him dance forgets it. ("Jazz should be danceable. That's the original idea.") He was dancing for quarters thrown out onto the dance floor in his mid-teens, completely self-taught. He could not not dance. He'd be leading his band, using his arms instead of a baton, signaling the accents with body language, until the band began to swing, and you could see the rhythm take possession of him: he'd forget the arm-waving and move into that whirling, hip-shaking, thigh-waggling, high-stepping boogie you couldn't see without a rush of pleasure. One night he was at Birdland with his quintet, on stage, between numbers, talking over what's next with his sax man, Shihab Sahib, when suddenly he shouted, "Boogie blues!" and the rhythm section began to cook and Dizzy began to dance, wilder and wilder the whirls, higher and higher the kicks, until a foot came down, flat, way up on Shihab's jacket lapel. Dizzy immediately collapsed into contrition, hugging Shihab, stroking him, all apologetic. It pleases me to note that descriptions of the high-kicking lowland fling that Jimmie Joyce would spontaneously erupt into, on a street in Trieste, say, after a night of too much white wine, are remarkably similar to descriptions of Dizzy's own Corybantics, for genius is exuberant, for Dizzy was to jazz what Joyce was to fiction, the greatest innovator of his time.

Birk's works share with Joyce's fiction (and Dylan Thomas' poetry) a maximum boundary-violating centrifugal force with a maximum centripetal force of formal cohesion. "Our music really exemplifies a perfect balance between discipline and freedom," he said; "I go for freedom, but freedom without organization is chaos. I want to put freedom into music the way I conceive it. It is free, but it's organized freedom." Yes, and I know I'm a bit deranged on this subject, but Dizzy, like Joyce, was a modernist, as free-form jazz is like postmodernist literature, freedom *without* form. Dizzy's feeling for form was not only aesthetic. It was to his music what self-possession was to his personality, an equal and opposite counterforce to the play of *Das Etwas.* Dizzy scared himself on those occasions when his self-possession was unequal to an aroused *Etwas,* as when he planted his foot on Shihab Sahib's clavicle.

Kenny Clarke tells the story of "one time in Sweden, I can't think of the name of the city, but the band was swinging so hard that Dizzy jumped up on the piano." Ray Brown tells a similar story:

> Dizzy was standing out in front of the band, and just looked at us, he just jumped off the bandstand and ran through the audience and went outside, like fifteen or twenty minutes. So when he came back, we said, "What happened?"
>
> He said, "Man, you were swinging so much I couldn't stand it," and he just jumped off, jumped off the stage and ran out.

There was the time that Dizzy was in a juice shop with some other musicians. The place "had one of those old time fans in the ceiling, like a windmill." A musician's wife came in with her baby. Dizzy took the baby and tossed it in the air, then tossed again, and again, higher and higher, until the fan clipped it. The "wife fainted out there in the middle of the floor. Yeah, we saw her laying out there on the floor, man . . . it could have been a tragic thing . . . but the baby wasn't hurt or anything."

In 1968 Dizzy renounced booze, for alcohol is a disinhibitor and disinhibition was not what Dizzy needed. "I'd lapse into getting drunk and act extremely uncivil," the anesthetized forces of restraint overpowered by the activated forces of violence, lip hanging from a split, head bloodied by a bottle, his knife confiscated by a nervous friend, no memory of anything the next day. "The most trouble I've ever been in is when I've had some of that juice in me. So I decided to leave it alone."

Then there is the bell of his trumpet, pointing up at a forty-five degree angle, like a young man's erection. It is usually understood as another one of Diz's zanies, the zoot suits and beret, the goatee and sunglasses. But the drab truth is that it was bent by accident, by the comedians Stump 'n Stumpy, who were clowning around backstage during a birthday party for Lorraine. There was no other trumpet around, and Dizzy had to perform. So he played the trumpet he had. "I played it, and I liked the sound. The sound had been changed and it could be played softly, not blarey." The bending up of the horn made the trumpet less of a weapon. "In small clubs, you'd be playing right up on people, and a trumpet is a very forceful instrument. If it's played straight at you, it can burst someone's eardrum. . . ."

It is my professorial opinion that the bent trumpet exemplifies Dizzy's way of dealing with the violence within him: sure, the inclined bell redirected the inherent force of the instrument and the particular violence of Dizzy's playing out of your face; but it also enhanced the priapic quality of the instrument, a ghost of a black power salute, a giving of the finger, a bit of Dada, of rule-breaking, pure Dizzyism. It asserts what it holds back, recovers what it gives away, the very type of symbolic gesture. Man, that trumpet was an achievement.

The mute Dizzy was always using worked the same way: it constricted the sound, but also made it rough around the edges, raspy and raucous, the voice of a trumpet with a jones for cigarettes sitting on a porch belting out the blues.

And it is my crackbrained opinion that the religion of Dizzy's later years worked for him in the same way, for it is a betrayal of my most fervent unbeliefs to say a good word for anyone's religion. In any case, there was already something offbeat about selecting, among all the world's religions, the Baha'i faith, which, however, is nothing if not ecumenical. It teaches "the truth of the oneness of God, the truth of the oneness of the prophets, the truth of the oneness of mankind," said Diz. The Spirit sends its prophets one after the other, like runners in a relay race, each taking humanity so far, before passing the baton on to his successor. "They never change, the spiritual laws of Moses, Abraham, Buddha, Krishna, Zoroaster, Jesus, Mohammad—all these people speak the same language. But the social order that goes with it changes with all the different prophets who come. They are the only ones who can do that." Yes, yes, I know, but the question to ask about a religion is not Is it true, for none of them are, but What does it do for believers. Here's Diz: "I believe in this parallel between jazz and religion. Definitely! Definitely! The runners on the trumpet would be Buddy Bolden, King Oliver, Louis Armstrong, Roy Eldridge, me. Miles, and Fats Navarro, Clifford Brown. . . ." That "me" looks pretty small amid all the caps, although Dizzy is claiming for himself the status of a prophet, even if only of one in a succession, even if his message is not the specialness of prophets, but "the oneness of mankind," muting the trumpet, but playing out of this world.

Even before he got religion, John Birks Gillespie had become Saint Diz. It turns out that the man who never did anything just to make people like him was universally loved. Try to think of another great artist about whom friends and acquaintances would say things like this:

> NAT HENTOFF: Seeing Dizzy, however casually, was like coming into sunlight. By the warmth of his greeting, his natural considerateness, and the keenness of his intelligence—which made his wit so sharp—he was a delight to be with.
>
> MILES DAVIS: It seems people loved Dizzy so much they used to just want to be with him, you know?
>
> CECIL PAYNE: Everybody just loved Dizzy; he was the whole thing.
>
> FATS PALMER: He was always a nice lovable cat.
>
> TEDDY REIG: He was just a happy cat, man; everybody loved him.

dickie wells: We were crazy 'bout Dizzy. Me specially. . . . He was the prettiest person in the world, and he still is.

gene lees: I have a very deep love for Dizzy Gillespie. He has contributed immeasurable joy to our troubled era.

mario bauza: Dizzy through his seventy-something years made everybody be happy when they heard his name.

daddy-o daylie: Diz has the biggest heart of any guy that I've known. . . . Diz seems as though he never had that same jealousy that so many professional musicians have, that I think is based on incompetence.

bob redcross: Another thing about Dizzy, and it fits right in: Diz was never envious.

rip tarrant: With his personality, everybody just took to him and really liked him, you know. . . . The personality is still there; it rubbed off on all of us.

sarah vaughan: There's nothing Dizzy does that I don't like. . . .

mary lou williams: He always looked out for me, and I never realized how wonderful he was until years later. Anytime he thought I wasn't working, or something wasn't happening right, he'd always come to my rescue.

chris white: He was never too busy to listen and help with questions of life and living when he could. Never sentimental, always supportive . . . he was the father I lost when I was eleven.

cab calloway: A very intelligent, fine-thinking person. A person that really knows what's happening in life. And he digs life more than anything else.

DR. LAWRENCE REDDICK: I liked his exuberance. In a way he has a sort of untainted sense of humor and love for life.

GROVER SALES: Dizzy differed from the majority of bebop pioneer outlaws in his refusal to seek refuge in self-pity, self-destruction and their handmaiden, drug abuse, which wasted so many of his compatriots. Thanks to vast reserves of mental health, a secure sense of his own value, a remarkable lack of envy and an irrepressible humor and gusto for living, Dizzy survives. . . .

GENE LEES: That man *is a* miracle of neurological organization.

That's enough. You get the picture: just being in his presence made people feel good. It was not so much anything he did, although much of what he did was easy enough to love. In trying to explain it, I fall back, almost seriously, on some Gnostic theory of emanation, or let's say good vibes, the spontaneous overflow of *Das Etwas*. You can spot traces of this emanation in the tributes to Dizzy's genius as a teacher, whether from pianists, bass players, drummers or horn men who, like Nat Adderly, agreed that "Dizzy's the greatest teacher in the world." As you are aware, this is a matter of some professional interest to me.

Teaching can be a species of violence, a trampling of students by the teacher's hobbyhorse, a force-feeding of alien corn. It can be totalitarian, the imposition through terror and preferment of righteous dogma upon a subject population, the fashion of the moment. It can be erotic, as good teachers since Socrates have admitted, insinuating yourself into the student's mind, which the pleasure of forebrainplay has made receptive, to discharge wisdom. It can be histrionic, the teacher's ego expanding like a noxious gas to fill the classroom; it can be cultic, aesthetic, anesthetic. . . . Dizzy's teaching was none of these things. It was a phase of his generosity.

"Dizzy is one of the greatest teachers, without teaching you. He shows you ways of handling life," said Flora Purim. Said Paul West, "He used to teach you so much but not ostentatiously. He doesn't make you aware that you're gonna get a lesson, you see. Because of his character and his personality, he's dropping stuff on you all the time, and all you have to do is be open and receive it." See what I mean? I hope you do, because this is not easy to put into words.

Another great modernist master, Willie Yeats, tried all his life, from his early interest in *sprezzatura,* "the old nonchalance of the hand," to put it into words. In one poem he imagines a setting in which

> Life overflows without ambitious pains;
> It rains down life until the basin spills,
> And mounts more dizzy high the more it rains
> As though to choose whatever shape it wills. . . .

He imagines

> That out of life's own self-delight had sprung
> The abounding glittering jet. . . .

In another poem he bequeaths to upstanding men his

> Pride, like that of the morn,
> When the headlong light is loose,
> Or that of the fabulous horn,
> Or that of the sudden shower
> When all streams are dry. . . .

In still another he admits that his mind has dried up of late,

> Yet knows that to be choked with hate
> May well be of all evil chances chief.

("I hardly ever remember a time when Dizzy didn't have someone white in his group," said Gene Lees.) Once hatred is driven out

> The soul recovers radical innocence
> And learns at last that it is self-delighting
> Self-appeasing, self-affrighting....
> And one's thoughts become like the linnet
> And have no business but dispensing round
> Their magnanimities of sound....

What I have been trying to say is that it was not only Dizzy's trumpet that was a horn of plenty dispensing magnanimities of sound, but the man himself. He had achieved in himself a condition of continuous *sprezzatura.*

You may wonder why I am telling you all this. One reason is that you don't know it, or didn't when you died: you always spoke to me about Dizzy the musician, never the man. Another reason is that Saturday night is the loneliest night of the week; I need someone to talk to; you're the only one I can talk to without hiding anything, and anyhow are the only one available. Another reason, and it is a trait of the literary mind that it can entertain two contradictory ideas without choosing between them, we both know that these letters, in form to you, are in content for me, commotions in my interior monologue. Verbal types often don't know what they think about something until they see it written out. I am trying to think through the problem of how to live. These last few days I have turned to Dizzy for help. I want to learn how to be at once tenderhearted and tough-minded. I want to be hard on myself, but easy on others. I want to attain a condition of exuberance with "equanimity," that shining word from *Ulysses.* I want to be a benign beserker—with self-possession to boot. I want to liberate my *Etwas.*

Why now? Well, Julie aroused me from my state of suspended animation, warmed me to life, then let go. I don't want to become freeze-dried again. I want to live. And that brings me to a crucial moment in Dizzy's life that was very like a crucial moment in my own. When Max Roach got seriously hooked on heroin, as he tells it, "Dizzy took me off the streets then. We went down South; he took me down South with him and nursed me like a baby till I got over that shit. I was working every night; he'd see that I got some swimming in, that I ate well, and really took care of me, man. Sometimes I couldn't make it, man, he was right there. I shook the habit and everything." The crucial moment occurred years later.

One night, between sets at Birdland, Dizzy went to Basin Street East, where his old friend Charlie Shavers was playing with Benny Goodman. Charlie Parker, in awful shape, fat, wobbling on bad feet, in debt to everybody, avoided by promoters, no regular gig, came over to Dizzy, and the two began to talk. Suddenly, out of the blue, Parker ("the other beat of my heart") said, "Save me.... Diz, why don't you save me?" Dizzy asked how. Parker said, "I dunno but just save me, save me, man." But Parker could not be saved. For one thing, his liver was shot. For another, Dizzy did not believe that Parker (unlike Max Roach) had it in him to stop using. "Regardless of how much someone does try to help you, if you've got it in your mind to keep using, it doesn't matter," he later said, looking back on too much exasperating experience with junkies. Shortly after that night at Basin Street East, Charlie Parker died, at age thirty-four.

I do not believe that Dizzy was ever as close to another man as he was to Charlie Parker, whose death threw him for a loop. "That broke me up. I couldn't help it. I had to go down in the basement and cry," he said, as though confessing to a moral lapse. Lorraine said, "That's the only time I've ever seen Dizzy sad. Only when his mama died and when Charlie Parker died." Just the same, he immediately got moving "to try to salvage something": he formed a committee to protect Parker's compositions; he arranged (and raised the money) to have the body sent to Parker's mother in K.C., for Dizzy believed that you were better off "lighting candles than cursing the dark." Listen to the tone of voice in which Dizzy concludes his account of how he reacted to Bird's death: "It was such a big shock, I went downstairs and had my little thing, got red-eyed crying and came upstairs." Yes, he came upstairs to take care of business, as he always did. "I maintain that society is largely responsible for Bird's demise," said Max Roach. "Dizzy maintains that Bird should've been stronger than to let them destroy him like that.... Dizzy just cannot stand weakness of any kind."

Think back to that spring twenty years ago when I had just come home from my junior year in college. I was on a two-week vacation, putting off my regular summer job working construction with the father of the meathead who married our sister. When you walked into my room, I was showered and shaved, sitting in my shorts, taking an air bath, cooling off, getting ready for my date with Donna, who had driven in her yellow VW Beetle all the way from Texas to New York so that she could spend the summer near me, and the generosity of women never ceases to take me by surprise. You sat down and offered me a Pall Mall, although you knew I never smoked, except for the one I always had before some serious kissing with Donna, so I wouldn't taste tobacco on her lips and in her mouth, on her lips and in her mouth, her mouth.

"I can't make it alone, Slim," you said. "You've got to help me. I want to live." You had access to a cottage on the west coast of Florida. You wanted me to drive down there with you, all expenses paid. We would swim, throw a football on the beach, as when we were kids, eat fish we caught ourselves, local vegetables. You would bring along a keyboard, teach me chord changes. And when the craving got bad or the sickness was on you, I would sit with you, hold your hand, talk to you, about college, about anything, for I had a silver tongue, could talk an unripe moth out of its cocoon.

You don't have to tell me: what I should have done was say, "Let's go." I should have called Donna, who would have understood, thrown some stuff into a carryall, and pulled you down the stairs to your microbus, before you could change your mind. But I did not; instead I said, "We'll talk about it in the morning." Why did I do that? Because waffling is my métier. Because, after a long drought,

I had a girlfriend and was getting laid regularly. The renunciation seemed beyond the call of brotherly love. You never mentioned the matter again. Six weeks later I stumbled over your body.

Ma and Pa needed me to lean on, but after one day of Pa's spectacular grief, I slunk off to Donna. She sat with me on a bench in Riverside Drive, holding my hand, while I smoked the last of your Pall Malls and watched the sun set over the Hudson. I think I'm still in the basement, Joel. It doesn't feel like I've been able to come upstairs, even if Julie has taken me by the hand and pulled me to the first step.

Tomorrow, when Julie comes home, I am going to ask her to marry me and I am going to swear eternal fidelity and I am going to mean it, for I want to live.

26

Dear Joel,

The sequelae to that Sunday's violence have kept me from writing to you this past couple weeks. For a while there it looked as though I might have to face a grand jury. I'd rather face a Ka-Bar pointed at my spleen anytime, or a Kilikang for that matter. I'd have a better chance of talking my way out of it, these New York ADA's have gotten so zealous about putting people away. Don't they know how expensive it is to build new jails?

I had my classes for the coming week prepared by about three o'-clock, so I was passing the time in my study, leafing through catalogues, Dizzy playing "Tin Tin Deo" on the boombox, a glass of beer on one side, a cigarette sending up smoke signals from an ashtray on the other, trying to relax, ears tuned up for the sound of Julie's key in the door lock, for I expected her to return before dark, longing for a set of dumbbells, anything! to drain off the tension, for I was by no means sure that Julie would not laugh at my proposal of marriage.

The buzzer sounded, making me jump, a communication from the nether regions, for my apartment is on the top floor. Naturally I assumed that Julie had lost or forgotten her key. But the voice that came back at me over the intercom was that of Teddy Nakatani. Before I was aware that I was doing it, I had buzzed him in, saying, "Cocksucking, motherfucking..."

I opened the door and there he was: pressed clean jeans, white shirt, denim jacket, thin black leather gloves, for fall had fallen upon us, and those old-fashioned white tennis shoes, skippies I think I once heard them called, with what looked like fresh mud on them, for it had rained that morning, a sudden downpour. Poor Julie, I thought, must have gotten caught in it. Well, she is not delicate, was my second thought, and she had her new green Gore-Tex parka (with zip-in Polartec fleece lining).

He flicked his left arm, and something white slid down from inside his sleeve: a half-dozen sheets of paper rolled up and kept that way by a rubber band. "I believe you will find this a good read," he said. "It is my dissertation proposal."

"After this long, it could have waited until tomorrow," I said.

"I'm on pins and needles," he said.

So was I, you presumptuous pup, and my proposal was a lot more important (to me anyhow). "Let's have it," I said, holding out a hand, "but I can't guarantee that it will be read tonight."

"I really must request two minutes of your time," he said. "A few words of background will point up the—"

I was about to scorch his eardrums for him, when I remembered my resolve to be like Dizzy, whose "unfailing kindness" to his ephebes has been well described by Gene Lees. "Come in, then," I said, stepping back and with a mock-ceremonious sweep of the arm showing him the way.

"After you," he said.

"After *you,*" I said. "Are you not my guest?" And I lightly pulled him forward by the elbow.

"It is a status I had begun to despair of ever attaining," he said.

We sat at opposite sides of my desk, studying each other. I broke the spell by lighting up. His eyes followed the pack, so I offered him one, which he took. I lit him up. He said nothing, not even "thanks."

"So," I said.

"Christopher North is dead," he said, with what is called a penetrating look.

Was he expecting some kind of give-away reaction? Just what is it he thought I had to give away? "I'm sorry to hear it," I said.

"He was killed by professors Terry Jones, Irenaus von Hartmann, and Marshall Grice," he said.

"Come now," I said.

"Bertil Lund, a man who has no mooring within himself, merely drifted which way he saw the wind was blowing," he said. "He is contemptible, but not criminal. Professor Frances Vocatelli alone affirmed the lofty precepts of our profession. I send her flowers on the anniversary of Christopher's defense, anonymously of course."

"Exactly how did Terry, Blinky, and Marshall kill Christopher North?" I said.

"I wonder if you would be so good as to turn off that music," he said. (Budd Johnson was taking his wild solo on "The Champ.")

"I'll turn it down," I said, doing so, but not by much, for I like my jazz loud. And the truth is that I needed the protection and support of Dizzy's spirit.

"It's not my kind of music," he said.

"Of course not," I said.

"When Christopher failed his dissertation defense, he was evicted from his university apartment," he said. "I admit that he had already been granted two extensions of his lease—upon petitions from Professor White. And it is true that he was years behind schedule in his progress toward the degree. So am I—but our profession is not best served by the most facile intelligences. I took him in."

"You have an affinity for waifs and strays," I said.

"You have not accepted invitations to visit me at my apartment, but I have described it to you," he said. "It is not spacious. Christopher and I slept back-to-back on my Castro Convertible, which was discarded by the previous tenant," and his look dared me to put on even a hint of a knowing smirk. "I don't have to tell you that our relationship was scrupulously chaste."

"I would not believe you if you said otherwise," I said.

"I tried to pull him out of his depression by taking him to wholesome cultural events," he said. "You are aware that every day in New York City there are free public lectures, free recitals, art exhibitions, poets and novelists reading from their work. . . ."

"Enough to throw anyone into terminal depression," I said.

"So it appears," he said. "Coming home from work one afternoon, I opened the door to be confronted by an unmade Castro Convertible. I was deciding on the words I would use to chide Christopher, for I believe that untidiness is demoralizing, when I saw that he was lying on the Castro, fully dressed." He slid his left hand under his jacket and began to scratch his right armpit.

"Why don't you take off your gloves and stay for a while?" I said.

"There was a plastic bag over his head tied tight around his neck with a shoelace," he said.

"I can imagine your shock," I said. "When I found Irene's body—"

"Can you imagine the self-control it took to stand in front of a mirror and tie a neat bow around your neck?" he said. "Can you imagine lying down and keeping your hands at your sides as you breathed in the air out of the bag and the plastic sealed your nose and mouth? Can you imagine not ripping—"

"No," I said. "Poor Christopher. Poor Teddy."

"That music makes a mockery of civilization," he said. (He meant "The Bluest Blues.")

"That's a lot of what I like about it," I said.

"Rigor mortis reaches a peak after twelve hours and remains that way for another twelve," he said. "That's on the average and barring faclicating comptors, you understand."

"Of course," I said.

"I tenderly rolled Christopher onto his side," he said. "I removed his belt, removed mine, joined them and used the resulting strap to bring his knees up tight against his chest. Those belts will embrace each other through all eternity."

"They will rot and fall from each other, the way of all flesh," I said.

"I tied Christopher's hands snug over his shins with the other shoelace," he said. "I went down to the basement, to the closet in which the janitor keeps his thick-skinned, fifty-gallon, black plastic garbage bags. I expect you to believe me when I say that only in an emergency would I steal so much as a packet of ersatz sugar from a greasy spoon."

"I believe you," I said.

"I will admit that to make tomato soup I did once appropriate a dozen of those little pillows of ketchup from a bin in a McDonald's," he said.

"Dear God," I said.

"I calculated that the scant cash in Christopher's pocket when added to my own small supply would be sufficient to fund my plan," he said. "I arrived at Collegiate Hardware just as the proprietor was locking the door. When I pointed out that his business depended on the goodwill of the University community, he consented to re-open, to sell me a grub hoe and a spade. I rented a car on a Hundred Thirty-first Street, and it is lucky that I owned a credit card, the unique occurrence of its use."

"Spare me the details," I said, quoting a character in Joseph Conrad.

"I buried Christopher in the Pine Barrens," he said, "where one idyllic Sunday afternoon Christopher and I went sightseeing in a borrowed car with a mutual friend named Alistair."

"Seems to me I've heard that name before," I said.

"I expect that the prayer I said over Christopher's grave is one of the details you would have me spare you," he said.

"And that is why you killed Terry Jones, Irenaus von Hartmann, and Marshall Grice," I said lightly, as though not much interested, idly pulling the rubber band off the roll of pages, flattening them out, but only glancing at them, for they were blank. When I looked up, Teddy flicked his right arm and a Ka-Bar slid down from inside his sleeve and into his hand. He placed it crossways on his thighs.

I opened the drawer to my desk and withdrew Uncle Alf's Ka-Bar. I placed it on the blotter crossways, for it is rude to point a knife at someone.

"How did you ever achieve that exquisite near-lavender patina on the blade?" he said. "Now just why would I have killed Terry, *et al.*?"

"To avenge Christopher partly," I said, "but mainly because you saw in them something you cannot abide in yourself. They were a temptation and a solicitation to sin. Can you write left-handed?"

"I am polydexterous," he said.

"I believe that you are projecting your own motives onto me," I said.

"Spare me the jargon," he said. "I *am* you."

"Not quite," I said.

"Close enough," he said.

"But you may be something in me that I shall have to exorcise," I said, standing, my hand on the Ka-Bar. "I want you to leave."

He stood and began to do some razzle-dazzle with his Ka-Bar, taking small steps toward me, twirling it like some martial arts asshole with a baton, stepping closer, spinning it like some gunfighter showing off with his Colt single-action, until we faced each other, thighs pressed against the desk on either side, for I held my ground, I held my ground. Then his left hand flicked out with the Ka-Bar and he cut me under the eye, over the cheekbone, where the flesh is thin. "It will be a worthy addition to your collection of scars," he said, stepping back to his chair, sitting.

I sat down and lit up, without touching my cheek. "Would you like one?" I said.

"Thank you," he said, withdrawing a cigarette from the offered pack. I lit him up.

We sat back and blew smoke at each other. "There's no wrong in being a homosexual, Teddy," I said, in the kindly voice I used to correct a student who has confused Joyce Kilmer with James Joyce, "any more than there is in being left-handed. In any case, where there's no choice, there's no culpability. But it's something you have not been able to accept about yourself." The blood began to drip off my chin, so I took out the bandanna to stanch it.

"Look what's calling the kettle black," he said. "I note with interest that this is the first occasion on which you have addressed me by my first name."

"You never cut me before," I said.

"As Jean-Paul Sartre truly observed, a homosexual is someone who does homosexual things," he said. "Latency is a myth. I can assure you that I have never committed a homosexual act. I consider homosexuality to be a sin. It is significant that you do not."

"You're a Christian?" I said.

"My family has been Christian for three generations," he said, scratching an armpit, his hand moving like a dog's paw.

"Sartre was a crackpot," I said, "like his consort."

"The fact remains that I have never cucked a sock," he said.

"Our emotions are closer to our true selves than our actions," I said. "What thoughts come to you involuntarily? What do you dream about? Who do your eyes follow before you realize what they are doing?"

"Let me have another cigarette," he said. I lit us up. "*Will that jungle cacophony never come to an end?*"

"Close your eyes," I said. "Just close your eyes, now. That's the way. And picture this: a faintly convex and gleaming belly, downy hair, a plump mons veneris, cleft like a peach and snug between smooth, soft thighs."

"So?" he said, opening his eyes.

"Close your eyes," I said. "Close *them.* Now picture this: a belly ridged with muscle, hair like a clump of furze, a cock still limp, but growing, balls as heavy in the hand as ripe plums, loosening thighs like—"

"You—!" he said, his eyes wide.

"See what I mean?" I said.

"You are about to die for your sins," he said, standing.

"Sins of omission at most," I said, standing.

He began to walk slowly toward me, like a bad dream, like a doom, smiling like a demon (the affrighted mind is superstitious), flipping the Ka-Bar from hand to hand without looking down at it, circling the right side of the desk to where there was nothing between us but smoky air.

The left side of the desk is up against a bookcase. I backed away from Teddy until my shoulders touched the shelf of books on the Society for Psychic Research, holding the Ka-Bar awkwardly in front of me with my right hand, my left hand trailing along the desk, coming to rest on one of the brass bison bookends Leonard had given me, a talisman, counter-magic. He advanced on me, feinting at my belly, my mouth, my eyes, my crotch. At each feint I flinched, overreacted, brought my Ka-Bar up to where his had been, but no longer was.

He stopped and let the Ka-Bar hang limply by his side. "Want to try your luck?" he said. "But I warn you that quick hands will always defeat thick arms," his eyes on the point of my Ka-Bar, his smile no longer demonic, merely superior. Man, that brass bison was at the end of an uppercut that could have toppled a gazebo. It caught him under the jaw, where it joins the neck. You are familiar with the sounds made by a person who has had the wind knocked out of him? Add a wettish gurgle. Then I let him have a kick in the fork that would have sent one through the uprights from fifty yards, for the aftermath of fright is humiliation and the aftermath of humiliation is revenge (and I don't want to hear you say that the kick put me on a level with Amabelle Bloor). He went down on all fours, somehow retaining his grip on the Ka-Bar. He rested his forehead on the floor.

I straddled him, bent over, reached my hands down and across his chest, laced my fingers, lifted him to his feet, which, however, were not functional. I dragged him to his chair and dropped him in it, but he slid to the floor, limber as an anesthetized snake. I pulled him back into the chair and said, "Show some spine." One hand flopped onto the armrest, the other still holding the Ka-Bar, his breath coming like that of a man in the throes of an asthma attack. I went back to my chair. He bent over, the hand on the armrest moving to cup his crushed jewels. I sat there smoking, finishing my beer, watching him come back to himself, the *Dee Gee Days* cassette ending with the last funky notes of "They Can't Take That Away From Me," his groans and wheezes loud against the silence, and where the hell was Julie?

You don't often see a person who has turned light green. Gradually his color returned to normal, except for his face, which as I watched became flushed and swollen. Finally he sat back, pulled out a clean, white handkerchief, and neatly spat a bloody oyster into it. "I had no idea you were so sneaky," he said, his voice like Louis Armstrong's.

"Only in self-defense," I said.

"Like Pearl Harbor," he said.

"You can't kill me," I said. "I am a mythological being."

"Pan is dead," he said, crushed rock under a tire after a heavy rain.

"Undead, I would haunt you through all eternity," I said.

"Let me have a cigarette," he said wearily. I lit us up. He puffed, coughed.

"Stab me and you will end up like William Wilson and Dorian Gray," I said.

"The mission of the hero is to rid the world of monsters, whatever the horrors," he said.

"Especially, if in the process he becomes monstrous himself," I said.

"I love you," he said. How does that grab you? After all this time, he was still capable of surprising me. Did he mean it? If so, what exactly was it he meant?

"Narcissus gazing into a stagnant pond," I said.

He let out a long shuddering sigh. "I haven't the heart to go on with this stichomythia," he said. "You are my advisor: tell me what to do."

"What would a Samurai do?" I said.

His eyes opened wide, eyebrows rising, the flush on his face fading away. "You *are* sneaky," he said. "Not a chance. No, I will not. I will not do that: I want to live."

"Are you one of these crass materialists who believe that nothing survives bodily death?" I said.

"You are counting on the fact that an intellectual is someone whose mind can be talked into something that everything else in him rejects," he said, his lower lip aquiver.

"Tell me," I said, for a malevolent imp playing around within me had taken charge: "are you equipped to spend the rest of your life in jail without sinning?" I had made cider of his Adam's apple and pureed his root, but it was mere words that brought tears to his eyes.

"Save me," he said, wearing an appeasement smile.

"That is what I'm doing," I said, very calm, "for there is no life without honor."

Was he coughing or was he sobbing?

"On your knees," I said.

He gave me a queer look. "Really, Wynn," he said, with a snuffle. "This is not the time or. . . . Besides, my throat is too sore."

"I sentence you to death," I said.

"Please," he said, now clear about what I meant, tears running down his cheeks.

"Come on, Teddy, be a man," I said.

He visibly pulled himself together. "You're right," he said, nodding, wiping his eyes with a handkerchief that was no longer starched, nor clean. "That was a revealing mistake I made just now. After such knowledge, what forgiveness?" He let out another of those long, shuddering sighs, his body at last relaxing in the chair. "Am I entitled to a condemned man's last cigarette?" and his face settled into that almost-smile of his.

I lit us up.

We smoked for a while in silence, except that he coughed lightly after every mouthful of smoke. "A half-dozen packs of these," he said, looking at the stub of his Pall Mall, "and I won't need the Ka-Bar."

"I've been smoking them for twenty-one years," I said.

"I read somewhere that smoking can cause erectile problems—constriction of the tributary blood vessels," he said.

"So I've heard," I said.

He bent over with a small involuntary groan and neatly broke the burning ash off the stub and into an ashtray he had placed on the floor by his chair. "I must have one more," he said. "Absolutely the last."

"You are not going to let me down again, are you?" I said. Had Julie run off with some aging con artist of a hippie?

"Absolutely the last," he said.

I lit us up.

After only two puffs, he resolutely ground out the remains. Then with a grimace he slid down out of the chair and onto his knees. "My life has been one sustained letdown," he said.

"All life is a preparation for something that never happens," I said.

"It's going to happen all right," he said. He opened his shirt and placed the point of the Ka-Bar against his bare skin, both hands on the hilt, the knife angling upwards. "I promise to haunt you through all eternity."

It was only then that the enormity of what was about to happen hit me. It was like snapping out of a trance. What had I been playing at, anyhow? "Wait," I said.

He straightened his arms, the knife still pointed at a spot just below his sternum, to give it a running start, I suppose.

"WAIT!" I said.

"For what?" he said.

The door burst open and Julie barged in, her hair curling every which way, saying, "The rain held us up." One quick look at the cut under my eye and a look at Teddy on the floor and she said, "What are you two playing at?" Then she saw the knife. She bent over neatly and took it out of Teddy's hand. He did not resist.

"Teddy wants to speak to Hector Suarez," I said, and I gave her Hector's card. "Here's his number." She went over to the phone, dialed.

I got up, walked over to him, put my hands under his armpits, lifted him into his chair. It was no use my trying to walk back to my own chair, for Teddy was holding on to my hand, tight. So I just stood there, looking out the window at empty space, while Julie finished her call. Then apropos of nothing, I burst into song:

Teddy learned to be a scholar
Couldn't make his verses scan (oh, woe)
I said Teddy learned to be a scholar
Couldn't make his verses scan
Teddy learned to be a murderer
Couldn't convince himself he was a man.

"He was a man," Teddy sang, in a voice that was surprisingly clear and strong, considering the circumstances.

Julie answered the door when Hector rang, for he had not yet finagled a key. She escorted him into the study, his partner one step behind; she gave Hector Teddy's Ka-Bar, nodded toward its owner. Hector looked over my bloody face and smiled evilly. "Martin," he said to his partner, who was black, slim, moved like a dancer, "suppose we put some cuffs on Mr. Nakatani here." Teddy couldn't stand on his own—Hector held him up while Martin cuffed him—but the look on his face was that of a religious nut about to be martyred. Once the cuffs were on, Hector just let Teddy drop back into the chair, tough on the coccyx.

"Don't be an asshole," said Julie.

"Let's have a little talk," said Hector.

"I want a lawyer," said Teddy.

Hector nodded, like a man who expects nothing from the world except the satisfaction of being right. "Martin, just keep Mr. Nakatani here company, will you?" With the crooked pointer finger of his left hand for Julie and the crooked pointer finger of his right hand for me, Hector signaled us to follow him. He led us into the kitchen, where he said, "For Christ's sake, Slim, do something about your face. I can't stand to look at you."

So while Julie washed my face with a dishwashing sponge and dishwashing detergent, while she fetched some adhesive tape and cut it into thin strips and stuck them slantwise across my cut ("You're going to need stitches"), while she fixed all three of us coffee and carrot cake that she had brought back from the Rainbow Gathering, awful stuff, I told Hector pretty much what I just told you, sparing him many details. I also told him that he would probably find Teddy's stash of Ka-Bars in the chamber built into the turret on the wall around Morningside Park.

As it turned out, the mud on his skippies was identical in composition to the soil outside the chamber. A key on his ring opened the padlocks on the door. Those signature sneakers of his left clear footprints all over the dirt floor. Under a pile of rotting burlap was a pine box with stencils on the outside and seven Ka-Bars inside. Teddy's fingerprints were all over it. Let's see: one for Terry, one for Blinky, one for Marshall, one for Teddy, and seven in the box: where was the twelfth Ka-Bar? Hector has still not tracked it down. While Teddy's father, a blustery sort of guy, was in New York to consult with lawyers, he admitted that the box was just the same as one he had ordered from Hylas Cutlery ten or twelve years ago. A call home verified that it was missing from the outbuilding in which Mr. Nakatani had stored it before forgetting about it entirely. A call to Hylas Cutlery confirmed that eleven years ago it had sent a "Presentation Case" of twelve Combat-Utility knives, number 269, the number on the case in the chamber, to a Mr. Hideo Nakatani.

The crime scene investigators recovered minute fibers of cotton denim from the backs of Terry's and Marshall's legs, above the ankles but below the knees. (Hector and I, in almost daily conversations, came to a complete agreement that Teddy dropped his pants, instead of just opening his fly, to bugger his victims.) "No contact without a trace," said Hector, quoting some French criminologist. The "nerds" in the FBI's Hairs and Fibers Unit, according to Hector, were able to establish that the dyes in the denim fibers were consistent with those used by the Wrangler Corporation for their jeans. Hard as he looked, Hector had never seen Teddy or me wear anything but Levis, for we were purists, but Teddy's valedictory jeans were Wranglers. Hector's theory is that Teddy, a careful man, bought a new pair of Wranglers before each transgression, ironed them to settle any loose fibers, and afterward threw them away, just in case. My theory is that Teddy kept the jeans in that haunted chamber, folded neatly on top of the presentation case, which was protected from dust and bat shit by a double layer of thick, black garbage bags, one inside the other. Among Teddy's books was found one with the title *Hard Evidence: How Detectives Inside the FBI's Sci-Crime Lab Have Helped Solve America's Toughest Cases.*

Before entry, Teddy donned a condom, of course, and I haven't the energy to eliminate the nasty chime of y's and n's in this sentence. He shaved off his pubic and leg hair. A thin smear of Vaseline glued his eyebrows to his head. It's likely that he put on a shower cap right after he stabbed his victims, for a shower cap (and a packet of condoms) was found in the back pocket of the Wranglers he wore on what was meant to be my last afternoon in this vale of tears. These details may eventually get cleared up: Teddy's lawyers seem to be going for a plea bargain—in return for a plea of guilty and a detailed confession, Teddy won't get the needle. It looks like I'm pretty much off the hook, despite pointed questions from the DA's office about the bruises on Teddy's neck and groin, despite rude questions from Hector's colleagues about my sexual orientation, for recent events have created a non-literary interest in Amabelle Bloor's wretched whodunit.

It helped that Hector Suarez and Frederick Grantwell were in my corner from the onset. Either to enhance his reputation or to deflect suspicion from me, Hector has let it be understood that he was the one who figured out where Teddy cached his Ka-Bars. I am under strict orders from Grantwell not to discuss any aspect of this case with anyone ("not even a significant other") although there have been numerous requests for interviews from print and broadcast journalists, some of the latter willing to pay. I have made an exception of you, for dead men tell no tales, and for Leonard Sistrunk, whose friendship has done more than anything else to keep me about as sane as I ever get. "Poor Teddy nearly died of Puritanism," Leonard said on one of the many afternoons we met in my office to have a glass or two (or three) of single malt Scotch whiskey together.

"Sooner murder an infant in its cradle than nurse unacted desires," I said.

"Amen," he said.

Julie and I still sleep back-to-back. My sneaky attempts to violate her no-touch policy have been firmly rebuffed. But her warmth, her fragrance, the good vibes emanating from her *Etwas*—these are still available to me.

I'm going to bed, Joel; I'm going to get as close to Julie as you can without touching.

27

Dear Joel,

Big fat snowflakes are falling, as they fell that night we gathered on the porch at Fern Hill Farm, the night I lost Julie. I expect I'll go for a walk later, for falling snow fits my mood, which I could not for the life of me define.

Classes are over; I have graded my term papers and final exams and turned in the results; Christmas has come and gone; on paper at least, the English Department is ready for the new term; for a couple of weeks I will have no pressing obligations . . . except maybe to myself. But then it is bad form to be scrupulous about meeting obligations to oneself.

Kay is pregnant. She has not yet begun to swell, but to a discerning eye there is a certain rosy bloom. . . . We are friends again, no more than that. It is understood that I will be the child's godfather. Serena is going to move in with Kay, the better to serve as her lady-in-waiting, I suppose. Zeno has got to be the father, or sperm donor let us say, although I see no change in Kay's attitude toward him or in his to her. He has been an irregular lunchmate recently for a rackety cough has taken hold of him and won't let go.

There will be no promotion to tenure for Malcolm Tetrault. I have gathered five years' worth of the students' teaching evaluation forms to use against him if he sues.

"Monsy" and "Fred" are cozy together. He has not made good on his threat to entice her away from the English Department, for reasons of decorum is my guess.

Angel Terrasco is also off the hook. There was noisy criticism and a small demonstration led by the Reverend Alphonse Sharp when the Manhattan District Attorney, overruling gung-ho assistants, dropped charges. But the promise of a named chair in the University's law school when the DA's term in office ends (for he is not likely to be re-elected) may have soothed the sting of those totally unwarranted charges of racism. Grantwell firmly advised against my appointing Angel vice-chair. I appointed Leonard, with a promise to handle all curricular matters myself. He will do it on the understanding that we hire another expert in African American Literature.

Amabelle's defense will be the Traumatic Stress Syndrome. Her brutal father, so she will claim, used to spank her viciously and often, his bare hand against her bare bottom, merely for the fun of it. This went on until she was sixteen, until, that is, a driver of one of the father's trucks backed over him, just possibly by accident. When that kid slapped her on the bottom. . . .

The kid has recovered entirely. He came around to show me his scar. I had surprisingly few books in my office that would be right for him to read, but I let him have an *Alice in Wonderland* and some of Conan Doyle's science fiction.

Lizzie spends a lot of time at the hospital, where Willi Heinfangl is fading fast, the end of an era, says Derwood Bobbie. (I must remember to visit him—and soon.) Lizzie is finding it harder to watch Willi die than she had expected.

I spent Christmas afternoon with the family. Nothing anybody said or did put me into a rage, although our brother-in-law came close. Whence this newfound equanimity? I owe it to Julie. On the night before the night before Christmas we decorated a tree together, laughing the whole time like kids, for my downstairs neighbor, an elderly widow whom I sometimes help out with this and that, gave me a big pot of a Swedish Yuletide concoction called "glug," as I heard it: raisins, cinnamon sticks, and you drink it hot. Man, that stuff is stronger than it tastes. In her condition of lowered resistance Julie allowed a couple of serious hugs and a kiss on the eyebrow.

We got up early on Christmas Eve, braving the hangovers, to begin work on what became a body-and-soul satisfying turkey dinner. My main job was to make the stuffing (the secret is too many onions and lots of celery), enough extra to mold into a neat little vegetarian turkey. I also got the bird ready for the oven, put it in, and when it was time, mashed the potatoes. Julie took charge of everything else, and there was an amazing amount else. She positively glowed in the well-deserved praise from our guests for dinner, Lizzie, Kay, Serena, Leonard, and Fawn. She felt so good that when everyone else had taken off and we were alone in the kitchen, cleaning up and putting away leftovers, she not only allowed me to hug her, but also to kiss her on the lips. When I reached down to cup her buttocks in my hands, however, she backed off.

We had a late and lazy breakfast together on Christmas morning (coffee, leftover pie and eggnog sans rum), a pale sun shining through the window to kiss her tumbled hair. She said the kinds of things good cooks say to elicit compliments after a triumphant dinner party—do you think there was too much lemon in the cheese sauce on the broccoli? and it's impossible to find decent pie apples anymore. I congratulated her at being a success at everything she set out to do: mastering the fine art of home cookery, solving my little problem, achieving grades of B+ (in French), A-, and A (from Zeno). Abruptly changing the subject, indirectly explaining why she was not in Middleburgh, she told me what Christmas at home with the Berceau family had been like before she struck out on her own. She was wry and she was witty, but she was not bitter. And I'll tell you, Joel, sitting there with Julie, saying nothing of importance, seemed so nice, so normal, so natural, so *right,* that I was overcome by a tremendous sense of well-being, aglow with the taken-for-granted affection between us. This is enough, I said to myself; I can limp by without the sex. (Among all my virtuoso displays of self-deception this was the most extravagant.) Thus the equanimity with which, later that day, I faced our family.

When I got back to the apartment, Julie was sitting next to the tree, a cold glass of glug in her hand, carols playing on her boombox, the lights casting red, green, blue reflections on her face, her eyes glistening. I heated the rest of the Swedish moonshine, poured myself a glass, filled hers, crawled under the tree for our presents. From me Julie got a dark green cashmere sweater set, one short-sleeved, one a cardigan, to do some justice to her chest, a jade necklace, homage to her neck, and a vial of perfume called "Abandoned," a hint. From Leonard she got an elegant silver pin in the shape of a slender guitar, a snake with emerald eyes coiled around it. From Julie I received a boombox on which you could play CDs, on which, in fact, you could transfer sounds from a CD onto a blank cassette, so I could listen to them in my Vanagon. Best of all, she let me give her a kiss by way of thanks.

She fetched a plate of Swedish meatballs she had made to go with the glug, half of them impaled with toothpicks wearing pantaloons, departed to try on the sweaters, returned looking terrific, but then I am no judge, for by my lights the less she wears the better she looks. I pressed my face against the cashmere, which felt delicious, but was no match for her skin. Over the glug and meatballs she told me how one year her father, to save money, waited until the last minute to buy a tree, couldn't find one, drilled holes in a broomstick, plugged them with branches from a ratty old fir tree growing in their backyard. I told her how you got me my first football for a Christmas present, how I couldn't make the pros because I lacked the killer instinct, how I discovered literature, which gives you in words what you can't get in the flesh, how I still haven't come up out of the basement. Then, just as I was suggesting that tomorrow we both put on our triple-laminate Gore-Tex parkas with the Polartec fleece linings and walk downtown through the whole length of Central Park, have lunch in a French—she put her hand on mine, said, "Want to fool around in bed for a while?" Oh, Joel!

You can imagine my feelings when I couldn't git the band up. But Julie snuggled up close and in a low voice began to babble, tickling my ear and neck, about how she was going on a bodybuilding kick and especially she wanted me to show her the best routines for developing big arms and shoulders, not like mine of course, for that would look ridiculous, and she closed a hand on my bicep, and by the way she wanted some credit for the fact that now when I lay on my back like this you could see my ribs, and she ran a hand over them, giving me gooseflesh, and I'll be damned if I didn't have a hard-on. After the usual preliminaries, which custom cannot stale, we once again demonstrated that Nature, more kindly than the Jewish-Christian-Moslem-Marxist God, has arranged things so that there is great pleasure in doing what She put us on earth to do, namely what comes naturally.

And once again, as usual, when she went off to tinkle, I rolled over on my stomach (and she is right: there's less of it), so she could stretch out on my back when she returned, and another way in which sex is like poetry is this: its rituals, as with the refrain of a poem, accrue new meanings with each repetition. She slipped her hands under my chest, hugged me, kissed my shoulders, said, "Cuz, could you lend me six thousand dollars?"

"Sure," I said.

"You mean it?" she said.

"Sure," I said.

She talked fast, as though I were already on my way out the door, and me not moving a muscle: the money will be put to good use, Cuz, for she had already been accepted by the New Mexico School of Natural Therapeutics, where tuition was only five thousand, but she needed some money to get there and get settled, even if Fawn had already found her a part-time job in a health food store, oh, thank you, Cuz, thank you.

I groaned.

"In six months' time I'll be a licensed massage therapist," she said. "I'm going to be a healer, Cuz."

"You've got a full scholarship to SAS," I said. "Do you know how much that's worth? And I don't mean the money."

"I know, Cuz, but I just don't think I'm cut out for college," she said. "It all seems like preparation for something that's not going to happen. Maybe if I was seventeen."

I groaned.

"Now don't try to make me feel sorry for you," she said. "The next best thing to starting an affair is breaking off. You'll see: there's this feeling of being let out of a cage."

"Will you marry me?" I said.

"What's that you say?" she said.

"Please marry me," I said.

"I thought you'd never get around to asking," she said.

"It took me a while to realize that I love you," I said. "I didn't recognize this thing called love, never having experienced it before."

"Love. . . . Well, yeah," she said. " 'Imprinting,' you called it."

"Whatever it is, it's real," I said.

"It's just, well, one of the reasons I came to college was to get away from all this sex and violence," she said.

I repressed the impulse to say Get thee to a nunnery, for there is no other refuge from sex and violence. Instead, I said, "The violence is over. After we've been together a while the sex will be less purely sexual—complicated by other emotions—more lovey-dovey, less agonistic."

"That's one thing I'll miss, the big words," she said.

I dropped onto my knees and clasped my hands in front of me, Al Jolson singing "Mammy." "Please, please, please," I said.

"Don't kid around, Cuz," she said. "This is serious."

I wrapped my arms around her legs, put my head down on her lap, saying "Please, please, please, please," aware of how preposterous I would look to a spectator, big as I am.

I could feel her idly curling a lock of my hair around her finger while she mulled it over. Finally, just as I was about to start with the pleases again, she said, "OK, here's the deal. One: no more monkey business with the Blonde Brobdingnagian."

"Agreed," I said.

"Two," she said: "you give up smoking."

"What's that got to do—?" I said. "Agreed."

"Three," she said: "You've got to write me at least two long letters a week."

"Letters!" I said. "Why letters? Can't I talk? What is this, the silent treatment in reverse?"

"I've got to have a career, Cuz," she said. "I've got to have something of my own, or you'll swallow me alive."

"Not true," I said. "Not fair: I'm pussy-whipped already."

"You're on six months' probation," she said. "If after that you still think you want me, you'll have to ask. Then we'll see."

"Agreed," I said, for sexual satisfaction makes me accommodating, especially when there is no alternative.

Eight days later I drove her to Newark Airport, whence she and Fawn departed for Albuquerque.

Dear Joel,

I know you will forgive me for writing my letters, one a day these past weeks, to Julie rather than to you. The self-imposed obligation to write Julie every day has been my only anchor; otherwise I'd be adrift entirely. (She has sent me a postcard with a picture of the desert—and three sentences.)

Here's how I waste my days: up late; breakfast in a coffee shop while I scan the *Times*; a long walk, usually down Broadway, striding in rhythm, for I can get so caught up in digging the scene that I forget about cigarettes; or three hours in the gym, where smoking is prohibited; coffee and an apple for lunch in my office; a session with Monika, who tells me what has to be done, so I can tell her to do it; drinks with Leonard, mutual commiserations, for Alistair has been giving him grief; dinner in one of the local dives, Indian, or Ethiopian, Italian, Greek, Chinese, Japanese, Korean, Thai (hold the pineapple and coconut), or native, so long as it is too cramped to have a smoking section; a movie, for smokers are no longer welcome in New York movie theaters; or another walk; home; a letter to Julie, for I can extract sentences from the ruck only when bodily fatigue slows down the churn of my spirit ("Those who see only difference between soul and body have neither," said Oscar); for cigarettes are an aid to concentration, for a cigarette is the sheepdog that herds your thoughts through the narrows of a pen. Which do I miss more, Julie or cigarettes? Well, every night I put pencil to paper, but I never put a Pall Mall to my lips.

I'm all at loose ends. Like Julie, I need something of my own. Teaching doesn't do it, now that I've learned how. I got my atheism from Pa, my corpulence from Ma, my taste in music and reverence for Diz from you. Oh sure, my lust is my own. But is that a career? Should I lose still more weight, learn how to dress, haunt singles' bars. ("Pardon me, Miss, but I have resolved to pay homage to beauty at least once each day. May I buy you a drink?") Bah. Ignominy is inevitable. There is no need for me to go looking for it.

Which reminds me—have I mentioned my date with Felicia Zhang for this coming Saturday? She graduated mid-year (a term early), and is therefore no longer off-limits. She's working downtown, at forty thousand a year, a stopgap, she says. In fact, she was the one who got in touch. She has an idea for a TV pilot and she wants me to help her develop it. Picture a big detective agency, does all kinds of work: industrial espionage; computer incursion; security for malls; tracing misplaced minors; tracking down heirs; entrapping errant spouses; building cases for lawyers; closing down the swine who's been using your long-distance calling card number; stalking stalkers. There will be violence and mystery in the detection, sex and intrigue among the agents. There will be nerds, yuppies, neurotics, an old-time dick with a fedora and a cigar, a muscular black homosexual dandy, a dissipated and irresistible Italian, a quick young Chinese American rookie (for Felicia can't see why she shouldn't have a go at acting), whom the Head, a big, strong guy modeled after me, takes under his wing. They have many adventures together.

Get that worried look off your face. I'm not going to have an affair with Felicia. My restraint in this regard is based not on morality, but on superstition. I'm afraid that some occult spirit floating in the ambience and looking for a pretext to do us harm will separate me from Julie if I cheat on her.

To get back to what I was saying before, I do have this small knack for improvising sentences—nothing secondhand about that. It's not much, but it's mine. I would try to write as Dizzy plays, if I had something to write about. Somehow my old idea of writing a screenplay of your life no longer beckons. But how about my letters to Julie? Suppose that instead of spilling my interior babble, as I did in these Dear Joels, I wrote with designs on my reader? Suppose I blew jazzy rhythms, the basal metabolism of four-to-the-bar, phrased them in vowel clangor and consonant congruence and strategic dissonance, in spooky augmented chords and solacing Picardee Chords and sustaining repeats, in whole tone runs and modal substitutions, in unsettling changes of key, in ornamental flurbles, in the long repressed truths of the *Diabolus in Scala*. Could I make it swing? Would it make Julie want to boogie?

The Diz and Stan cassette, one of my two favorites, has this minute ended with the raucous conclusion to "Lover Come Back to Me." I only allow myself to play these favorites once a month, for it is only sex of which one may truly say that age cannot wither nor custom stale its infinite variety. There: I just put on *The Modern Jazz Sextet*. Soon I'll be listening to the calls that open "Blues for Bird," give me the chills—reminds me of a conversation I had over drinks with Leonard this afternoon.

He was wearing a black suit, a dark gray shirt, a silver tie, and pebble-grained chukkas of a kind I had looked over myself in Eddie

Bauer (with a Gore-Tex bootie and a Cambrelle lining that wicks away perspiration). He listened patiently when I once again told him how Julie's departure has left me suspended between life and death.

"I know what you mean," he said.

What's this? One-upmanship in misery is not Leonard's style. "Alistair's flown the coop?" I said.

"I showed him the door," he said. "First I gave him a good beating—man, I tenderized him all over, then kicked him out, dislocating my big toe in the process."

"Is he the kind of pip-squeak to bring charges?" I said.

"I'd bring a counter-charge of assault with a deadly weapon," he said.

"He came at you with a knife?" I said, for our expectations are based upon our experiences.

"He infected me with the AIDS virus," he said. "I was feeling poorly, so I had some tests. It turns out I'm HIV positive."

"Dear God," I said, for there are times when it seems there ought to be one.

"My opinion is I'm too young to die," he said. "What's yours?"

Right there in the bar I put my hand on his neck and pulled his head toward mine until they bumped.

Yes he was. So was Marshall. So is Teddy. "So was Methuselah," I said.